Michael Robotham is a former feature writer and investigative reporter who has worked in Britain, Australia and America.

His debut thriller, *The Suspect*, introduced clinical psychologist Joe O'Loughlin and sold more than a million copies around the world, launching a nine-book series. It has been adapted into an ITV series starring Aidan Turner. Michael's standalone thriller, *The Secrets She Keeps,* has also been the basis of two BBC TV series.

He has twice won the prestigious UK Crime Writers' Association Gold Dagger Award for best crime novel, as well as the Ian Fleming Steel Dagger for *When She Was Good*, a Richard & Judy Book Club pick.

Michael lives in Sydney.

## Also by Michael Robotham

### Joe O'Loughlin series
The Suspect
The Drowning Man (aka Lost)
Shatter
Bleed for Me
The Wreckage
Say You're Sorry
Watching You
Close Your Eyes
The Other Wife

### Cyrus Haven series
Good Girl, Bad Girl
When She Was Good
Lying Beside You
Storm Child

### Philomena McCarthy series
When You Are Mine

### Other fiction
The Night Ferry
Bombproof
Life or Death
The Secrets She Keeps

# MICHAEL ROBOTHAM

# THE
# WHITE
# CROW

SPHERE

SPHERE

First published in Great Britain in 2025 by Sphere
1 3 5 7 9 10 8 6 4 2

Copyright © Bookwrite Pty 2025

The moral right of the author has been asserted.

*All characters and events in this publication, other than those
clearly in the public domain, are fictitious and any resemblance
to real persons, living or dead, is purely coincidental.*

All rights reserved.
No part of this publication may be reproduced, stored in a retrieval system, or
transmitted, in any form or by any means, without the prior permission in
writing of the publisher, nor be otherwise circulated in any form of binding or
cover other than that in which it is published and without a similar condition
including this condition being imposed on the subsequent purchaser.

A CIP catalogue record for this book is available from the British Library.

Hardback ISBN 978-1-4087-2725-6
Trade Paperback ISBN 978-1-4087-2724-9

Typeset in Bembo Std by Palimpsest Book Production Limited,
Falkirk, Stirlingshire
Printed and bound in Great Britain by Clays Ltd, Elcograf S.p.A.

Papers used by Sphere are from well-managed forests
and other responsible sources.

Sphere
An imprint of
Little, Brown Book Group
Carmelite House
50 Victoria Embankment
London EC4Y 0DZ

The authorised representative
in the EEA is
Hachette Ireland,
8 Castlecourt Centre,
Dublin 15, D15 XTP3, Ireland
(email: info@hbgi.ie)

An Hachette UK Company
www.hachette.co.uk

www.littlebrown.co.uk

For Lesley Poole

He was a killer, a thing that preyed, living on the things that lived, unaided, alone, by virtue of his own strength and prowess, surviving triumphantly in a hostile environment where only the strong survive.

Jack London, The Call of the Wild

# 1

In a real dark night of the soul it is always three o'clock in the morning. F. Scott Fitzgerald wrote that line almost sixty years before I was born but it's true enough today. London is not asleep at this hour. Merely resting her eyes and humming impatiently, waiting for the sun to rise. She is like an aging toothless beast, chewing through years that she struggles to swallow.

I'm behind the wheel of a police car, driving along Prince Charles Road towards Hampstead in North London. The headlights sweep across the wet asphalt, reflecting from the polished surfaces of parked cars whose bonnets are beaded with raindrops. Beside me, PC Rowan Cooper has a mobile phone tucked against his ear taking down food orders.

We are on a breakfast run to a Jewish bakery in East Finchley that serves the best salt beef bagels in London outside of Brick Lane. Our colleagues at Kentish Town police station are hungry, or bored, or both, although boredom is not a word that is ever used. A quiet night is a good night. Good nights are rare.

'What do you want?' asks Coop.

'Smoked salmon and cream cheese.'

'You're such a girl.'

'I'm a pescatarian.'

'Is that like being an Anglican?'

'No, but I *am* going straight to Heaven.'

Coop is one of the few people who call me Philomena rather than Phil. My mother is another one. She insists upon it. She rang up my station sergeant on my first day at Kentish Town and told him that I should be addressed as *PC Philomena McCarthy*. The sergeant thought it was a wind-up and I was teased for weeks.

Coop is fresh out of training college, but with the self-confidence of someone much more experienced. Maybe it's a male thing. When I graduated from Hendon and became a trainee, I was desperate to fit in rather than stand out, which is a female thing. That was four years ago and I'm more comfortable in the uniform now, but still wary of drawing attention. With a family like mine, it's best to keep a low profile.

This is my last shift on a six-day roster that began with two early starts, followed by two afternoons and now two nights before a four-day break. Tomorrow, by which I mean today, I have a family event – a christening at a church in Greenwich – when I'm going to be a godmother to my cousin Rosie's first baby.

After that, Henry is spiriting me away for a romantic weekend in Paris, which is supposed to be a secret, but I found a printed receipt for Eurostar tickets in his jacket pocket when I was looking for cash to pay our cleaner. I also saw clues on his Facebook feed – Airbnb apartments in the Latin Quarter. There are no secrets from Siri.

It will be our first trip abroad since our honeymoon – an extremely wet ten days in the Maldives, when a tropical storm called Bethany broke rainfall records. We spent the entire time in bed, binging Netflix and having sex, in between shoving towels against the balcony doors and dodging drips in the restaurant.

Sex is also high on the agenda this weekend, I suspect, because we've both been so busy of late; and Henry wants to sell me on the idea of starting a family. The seduction will be nice – the champagne, caviar, and a view of the Seine – but I'm not going to change my mind. Not yet.

We've only been married a year and I'm quite happy to keep

practising. It's not as though my biological clock is ticking loudly in my ears. I'm twenty-nine. Henry is thirty-one, and we have a mortgage that needs two incomes to manage. Don't get me started on the spousal maintenance payments to his ex-wife, who treats Henry like her personal ATM.

When it comes to babies, my answer is 'not yet', but I do have a rough timetable in mind. Thirty-four for the first, another at thirty-six. One girl. One boy. If only I could order them on Uber Eats with a side order of garlic bread.

For now, I'm enjoying my career. I transferred from Southwark to Camden eight months ago, and nobody at Kentish Town police station has mentioned my family connections – although a few of them will know. Some children have to live up to parental expectations. I have to escape mine.

My father is Edward McCarthy and my uncles are the McCarthy brothers, whom the tabloids refer to as 'colourful local identities' or 'ex-cons' but never 'gangsters' because my father has a barrister on speed-dial.

I have never understood why people use the term 'organised crime'. They never talk about 'organised nursing' or 'organised teaching' or 'organised accountancy'. Why do criminals get this added descriptor? Maybe because most crimes are chaotic and impulsive and stupid, which is why the perpetrators get caught. Not Edward McCarthy. Accusations and insinuations slide off him like he's John Gotti, the Teflon Don. Nothing ever sticks.

'With extra mustard,' says Coop, relaying the last of the order. 'We'll be there in fifteen.'

Satisfied, he puts his phone away and drums his hands on the dashboard. Eating is like a competitive sport for Coop, a reality that's beginning to show around his midriff, although he keeps telling me he's training for the London Marathon.

At this hour, the roads are mostly deserted, except for garbage trucks and street-sweeping vehicles and the occasional black cab, which come in all colours these days. The rain has stopped and misty yellow halos glow around the streetlights that reflect from puddles on the road.

We're on Haverstock Hill, not far from Belsize Park station, when a cyclist hurtles out of a side street, running a red light. I see a flash of yellow and hit the brakes. Wheels lock. Rubber squeals. The cyclist swerves and turns his head at the last moment, his eyes full of fear. The car nudges his back wheel. The bike wobbles, but the cyclist stays upright and carries on riding down Haverstock Hill, pumping on the pedals, his Lycra-covered arse swaying.

'Fuck!' says Coop, bracing his hands against the dashboard. His notebook and phone have fallen into the footwell.

'Maniac,' I say, sucking in a breath.

'You want to go after him?'

We both consider the question, while thinking the same thing. Paperwork. If we catch up with the cyclist, we'll spend the rest of the night writing reports, preparing statements and filing formal charges. After twelve hours of work and half a day at court, we'll watch him act like a choirboy in front of the magistrates, who will give him a rap over the knuckles and tell him to be more careful next time.

'I think we scared him,' I say.

'Shat himself,' says Coop.

The police car is idling in the middle of the intersection. I look in the mirrors before moving off.

'Did you see that?' I ask, turning my head.

'What?'

'On the road. Behind us. A child.'

'You saw a kid?'

'Yeah.'

He follows my gaze. The road is empty.

'Are you sure?'

'Yeah.'

I pull over and park on the corner, before walking back to the intersection. Coop jogs to catch up.

'When you say a kid, how old?'

'Young. A boy, I think.'

'Where was he?'

'Standing on the corner.'

We've reached the place. Most of the houses are set back from the road with railing fences or brick walls or neatly trimmed hedges surrounding small front gardens. We look up and down Haverstock Hill.

'Maybe it was a dog,' says Coop.

'No.'

Our shoulder radios crackle and buzz in unison.

*'All cars. All cars. Emergency attendance. Major incident in progress. Hatton Garden. Please proceed to Holborn Circus and establish a perimeter.'*

Coop on the radio: 'Kilo Quebec Three Zero, responding. Twelve minutes away. Over.'

'You go,' I say.

'We should stick together.'

'I'm not leaving a child out here.'

I talk into my radio. 'Kilo Quebec Three Zero. This is PC McCarthy. I've spotted a missing child dressed in pyjamas. I'm searching on foot.'

'What is your location?'

'Haverstock Hill at England's Lane.'

'Do you have a description?'

'A little boy wearing long pyjamas.'

'Approximate age?'

'Hard to say. I only got a glimpse.'

'Do you need assistance?'

'I'll let you know.'

'Understood. Control out.'

Returning to the patrol car, I collect a torch and a thermal blanket before watching Coop drive away. My radio is broadcasting comms chatter about the Hatton Garden call-out. Some sort of robbery. So much for a quiet night.

Back in England's Lane, I walk slowly along the footpath, searching under cars and peering over hedges. The roots of trees have pushed up under the paving stones, making it uneven in places. Red-brick mansion blocks line both sides of the road, broken by the occasional free-standing house or semi. Most are probably heritage listed. Expensive. Darkened. Asleep.

Coming to a partly open gate, I step inside and hear a rustling sound in the undergrowth, among the soggy leaves. It could be a cat or a fox. London is full of foxes, which have become experts at urban living, raiding rubbish bins and breeding in the parks and heathland.

Sweeping my torch back and forth, I crouch and look under the hedge. The beam of light picks up a pale white foot. A shin. An ankle. Five muddy toes. Pyjama bottoms.

'Hello,' I say.

The foot disappears.

I sit on the damp grass, feeling it soak through my trousers. The garden smells of compost and grass clippings.

'My name is Phil. Do you have a name?'

Silence.

'Let me guess. Perhaps you're Peter like Peter Rabbit, or Stuart like Stuart Little. Are you a rabbit or a mouse?'

A small voice says, 'No.'

'You sound like a mouse. Mice make me jump. I'm always scared they're going to run up my trouser leg. You wouldn't do that, would you?'

'No.'

'I think I need some proof that you're not a mouse. Maybe you could show me your fingers. Mice don't have fingers.'

There is a pause and a rustle of leaves. A small hand appears from under the bushes.

'Mmm,' I say. 'Maybe mice do have fingers. They definitely don't have toes. Do you have toes?'

After another pause, two pyjama-clad legs appear from under the hedge.

'I guess you're not a mouse. But what else could you be?'

'I'm a little girl.'

'No. That's not possible. Little girls don't live in hedges. Little girls should be tucked up in bed.' I slide a little closer. 'I'll have to start again and guess your name. You sound like a Jasmine, or an Ariel, or an Elsa. Definitely a princess?'

'I don't want to be a princess.'

'I see. Then maybe your name is Ninty Minty or Cutie Patootie?'

'I'm Daisy,' says the voice.

'That's a pretty name. Like the flower. I love daisies. What are you doing out so late?'

'I couldn't wake Mummy.'

'Oh, I see.'

'And I'm not allowed to talk to strangers.'

'That's very good advice, but I'm not a stranger. I'm a police officer. And I want to take you home.'

Again, I wait, but nothing moves inside the hedge.

'I tell you what I'm going to do, Daisy. I'm going to lie down and have a sleep. I'd rather it be somewhere warm and dry, but I can't leave you out here.'

Unfurling the silver foil blanket, I lay it on the grass and curl up.

After a while, the leaves begin to move. I partially open my eyes and watch a small face appear. Daisy crawls out of the hedge and kneels next to me, gently shaking my shoulder. She has a pageboy haircut and a smudge of mud on her cheek.

'I need to do a wee,' she says.

'OK, well let's get you home.'

Daisy shakes her head. She is squeezing her thighs together, holding it in.

'You could go just here,' I suggest.

'In the garden?'

'I was always weeing in the garden when I was your age.'

Daisy looks at me dubiously.

'You have to be careful not to splash your feet,' I say. 'Pull down your pyjama pants and squat down. I'll hold your arms so you don't fall over.'

Daisy does as she's told. Her little bottom is sticking out towards the hedge.

'Nothing is coming,' she says.

'Think of running water.'

'Why?'

'It helps.'

I begin singing a nursery rhyme from my childhood. 'Rain is falling down. Rain is falling down. Pitter patter, pitter patter, rain is falling down.'

Soon I hear the tell-tale splash of urine on the grass.

'What am I going to wipe with?' asks Daisy.

'With a tissue,' I say, pulling one from my pocket.

She tugs up her pyjamas and I wrap her in the foil blanket.

'When you said that you couldn't wake Mummy, was she in bed?'

'No.'

'Where was she?'

'In the kitchen.'

My heart sinks. 'Where do you live?'

She points into the darkness.

'Can you show me?'

Daisy takes my hand and leads me onto the pavement, limping slightly. Her hand is freezing.

'How old are you?' I ask.

'Nearly six.'

'What's your last name?'

'Kemp-Lowe.'

'Is that two names or one?'

'It's my name.'

We turn into Antrim Road, walking past red-brick mansion blocks and Victorian mid-terraces, most of them converted into flats.

Daisy stops outside a large private house. The painted iron gate is open and stone paving leads to a door framed by wisteria.

'Is this your house?'

She nods.

'How did you get out?'

Daisy points to the front door, as though it should be obvious.

'Does one of these cars belong to Mummy or Daddy?' I ask.

She looks up and down the road and indicates a silver Mercedes, top of the range. Clearly, her family has money. I punch my call button. 'Kilo Quebec Three Zero to control.'

'Control, receiving.'

'I've found the child. Her name is Daisy Kemp-Lowe. Aged five. She says she couldn't wake her mother. I'm outside the house now. Can you run a plate for me?'

'Control received.'

'Silver Mercedes. Hotel Victor Six Three Golf Mike Charlie.'

We wait, sitting on the front steps. I wrap the foil blanket more closely around Daisy, before noticing blood on the sleeve of her pyjamas.

My radio squawks. 'Control to Kilo Quebec Three Zero. That vehicle is registered to a Russell Kemp-Lowe. Seventy-five Antrim Road.'

'Received.'

I look at Daisy. 'Let's get you back to bed.'

# 2

Three miles away as the crow flies, Detective Chief Inspector Brendan Keegan steps through the door of a jeweller's in Hatton Garden, crushing broken glass beneath his shoes. He is filming on his mobile phone.

'Hi, how are you doing?' he asks a man, who is sitting in a swivel chair above a puddle of urine.

The man cannot reply because packing tape covers his mouth and binds his wrists and ankles to the chair. He's in his late forties and slightly overweight in a going-to-seed sort of way that suggests he exercises by running for the bus or reaching for the TV remote.

A fringe of hair is plastered to his forehead by perspiration that has run down his face to the corners of the packing tape. A bike chain is wrapped around the man's waist and threaded through the sleeves of a bulky black vest that is fastened in the centre of his chest by three plastic clips. Wires are attached, leading to a small glass vial shaped like a cigar that is perched on the man's right thigh. It has liquid metal inside. A tilt switch. If he moves, the mercury metal will slide down the tube, closing the circuit.

'I'm DCI Keegan. You can call me Brendan.'

The man in the chair doesn't move. If the eyes are a window to a person's soul, then this one needs Windolene and a squeegee because his are clouded with torment and bereft of reason. He cannot move. He must not move.

Keegan continues filming the shattered display cases and open drawers. A single teardrop pendant, dropped in haste, lies amid the broken glass and splintered wood. The man is sitting at a desk in the rear office. Behind him, a large iron safe is bolted to the floor, open, empty. An intruder alarm is sounding constantly, rattling the calm, and a flashing yellow light is strobing across the wet footpath and the cars that are parked outside.

Two constables, responding to the alarm, had discovered the open door and the looted shop and the man in the chair. They called for back-up and mentioned the word 'bomb', which got everybody's attention, including Keegan, who was the senior detective on duty at Kentish Town police station. Now there are ten officers outside and more coming, evacuating the surrounding buildings and diverting traffic away from Hatton Garden. Control will be cutting off gas lines and electricity, and jamming mobile phone signals to prevent anything triggering an explosion.

The jewellery store takes up the entire ground floor of a four-storey Regency-style building with flats on the upper levels. There are more jewellery shops on either side and opposite. Holborn is the centre of Britain's diamond trade, with more than three hundred jewellers within five hundred square yards.

Keegan looks around his feet, checking for any tripwires or pressure plates that could detonate the vest. He can feel blood passing from his heart along his arteries, through smaller and smaller vessels, until it pulses directly beneath his skin. Moving carefully forwards, he examines the vest, which has multiple pockets, some with zips and others sealed by Velcro flaps. Circling the chair slowly, still filming on his phone, he gives a running commentary.

'The vest has one, two, three, four, five, six pockets. Plastic clips at the front and the sides. There is a wire attached to a small glass tube resting on his right thigh.'

He also describes the showroom and the rear office. 'One entrance to the street. Display cases along the walls and at counter height. The office has a desk, a chair, filing cabinets and a freestanding floor safe. Open. Empty.'

At that moment, the alarm stops ringing. The silence is so sudden it feels as if something is falling from a great height and everybody is waiting for it to land.

Keegan raises his gloved hands. 'I need you to remain very still. Understand?'

The jeweller nods.

'If that switch moves, we're going to be seeing each other around . . . and I mean everywhere.'

His attempt at humour is lost on the jeweller.

'Normally, I'd do this quickly, but I'm going to take it slowly.'

He reaches for the tape covering the jeweller's mouth and begins picking at one corner with his fingernail. Pinching it between his thumb and forefinger, he slowly peels it away. The man groans and sucks in a breath. The tilt switch moves on his knee. Keegan thrusts out his hands, ready to catch it. They're both staring at the glass tube.

'My wife,' croaks the man. 'They're holding her hostage. Help her.'

The words come out in a sob and the chair sways.

'Don't move!' pleads Keegan. 'Please. Relax. Now tell me your name.'

'Russell Kemp-Lowe.'

'Is this your shop?'

'Yes.'

'Where do you live, Russell?'

'Belsize Park. Antrim Road. Number seventy-five.'

'Is that where you last saw your wife?'

He nods. 'And my little girl.'

'What's your wife's name?'

'Caitlin.'

'And your daughter?'

'Daisy.'

'When did you last see them?'

He looks lost, as though unable to measure time. 'They were at the house. The men had guns. They forced me to come here.'

A woman's voice cuts through the radio chatter. 'This is EXPO1, EXPO1. Are you receiving?'

'That's the bomb squad,' says Keegan, trying to reassure the jeweller. He answers his radio and the woman introduces herself as Sergeant Christine Blainey and asks him about the device. Keegan gives her a description, gently lifting one of the pocket flaps of the vest. Inside is a small brick of what could be plastic explosive. He describes the tilt switch and the bicycle cable threaded through the arms of the vest and around the back of the chair. The cable is made of woven steel covered in vinyl. It has a combination lock with four numbered wheels.

Keegan studies the numbers and makes a mental note: 4, 8, 7, 2. Then he tries a few different combinations – the obvious ones like four zeroes, or four nines, and 1, 2, 3, 4.

'Any possibility of other devices?' asks Blainey.

'I haven't seen any.'

'What about pressure pads or tripwires?'

'Nothing obvious.'

A bubble of snot pops in the jeweller's nose and his right knee begins to jiggle up and down. The tilt switch moves. Keegan reaches out and holds it against the jeweller's leg, watching the mercury in the tube.

'I'm sorry. I can't help it,' says Russell, choking on the words. 'I can't feel my legs.'

'You're doing great,' says Keegan. 'Wiggle your toes to get the blood flowing. Gently. That's it.'

His radio gives him regular updates. Surrounding properties are being evacuated and an armed response unit has been sent to the address in Belsize Park.

Keegan tries to distract the jeweller, asking him about his daughter.

'She's almost six. Her birthday is in December. Christmas

Eve. She thinks it's cool to have a birthday so close to Christmas. One day she'll realise the drawbacks.'

'What does she want?'

'She keeps changing her mind. I've promised to take her to the Shake Shack in Leicester Square. She loves the crinkle-cut fries and milkshakes.'

Keegan has a little boy, who just turned three, and a wife who walked out on him six months ago. She wants a divorce. He wants to try again. He knows the marriage is broken, but some things still work when they're incomplete or incompatible. His OCD is the problem – his obsessive cleanliness and other compulsions. His 'foibles' once amused her, until they did the opposite.

Christine Blainey is back on the radio. She and her team are outside. 'You can leave this to us,' she says.

Keegan moves towards the door, but Russell reacts. 'You're not leaving me!'

His chair moves. His knee. The tilt switch. Keegan catches it as it falls, cradling it in his hands, watching the mercury move in the glass bulb, running towards the trigger and back again. Both men breathe again.

'I'm sorry,' says Russell.

'That's OK.'

'Don't leave me.'

'I'm staying right here.'

Keegan relays the information to Blainey. Moments later, a black-clad figure appears in the doorway. Bulked up by cladding and body armour, she is carrying two enormous metal plates, strapped to her forearms.

'Can I join the party?' she asks, her voice muffled inside a full-face helmet.

Stepping into the store, moving like a stop-motion puppet, she pauses and scans the room. 'OK, what do we have here?' she asks in a West Country accent, rough and mellow at the same time. 'Your name is Keegan, right? And you must be Russell.'

'I can't feel my legs,' moans the jeweller, blinking at her helplessly.

'You still have them. Let's keep it that way.'

Blainey carefully arranges the blast shields around the seated jeweller and takes a small penlight torch from her pocket. Crouching next to Russell, she examines the tilt switch and gently lifts the pockets of the bomb vest, peering inside. With her gloved fingertips, she traces each of the wires, following them from the switch to the pockets and back again.

'OK, here's what we're going to do. I'm going to cut the bicycle lock and release your hands and feet, but you must remain perfectly still. Understand?'

Russell nods.

Blainey addresses Keegan. 'I want you back behind the shields. They won't provide much protection, but it might save your bollocks from coming out the top of your head.'

'Good call,' says Keegan, still holding the tilt switch against the jeweller's thigh. 'But maybe I should just stay here.'

'Your choice, but I want you to imagine that glass tube is the most expensive tumbler of single-malt whisky in the entire world and it's filled to the very brim. You can't spill a single drop.'

'I could do with a drink,' says Keegan.

'I'll buy you one when this is over.'

'Single malt.'

'Not on my wage.'

She takes a set of bolt cutters from the satchel slung around her waist.

'Now gently, gently, lift the tube away from his leg. Hold it steady. Good lad.'

Blainey lifts the bicycle chain and opens the cutters. She squeezes the cable between the jaws and presses the arms, snipping it easily. Then she slowly pulls the cable through the arms of the vest and unwraps it from around the chair.

'OK, Russell, now it's your turn. Carefully lift your arms. Slower. Slower.'

Russell complies, exposing the sweat stains under his armpits. Blainey gently undoes each plastic clip on the vest, starting at the top. The two sides separate and she begins to lift the vest from Russell's shoulders and over his head. Keegan is holding the tilt switch. The wire lengthens. He moves his hands higher but keeps them steady.

Blainey lowers the vest onto the desk and asks the jeweller if he can stand. Russell tries, but his limbs have atrophied. His brain sends the message again and he lifts himself upright, swaying. He over-corrects and loses his balance, stumbling, falling towards Keegan.

Blainey reacts instinctively, slamming her forearm into the jeweller's chest, changing his direction. He topples backwards, over the chair, away from the tilt switch. His head hits the corner of the safe with a sickening thud and he's out cold before he crumples to the floor.

The two officers take a moment to exhale.

'I almost spilled my drink,' says Keegan.

'I almost shat my pants,' says Blainey, checking on the jeweller. Russell has a gash on his head that is bleeding profusely, but he's breathing steadily.

'What happens now?' asks Keegan.

'This is when I decide whether to cut the red wire or the blue wire.'

'You don't know?'

'I normally choose blue.'

'You a Tory voter?'

'A Chelsea supporter.'

She is holding a small pair of pliers with rubber handles. She pulls off her heavy gloves. Her fingernails are painted red. The pliers squeeze the wires and Keegan closes his eyes.

When he opens them again, he sees that Blainey has taken off her helmet, and dark hair spills to her shoulders. She has a round face and freckles on her nose and a slightly crooked smile.

She hands him an evidence bag. 'You do the honours,' she says, indicating the tilt switch.

Meanwhile, she picks up the vest and begins opening the pocket, making a humming sound as she pulls out a brick-shaped square of putty.

'Plastic explosives?' asks Keegan.

'Made to look like it.'

'A fake bomb?'

'A good one.'

'Jesus. My whole life just flashed before my eyes.'

'I hope it was a good one.'

'The second half was going to be better.'

Keegan presses the button on his shoulder radio and tells the teams outside to stand down. He looks at Russell's unconscious body. 'I need a paramedic in here.'

Blainey is packing up her gear.

'What do we know about his wife?' she asks.

'Still no word.'

# 3

'Wait here,' I tell Daisy, leaving her on the lowest step.

I press the doorbell and wait. Nobody answers.

Daisy said her mother was in the kitchen. She could be unconscious. Bleeding. It could explain the blood on the girl's pyjamas.

Stepping back from the door, I study the bay windows at the front of the house. They are double-glazed and stickered with a security company logo, stating that the premises are guarded by CCTV cameras. The interior wooden window shutters are angled downwards and I can't see inside.

Can I justify breaking into the house? Forced entry is allowed when there's an immediate threat or if a delay could be detrimental to the health of the occupant, or any other person.

I return to Daisy. 'Do your mummy and daddy keep a key in a secret place in case one of them gets locked out?' I ask. 'Under a pot plant? In Daddy's car?'

She shakes her head.

'OK. Wait here a little longer.'

I climb the steps again.

Into the radio: 'Kilo Quebec Three Zero to control. Officer on foot in Antrim Road. No answer at the house. Permission to enter.'

'Granted. Do you need a locksmith?'

'Eventually.'

I remove a rubberised claw hammer attachment from my

vest pocket and screw it into my extended baton. Wedging the claw against the frame, I begin prising it back and forth, jamming it further into the gap. Stepping back, I aim a kick at a spot just below the lock. The sound echoes through the darkness and a neighbourhood dog begins to bark.

I have studied karate since I was nine and know how to channel my energy into a kick that can knock down a charging ice addict or open a door if necessary. This one is stubborn. I try again. Wood splinters and the door swings inwards, banging against the internal wall.

'Police! Anybody home?'

The entrance hall has a high ceiling and chequerboard-patterned tiles, and a wide staircase leading to the upper floors. Everything about the decor is elegant and expensive like something out of an interior design magazine. My stepmother would approve because she knows the difference between glass and crystal, porcelain and fine bone china, hand-knotted and hand-woven, which is why my uncles call her 'the duchess'.

Daisy's shoes are lined up on a rack beneath a row of coat hooks. A bright pink schoolbag is hanging next to a red woollen coat with a fleecy collar, which is about her size. Why didn't she think to put on something warm when she left the house? She was in a hurry. Frightened.

I look into the drawing room, which is clearly off-limits to children. Not a toy to be seen. There are family photographs on the mantelpiece, documenting Daisy's life. Her birth, her first steps, riding a three-wheel scooter along a footpath. The next room is a playroom, with a toybox and painting easel and artworks pinned to a corkboard.

My shoulder radio squawks. An urgent voice. 'Control to Kilo Quebec Three Zero, the officer on foot.'

'Kilo Quebec Three Zero, receiving.'

'Where are you?'

'Inside the house.'

'Get out! Armed response units are responding to that address.'

'Why? What's happened?'

'A reported home invasion. Evacuate the premises. Wait for them. Do you copy?'

'Kilo Quebec Three Zero. Copy that. Over.'

Ahead of me is the kitchen. I can almost reach out and touch the door. I look over my shoulder. Daisy is still sitting on the steps. I can see the top of her head, poking out of the thermal blanket.

I take out a pack of silicone gloves and pull them over my hands, stretching my fingers. Using my foot, I nudge open the kitchen door, watching as the light from the hallway spills across the tiled floor. It falls diagonally over the legs of a woman sitting in a chair facing me.

She is wearing a nightdress. Her legs are bare to mid-thigh. Knees open. Face in darkness.

I step fully into the kitchen and reach for the light switch. It blinks on. My eyes adjust. The woman is staring at me with wide, dull eyes. Her mouth is covered by plastic packing tape. Her feet are bound together and her hands are pulled back behind her and taped at her wrists.

Ripping the tape from her mouth, I press my cheek to her chest, listening for a heartbeat and feeling for a pulse in her neck. Nothing. Her body is cold. Her lips are blue. A soft toy is lying on the floor next to her. A squashed-looking hippo with googly eyes and sticky-out ears. It must belong to Daisy. She was here. She tried to wake her mother.

'Kilo Quebec Three Zero. The officer on foot at Antrim Road. SCD1 required. Deceased female. Located in the kitchen. Ground floor. Rear of the address.'

'You were told to wait for the armed response unit.'

'I had reasonable cause. The little girl couldn't wake her mother.'

'Stand down. Wait for back-up.'

'Received.'

I release the button of the radio and look again at Daisy's

mother. I don't even know her name. I wish I could close her knees and her eyes and give her some dignity in death, but I've already risked contaminating a crime scene.

'You have a lovely house,' I whisper. 'And a lovely daughter. We'll find out who did this and make them pay.'

# 4

'So, you're the famous "officer on foot",' says Brendan Keegan, who hands me a takeaway coffee.

I stand a little straighter and introduce myself. 'PC Philomena McCarthy.'

'At ease,' he says, but not in a mocking way.

I study the detective out of the corner of my eye. He's in his early forties, of average height with dark hair and a wide mouth and slightly crooked lower teeth. His brown eyes are inquisitive and strangely melancholic and make me think of Patch, a dog I once owned that 'went to live on a farm' according to my father.

Keegan is young to be in charge of a murder investigation, but he's confident, maybe even cocksure, which could be a front to hide his insecurities. He's dressed business casual, in a blazer and black jeans, which seems rather progressive when most of his peers are wearing rumpled suits that have grown shiny on the elbows and backside.

Keegan motions me to a low stone wall. We sit side by side, sipping lukewarm coffee and watching SOCO officers in white chemical coveralls enter and leave the house.

The sky is growing brighter in the east, etching out the skyline and giving definition to the clouds. Daisy is asleep on the back seat of a nearby police car, curled up under a blanket with her hippo tucked under her arm. The soft toy is the only thing I took from the house.

'You broke in,' says Keegan, without sounding judgemental.

'I suspected the occupant might be hurt.'

'What made you think that?'

'Daisy said that she couldn't wake her mother.'

'Did you see any sign of forced entry?'

'No.'

'How did the girl get out of the house?'

'She's tall enough to reach the latch on the front door.'

DCI Keegan nods, as though satisfied with my answers.

'What was her name?' I ask, meaning the victim.

'Caitlin Kemp-Lowe. Her family owns a jewellery store in Hatton Garden.'

'This was a robbery.'

'A home invasion. They forced her husband to drive to the store and open the safe.'

I study the house, which is being touched by sunlight. Keegan seems to read my mind. 'They took precautions. There are motion sensors on the windows. Panic buttons. CCTV cameras.'

'The alarm wasn't sounding,' I say.

'The system was disabled and the cameras were spraypainted. It was the same at the jewellery store.'

He tips out the dregs of his coffee into a garden. 'Did you go upstairs?'

'I was asked to leave the house.'

'That wasn't my question.'

'I wanted to make sure nobody else was inside.'

'Touch anything?'

'I wore gloves.'

'What do you remember?'

*Why is he asking me this? He could go into the house himself and see the rooms.*

I tell him about climbing the stairs to the first landing and entering the master bedroom. One side of the bed was turned down. There were make-up wipes crumpled on the vanity, next to jars of night cream and cleanser. A single earring, a lotus cluster, was sitting inside the lid of a jewellery box.

'A lotus what?'

'The diamonds were arranged to look like the petals of a flower.'

'One earring?'

'Yes.'

'You have an eye for detail.'

Again, I don't know if he's teasing me. A scene of crime officer emerges from the house, pushing back the hood over her coveralls and removing her safety goggles. She signals to Keegan.

'We're still working in the kitchen, but the rest of the house is yours.'

He turns back to me. 'Come on.'

'Where?'

'You're going to show me through the house.'

'Why?'

'Because you've been here before.'

He pulls a pair of latex gloves from his pocket and offers them to me, but I have my own. We climb the front steps and navigate the hallway using duckboards arranged like stepping stones. Ahead of us, the kitchen door is open. I catch a glimpse of Caitlin Kemp-Lowe's body. She is now lying on a plastic sheet in the middle of the floor. A camera flashgun lights up her face. Moments later, the corners of the sheet are pulled across the body.

'This way,' says Keegan, taking me up the stairs.

The main bedroom is as I remember. One side of the bed has been turned down. A woman's reading glasses are resting on a novel by Ann Patchett.

'They had been out that evening,' I say. 'Somewhere fancy.'

'What makes you say that?'

'She removed her make-up and took off her jewellery. She also hung up her cocktail gown, but not in the wardrobe. She wanted to get it dry-cleaned.'

'You're good at this,' says Keegan.

'She had a shower and changed into a nightdress, but I don't think she'd gone to bed because there's no depression in the pillow.'

'What about her husband?'

'Not many signs of him in the room. Maybe they were sleeping separately.'

Keegan is standing in the walk-in wardrobe, examining the couple's clothes. Hers to the left. His to the right. He seems to admire the sense of order. Laundered business shirts are hanging next to suits and casual jackets. Jeans and jumpers have their own drawer.

'Why does anyone need seven cashmere sweaters?' he asks.

'One for each day of the week.'

Pushing shirts aside, he reveals a square safe embedded into the wall. A combination lock and handle. Unopened.

'A missed opportunity or they didn't know it was here,' I say.

'They knew about everything else – the security cameras, the alarms.'

Leaving the main bedroom, we visit the other rooms on the first floor. One of them shows evidence of occupancy – male pyjamas beneath a pillow. Sleeping tablets, a TV remote. Keegan turns it on. A sports channel appears on screen.

'Maybe he's a snorer,' I say.

'You have experience of that?'

'Periodically.'

The last bedroom is closest to the rear of the house. There is a picture of a unicorn on the door and a painted sign saying, 'Daisy's Room.'

'I checked. It was locked from the outside,' I say, pointing to the key.

'Which begs the question – how did she get out?'

We enter the little girl's room, which is decorated in pastel colours and populated by a rocking horse, a doll's house and soft toys covering a large single bed. Daisy's slippers are on the rug, and a robe is lying across the duvet.

'Why lock the bedroom door?' asks Keegan.

'They wanted to keep her here.'

I pull back the curtains and examine the sash window, which can only be opened only a few inches. The garden is twenty feet below.

'Maybe Daisy locked the door as she left,' he says.

'Why would she do that?'

I keep scouring the room, considering the possibilities. It is like one of those locked room mysteries that Hercule Poirot or Miss Marple is always solving.

'Something made Daisy wake,' I say, thinking out loud. 'Maybe she had a nightmare or needed the bathroom. If the door was locked, she would have called out.'

'Her mother couldn't answer.'

I picture Daisy, trying the door and calling for help.

'What does she do then?' asks Keegan.

I notice a tall cupboard beside the bricked-up fireplace. The door is unlatched. I expected to find a wardrobe with more toys, but the interior is a dark shaft that runs vertically from the lower floor. Two ropes are visible, running down the sides of the shaft.

'A dumb waiter,' I say. 'The kitchen must be directly below us.'

'This must have been a dining room,' says Keegan, looking past me. 'Is she strong enough?'

'Her weight would have helped,' I say. 'A counterweight kicks into gear when you pull on the ropes.'

'How do you know?'

'My father has one of these.'

'You come from money.'

'Not when I was growing up.'

Keegan pulls on the rope, triggering the counterweight, and a small wooden box appears.

'OK, let's say you're right – and Daisy lowers herself to the kitchen. What does she see?'

'She said she couldn't wake her mother.'

'Which suggests that Caitlin Kemp-Lowe was already dead.'

We retrace our steps to the lower floor, pausing on the stairs to watch as Caitlin's body is carried outside in a zipped body bag.

'Where is the husband?' I ask.

'At the hospital.'

'Does he know about his wife?'

'Not yet.'

We're outside again, standing on the front steps. Daisy is still asleep in a police car, drooling onto Hippo's head.

'What's she like?' asks Keegan.

'Bright and brave.' I feel my throat closing.

'She could be our only witness.'

'What happens to her now?'

'Child services are sending someone. If you could stay with her until then.'

'I'm going to Paris today,' I say. 'With my husband,' I add, as though it has to be explained. *Why am I telling Keegan that I'm married? What difference does it make?*

'You'll have to postpone that trip,' he says.

'Henry won't be happy.'

'What does Henry do?'

'He's a firefighter.'

'He'll understand.'

Keegan is called away by the crime scene manager. I sit next to Daisy, resting her head on my lap. She murmurs something in her sleep but doesn't wake. Around us, the street has slowly woken up. Neighbours are gathering at roadblocks, gossiping and speculating about what might have happened.

Already, detectives are going door-to-door, collecting statements and security footage from video doorbells and cameras, confirming what people saw and heard in the hours after midnight. Alarms. Screams. Arguments. Unfamiliar cars. Faces. Deliveries.

I phone Henry. He's half asleep. 'Hey, Wombat,' he says —
today's pet name. 'What time is it?'

'Almost eight.'

'Are you on your way home?'

'No. I'm caught up. There's been a murder. I found the body.'

'Shit! Are you OK?'

'I'm fine, but we can't go away today. They want me here.'

'But it's all planned.'

'We can postpone.'

'We won't get our money back if I cancel, not this late.'

'We can go to Paris another time.'

'How did you know we were going to Paris?'

'Lucky guess.'

'Did your father tell you?'

'No. And why would he know?'

'He gave me the names of some restaurants.'

'I'm not sure I like the idea of my father helping plan our
romantic weekends.'

'He didn't plan all of it,' says Henry, sounding disappointed.

'I'll make it up to you,' I say. 'I'll wear my French maid's outfit.'

'You don't have a French maid's outfit.'

'That might be *my* surprise.'

Keegan clears his throat and I hang up quickly, feeling my
cheeks glow. Blushing has been the bane of my life since adoles-
cence when I lit up like a human traffic light every time a
good-looking boy spoke to me. I just hung up on Henry. I'll
have to apologise later. More guilt.

Keegan is with a matronly woman whose dyed black hair is
pulled back from her face so severely that her eyebrows are
clefs on her forehead.

'This is Mrs Manifold from child services. She's come to
collect Daisy.'

I shake Daisy's shoulder. She doesn't want to wake. I lift her
chin. 'Hey! Sleepyhead. Time to go.'

She blinks and rubs her eyes.

'This nice lady is going to take you somewhere and put you in a proper bed.'

'I don't want to go,' says Daisy. 'I want Mummy.'

'Your mummy isn't here.'

'Where has she gone?'

My heart flips. During my police training we were taught about bereavement counselling. Children should be told as soon as possible. The longer you leave it, the greater the likelihood they will overhear a conversation or find out in some other inappropriate way. At the same time, I realise that the news should come from somebody that Daisy loves and trusts, like her father or her grandparents.

'Is she dead?' asks Daisy, her big eyes demanding the truth. 'Fleabag died. We buried her in the garden beside the goldfish pond because she was always trying to catch those goldfish. Mummy said she'd gone to Heaven.'

'Your mummy is in Heaven too,' I say.

'With Fleabag?'

'Yes.'

Daisy's bottom lip quivers. 'I want Daddy.'

'He's at the hospital, but you'll get to see him very soon. Right now, you have to go with the nice lady, just until your daddy comes to get you.'

'Why can't I stay with you?'

'I'm a police officer and I'm very busy.'

'You look after people?'

'Yes, but Mrs Manifold will find you a nice family.'

Daisy looks at the woman and is clearly unimpressed.

Growing impatient, Mrs Manifold takes matters into her own hands. She leans into the car. 'Hello, young lady, aren't you a pretty thing?'

'Fuck off!' says Daisy.

The look of shock on Mrs Manifold's face makes me giggle.

'That's not very polite,' I say, trying to recover. 'You should apologise.'

'I want to stay with you.' Daisy flings her arms around my neck and tightens her grip until it hurts. I slide out of the police car, carrying her with me, and try to hand her over, but Daisy clings even more tightly. Three people are trying to prise her loose, unpeeling her fingers and limbs. Meanwhile, Daisy is screaming and bystanders are watching.

'Maybe we should do this somewhere else,' I say.

Mrs Manifold has one arm wrapped around the little girl's waist and manages to unlock her legs. Daisy is screaming and kicking. Tears stream down her cheeks.

Suddenly, she's pulled free and Mrs Manifold makes a triumphant sound. At that same moment, Daisy locks her teeth onto the woman's hand between the thumb and forefinger.

'Get her off! Get her off!' screams the social worker.

Mrs Manifold raises her hand, ready to lash out, but stops herself. Instead, she shoves Daisy, who falls backwards, bouncing off the car and crumpling into the gutter. The child blinks in shock and then leaps back into my arms, pressing her face into my chest and wrapping her legs around my waist.

'The little bitch!' mutters Mrs Manifold.

'You pushed her,' I say, incredulously.

'She bit me.'

'I don't care. I could arrest you for assault.'

'Oh, don't be so melodramatic.' She turns to DCI Keegan. 'You saw what happened.'

'I did, and the constable is correct. I suggest you apologise to Daisy and change your attitude.'

Mrs Manifold glares at the child, muttering under her breath. It could be an apology or it could be a death threat.

I pull Keegan to one side. 'You can't let her take Daisy.'

'What else can I do?'

'I can take her home with me.'

'You're part of the investigation.'

'I found her, that's all. She trusts me.'

Daisy still has her face buried into my neck but has stopped crying.

'Will you come home with me?' I ask.

She sniffles and nods.

'OK, take her for now,' says Keegan. 'But we still need to find her a placement.'

# 5

Edward McCarthy is standing at the edge of a muddy, water-filled pit where an earth-moving machine is half submerged, looking like a fossilised dinosaur exposed during an archaeological dig.

He's dressed in an oilskin jacket with a fur collar and a trilby that looks too small for his head, and his Wellingtons, recently purchased, are caked in mud.

'How do we get it out?' he asks.

'A crane,' says his brother Clifton, who is peering into the same hole.

'Can it be repaired?'

'Too soon to say.'

Clifton is taller by a foot and has a scar that curls from his mouth across the middle of his left cheek, which he calls his 'Glasgow smile'. He's dressed in a brown trench coat and has a shock of dark hair that spikes up whether he uses gel or not.

McCarthy turns away and splashes through puddles as he walks to a torn and twisted metal fence that has collapsed under the tracks of the excavator. The path of destruction continues across the construction site where iron formwork has been ripped up and pylons knocked over. A chemical toilet is lying on one side, leaving the smell of shit in the air.

'What else did we lose?' he asks.

'A pile driver, a skid loader and a trencher.'

'How much?'

'If they're unsalvageable – two hundred thousand.'

'Insurance?'

'Doesn't cover vandalism.'

'This isn't vandalism – it's sabotage.' McCarthy kicks aside an empty Coca-Cola can, which rattles against the fallen fence.

Nearby, the site office has one wall torn away, exposing the inside like a gutted whale. Sodden papers and broken computer equipment are strewn across the floor.

'Where were the security guards?'

'A car was set alight opposite the old ironworks,' says Clifton. 'It was a diversion. When the guards went to investigate, this happened.'

'We must have CCTV?'

'Three men in black, wearing balaclavas and gloves.'

If it isn't one thing, it's another, thinks McCarthy. Rain. Supply-chain issues. Cost overruns. Environmental regulations. Heritage orders. Now vandalism. Not the first attack. Three in the past month. Each more serious than the last. Escalation.

The unknown saboteur has yet to make any demands. Clearly, a sub-species, someone lower down the food chain, trying to knock him off his perch. Envy is a terrible thing – a cancer on the soul.

On days like today, McCarthy wishes he'd done something simpler with his life, like becoming a postman or a bookkeeper or a train driver. His grandfather had spent forty years driving the sleeper service from Euston to Edinburgh. Maybe not an easy life, but one less complicated. One track. A timetable. A beginning and an end.

Instead, McCarthy became a property developer, a euphemism for various activities, before leveraging everything on the Hope Island development – a mix of commercial and residential towers within spitting distance of London City Airport. This all-or-nothing play should have been a licence to print money but had become a recurring nightmare, what with Brexit, then Covid and soaring interest rates and no end of fuckery. Balls have to be kept in the air – employees, unions, creditors, bankers and suppliers – all while somebody is trying to cut off his arms with a chainsaw. The million-quid question: Who?

Up until now, anyone stupid enough to challenge the McCarthy family had been quickly re-educated. A visit from Daragh, brother number two, had sorted out the problem. A word in his shell-like and the sub-species would duly shit themselves, or spend the next ten years in hiding, hoping Daragh would never visit them again.

For the most part, McCarthy had avoided creating rivalries. He didn't flaunt his success by flashing his money around or rubbing the law's noses in his new-found prosperity. Yes, he had a nice gaffe and a few showy motors – but he was still a barrow boy at heart, who preferred fish and chips to foie gras.

When he married Constance, a minor blue blood, it wasn't because of status anxiety or to raise his social standing. He preferred to avoid the limelight, and to hire the best lawyers to keep people from asking uncomfortable questions about his business interests.

To this end, he cultivated powerful friendships with politicians, councillors and senior police officers. Wheels were oiled, of course, but unlike the old days, favours didn't require brown paper bags bulging with cash. His largesse might be a platinum membership to Chelsea or Arsenal FC or tickets to the Royal Opera House or racing tips straight from the horse's mouth. McCarthy had done the same for several national newspaper editors, but they change more often than engine oil and are usually oily little cunts.

Having his only daughter join the Metropolitan Police had been problematic, but McCarthy had tried to respect Philomena's choices without compromising his own ambitions. And although he hated her chosen career, he was proud of her and loved her and he hoped that one day she'd see the error of her ways.

Clifton has been waiting for instructions.

'This fuckery has to stop,' says McCarthy, breaking his silence. 'Double the security teams. Round the clock. Head-kickers.'

'And if they catch anyone?'

McCarthy motions to the water-filled pit. 'Bury 'em.'

A Range Rover navigates through the fallen fence and splashes through puddles, pulling up next to McCarthy's own Range Rover. Out of the car now, Daragh tiptoes through the mud, trying not to dirty his Oxford brogues. He looks like Bob Hoskins on steroids, with a short square body, balding head and the lumbering swagger of a sumo wrestler.

'You 'eard the news?' he asks.

'We're lookin' at it,' says Clifton.

'Nah, not that,' says Daragh, ignoring the sunken excavator. 'Kemp-Lowe got turned over early 'ours. Cleaned out. One white male taken to 'ospital.'

Daragh has never bothered sounding out the letter 'h' and certain other consonants. In his lexicon 'fings 'appen' for a reason and situations have to be 'andled or people get 'urt.

McCarthy is no longer interested in the vandalism. 'What happened?'

'Dunno all the details. The filth is crawling over 'Atton Garden. I picked up scanner chatter about a bomb. The what-nots 'ad to be called.'

Clifton: 'The bomb squad?'

'Yeah, that's what I said.'

'What was taken?' asks McCarthy, an edge to his voice.

'Too soon to tell, but there was some sort of 'ome invasion in Belsize Park. A woman is dead.'

'That's where Russell lives,' says Clifton.

'His wife?' speculates McCarthy. 'They must have held her hostage.' He turns to Clifton. 'When did Russell get back from Antwerp?'

'Thursday. I transferred the cash Tuesday.'

'How much did we give him?'

'Eleven million.'

They look at each other grimly. No words necessary.

McCarthy to Daragh. 'Go to the hospital. Find out what you can.'

'But I got the christening and the whatnot.'

'Tell Finbar he's up.'

# 6

I should call Henry but I don't want Daisy overhearing the conversation. She hasn't let go of my hand since the incident with Mrs Manifold. We catch a lift in a patrol car, riding in the back seat. Daisy is wearing a pair of jeans, a unicorn sweatshirt and her red woollen overcoat. I collected some spare clothes from her room, along with an overnight bag. Her bloodstained pyjamas were taken for testing after they swabbed her fingernails and her mouth for DNA.

At the terrace house in Clapham, Daisy follows me through the front door and immediately takes off her boots as though she's been here a hundred times before. I put them on the shoe rack that Henry built. When he's not fighting fires, my husband doubles as a handyman.

'You should have been a carpenter,' I once told him.

'Like Joseph,' he added.

'That would make me Mary.'

'And pregnant.'

'But still a virgin.'

'OK, let's stop the analogy there.'

Today's post is still waiting to be opened on the doormat. Energy bills, bank statements and flyers for local restaurants and tradespeople.

Henry looks over the banister. 'Hey, stranger. I thought you were at a crime scene.'

Daisy appears from behind me. She blinks at Henry with her impossibly long eyelashes.

'This is Daisy,' I say. 'She's come to spend the day with us.'

Henry looks puzzled and quickly checks that he's wearing more than just his boxer shorts.

'He might look scary, but he's a big teddy bear,' I tell Daisy.

'Is he your boyfriend?'

'No, I married him.'

She holds up her stuffed toy. 'This is Hippo.'

'Is Hippo a boy or a girl?' he asks.

'A boy, of course.'

'Well, Hippo looks hungry. What would he like to eat? Porridge? Scrambled eggs? Baked beans?'

'Daddy says baked beans make you fart.'

'That's very true,' says Henry. 'Unless you're Philomena. She never farts.'

'Very funny,' I say.

The two of them laugh because they clearly share the same childish sense of humour.

'OK, what *would* you like to eat?' he asks.

Daisy frowns in concentration and then announces, 'Pasta with dusty cheese.'

'What's dusty cheese?' I ask.

'I think she means Parmesan,' says Henry.

A perfect description.

Henry fills the kettle and lifts Daisy onto a stool. He's barefoot in faded jeans and a cotton shirt rolled to his elbows. It takes me by surprise sometimes – how handsome he is. Normally, it's only when I catch women staring at him or one of my friends makes some comment about my 'hot husband'. Henry doesn't seem to notice, which is another reason I love him.

He and Daisy are negotiating about what sort of pasta he should make. She chooses fusilli, calling it 'spirals'. They chat while he cooks. Henry is comfortable around children, having more experience than me. He has Archie from his first marriage, a sweet little boy, who sleeps over two nights a week and treats me like a big sister rather than his stepmother, which I don't mind, although he does call me his 'daddy's girlfriend' rather than his new wife. That's Roxanne's doing. Henry's ex. She doesn't seem to regard their divorce as being final, either financially or emotionally. As a result, she treats me like I've borrowed one of her sweaters and will give it back eventually.

Daisy notices a crayon drawing is pinned beneath magnets on the fridge.

'Who did that?'

'My little boy,' says Henry.

'Where is he?'

'He doesn't live here. Not all the time.'

'Henry has been married before,' I explain.

'Do you have any children?' asks Daisy.

'No.'

'Why not?'

Henry leans forward, elbows on the bench. 'Yes, why not?'

'Because I'm not ready,' I say, glaring at him.

'I need to do a wee,' says Daisy, sliding off the stool.

'It's two doors down. Past the stairs. Do you need my help?'

'No, but don't leave me.'

'I'll be right here.'

When she's gone, Henry whispers, 'Who is she?'

'Her mother was murdered. Her father is in hospital.'

Shocked: 'Does she know?'

'She found the body, but I'm not sure she fully understands.'

*Can a five-year-old comprehend the finality of it?*

Henry glances along the hallway. 'Why bring her here?'

'She refused to go with child services and it's only for a few hours.'

'What about the christening?'

I hadn't thought about that. 'She'll have to come with us.'

'Where?' asks Daisy. 'You whisper very loudly.'

'And you have very big ears.'

'Yes, but they're very clean.' She lifts her hair and shows me her ears.

'Do you take everything so literally?' I ask.

'What does that mean?'

*Where do I start?*

'Josie says I'm a pedant,' says Daisy. 'What's a pedant?'

'Who is Josie?'

'My babysitter, but I'm not a baby any more.'

Henry laughs and serves Daisy a plate of pasta, with grated Parmesan on the side.

'Where are we going?' she asks again.

'To church. A baby is being baptised today.'

'What's that?'

'Holy water gets poured on them.'

'Why?'

'To wash away their sins.'

'What sins?'

I'm lost. I look at Henry, hoping he might explain.

'It's more of a welcome ceremony,' he says. 'God says hello to the new baby.'

'And I get to become a godmother,' I add.

Daisy's eyes light up. 'I have a godmother. Her name is Amber. She has a moggy called Marmalade who gets in trouble for scratching her sofa.'

'Where does Amber live?' I ask.

'At her place.'

'Do you know her last name?'

'She doesn't have a last name,' says Daisy.

I make a mental note to call Keegan and tell him about the godmother. In the meantime, Henry has gone to get changed. I wait for Daisy to finish her pasta spirals.

'Do you go to preschool?' I ask.

'Two days a week.'

'Who normally takes you?'

'Mummy or Josie.'

'Does Josie live with you?'

'Sometimes she sleeps over.'

My heart skips a beat. 'Did she look after you last night?'

Daisy nods. 'We watched *Frozen* and had a hot chocolate. She let me have two marshmallows.'

'What is Josie's last name?'

Daisy shrugs.

'What about her phone number?'

'I have it in my schoolbag in case of an emerging-sea.'

'Emergency,' I say, remembering the schoolbag on the coat hook in the entrance hall.

I call Keegan. He answers on the third ring.

'Sorry to bother you, sir. There was someone else at the house last night – a babysitter called Josie. I don't have a last name, but her phone number is written in Daisy's schoolbag, which is hanging in the hallway. Daisy also mentioned a godmother, Amber. She can't tell me any more.'

'I told you not to question her,' says Keegan.

'It came up in conversation.'

He accepts the explanation but cautions me to be careful about tainting her memories or adding to her trauma.

Daisy has spied a cup of crayons on a shelf and asks if she can draw. I find her some paper. Kneeling on the stool, she leans over the bench, drawing with the intensity of a portraitist. While she's occupied, I quickly shower and get changed for the christening, wearing a floral knee-length dress and boots. Henry is using a lint brush on his jacket.

'Did Daisy see the killers?' he whispers.

'I don't know. I'm not supposed to ask her. She has to be properly interviewed.'

'When does that happen?'

'Tomorrow, maybe.'

'Where will she stay?'

'They're looking for a family member or close friend who can take her.'

Daisy has finished one drawing and begun another. She takes a black crayon and begins scrubbing it over the image, as though angry at what she's drawn. I step closer.

The image shocks me. It shows a stick figure with a round face, a gaping red mouth and large black eyes. A second smaller figure has long hair and is sitting on a chair.

'Who is that?' I ask.

'Mummy.'

'And that?'

'The bad man.'

'Did you meet the bad man?'

'He tucked me into bed.'

'Can I keep this drawing?' I ask.

'Do you want me to sign it?'

I laugh. 'Absolutely.'

She slowly spells out her name in wobbly capital letters in the lower right-hand corner.

# 7

DCI Brendan Keegan flashes his warrant card at a hospital security guard and follows a heavily pregnant woman into a lift. She arches her back as though counterbalancing the weight and smiles. He smiles back and thinks about asking when she's due, but what if there are complications? What if it's bad news? He remains silent. The lift climbs. The doors open. He steps out. She's gone.

A uniformed constable is slouched in a chair outside a private room. He stands quickly and pockets his phone, sucking in his stomach, and addressing Keegan as 'guvnor'.

'Is he awake?'

'Yes, guv.'

Keegan knocks and enters. Russell Kemp-Lowe has a white bandage wrapped around his head, which crosses his forehead diagonally making his eyes look lopsided. He is in an armchair near the window, dressed in pyjamas, a hospital gown and slippers. The remains of a meal are on a tray beside the bed. Untouched.

The jeweller looks up, hopefully. 'My wife. Is she OK? And Daisy? Where are they?'

Keegan pulls a chair closer. Sun slants through the Venetian blinds, throwing patterns on the floor. It's too nice a day for this.

'Russell, I'm very sorry to inform you that your wife is dead.'

Kemp-Lowe blinks at him in disbelief and begins shaking his head, repeating the word 'no' and trying to stand. Then another degree of horror clouds his face. 'Daisy?'

'Your daughter is unhurt. We're looking after her.'

The relief is short-lived. The jeweller begins to sob quietly, burying his face in his hands. 'They promised. They promised.'

'What did they promise?' asks Keegan, pressing the record app on his phone and placing it on the low table.

'They said they wouldn't hurt her.'

'Who?'

'The men who broke into the house. They said if I did as I was told, nobody would get hurt. Caitlin and Daisy would be safe. They only wanted the jewellery—'

Keegan stops him. 'I know it's difficult to talk about these things so soon after learning about your wife, but it's important that we get information quickly if we're going to catch these men. Your recollections are vital.'

'I didn't see their faces.'

'OK, but you talked to them. You travelled with them. You can help us.'

The jeweller nods and takes a shuddering breath.

Keegan begins. 'Take me back to Friday evening?'

'We were at a charity gala at the Banking Hall. Caitlin was one of the organisers. It was for the homeless or something like that. Philanthropy is one of her hobbies.'

'What time did you get home?'

'Earlier than expected. Caitlin had a headache. We caught a cab and got home around ten-thirty. I drove Josie back to her place.'

'Josie?'

'Josie Sheldon. She babysits for us. She used to be Daisy's nanny.'

'Where does she live?'

'Kilburn.'

Keegan makes a note of the address. 'You dropped her home and then what?'

'I drove back to the house.'

'What time was that?'

'Some time after eleven. I parked and locked the car and walked up the path.'

'Did you notice anyone else in the street? Any strange cars? People watching?'

'No.' Kemp-Lowe pauses and frowns. 'I remember the lights were off downstairs. Caitlin normally leaves them on in the entrance hall and on the landing in case Daisy needs the bathroom at night.'

'Then what?'

'I had my key in the door and they jumped me. They must have been hiding in the garden. They wore masks. One of them put his hand over my mouth and a gun to my head. He used my keys to unlock the door and pushed me inside. I tripped. Fell. One of them sat on my back and pulled my arms behind me.'

'How many?'

'Three, maybe four. One grabbed my hair and yanked my head up. He told me to call out to Caitlin, but not to warn her. They wanted her to come downstairs. I used an old pet name for her, hoping she might realise that something was wrong and press the panic button, but she appeared on the landing. Once she saw the gun, it was too late.'

'You said they wore masks.'

'One was a zombie, another was a skull, and there was a Joker, like in *Batman*.'

'So, three men?'

He looks confused. 'Maybe. Yes. Three.'

'What about their clothes?'

'Dark colours. Jackets, boots. Paramilitary stuff.'

'They spoke English?'

'Yes.'

'Accents?'

'Foreign sounding.'

'Did they use any names, nicknames?'

'No.'

Keegan doesn't press for more because he knows that Kemp-Lowe will have to be interviewed again, multiple times, as

investigators mine his memories for even the smallest details –
distinguishing features, phrases, smells, tattoos, teeth, jewellery . . .

'You mentioned a gun – what did it look like?'

'A pistol. I don't know anything about guns.'

'Where was Daisy?'

'Asleep upstairs, thank God. I told them they could have
whatever they wanted. My wallet. My car. We have a safe in the
main bedroom. I told them the combination.'

'What's in there?'

'Papers. Wills. Birth certificates. Caitlin's jewellery.'

'How much is that worth?'

'It's insured for half a million.'

Keegan types a note to himself on his phone. Why would
they leave the safe untouched? He wants it opened and the
contents checked.

'You said your wife came downstairs.'

'They took us to the kitchen and sat us on chairs. Caitlin was
in her nightgown. One of them put his hands on her breasts and
made some horrible remark about her being a . . .' He chokes
on a sob. 'I thought they were going to . . . to . . .' He looks up
from his hands. 'Tell me she wasn't . . . they didn't . . .'

'There's no obvious evidence of a sexual assault,' says Keegan.

Kemp-Lowe drags his fingers down his pale cheeks, leaving
marks on his skin. He takes a sip of water, spilling some onto
his hospital gown.

'You were in the kitchen,' says Keegan.

'I kept begging them to leave us alone, I offered them
everything, but they put tape over my mouth and threatened
to hurt Caitlin if I caused any trouble.'

'What happened then?'

'Nothing. Not for a long while. Hours. Daisy woke up. She
came downstairs. We were terrified. Caitlin begged them not
to hurt her.'

'Did Daisy see you?'

'She came to the kitchen door. She was asking for her

46

mummy.' His voice breaks. 'Caitlin told her to go back to bed. One of the men took her upstairs.'

'Did you see her again?'

'No.'

'What did these men say they wanted?'

'I had to open the safe at the store. They said that Caitlin was going to stay behind and that if I did what I was told she'd be left untouched.' He utters a broken sob.

'What time did you leave the house?'

'Two o'clock.'

'How can you be so sure?'

'The clock on the wall oven.'

'Did you leave through the front door?'

'No. We used the side path. I had a hood over my head. I was hoping one of the neighbours might see us leaving and call the police. They bundled me into the back of a van.'

'Make? Model? Colour?'

'I can't tell you.'

'How many men got into the van.'

'Two of them. One driving. Another in the back with me.'

'They left someone behind?'

'That's what they said.'

At least three men, thinks Keegan as the jeweller continues.

'They told me that if anything went wrong – if the alarm sounded, or the safe didn't open, or the police showed up – Caitlin would be dead.'

'Who did the talking?'

'The one in charge. He wore the Joker mask.'

'You said he sounded foreign.'

'East European or Russian or maybe Polish.'

'You sound Australian.'

'I came to London in my twenties to study acting at RADA, the Royal Academy of Dramatic Arts. I met Caitlin and the rest is . . .' He doesn't finish. He sniffles and wipes his nose on his pyjama sleeve. 'Where's Daisy?'

'She's with a young police constable.'

'When can I see her?'

'Soon, but let's get back to the robbery. What happened when you got to the store?'

'They removed the hood and cut my bindings and told me to turn off the alarm system and the CCTV feed.'

'You could have triggered the silent panic button.'

'Yes, but if the police showed up, they were going to kill Caitlin.' His eyes are shining. 'I told them that the safe had a timer mechanism and it couldn't be opened until eight, but they didn't believe me. That's when I got this.' He lifts his pyjama top and shows an ugly purple bruise below his ribs.

'They hit you?'

'With the pistol.'

'Why did you lie to them?'

'I thought they might just take the jewellery in the display cases and leave the safe alone, but they insisted.'

'What was in the safe?'

'The high-value pieces.'

'How much are we talking about?'

He hesitates, either reluctant to say or calculating a figure.

'Three million pounds – give or take.'

'Any cash?'

'No.'

'What about the jewellery in the display cases?'

'Maybe another million.'

'Insured?'

'Yes, but not for the full value. The premiums are too expensive.'

'What happened after you opened the safe?'

'They made me put on the vest and told me that if I moved the entire building would come down, killing everyone. There are people living upstairs. Families. Old people . . .'

'The guy in the Joker mask – had you ever heard his voice before?'

'No.'

'Think back – over the past month or so – did anybody come into the store that might have been planning this; someone who took an interest in the cameras, or the alarm system? Someone watching you . . . following you?'

Kemp-Lowe shakes his head.

'What about Caitlin? Could she have been followed?'

'She only comes to the store on Fridays, to do the payroll and bookkeeping.'

'She was in yesterday?'

He nods.

Keegan stops recording and pockets his phone. 'We're going to need a full inventory for what's been stolen – including photographs and valuations.'

'I don't have photographs of everything. Some of the pieces don't belong to us. They were being cleaned or valued.'

'Do what you can.'

A nurse appears. She has green eyes and a Portuguese accent. Smiling apologetically, she checks the stitches on Kemp-Lowe's head, slowing unwrapping the bandage. A patch of his head is shaved. Ugly black stitches crisscross behind his right ear.

'How are you feeling?' she asks.

'I need something for the pain,' says the jeweller.

She checks his chart. 'You're not due for another two hours.'

'It hurts.'

'I'll talk to the doctor.'

Keegan steps out of the room. He has a missed phone call from his estranged wife, Veronica. She has left a voice message. The same one that she's been leaving every day for a month. She wants to know if he's signed the divorce papers, which were due back two weeks ago. He's been putting it off, hoping Veronica might change her mind, but that's not going to happen. It's also difficult to sign a document that is lying in torn pieces in the wastepaper basket beneath his desk.

An elderly patient hobbles past, lifting and placing a Zimmer frame like he's measuring the length of the corridor. The patient pauses and coughs into his pyjama sleeve. Keegan holds his breath and feels his skin crawl with germs and infection. He squeezes a drop of hand sanitiser onto his palm and rubs them together, working the pungent gel into every wrinkle and fold of skin.

His phone rings. A name appears on screen. Assistant Commissioner Colin Duckworth is in charge of specialist operations. He's one of the rising stars of the Met – young, Black and state-school educated – an officer who ticks all the boxes. Is that a racist thing to think?

'What have we got?' asks Duckworth.

'A home invasion. Robbery. One dead. One injured. Four million taken.'

'You sure you can handle this?'

'Yes, sir.'

'Brief me on Monday morning. My office.'

# 8

More than a hundred people have gathered at St Alfege Church in the centre of Greenwich. Uncles. Aunts. Cousins. Family friends. The McCarthys love a party and Uncle Daragh has arranged this one. His eldest daughter, Rosie, has given him his first grandchild, a baby girl, and Daragh is handing out cigars like he's the father or deserves some of the credit.

He's dressed in pinstriped trousers and a fawn coat with a crimson velvet collar – an ensemble that fits him like a brick because of his body shape. If ever a man looked like a dangerous psychopath, it's Daragh, but in my experience, he's as gentle as a lamb, full of big hugs and magic tricks.

'I don't think you should be encouraging smoking,' I say.

'Yeah, my Rosie said the same fing,' he replies, tucking a cigar into Henry's coat pocket. 'How's my favourite water fairy?'

'I'm a fireman,' says Henry.

'Same fing. Firebugs. Water fairies. Daffodils.'

'Why daffodils?' I ask.

'Cause they wear yellow 'ats and stand around in bunches.'

I can't help but laugh, which annoys Henry.

Daragh spies Daisy. 'Who do we 'ave 'ere?'

'This is my friend, Daisy. I'm looking after her for the day.'

He squats on his haunches. 'Nice to meet you, Daisy.'

Reaching into the fob pocket of his waistcoat, he takes out a wrapped sweet. Holding it between the thumb and forefinger of his left hand, he closes his right hand over the sweet and makes it disappear.

Daisy points to his right hand. He opens his palm. Empty. She points to his left hand. The same thing.

'Where did it go?' she asks.

'Right here.'

He pulls the sweet from behind her ear. I've seen that trick a thousand times, but it still feels new. He hands it to Daisy.

'I'm not supposed to take sweets from strangers,' she says.

'Very wise advice,' says Daragh. 'Give it to your mummy.'

'My mummy is dead.'

The statement knocks the air out of Daragh, but the only outward sign is a creasing around his eyes. A silence follows. A mumbled apology. I change the subject quickly and ask about Rosie.

'She's inside with the aunts,' says Daragh. 'And your old man has gone to the pub with Clifton and Finbar. Quick bevvy before the whatnot.'

'Typical.'

Nudging Daisy towards the church, we enter the arched doorway into a cool dark interior full of flowers and coloured light from the stained-glass windows. People are milling in the aisles and nieces and nephews are chasing each other between the pews. I'm greeted by aunts and cousins and family friends. My childhood doctor, now retired, is in a wheelchair, and some of Daragh's old mates from the markets have come to wet the baby's head.

Most children of divorce have blended families. Mine is more jumbled or mashed. My mother hasn't spoken to my father since they divorced more than a decade ago. At my wedding, they sat on different sides of the church and at separate ends of the top table, never making eye contact.

They loved each other once. According to Daddy, they had sex in the limousine on the way to their wedding reception, which was more information than I needed to know, and quite the feat considering the layers of organza and lace that my mother was wearing. Now they live in different postcodes, physically and morally. Mummy is a Mass-every-Sunday Catholic while Daddy worships Plutus, the god of abundance and wealth.

I've always known he was different. At five years old, I sat on his knee in the visitors' room of HMP Wormwood Scrubs, visiting Daragh, Clifton and Finbar, who were big hard men, but never criminals – not in my mind.

The law thought differently. The McCarthy brothers were the most notorious criminal gang in the south-east of England, who were still in their teens when they were selling counterfeit and pilfered goods at market stalls in the East End of London. They graduated to hijacking trucks and eventually controlled the movement of every shipping container that passed through ports like Harwich and Dover, collecting fees to allow stevedores to load and unload them.

The extortion racket was broken in the late nineties and Daragh, Clifton and Finbar were sent to prison. Not my father. He escaped unscathed. My uncles served ten-year sentences. Hard time. When they finally came out, Daddy had transformed the 'firm'. Instead of 'taxing' shipping containers, he provided building services. Anyone who wanted to lay a concrete slab, or erect a piece of scaffolding, or hire an excavator, or protect a worksite in Central London had to use his contractors. It wasn't a choice.

These days he calls himself a property developer and a 'facilitator', although I don't know what a facilitator does and have no desire to find out. It's like that famous quote about sausages. Sometimes it's best not to see how they're made or what goes inside.

Finbar's oldest boy, Toby, puts his arm around my waist and kisses me. My cheeks always colour when I'm around Toby because I remember how we used to practise snogging when we were thirteen. It happened one summer when our families went to Cornwall and rented a big house and I learned how to sail. I had braces, and eczema on my elbows. Toby tasted of bubblegum and wanted to be a professional footballer. Now he manages a car salesroom in Romford and has a wife and three children and thinning hair.

My stepmother, Constance, breaks from a group and sashays towards me. She's dressed like she's going to Ascot for the races, in a body-hugging white dress and an enormous hat that almost takes out an eye when she leans in to kiss my cheeks.

'Philomena, you look lovely. It's so nice to see you in a dress.'

I ignore the passive-aggressive compliment and instead admire her hat and her shoes. High heels, of course. She has the calves of a dancer.

'I hope you're coming back to the house afterwards.'

'Sadly, I can't. I'm looking after Daisy.'

'Daisy?'

I point to the little girl with a hippo under her arm. She is with Henry, watching the other children playing.

'Who does she belong to?' asks Constance.

'Her father is in hospital. We're going to visit him.'

Thankfully, she doesn't ask any more questions. Instead, she looks past me, searching for my father.

'If he's late, I'll kill him,' she says.

'He won't be late.'

Daddy has many faults, but tardiness is not one of them.

I look for Rosie, who is holding a baby girl, swaddled in an antique lace christening shawl that has been in the family for generations. I was baptised in the same shawl.

Rosie is talking to her mum, Auntie Mary, who was diagnosed with cancer six months ago. She has lost weight and her head is covered by a brightly coloured turban, but she looks radiant. Rosie also looks amazing, blooming with happiness, and I wonder if those horror stories about motherhood, the sleepless nights and cracked nipples are exaggerated. Her husband, Terry, is hovering, probably wishing he'd gone to the pub with Daddy. Terry is a social worker for Lambeth Council, and I can't imagine what he must have gone through to marry Daragh's eldest daughter. Most men would have run a mile when they met him as their future father-in-law.

'What do I have to do?' I ask Rosie.

'The vicar will talk you through it,' she says. 'You can ignore all the "walking in the way of Christ" stuff. You're going to be the cool godparent.'

'Me? Cool?'

'Yeah, you get to give her the proper sex talk and can get her stoned when she turns eighteen.'

'I'd best do the sex talk before the dope.'

'That might be safer.'

The volume suddenly rises and I know that my father has arrived because his voice booms above all the others.

'OK, let's pour some magic water on this baby's head,' he says, striding down the aisle. Uncle Finbar and Clifton are close behind. Finbar is the youngest and tallest of my uncles, with a shaved and oiled scalp and a bushranger beard. Clifton has dressed in a suit and open-necked white shirt, and has unsuccessfully tried to tame a cowlick that makes his hair stick up like a dorsal fin. He's with his partner, Morris, who looks like George Clooney and dresses like David Beckham.

Henry sidles up next to me and nods towards the baby. 'I want one of those.'

'You can't have one.'

'But you can.'

'Yes. One day.'

Daisy has gone quiet, overawed by the number of people. Henry can see the problem and takes her outside.

The vicar arrives. A grey-haired woman in black robes, she summons the parents and godparents to join her. We stand around the baptismal font, a silver bowl on a stone plinth. Rosie is holding the baby, who has the sweetest button nose and liquid brown eyes. Her hands are so tiny.

My phone begins vibrating in my blazer pocket. I want to

check who's calling, but don't want to interrupt. It stops and rings again. I sneak a glance and see Keegan's name on the screen.

The vicar is giving instructions to the godparents, telling us we are responsible for protecting this 'new young soul' and guiding her on 'God's path'.

'I'm really sorry. I have to take this,' I whisper to Rosie.

I step to the side, beside the choir stalls, and answer the call. Keegan doesn't bother with pleasantries: 'Bring Daisy to the Royal Free. Her father is awake.'

'I'm busy now . . . at a christening.'

'Is it your baby?'

'No.'

'Then you can bring her.'

He hangs up before I can argue. I return to the gathering. The vicar is still speaking.

'Will you be responsible for seeing the child is brought up in the Christian faith?'

The other godparents answer in unison: 'I will with God's help.'

I lean close to Rosie.

'I have to go.'

'Now?'

'Uh-huh. It's work.'

'But?'

'I'm sorry.'

I begin walking up the centre aisle, aware that everybody is staring at me.

The vicar continues. 'The Christian community welcomes you with great joy as I christen you Victoria Mary Alcott, in the name of the Father, and of the Son, and of the Holy Spirit.'

'Amen,' is the chorus.

Henry and Daisy are sitting on the stone steps. Henry stands and wipes the back of his trousers. 'Has it finished?'

'Not yet. They want Daisy at the hospital.'

'I can drive you.'

'No. You stay. Apologise for me.'

He looks nervously into the church.

'They won't bite,' I say. 'They like you.'

'Only when you're around.'

Reluctantly, he hands me the car keys and I walk Daisy out of the gates, turning right into Roan Street. A car is parked across the road. The driver is holding up a phone, as though filming us. I walk along the opposite side of the road and he pans the phone, following our progress. There is no law against filming someone in public unless it is stalking behaviour, but I feel uncomfortable and hold Daisy's hand a little tighter.

'Come on, sweetheart. Let's go and see your daddy.'

# 9

We're stuck in traffic on Finchley Road.

'We should have caught the Tube,' I say.

'Mummy doesn't like the Tube,' says Daisy. 'She says it's full of Germans.'

'You mean germs.'

'Uh-huh.'

She holds Hippo up to the window, as though showing him this part of London. This is the first time she's mentioned her mother in the past few hours but has spoken in the present tense. I wonder if she's forgotten or if she's still processing what happened and doesn't realise the cause and effect or the finality of death.

Turning into Pond Street, I glimpse photographers and reporters milling outside the main hospital entrance. Carrying on, I park in the visitors' area, before taking Daisy through a different door, avoiding the cameras and the scrutiny.

I know the Royal Free Hospital because two of my friends have had babies here in the past year. I've also visited as a police officer, conducting interviews with battered wives, failed suicides, crime suspects and rape survivors. The ground floor has a history wall. It reveals how the Royal Free was founded in 1828, by a surgeon called William Marsden. He discovered a diseased and hungry young girl lying on the steps of a nearby church, but she died because nearby hospitals had turned her away. Outraged, Marsden set up a small dispensary in Holborn, which he called the London General Institution for the Gratuitous Care of

Malignant Diseases. Later, thankfully, it was renamed the Free Hospital and, later still, given the royal charter by Queen Victoria.

Keegan is waiting for me in a patient lounge on the sixth floor. I settle Daisy on a chair and step into the corridor, showing him the crayon drawing.

'She called him the bad man,' I say, pointing to the figure with black holes for eyes.

'Did she see his face?'

'I didn't ask. What about the babysitter?'

'Josie Sheldon shares a house in Kilburn. She and her boyfriend left London early this morning for a planned weekend away. Both have their phones turned off.'

'That's unusual.'

'We're interviewing their housemates.' Keegan motions along the corridor. 'Russell Kemp-Lowe is awake. I've told him about his wife.'

'How did he take it?'

'As well as anyone could, given the circumstances. I want you to stay close to Daisy. Listen to what they say.'

'You *suspect* him?'

'I suspect everybody.'

The answer seems too flippant, but Keegan doesn't resile from it. I collect Daisy from the lounge and knock on the door. Russell Kemp-Lowe is bandaged and bruised, sitting in a chair beside the bed. He stands stiffly and scoops Daisy into his arms. I remember being hugged by my father – the sandpapery stubble on his cheeks, the strength of his arms, his smell of Old Spice and cigar smoke and breath mints.

Kemp-Lowe is crying quietly. He wipes his eyes and forces himself to smile, calling her Poppet. Then he acknowledges me for the first time.

'Are you the officer who found her?'

'Yes, sir.'

'I can't thank you enough . . . to lose her would . . .' He doesn't finish.

Still in pain, he lowers himself into the chair and Daisy crawls onto his lap, settling into his arms.

'Mummy is with Fleabag,' she says, as though breaking the news to her father. He takes a moment to understand the reference. Daisy continues, 'The bad men hurt her, but Phil is going to catch them.'

'Phil?'

'That's me,' I say, embarrassed. 'I'm not really part of the investigation.'

'But you're a police officer?'

'Yes.'

'They won't let me leave the hospital until tomorrow at the earliest. Where will Daisy stay?'

'Do you have any other family?'

'Caitlin's parents live in Golders Green, but her dad has dementia and her mum has her hands full already.'

'What's dementia?' asks Daisy.

'It means you forget things,' says her father.

'Is there anyone else?'

'I gave Detective Keegan a name. Caitlin's best friend. Amber Culver.'

'Auntie Amber!' says Daisy, excitedly.

'Would you like to go and stay with her?' he asks.

'And Marmalade?'

'That's a tabby cat,' he explains.

'Is she Daisy's aunt?' I ask.

'Just her godmother. She and Caitlin were at school together. I could call her, but I don't have my phone.'

'You'll get it back. It's with forensics.'

'Why?'

'We need to trace your movements. The gang could have followed you or your wife.'

A knock on the door. Keegan motions me into the corridor. 'Amber Culver is here.'

'That was quick.'

'She turned up at the house and saw the police cars.'

'Does she know Caitlin is dead?'

'Yes.'

Glancing past him, I see a woman waiting at the far end of the corridor. Late-thirties. Curvy. Agitated. She's dressed in black exercise wear, white trainers and a sleeveless puffer that bulks out her chest.

'Talk to her,' says Keegan. 'Make sure she doesn't say the wrong thing in front of Daisy.'

*Is there a right thing?*

I introduce myself to Amber and take her into the lounge. We sit side by side on a sofa, knees almost touching. Her make-up is deftly applied, accentuating her large brown eyes, but she looks tired and fearful.

'Where is Daisy? Is she OK? Can I see her?'

'Soon. How did you hear the news?'

'On the radio. It mentioned a jewellery-store robbery. I thought of Caitlin and Russell. I called Caitlin's number but it kept going to her voicemail.'

Late afternoon sun is streaming through the Venetian blinds, creating vertical stripes on the floor and far wall. Angles within angles. Light and shade.

'Daisy found Caitlin's body,' I say, watching the news contort Amber's face. 'We don't know how much she witnessed, or if she can identify any of the attackers, which is why you can't mention the robbery to Daisy. You can't ask her questions or make comments that might influence her memories until she's been formally interviewed.'

'But she's a child. You can't make her relive what happened.'

'We do it very gently.'

'When?'

'Possibly tomorrow.'

'Who's looking after her? She can stay with me.'

'One thing at a time.'

I take her along the corridor and knock gently on the door.

As we enter the room, Daisy lets out a squeak and throws her arms around her godmother. Amber picks her up, balancing her easily on her hip, and goes to Russell Kemp-Lowe. They embrace, arms interlocked, Daisy in the middle.

Eventually, they separate, but Daisy keeps hold of Amber's hand.

'You'll do it, won't you? Look after her,' says Kemp-Lowe.

'For as long as necessary,' says Amber.

'Can Marmalade sleep on my bed?' asks Daisy.

'Marmalade sleeps wherever he wants to,' says Amber. She studies the jeweller. 'How are you feeling?'

'Bruised. Heartbroken. Angry.' He plucks a few other words out of his vocabulary, before taking a ragged breath. 'I should have stayed at the house. I should never have left her.'

'Was that an option?' asks Amber.

I interrupt them and shake my head. They look at me apologetically and begin talking indirectly, using euphemisms and codes, but I sense that Daisy is soaking up information, picking up on the unspoken signals.

'Maybe I should take Daisy out for a walk,' I say. She's about to protest. 'Or a hot chocolate.'

'With two marshmallows?'

'We can ask.'

Daisy takes my hand as we walk towards the lifts. As we wait for the doors to open, Daisy looks up at me, earnestly. 'Mummy isn't coming back, is she?'

'No.'

'Because of the bad men.'

'Yes.'

Her fingers tighten on mine.

Downstairs, Keegan is talking on the phone. He ends the call and motions me aside. 'That was child services. They want us to check out Amber Culver's house. You go. Make sure it's OK for a short-term placement.'

'Yes, sir. When do you want to interview Daisy?'

'First thing Monday morning. You bring her.'

'Where?'

'To the house.'

'That could be triggering.'

'It could also help her remember.'

'Will her father be present?'

'No. A child psychologist. I want you there, too. Bring her at ten.'

# 10

I order a hot chocolate for Daisy with an extra marshmallow, which she nibbles like a mouse with a piece of cheese.

'Auntie Amber seems nice,' I say. 'Have you stayed with her before?'

'Lots.'

'Does she have children?'

'She says I'm her baby, but I'm not a baby. I'm a big girl.'

'Yes, you're very grown-up.'

From the café, I can see the reporters and cameramen still milling outside the hospital. A man pushes through them. It takes me a moment to recognise Uncle Finbar because I don't associate him with a place like this. He must have left the christening party.

I call out to him when he's halfway across the foyer. He does a double-take before giving me a hug that smells of whisky and throat lozenges.

'Fancy seeing you here,' he says. 'Are you working?'

'Yes. You?'

'Visiting a friend.'

'Somebody I know?'

'A geezer I drink with. Had a stroke, poor bugger.'

Finbar lies so easily. They all do. My father. My uncles. My aunts. Maybe it's a family trait. Did I get the same genes?

'This is my uncle, Finbar,' I say to Daisy, who is hiding behind me, her fists holding the fabric of my dress. 'And this is Daisy,' I tell Finbar.

Recognition flares in his eyes. It's like watching the inner workings of a cuckoo clock, the cogs and wheels turning, before the bird pops out on a spring.

He crouches to her level. 'What's your last name, Daisy?'

'Why?' I ask.

'She just looks familiar, you know. I thought she might go to school with one of my hatchlings.'

He means his grandkids. He has eight of them, produced by his five children, who consist of a son, Toby, three daughters and a non-binary 'them' or 'they', George, who was once Georgia.

Finbar straightens and looks past us to the reporters outside. 'Well, I best be off.'

'To visit your sick friend?'

'Yeah.'

I watch him cross the foyer and approach the information desk. A receptionist shakes her head, but Finbar keeps her talking. She blushes and smiles and taps at a computer screen. Finbar is such a charmer.

'Is he really your uncle?' asks Daisy.

'Yes.'

'He's scary but nice.'

*Out of the mouths of babes.*

Upstairs, Russell Kemp-Lowe and Amber are deep in conversation, but they stop talking when they see Daisy.

'Are you ready to go home?' asks Amber, brushing hair from Daisy's forehead.

'I have to tag along to do a security check,' I say.

'You'll get to meet Marmalade,' says Daisy. Taking hold of our hands, she swings between us, letting her legs leave the ground.

I choose the same side entrance, avoiding the media, and I follow Amber's directions to Sutherland Avenue in Maida Vale, pulling up under plane trees that are changing colour and shedding leaves onto the pavement and grass verge. Amber lives in a garden flat with a cluttered hallway that leads past a cluttered sitting room to a cluttered kitchen that overlooks a cluttered garden.

Daisy calls out for Marmalade.

'He'll be sleeping in the drying cupboard,' says Amber. 'He knows every warm place.'

Amber apologises for the mess, nervous around me. 'Would you like tea or coffee? I know you can't drink on duty. Are you on duty? I don't have any alcohol. I don't know why I asked. Silly, really.'

'I'm fine with water,' I say, taking a seat at the kitchen table. 'How long have you lived here?'

'Since my divorce.'

'I'm sorry.'

'Don't be. I'm happier on my own.'

'No children?'

'Not of my own.'

'You have stepchildren?'

She laughs and shakes her head.

Daisy appears with a cat draped over her shoulder. Marmalade is almost half her size and still half asleep.

'Don't worry,' says Amber. 'He's used to being treated like a rag doll.'

'I'm hungry,' says Daisy.

'You're always hungry.'

'I'm a growing girl.'

Both of us laugh and Amber begins peeling an apple and cutting it into quarters. Meanwhile, Marmalade escapes through the cat flap into the garden.

'Is it OK if I look around the flat?' I ask.

'Of course, I'll show you the spare room,' says Amber.

We leave Daisy at the kitchen table and I get a guided tour. It doesn't take long. The second bedroom has a single bed and two enormous chests of drawers. There are photographs on a dresser – pictures of Amber graduating university and working as an airline stewardess and skiing in the Alps. No marriage photos, but there are some of Daisy.

I pick up one picture that shows a newborn baby, still covered in gunk, nestled in her mother's arms. Amber is alongside them and both women are wearing hospital scrubs.

Amber has followed me to the bedroom. 'That's Caitlin and Daisy,' she says, explaining the photograph.

'You were at the birth?'

'Yes.'

'Where was Russell?'

'He didn't want to be there. He said something about hating the sight of blood.'

Amber takes the photograph from me and replaces it on the dresser. 'I know this place is untidy, but that's what happens when you divorce and have to squeeze too much furniture into a smaller flat. But it's clean and warm and safe, and Daisy has stayed here before.'

'How did you and Caitlin meet?'

'At school. Godolphin and Latymer.'

I know the place. It's a private girls' school in West London. Expensive. Sought after.

'I was a scholarship girl,' says Amber, as though reading my mind. 'My parents don't have that sort of money. I met Caitlin on my first day. She didn't know anyone either. We both loved drama and dancing. After our A-level exams, we took a gap year and went travelling through South-East Asia and Australia.'

'Is that where she met Russell?'

'No. They met in London. I introduced them. He was a young Aussie actor, appearing in his first West End production.' She drops her voice conspiratorially. 'He wasn't very good, but by God he was handsome and something of a player. Caitlin took one look and said, "He's the one for me."'

'What happened to his acting?'

'Oh, that was never going to last. Once his looks began to

fade, he joined the family business. He even took Caitlin's surname.'

'Why?'

'I think he liked being part of a famous jewellery dynasty.'

'Does he run the company?'

'Heavens, no. Caitlin is the boss. She took over when her father was diagnosed with dementia.'

'Any other siblings?'

'A brother, but nobody talks about him.'

'Why?'

'He's the black sheep or maybe he's the prodigal son. I can never remember my Bible stories.'

'I don't think black sheep were in the Bible,' I say, although the term does have ancient roots, dating back to when black sheep were seen as being marked by the devil because their wool couldn't be dyed.

Amber smiles. 'Noah gave his parents no end of trouble. Drugs. Alcohol. Petty crime. He was expelled from four different schools and had two stints in rehab, before going to prison.'

'What for?'

Amber hesitates. 'I'm not sure I should be talking about it.'

'I can look it up easily enough.'

She sighs grudgingly. 'He was convicted of supplying heroin to a woman who died of an overdose. His girlfriend. Then he breached parole and ran off to America. By then, his parents had disowned him. Written him out of their will. Once a junkie, always a junkie, that's what Caitlin said.'

Not in my experience, I think. Three out of four addicts recover, but I let it pass.

'How did Noah feel about that?' I ask.

'No idea.'

'Has he ever asked Caitlin for money?'

'He wouldn't dare.'

My phone is vibrating. A photograph of my father appears on screen. I answer.

'Where did you run off to?' he asks.

'Work called.'

'You're missing the party.'

'Has anyone disgraced themselves?'

'Daragh fell in the pond when he unsuccessfully tried to launch a kite.'

'Lack of wind?'

'Surfeit of alcohol. When are you off to Paris?'

'We're not going.'

'But I thought—'

'Does my entire family know about my romantic weekend away?'

'Only me . . . and, um, Constance.'

'Everybody, then.'

# 11

Late-afternoon shadows are drawing a blanket over the soggy lawn and trimmed hedges and raised garden beds. It should be too cold to sit outside on the terrace, but Edward McCarthy prefers to talk outdoors.

The guests have gone and Constance is inside, unloading and reloading the dishwasher with plates and glasses. Outside, the gardeners are packing up the badminton net and croquet hoops and fishing a sodden kite from the pond.

Daragh is dressed in a tracksuit and slippers, having ruined his own clothes. He rests his feet on the railing fence. 'Imagine mowing this gaffe. You'd finish and have to start again.'

'You don't have a garden,' says Clifton. 'You paved paradise and put up a parking lot.'

'It's an all-weather tennis court.'

'You don't play tennis.'

'Yeah, but I'm gonna get lessons.' He hits a forehand with an imaginary racquet. 'I reckon I'd be quite good.'

Constance joins them on the patio. She's wearing padded jodhpurs, riding boots, a fitted blouse and a short red jacket. Her long dark hair is pinned up in a bun.

'Shall I turn on the lights?' she asks.

'Nicer in the dark,' says McCarthy. 'We can see the sunset.'

'What sunset?'

'It's going down somewhere.' McCarthy rattles the ice in his tumbler. 'I could do with a top-up.'

Constance disappears through the French doors and returns with a decanter of whisky. As she crosses the patio, all eyes follow her. McCarthy doesn't mind. Constance is a beautiful woman and dresses for attention.

'How was your ride?' asks Daragh.

'My ride?' asks Constance.

'Your horse.'

'Oh, I don't have a horse. Evil creatures. Such horrible eyes.'

'Why are you wearing the clobber – the jodhpurs and what-nots?'

'Because I look good in them,' says Constance, as if the answer were obvious.

The men laugh. She smiles. Her accent is pure Sloane Square, whereas McCarthy is an Eastender through and through, born within earshot of the Bow Bells. They met fifteen years ago, when Constance was working as a paralegal in a law firm in Chancery Lane. McCarthy was contemplating divorce and looking for a new secretary. Constance was single and seeking a rich husband. Not quite yin and yang, but good marriages are made in the head as much as the heart.

Constance tops up every drink but skimps on McCarthy's pour. He rattles the ice again. After a sigh, she allows him another finger of whisky. 'Remember what the doctor said.'

'It's tattooed on my chest,' he says, tapping the buttons of his shirt, which covers the pale, puckered scar of a heart bypass.

The intercom chimes. Someone at the gates. Constance leaves the whisky decanter and goes inside to answer the summons. Moments later, an Aston Martin convertible rumbles into view with Finbar at the wheel. Realising that he has an audience, he does a quick spin around the circular fountain, spraying gravel onto the grass. McCarthy swears under his breath. The gardeners will now spend hours picking stones out of the lawn.

Jogging up the stone steps, Finbar bumps fists with his brothers and pours himself a drink.

'How is our sick friend?' asks McCarthy.

'Bump on the head. Mild concussion. Ten stitches.'

'Did you talk to him?'

'Couldn't get near him. Filth all over the place. One of the nurses, a Nigerian lass, said he should be out in a day or two.'

'What about the wife?' asks Daragh.

'Dead at the house. Tied to a chair.'

The men offer a moment of silence before speaking again.

Finbar continues. 'I talked to a scribbler from the *Daily Tele*. Caroline Davis. She heard they cleared out the safe and took jewellery worth four million quid.'

'Any mention of loose diamonds?' asks McCarthy.

'Nah.'

'How do we know they were in the whatnot?' asks Daragh. 'Maybe he took 'em 'ome.'

'They would have robbed the house as well,' says Clifton.

Finbar interrupts. 'I saw your lass at the hospital.'

McCarthy raises an eyebrow. 'Philomena?'

'Yeah. She was with that little girl, Daisy. The one she brought to the christening.'

'Russell's daughter,' says Daragh, slapping his forehead. 'I shoulda known.'

Constance appears again, this time carrying a tray of small sausage rolls and other snacks, including carrot sticks and hummus. The boys descend on the sausage rolls, two-handed eating.

Clifton, with his mouth full, 'You are a true princess.'

'A lifesaver,' echoes Finbar.

'An angel of whatnot,' says Daragh.

Constance makes a point of keeping the sausage rolls away from McCarthy, giving him the carrot sticks. Ever since his bypass, she's been on a mission to improve his diet and limit his drinking. The cigars have already gone. Well, almost gone. He has a secret stash in the garage, available for his evening walks when Constance is at her Pilates class, or book club, or whatever charity committee has attracted her patronage.

Finbar reaches for another sausage roll.

'Maybe you could ask Phil about the robbery. She could tell us what the filth is thinking.'

'Suspects and whatnot,' says Daragh.

'I can't do that,' says McCarthy.

'But if she's part of the investigation.'

'I won't ask and she won't tell,' he says, sternly. 'That is the deal, OK? Unbreakable.'

Getting to his feet, he walks to the edge of the patio. 'Who do we know could have pulled off a robbery like this?'

Clifton speaks first. 'What about Paddy Gallagher's crew in Birmingham?'

'Paddy couldn't tell a gemstone from a gallstone.'

'There's Danny Hammer in Glasgow, but he doesn't like coming south of Hadrian's Wall.'

'And Danny isn't gonna kill an innocent woman,' says Finbar. 'He's a psycho, but he's not crazy.'

'Think further afield,' says McCarthy.

'You mean across the ditch?' asks Clifton. 'Romanians. Albanians. Russians. Could be any of them.'

'So much for Brexit,' says Finbar.

Daragh begins clicking his fingers, trying to summon up a memory. 'Remember that gang that was knocking off celebrity whatnots a few years back? One of them Kardashians got robbed in Paris. The one with the big arse.'

'I don't know if you're allowed to say that any more,' says Finbar.

'Which bit?'

'Her having a big arse.'

'Why not? It's true, in'it?'

'They were Serbs,' says Clifton, interrupting their discussion on political correctness. 'And most of 'em got caught.'

'Given the general fuckery of late, a paranoid man might think this latest robbery is part of a pattern,' says McCarthy.

'You think they knew the diamonds were in the whatnot?' asks Daragh.

'I'm fuckin' sure of it. And I want their heads on pikes.'

'What's a pike?'

'It's a long stick,' says Clifton.

The brothers fall silent. There is a lone sausage roll left on the platter. All four of them have been eyeing it up.

Daragh breaks first. His hand shoots out. At the same time, Finbar drags the table closer with his foot, while Clifton tilts it up and the tray slides towards him. Out of nowhere, McCarthy thumps the edge of the tray with his fist. The sausage roll leaps and he plucks it out of mid-air, examines it for a moment, and pops it into his mouth.

'You don't reach the top of the fuckin' food chain by eatin' carrot sticks.'

# 12

Brendan Keegan slips out of bed at six-thirty on Monday morning and trips over his shoes in the dark. He curses his soon to be ex-wife because she was always complaining about him leaving his stuff lying on the floor. He can hear her laughing now from Brighton, where she lives with her new boyfriend.

Standing over the toilet bowl, waiting for something to happen, he catches a glimpse of himself in the mirror. He sucks in his stomach but doesn't have the energy to hold the pose. He didn't have to get up this early, but he woke and his brain slipped into gear and going back to sleep was an impossibility.

Barefoot, in his pyjamas, he pads to the kitchen and starts the coffee, checking his phone. His last text message was delivered just before midnight. It came from the Home Office pathologist Gerard Noonan, saying he conducted the post-mortem on Caitlin Kemp-Lowe.

*Victim died in the early hours of Saturday morning. Suffocation. Talk to me after eight.*

Keegan wants to call Noonan immediately but decides to wait. The coffee machine hisses and spits. He sniffs the open carton of milk and pours a splash into a mug. Smell is a bachelor's most important sense – honed by having to check leftover food, out-of-date produce, unwashed shirts and reused underwear. Returning the milk to the fridge, he lifts the lid on a chicken curry, but won't take the risk. The eggs are past their use-by date, but close enough. He has them scrambled on toast, doused in tabasco sauce, tasting only heat.

Noonan answers his call. 'I told you after eight.'

'It's close enough,' says Keegan.

'Give me a minute.'

He hears a toilet flushing.

'How much you want?' asks Noonan.

'The highlights.'

'Cause of death was asphyxiation. There was evidence of petechial haemorrhages on her face, a blue discoloration of the skin and engorgement of the right side of the heart.'

'I didn't see any ligature marks.'

'The killer likely used a plastic bag. It was placed over the victim's head and held tightly around her neck. The abrasions on her wrists showed that she fought against the bindings as she died.'

'We didn't find a plastic bag?'

'There was one in the pedal bin. We're testing it for DNA and fingerprints.'

'Time of death.'

'Her body temperature and stomach contents indicate three a.m. but the house was cold, so it could have been later. She died where you found her.'

'Any other injuries?'

'Some bruising on her cheek. Fading.'

'How old?'

'A few weeks.'

'What about the blood on the kid's pyjamas.'

'It most likely came from the mother. Caitlin had a nosebleed at some point. There was blood on her nightdress.'

Keegan makes a note to chase it up. 'What about the tox screen and swabs?'

'Later today, if you're lucky. Give me a call.'

The samples have gone to a Central Forensic Crime Lab in South London, along with the fake bomb and tilt switch. Every component will be examined and traced. Someone bought them and assembled them. That chain can be traced. All Keegan needs is a name, an opening, a scent to follow.

At nine, he is picked up from his house and driven to the jewellery store because he wants to view the scene again in the daylight. So much of the robbery was slick and well coordinated – the timing, the speed, the attention to detail – everything except for the death of Caitlin Kemp-Lowe, which was ugly and unnecessary, raising the stakes.

Detective Sergeant Warwick O'Neil breaks open the crime-scene tape and follows Keegan into the store. Older by a dozen years, O'Neil has a weathered face, greying hair and a suit jacket that won't button over his gut.

Broken glass crunches beneath their shoes. Keegan glances at the CCTV camera in the corner of the ceiling. The gang spraypainted it when they first entered, just as they'd done at the house.

'What do we know about the footage?' he asks.

'It gets looped every forty-eight hours onto a hard drive in the office. The archival stuff is transferred automatically to a security server in Watford. It has been collected.'

Keegan looks out of the window. Hatton Garden has returned to normal. Pedestrians fill the footpaths and traffic is banked up at the red lights.

'What about neighbouring businesses – any cameras?' he asks.

'One over the road and another on the corner at Holborn.'

'I want them all checked. Every CCTV and camera doorbell along the route from the house to here.'

Keegan crouches and examines the safe. 'Four million in jewellery, some of them designer pieces. Easy to trace.'

'Unless they break up the stones.'

'And diminish the value.'

He picks up a fallen chair and remembers the bomb and the blast shields. 'What do we know about Russell Kemp-Lowe?'

'He was born in Australia and moved to the UK about fifteen years ago. Originally, he was Russell Holcroft, but he took his wife's name when they married.'

'Unusual.'

'Or progressive. He went to drama school in London and spent a few years acting, mainly smaller TV productions and on stage. He played Marius in *Les Mis* for a season and was one of the ex-husbands in *Mamma Mia!* Took the wife to see that. I thought it was hokey and silly, but she liked the music.

'Caitlin met Russell at some after-party. They married nine years ago and he gave acting away to work for her old man. She took over the business when her father retired.'

'How solvent is the business?'

'You saw the house.'

'Means nothing. Talk to their accountant and check their tax records.'

'You think this was an insurance job?'

'I want to rule it out.'

The two leave the store and walk to a waiting unmarked police car. It pulls away and turns into Holborn, heading for New Scotland Yard. Keegan stares out of the window at the passing pedestrians who are like schools of fish surging over crossings and pausing at the next 'don't walk' sign. *Are they happy?* he wonders. *Do they have a purpose?* Ever since Veronica walked out on him, he has felt aimless and drifting, uncertain about what comes next. Fatherhood had plotted out the next fifteen years, but now he has no landmarks or milestones to guide him.

Taking a bottle of sanitiser from his jacket pocket, he squeezes exactly three drops onto his hand, sealing the bottle before rubbing the gel into his palms and between his fingers and up his wrists.

'Why do you do that?' asks O'Neil.

'Do what?'

'Clean your hands. Is it a Covid thing?'

'Something like that.'

The men drive in silence, passing Trafalgar Square and heading along Whitehall.

'They're itching to take this away from me,' says Keegan. 'They'll bring in someone from SCD7.'

'We don't need the Specialist Crime Directorate,' says O'Neil. 'You can run this.'

'I've been a DCI for less than a year.'

'And look at your stats.'

Keegan gives him a mirthless smile. 'You know my biggest fear? They'll focus on the robbery and not the murder. The Met does it all the time – treats property crimes as being more serious than crimes against a person. I blame the class system.'

'How do you figure?'

'The rich don't like being robbed.'

'Spoken like a true working-class boy.'

'I'm serious. Fifty years ago, eleven men stole two and a half million pounds in the Great Train Robbery and the most violent act they committed was coshing the engine driver. They were treated like folk heroes by the public because the money didn't belong to anyone. It was being sent to incinerators because it was old and dirty.'

'The engine driver died,' says O'Neil.

'Seven years later, of an unrelated illness. When the sentences were handed down, they added up to more than three hundred years. Why? Because the rich are frightened of the poor and they don't want to see criminals treated like folk heroes.'

'This case isn't the same, boss.'

'You're right, but a woman is dead and her life is more important than a safe full of jewellery.'

The car pulls onto a ramp that they descend into an underground parking area beneath New Scotland Yard. Warrant cards are checked at a boom gate. The guard waves them through.

'You want me to come with you?' asks O'Neil.

'No. It only needs one of us to mess this up.'

'Good luck.'

# 13

There are reasons for staying in bed and reasons for getting up. It's snug and warm lying next to Henry, and cold outside. I also need to wee and to get to work. I'm supposed to take Daisy back to the house this morning.

Henry has his right arm draped across my stomach and curled beneath my pyjama top where his hand is cupping my left breast. It's a big hand and a smallish breast, but he says, 'any more than a handful would be a waste'. Men are such simple creatures, by which I mean idiots.

My pyjamas are silk and embroidered with my initials, PM. They were a wedding present from Constance – which I've fallen in love with, even if I haven't fallen in love with my wicked stepmother. She isn't really wicked, just vain and snobbish and too young for my father, but she loves him and looks after him. Somebody has to.

I thought the pyjamas were an odd gift, but now I'm worried that I won't be able to afford another pair when this pair wears out. I'm usually a flannelette sort of girl. And don't get me started on lingerie. Henry once suggested he might buy me something 'sexy' for Valentine's Day and I had fever dreams for a week about ill-fitting bras and absentee crotches.

The alarm is on snooze. It will sound again in three and a half minutes. My nose is cold, which is a much better judge of the temperature than any thermometer. Autumn in London isn't about numbers, but how cold it feels.

Henry groans when I lift his hand away. He pulls me back. I squirm more forcefully and roll free, slipping my feet into Ugg boots and my arms into a dressing gown.

Thirty minutes later, wearing my half blues, I'm on the Tube train on the Northern Line from Clapham Common to Kentish Town. I scan a copy of the *Guardian*, looking for any mention of the home invasion and robbery. Page three. There's a photograph of Caitlin Kemp-Lowe, taken at the charity ball on Friday night. She's wearing a black and gold sequin flapper dress with a deep V at the back. Her hair is pinned tightly to her scalp and she looks like she's stepped out of a party at Jay Gatsby's mansion.

There is a side-bar story about the Kemp-Lowe family. Caitlin's great-great-great-grandfather made a fortune trading Persian pearls for blue star sapphires from India in the 1850s. The family set up its first London store in Park Lane in the 1950s, before moving to 'the Garden' in 1985.

At university, Caitlin was romantically linked to Prince William when they were photographed together at a polo match at Windsor. And the media also speculated that her father had helped source the stones for Princess Diana's engagement ring, although it was never confirmed.

The only negative angle is a reference to Noah Kemp-Lowe, Caitlin's younger brother, who had been in and out of rehab in his twenties. The low point came when Noah was found in a filthy bedsit in Kennington beside the decomposing body of his then girlfriend. The *Daily Mail* snapped a photograph of him, dishevelled and hollow-eyed, being arrested by police. He was convicted of constructive manslaughter and supplying a class A drug. That was seven years ago. He should be out by now.

At eight-thirty, I pick up Daisy from Maida Vale in an area vehicle. She seems different today. Smaller. Quieter. The clothes I chose for her on Saturday don't seem to suit her any more. They're too bright and colourful.

Amber Culver pulls me aside. 'She had a difficult night. Nightmares. I let her sleep in my bed. She ate nothing for breakfast.'

Daisy has a small backpack. 'Are you going somewhere?' I ask.

'Home,' she says, as though it should be obvious.

'We're only going back there for a few hours,' I explain. 'You'll be coming back here.'

'But Daddy said.'

'When did you talk to him?'

'He called last night,' explains Amber. 'He's being released from hospital today.'

'The house is still a crime scene. He won't be allowed to go home.'

Daisy looks at Amber and back to me, not understanding.

'We'll sort it out,' I say, not wanting to upset her. I try to make conversation on the drive but the chatterbox child of yesterday has been replaced by a pensive, more anxious version. Perhaps the magnitude of her loss is sinking in.

As we turn into Antrim Road, we are surrounded by reporters and photographers, yelling questions and snapping photographs. Instinctively, I tell Daisy to duck. She doesn't hesitate, pushing her face over her knees.

Two police constables come to my aid, clearing a path through the scrum and pointing me to a parking spot outside the house. More officers are standing guard on the front steps. Colleagues. I don't know any of them well. Most of my new workmates regard me as standoffish or aloof because I keep to myself and rarely go to the pub after work. I should make more of an effort. I could join one of the sporting teams, or the football tipping competition. I could take an interest in their lives, but I'm worried they might take an interest in mine.

Keegan is waiting in the entrance hall. The duckboards and evidence markers have gone, and the fingerprint powder has been vacuumed away, but the house still feels like a crime scene.

A woman is waiting with the inspector, a child psychologist, who introduces herself as Imelda Thomas and takes my hand like she's doing a palm reading, studying my 'money line' and my 'marriage line'. When she gives it back, I want to count my fingers.

Imelda is in her late thirties, dressed in a blue blouse, tailored trousers and black patent shoes. She speaks in the sing-song voice of a kindergarten teacher as she comments on Daisy's 'pretty clothes' and 'lovely hair'. Daisy doesn't respond to the praise. If anything, it makes her wary.

'How about you come with me?' she says, pointing to the front reception room.

'I'm not allowed in there,' says Daisy. 'Mummy says that's for visitors.'

My childhood comes rushing back to me, when our parlour was off limits to children and kept spotlessly clean and decorated with cut flowers in case the parish priest or the Queen dropped by for afternoon tea.

'Mummy won't mind,' says Imelda, leading Daisy to a rolled arm sofa, which is so deep that Daisy's legs stick straight out like a doll sitting on a shelf.

'Don't go,' says Daisy, fearing I might leave.

'Philomena will sit right next to you,' says Imelda, who purposely uses first names. DCI Keegan is 'Brendan' and is directed to a chair behind Daisy, out of her line of vision.

I have watched children being interviewed before, but never one this young. It is laborious and time-consuming, aimed at eliciting information without adulterating the memories or traumatising the child. Imelda sits directly opposite Daisy, making constant eye contact, but not invading her space. She begins by establishing whether Daisy knows the difference between right and wrong, real and pretend, and the truth and a lie. Taking a picture book from her handbag, she points to a drawing.

'What is this a picture of?'

'A fish,' says Daisy.

'And this is a bird?'

'No, silly, that's a lion.'

Imelda turns a page. 'What if I tell you this is a picture of a cow?'

'No, that's an elephant.'

Imelda asks me to leave the room for a moment. I walk outside into the hallway until she calls me back again. My hat is no longer on the sofa where I left it. I look at Keegan, wondering if this is part of the interview.

I play along. 'Where is my hat?'

Imelda points at Daisy. 'She took it.'

Daisy's hand goes to her mouth in surprise and she shakes her head. 'No, I didn't.'

Next Imelda points to Keegan. 'It was him.'

'No. It was you,' says Daisy. 'You're telling fibs.'

The psychologist smiles and retrieves my hat from under her chair.

'It was a test,' she says. 'I wanted to be sure that you'll tell the truth – even if it might get someone else in trouble.'

'You were being tricky,' says Daisy, narrowing her eyes.

'Yes, I was.'

Imelda nods to Keegan, who turns on the recording app on his phone. 'I'm going to ask you some questions, Daisy. If you don't know the answer, you say, "I don't know." And if you don't understand, you say, "I don't understand." But you must never make things up. Understand?'

'Yes.'

Imelda begins asking her about Friday night and her usual routines – dinner, bathtime, TV watching. The questions are simple with no forced choices or yes or no answers.

Daisy had mac and cheese for dinner (which she calls 'monkey cheese') and watched *Frozen* on the TV in the play-room. At eight o'clock she went to bed. Josie helped her clean her teeth and read her a chapter from *Charlie and the Chocolate*

*Factory* – the scene where Violet Beauregarde turns into an enormous blueberry.

'Do you really think she got juiced?' Daisy asks me, frowning seriously.

'I think she was OK,' I say, unsure if I'm supposed to interact or be silent.

Imelda: 'Do you ever wake up at night, Daisy?'

'Sometimes.'

'Did you wake up on that night?'

'I don't know.'

'Did you hear your mummy and daddy come home?'

'Mummy came and kissed me goodnight.'

Daisy's crayon drawing is placed on the coffee table in front of her.

Imelda points to the figure with the black eyes. 'Who is this?'

'The bad man.'

'Why is he bad?'

'He made Mummy cry.'

'Where did you see him?'

'In the kitchen. Daddy was shouting.'

'What was he shouting?'

'Don't hurt her.'

'Is that why you went downstairs?'

Daisy nods.

'How did you get to the kitchen?' asks Keegan.

Daisy turns her head. 'The stairs.'

'When you went downstairs, did you see your mummy or daddy?' asks Imelda.

'I saw Mummy.'

'What about the bad men?'

'They were scary.'

'What made them scary?'

Daisy covers her face, looking through her fingers. She doesn't have the vocabulary to describe the masks.

'What happened then?' asks Imelda.

'Mummy told me to go back to bed.'

'What was she doing?'

'Sitting down.'

Imelda points to the other figure in the drawing. 'Is that your mummy?'

Daisy nods.

'What about your daddy?' asks Keegan, interrupting.

'He was sitting next to Mummy.'

Daisy's bottom lip begins to wobble and tears fill her eyes. Imelda takes a tissue from a packet and waits for Daisy to blow her nose. After she settles, the interview begins again.

'Did you go back to bed?' asks Imelda.

'The bad man took me. He tucked me in and told me not to come out again.'

'Did he say anything else?'

'I asked him if he was a monster, but he said he was only pretending, like playing a game, and that under the mask he wasn't scary at all. He showed me.'

'Showed you what?'

'His face.'

Keegan leans forward in his chair, unable to help himself. 'You saw his face?'

Daisy nods, uncertain if she's done something wrong.

Now the questions focus on the man's appearance, trying to draw out any detail that Daisy might remember, but she doesn't have the vocabulary or the experience to understand the difference in someone's eye colour or the shape of a mouth or the size of a nose. Just when it seems pointless, the little girl says, 'He had a drawing.'

'What sort of drawing?'

'Here.' She points to her right wrist.

'A tattoo,' says Keegan. 'What did it look like?'

'Like in my ladybug game. You count the dots.'

The psychologist and detective look at each other blankly.

'I think she means dice,' I say.

Daisy nods and begins telling me about the game, asking if I'll play with her. Keegan leaves the room and makes a phone call, no doubt asking the database manager to run the details of the tattoo through HOLMES 2, searching for a match on the database.

In the meantime, Imelda suggests we take a break. Daisy has a plastic lunchbox full of snacks that Amber packed for her. A boxed juice, a banana and a packet of teddy bear biscuits. She sits on the sofa, trying not to spill any crumbs on her lap. I help put a straw in the juice and to peel her banana.

When the interview begins again, we take Daisy up to her bedroom, trying to recreate the events. She takes me on a tour, showing me her doll's house and her rocking horse and her favourite toys. Finally, she sits at a child-sized table. Imelda and Keegan join her, looking somewhat ridiculous because their knees almost touch their chins.

'What happened after the bad man took you back to bed?' asks the psychologist.

Daisy doesn't know how to answer.

'Did you go back to sleep?'

'I don't remember.'

'Did you wake again?'

'I had a bad dream – a real one, not a pretend one. I called out for Mummy, but she didn't come.'

'What did you do?'

'I cried.'

'Did you get out of bed?'

Daisy nods. 'My door wouldn't open.'

'How did you get out?'

Daisy lowers her eyes.

'Is it a secret?' I ask.

She nods.

'You're allowed to tell us.'

Daisy walks to the cupboard beside the fireplace, opening the sliding doors, revealing the dumb waiter.

'I use it to play tricks on people, but I hurt my finger and Mummy said I couldn't do it again.'

'It's very small,' says Imelda.

'So am I,' Daisy replies. 'I can show you.'

'That's OK,' says Keegan. 'Come back and sit down.'

Daisy returns, holding Hippo on her lap.

'What did you see when you went downstairs?' asks Imelda.

'Mummy.'

'Did you talk to her?'

'She was being silly.'

'Silly? How?'

'She had a bag on her head.'

'What sort of bag?'

'A bag.'

'Was it made of paper?'

'No, plastic? Mummy told me I should never put a bag like that on my head or I might suffer like Kate.'

'You mean, suffocate?'

Daisy nods.

'What did you do?'

'I went to look for Daddy.'

'Is that when you went outside?'

'Yes.'

Keegan's knees are beginning to seize up. He gets off the child-sized chair and stretches, rubbing his thighs. I keep going over the details, remembering when I entered the house and searched downstairs. Caitlin was sitting in a chair in the kitchen, her hands and feet bound with packing tape. Staring at me.

I clear my throat. 'Can I ask Daisy a question?'

Keegan nods.

'You said Mummy had a bag over her head and you couldn't wake her.'

Daisy nods again.

'Did you take the bag off Mummy's head?'

'No.'

'Are you sure?'

'Yes.'

I look at Keegan, aware of the significance. Caitlin's head was uncovered when I found her in the kitchen. Her mouth was taped. Her eyes were open. The image is burned into my brain.

Would Daisy have forgotten a detail like that? I wonder. If not, then somebody else was in the house when Daisy came downstairs. They were there when she left. Waiting. Watching.

# 14

Edward McCarthy thinks all bankers are thieving bastards, but he tries not to let his feelings show when he welcomes three of them into the boardroom on the thirty-fourth floor of Hope Island House. All of them admire the view from the floor-to-ceiling windows. On a clear day it stretches west as far as the Houses of Parliament and east over London City Airport towards the Thames Estuary.

Hope Island is a small peninsula created by the River Lea on the northern bank of the Thames, opposite the O2 Arena. This area of London was once at the beating heart of Britain's maritime supremacy, when the sun never set on the empire, but now the old wharves and soot-blackened warehouses and tenements have been bulldozed and replaced by gleaming glass and chrome towers. Many of the buildings are finished or being fitted out, while others are still under construction, flanked by cranes and shielded in scaffolding.

The most senior of the bankers, George Carmichael, imagines he can see his house in the distance. His colleague, Aaron Morby, takes a photograph on his phone. The third visitor, a woman, Charlotte Farley, is the only one without a briefcase. She has an iPad.

'You didn't have to come here,' says McCarthy. 'I would have gladly made the trip to the City.'

'It's nice to get out,' says Carmichael, unbuttoning his suit jacket to reveal a matching waistcoat with a small pocket for a non-existent fob watch. He takes a seat at the circular board table, resting his hands on his stomach.

'What can I get you?' McCarthy asks. 'Tea. Coffee. Soft drinks. Water.' Silently adding, *Arsenic. Shit sandwiches. Personalities.*

Only Charlotte Farley has remained standing. She is still at the window, tapping at her iPad as though measuring it up for curtains.

There is small talk among the men, discussing weekend activities, football results and the weather, before McCarthy gets to the point.

'You wanted a meeting. How can I help you?'

'You can allay our concerns,' says Carmichael. 'Your companies are in default of their loans.'

'Only by three months.'

'Six months,' says Morby.

McCarthy waves his hand dismissively. 'We have had some cashflow issues. Nothing we can't handle.'

'The project is sixteen months behind schedule,' says Carmichael.

'Because of lockdowns and supply-chain problems.'

'Half of your completed buildings are empty.'

'We are negotiating with tenants.'

'Who are being offered rents that don't match your projections.'

'Introductory offers.'

The two men pause, as though reloading. Carmichael speaks first. 'I appreciate that times are difficult. Brexit, inflation, pandemics, lockdowns, skills shortages, supply disruptions, etcetera, but we need to be sure that our investment is safe.'

'As houses,' says McCarthy.

'Quite a few of those are being handed back,' says Morby, whose nose twitches like a ferret.

'You will get your money.'

'Oh, of that I'm sure,' says Carmichael. 'That's one of the great advantages of being a bank – we're always first in line.'

They laugh. But not McCarthy. He has noticed that Carmichael doesn't seem to blink. Maybe he has no eyelids or he is one of those lizard people that conspiracy theorists go on about. But the person who intrigues him most is the woman, who is still standing at the window, taking notes.

He begins again. 'This development is worth seven hundred million pounds and will transform this part of the city. Opening up new areas. Continuing the gentrification of the East End—'

Carmichael interrupts. 'You're preaching to the choir, Edward. We bought the sales pitch five years ago. Now you're haemorrhaging money and the business case you put forward is no longer relevant. Times have changed. This country has changed, along with our appetite for risk.'

He motions to his colleague Morby, who takes a page from his briefcase and hands it to his boss. Carmichael studies the letter.

'When we entered into a loan agreement with your companies, you were given very generous fixed interest terms for the first five years. Those interest rates were historically low, but now those agreements are due to expire and your loans will become variable, at which time your repayments will quadruple. Since you are already in arrears, you can appreciate our concern.'

'The bank could make it easier – a loan holiday or an interest rate freeze. I'm happy to renegotiate,' says McCarthy.

A wry smile. A banker's smile. Cunt!

'There will be no renegotiation,' says Carmichael. 'We too are under pressure to meet our obligations to shareholders and to the Financial Conduct Authority. Do you have any idea how many insolvencies there have been in the construction sector? More than five thousand in the past year. Most made the same mistakes that you have, overpromising and underdelivering.'

'We can take out a bridging loan.'

'Nobody will extend you credit and there are clauses in your original loan contracts that limit such activities. We also have the legal right to intervene if we feel that our investment is at risk.'

'There is no risk. You'll be paid.'

'When?'

'I have the matter in hand.'

All sense of bonhomie and professional respect has evaporated, replaced by a mixture of hatred and mistrust.

Carmichael continues. 'Your insurance companies are abandoning you, Edward. I don't blame them, what with the fires, workplace accidents, vandalism and industrial disputes. We suspect your company is effectively insolvent and trading illegally.'

McCarthy reaches across the table and grabs Carmichael by the throat, lifting him out of his chair and shoving him hard against a wall. His fingers close around his neck. Squeezing.

A heartbeat later, he realises this is all in his imagination. The men are still sitting at the conference table, eyeballing one another. Charlotte Farley turns from the window and crosses the room, taking a seat next to McCarthy. Her hand rests on his forearm. He can smell her perfume.

'We are not the enemy, Edward.' Her smile is all teeth, no gums. 'We are here with solutions, not problems.'

'What solutions?'

Her hand moves down his arm, until her long, tapered fingers are stroking the hairs on his wrist. 'We have been approached by a potential suitor, someone who wants to buy a considerable stake in Hope Island Developments. The sale would generate capital and reduce your debts.'

'What sort of stake?'

'Forty-nine per cent.'

'Who is it?'

'We are not at liberty to give you a name at this stage.'

'You want me to agree to a marriage without telling me who I'm sleeping with.'

'We would like your permission to negotiate.'

'You have my permission to fuck off,' says McCarthy, the

statement rumbling from deep in his chest. 'Get out of my office.'

'You cannot threaten us,' says Carmichael, trying to save face, but the bankers are bundling papers into briefcases.

'This is not a threat,' says McCarthy. 'Somebody wants half of my business. I want to know his name.'

'He will take on half of your liabilities.'

'And pocket half of my profits. His name?'

'Good day, sir,' says Carmichael, opening the door and ushering the others out of the conference room. Charlotte Farley hasn't moved. She is less fearful and more confident, despite her youth. Where did she get that sort of coolness? Not in a boardroom.

'Please, consider this proposal,' she says calmly, dabbing at the edge of her painted mouth with a fingertip. 'You are in arrears and your insurance has lapsed. Any more problems and the bank will call in an insolvency team.'

'Are you a lawyer?' asks McCarthy.

She raises one eyebrow. 'What makes you think that?'

'Call it intuition.'

She smiles and stands, smoothing down her pencil skirt. Reaching into the top of her blouse, she takes out a business card that has been tucked into her bra. Still warm from her skin, it has her name, legal qualifications and mobile phone number, but no address.

'Call me. I'm sure we can come to terms.'

The bankers are waiting at the lift, holding the doors open.

After they're gone, McCarthy goes to his office and takes a burner phone from his desk drawer. Inserting a fresh SIM card, he texts Clifton's number and then calls him immediately.

'This fuckery at the building sites and the robbery – I know the reason.'

'Why?'

'It's a shakedown.'

# 15

After dropping Daisy back to Amber Culver's flat, I drive to Kentish Town station and pull into the police parking area. It's lunchtime and I haven't eaten all day. I buy a salad sandwich and fruit juice at a nearby café, taking a seat at the front window.

I wanted to talk to DCI Keegan at the murder house, but he left quickly before I could get him alone. Now I'm not sure what I'm going to say – that I want to be a detective, or I think I can help the task force. I've only been a constable for four years.

I'm walking back towards the station when I hear someone calling my name. A man is standing across the road, waving. A fringe of foppish hair covers his forehead, almost shielding one eye. He tucks it behind his ear in a gesture that is immediately familiar, before dashing between stationary cars and crossing to my side.

'If it isn't Philomena McCarthy. As I live and breathe.'

'Jamie?' I say tentatively.

He grins. 'Do I get a hug?'

'I don't know,' I say. 'Remember the last time?'

'That was more than a hug.'

Jamie Pike was my first boyfriend. I was fourteen, or maybe fifteen, when Daddy caught us snogging in the front room. To be fair, it was more than snogging. Jamie had his hand down my knickers, having reached third base, and was turning for home. Daddy picked him up and threw him against an antique sideboard, shattering several plates. Then he marched Jamie out of the house and gave him a lecture that put the fear of God into him. That was the end of the relationship and I've only seen Jamie once since then. We bumped into each other outside a cinema in Leicester Square and Jamie almost ran away – clearly still traumatised by his teenage memories.

Now he's here, standing in front of me, looking older, but just as charming and handsome in a casually licentious sort of way. He crushes me against his chest. He always did smell good.

Untangling myself, I step back and hope I'm not blushing. 'What are you doing here?'

'I live around the corner. How about you?'

'I work over there.' I point across the road to the police station.

'Doing what?'

'I'm a police officer.' I do a pirouette, showing off my uniform.

'I thought that was fancy dress,' he says, laughing. 'What did your father say?'

'It wasn't his decision.'

Jamie can see I'm annoyed. 'Well, good for you. Do you have time for a coffee or lunch?'

'I've just eaten.'

'A drink then. Later. I could take you to dinner.'

I hold up my left hand, showing him my wedding ring.

'You're married. What a shame.'

'Not for me.'

He grins. I remember that smile. 'We can still be mates. Meet me later.'

'No.'

'Well, at least give me your number.'

'Why?'

'Because we're old friends.'

'I'm not sure my husband would approve.'

'And he rules the roost?'

'No.'

He's teasing me. He was always the cool boy, who flirted by playfully mocking the girls he liked. I was flattered then and a part of me is flattered now.

'Give me your number,' I say. 'If I'm interested, I'll call you.'

'Fair enough.'

I hand him my phone. He types his number into my contacts.

'Well, it's been lovely seeing you again,' I say, as I put the phone away.

'Let's do it again soon,' he echoes, with a wink. Could he be any more obvious?

'I'll tell Daddy I bumped into you,' I say.

'Please don't.'

I laugh. 'Goodbye, Jamie.'

Kentish Town police station is in Holmes Road and looks like something out of an Arthur Conan Doyle story. Built in 1896, it has the word 'Police' carved in stone above the doorway and an iron arch supporting an old-fashioned blue lamp. A second, wider entrance is too narrow for a police car, but perfect for a horse and carriage.

A young couple is deep in conversation on the front ramp. She's wearing leggings and a baggy sweater with a baseball cap pulled low over her eyes. The boy is a foot taller, in jeans and a scuffed leather jacket. She seems upset and, for a moment, I think they're arguing. He raises his hand, as if to threaten her, but she pulls it down and wraps it around her waist and kisses him.

Inside the station, I nod to the front desk, which is staffed by two constables and a civilian worker. I go looking for the duty sergeant, whose name is Baird, but everyone calls him 'Big Bird' because of his size and his yellow hair and his natural gentleness.

He looks up from his desk. 'You're not rostered on today, McCarthy.'

'No, Sarge. I wanted a word.'

'Is this a door-closed or a door-open sort of word?'

'Either.'

He motions to a chair.

'I was hoping I could help the murder investigation team, sir. I found the little girl and I want to stay involved.'

'Has DCI Keegan asked for you?'

'Not exactly.'

'What does that mean?'

'I've been chaperoning the girl to interviews.'

'Well, I can't spare any officers. I'm already short-staffed.'

'What if DCI Keegan were to ask?'

'I'd tell him you're needed here.'

Baird can see I'm disappointed. 'I suppose if he were to make an official request . . . But I think you should stick to one job at a time.'

'Noted.'

'You're going to ask him.'

'Yes, sir.'

He laughs. 'Away you go.'

# 16

Keegan washes his hands, working the soap into his fingernails and cuticles. Rinsing off the lather, he repeats the process, counting the seconds. During the Covid pandemic, people were encouraged to sing two verses of 'Happy Birthday' to time how long they washed their hands. They were the good old days when Keegan didn't have to make excuses for his compulsive behaviours. He would even joke about his OCD, telling people he had CDO, which was preferable because it was in alphabetical order.

As a child he had feared handling doorknobs and dirty glasses or eating food that had touched on his plate. Later, as a teenager, he walked around with his hands in his pockets, convinced he was going to contract some flesh-eating disease from unwashed surfaces or random handshakes or a rogue cough.

Therapy helped. Cognitive training. For years he wore a thick elastic band around his left wrist, which he snapped whenever he had a negative thought, using pain to train his mind. These tricks allowed him to fight back and he dared to believe he was cured.

Then Rafa was born and surgeons operated within hours to fix a congenital heart defect. During a month in hospital, Keegan and Veronica took turns to sit beside their newborn baby, talking to him and touching his tiny hands. But even wearing surgical mask and gloves, Keegan was convinced that he would pass on some deadly infection to Rafa.

His OCD came roaring back. When they took Rafa home, Keegan had the baby's room scrubbed and disinfected. Every toy or spoon or piece of clothing that touched the floor and went close to the baby's mouth was a potential killer. His cleaning rituals became more and more elaborate. Unable to sleep at night, he would scrub the kitchen and bathroom, scouring the grouting between the tiles to keep the germs at bay.

It wasn't the ritual that captivated him. It was the thought of what might happen if he didn't clean. The disasters it would trigger. The bad luck that would result.

The murder investigation team (MIT) has taken over the entire upper floor of Kentish Town police station, an open-plan space divided by desks, partitions and whiteboards. The team has thirty detectives, including two inspectors, five detective sergeants and eighteen detective constables. They are supported by civilian analysts, indexers, exhibit officers, PIP2 investigators and a HOLMES manager, whose job is to get the best information from the HOLMES 2 computer system.

The team has been divided into four groups. One has spent the last couple of days going door-to-door, interviewing neighbours and shopkeepers, collecting footage from private CCTV cameras and digital doorbells. Another team has been identifying everybody who visited the house in Antrim Road and the jewellery store in the weeks leading up to the robbery. The third group is examining the couple's movements in the days beforehand. And a fourth is looking at similar robberies, trying to find patterns in the data.

People watch TV cop shows and imagine that investigations are full of brilliant deductions and eureka moments, punctuated by car chases and interrogations. The reality is mind-numbing tedium and legwork, with occasional flashes of interest and intuition. Some of these officers will spend days studying a single CCTV feed of the same street, hoping someone of interest might walk past.

DS O'Neil looks up from his desk. 'What did the assistant commissioner say?'

'This is my case to fuck up.'

'Congratulations.'

'That might be premature. Briefing in fifteen.'

'Everyone?'

'Just the team leaders.'

Keegan goes to his office and closes the door, wanting to lock it, but fighting the urge. He names the compulsion out loud. Psychologists call it the Rumpelstiltskin effect: the idea that if you can name something, you can have power over it.

The detectives arrive. Three men and two women. They take their favourite seats. Some have been on the job longer than Keegan, but he has been promoted ahead of them. No hard feelings on his part. He can't speak for them.

O'Neil goes first. 'Caitlin and Russell Kemp-Lowe were at a charity dinner at the Banking Hall on Friday night. Russell bid on centre-court tickets to the Wimbledon finals. Made a big show of losing. They shared the table with ten friends. We've interviewed all but two of them.'

'How did the couple seem?' asks Keegan.

'Depends on who we asked. Some people said they were tickety-boo – all sweetness and light – but others reported tension. Caitlin was complaining about Russell bidding on the tickets. She called it a "swinging dick" contest.'

'Was he drinking?'

'No more than usual, according to friends.' O'Neil glances at his notes. 'A coat-check attendant heard them arguing in the foyer. Caitlin was angry about something Russell had done, saying that he embarrassed her. He accused her of being hysterical.'

'Oh, that would have helped her calm down,' says DS Trisha Hobson. Only her female colleague laughs.

O'Neil continues: 'They left the Banking Hall at ten-fifteen and caught a cab home. We talked to the driver. Not much

101

chat between the two. He dropped them outside the house just before ten-thirty. Kemp-Lowe tapped his credit card.'

Keegan asks about the babysitter.

Hobson answers. 'Josie Sheldon. Twenty-four. She worked on Friday night and Kemp-Lowe drove her home. On Saturday morning she and her boyfriend went away for the weekend, somewhere up north. She didn't return our calls until last night. She's downstairs now.'

Keegan nods and turns to another detective, DS Andrew Pearson, whose prominent Adam's apple bobbles when he speaks.

'SOCO pulled eight unique sets of prints from the house, as well as six partials. The partials include a thumbprint on the plastic tape covering the victim's mouth. It's notable because the gang members most likely wore gloves. SOCO also recovered hair samples and fibres that are being analysed. And they found semen on Caitlin Kemp-Lowe's dressing gown and her bedspread.'

'How old?'

'Recent.'

'She and Russell were sleeping in separate bedrooms,' says Keegan.

'Maybe they kissed and made up,' says O'Neil.

'When did they have the time? Russell drove the babysitter home and came back to the house. He was attacked as he reached the front door.' He turns to O'Neil. 'Lean on the crime lab. I want the DNA results ASAP.'

'Yes, boss.'

The next detective, Cliff Baxter, is six-three with the gait of a giraffe. He gets to his feet and approaches a TV, remote control in hand. He presses play. The colour footage is grainy and lacking contrast. It shows the front steps of the Kemp-Lowe house, the path and the street beyond.

'This is the camera linked to the Kemp-Lowes' security system. It recorded everything up until the home invasion but was disabled once the gang entered the house.' He runs through the timeline. 'The babysitter arrived just after six. The couple left for the charity dinner at seven-eighteen, picked up by a cab, ordered on their account. The only other arrival was a food delivery rider, who dropped in a pizza and garlic bread at eight forty-five.'

They're watching the screen. The camera over the front door shows the motorbike rider climbing the steps and ringing the doorbell. Josie answers and takes the food.

'This is when the couple get home,' says Baxter, fast forwarding to 22.34. The footage shows them at the gate. Caitlin searches her handbag, finds her keys, and opens the door. Russell is behind her, looking at something on his phone.

'And this is eight minutes later,' says Baxter.

The front door opens and Russell Kemp-Lowe leaves the house with Josie Sheldon. Josie is putting on her overcoat, silhouetted by the light from inside. Russell puts his hand on her lower back, as they descend the steps. His fingers slide lower, as they turn along the footpath.

'Go back. Play it again,' says Keegan, peering more closely at the screen.

At the very last moment, Josie leans into Russell, and he slips his hand around her waist.

'They seem rather friendly,' says Hobson.

'Smells like sex to me,' says O'Neil.

Baxter hits fast forward. Sixty-six minutes have elapsed. Russell Kemp-Lowe appears at the front gate, pausing and looking to his right, as though something has caught his attention. A moment later, he walks up the steps, keys in hand. Two black-clad figures step from the shadows on either side of the path. One of them holds a pistol against Russell's head. A third man joins them – all wearing Halloween masks, dark clothing and gloves. The Joker takes the house keys and unlocks the door. Immediately, another reaches up and spraypaints the camera above the entrance, sweeping the nozzle back and forth until the screen goes dark.

The time code on the footage is 23.50.

Keegan checks his notes. 'How long is the drive from Antrim Road to Josie Sheldon's house in Kilburn?'

'Fourteen minutes,' says Hobson.

'So there and back should have taken him less than half an hour. We're missing forty minutes.'

'Dirty bugger,' says O'Neil.

Keegan ignores him. 'Let's see what Josie Sheldon has to say.' He motions for the briefing to continue. Trisha Hobson takes over.

'We've identified two possible vehicles used in the robbery – a dark-coloured BMW and a Ford Transit van,' she says, taking the remote control. 'This came from a traffic camera on the intersection of Crowndale Road and Camden Street at two twenty-four a.m.'

A driver is visible in the BMW, but the angle and the darkness of the tint make it impossible to see his face clearly. The Transit van has a driver and passenger, whose faces are also indistinct.

'Plates?' asks Keegan.

'Cloned from different vehicles and registered to owners in Birmingham and Manchester.'

'Any similar vehicles reported stolen?'

'Three BMW i4s in the past month and a Ford Transit van ten days ago.' Hobson points to the screen. 'This is twelve minutes later in Holborn.'

The same two vehicles are shown turning left into Hatton Garden. The BMW pulls over almost immediately, but the van carries on and crosses Greville Street before parking outside the jewellery store.

'This is from a store security camera at a café two doors down,' says Hobson. The footage shows Kemp-Lowe being bundled out of the van and marched across the footpath by two masked men. The van stays parked, blocking the camera's view of the jewellery store. 'And this came from inside the jewellery store.' A man in a zombie mask walks between jewellery cases and stands on tiptoes to point the nozzle of a spray can at the camera. The spray of paint zigzags over the lens. Moments later, the sound is also disabled.

Four men in total, thinks Keegan. Two in the van. One in the BMW. And a fourth left at the house, guarding the wife. Professionals. Forensically aware. They spent more than two hours at the house before leaving for the store. That takes patience. Discipline.

A final detective speaks. Yvette Combes. She's been collating what was stolen in the robbery, itemising the list of jewellery and uncut stones.

'Some of the pieces belonged to clients, who were having them cleaned or valued,' she says. 'Mr Kemp-Lowe has been rather reticent about giving us their names. He wants to seek their permission first.'

'Maybe it's a tax dodge,' says O'Neil.

Keegan: 'Was any of this jewellery well known? Recognisable?'

'A sapphire and diamond necklace belonging to Amanda Coulter.'

'The oligarch's wife?'

'Valued at more than a million.'

'That's going to be hard to flog,' says O'Neil.

'OK, let's liaise with Interpol,' says Keegan. 'Send them photographs of the notable pieces.'

He issues new orders, wanting to concentrate on CCTV footage from the jewellery store.

'The gang must have done reconnaissance. Maybe they made an appointment to view engagement rings or put jewellery in to be cleaned. I want the names of every visitor.'

'How far back?' asks Hobson, not relishing the task.

'Ten days. If that doesn't work – go back twenty.'

Groans around the room.

'What about the Gang Intelligence Unit?' asks Baxter.

'This wasn't some street gang,' says Keegan. 'It feels old school.

Someone with organised crime connections. Lean on your informants. Somebody will be celebrating a robbery like this, getting drunk and cocky and letting details slip. That creates jealousy and fosters greed. It attracts carrion.'

'What's carrion?' asks O'Neil.

'Scavengers.'

'You mean like vultures.'

'Exactly. Right now, they think they're going to get away with this. Let's prove them wrong.'

# 17

I'm waiting outside Keegan's office as the detectives file out. A few make eye contact with me, but most are deep in conversation. The door is still open. I knock and step inside. Keegan straightens quickly. Surprised. 'Constable McCarthy.'

'I was hoping to have a word, sir.'

He slips a bottle of hand sanitiser into his pocket.

'I wanted to offer my services,' I say.

'Your services.'

'To the task force. I know you're short-handed. I'll do anything. Data entry, door-knocking, answering phones, making coffee.'

'You want to be reassigned?'

'Yes, sir.'

'What does your duty sergeant say?'

'He doesn't want to lose me, but if you put in a request . . .'

Keegan smiles knowingly. 'Why is it so important?'

'Well, I found Daisy because I trusted my instincts. And now I feel close to the case. Invested.'

'You're not supposed to get personally involved.'

'That's not what I meant,' I stutter. 'You said I had a good eye for detail.'

'And you want to be a detective?'

'I think so, yes.'

'You think so?'

'I do. Definitely.'

Keegan looks at his fingernails. 'I'm about to interview Josie Sheldon.'

'The babysitter?'

'You can sit in and give me your impressions afterwards.'

'Does that mean you'll—?'

'I haven't decided.'

'Yes, sir, of course.'

I look over my shoulder, wondering if I should leave or wait to be dismissed.

Keegan looks amused. 'I'll see you outside, Constable.'

'Yes, sir.'

The girl in the interview room is the same one I saw outside the station. She has taken off her baseball hat, revealing blonde hair pulled into a ponytail and wound into a bun and pinned high on her head. She is attractive with an overly large mouth and widely spaced, almond-shaped eyes. And the gap between her two front teeth makes her look younger and tomboyish.

Keegan introduces himself and I do the same. We're sitting in an interview room with three chairs and a table and recording equipment. Josie is pulling the sleeves of her sweater into her fists, stretching the neckline, revealing love bites on her neck. She notices me staring and covers the marks with her hand.

'It's terrible, about Caitlin, I mean Mrs Kemp-Lowe. I didn't know – not until we were coming home.' She is speaking quickly, nervously, rushing to get the words out. 'I turned my phone on and got your messages. I called the station. Someone said Caitlin was dead. I cried all night. I've never had someone die like that. Murdered, I mean.' Josie takes a tissue from the sleeve of her jumper and blows her nose. Keegan gives her a moment to settle before he turns on the recording equipment.

'How long have you worked for the Kemp-Lowe family?'

'Since Daisy was born,' says Josie. 'Full-time at first, then a few days a week, or at weekends if her parents were going away. Sometimes they took me on holidays with them. Skiing in Italy. On safari in Africa.'

*Lucky girl*, I think, watching how eager she is to tell her story.

'Now I babysit when they need me.'

'You worked on Friday evening?'

Josie nods.

'When did you arrive at the house in Antrim Road?'

'Early. Around six. Caitlin wanted me to bathe Daisy and get her dinner. She eats the same thing every night. Chicken nuggets or macaroni and cheese. Afterwards, we played games and watched a movie, and I read her a bedtime story.'

'Have you ever known Daisy use the dumb waiter?' asks Keegan.

'Huh?'

'The small lift in her bedroom cupboard.'

'Oh, that weird thing! Daisy isn't allowed to go in there – not after the last time. She caught her fingers in the doors and howled the place down. Lost a fingernail. I felt awful.'

'Why?'

'I was looking after her.'

Keegan moves her forward. 'Did you talk to Caitlin on Friday?'

'Not really. She was rushing to get ready. She's always running late. Russell complains, but I think he's used to it now.'

'They argued?'

'No more than usual.'

'Is that a lot?'

Josie shrugs. 'I don't know. I've never been married and my parents barely speak to each other.'

'What time did they leave?'

'The car came around seven. I was giving Daisy her bath.'

'Did you notice anything different during the evening? Anyone waiting outside? A strange car, or people loitering?'

'No.'

'Any visitors?'

'None.'

Keegan waits, letting silence do the heavy lifting. Josie fidgets and then remembers. 'I ordered some food. This local place does sourdough pizzas and a salt and rosemary bread that is to die for.' Her hand goes to her mouth in shock. 'I didn't mean . . . that's a terrible thing to say. I'm sorry. Can you edit that out?'

'This isn't a performance,' says Keegan. 'What time did Mr and Mrs Kemp-Lowe arrive home?'

'They told me it could be late, but they were home by ten-thirty.'

'Why?'

'Caitlin said she had a headache.'

'Did she have a headache?'

Josie gives a non-committal shrug.

'How did they seem? Happy? Affectionate? Drunk? Arguing?'

'I wouldn't know.'

Keegan waits, wanting more.

'Does it matter?' asks Josie. 'I mean, I don't like talking about them like this.'

'I'm investigating a murder and everything matters until it doesn't,' says Keegan. 'This robbery was well planned and executed. The gang knew about the alarm system and the security cameras and the layout of the house. They could have spent weeks watching the family come and go. Watching you, too.'

Josie looks alarmed. 'Me?'

'That's why it's important you tell us everything.'

Josie toys with her phone, as though mulling over her next words. 'They were arguing.'

'What about?'

'Caitlin accused him of flirting with some woman and drinking too much.'

'What woman?'

'I don't know.'

110

'Was he drunk?'

'No. I don't think so. He drove me home.'

'Was that always the plan?'

'He could have ordered an Uber, but Russell insisted. I mean, Mr Kemp-Lowe.'

'Did you normally call him Russell?'

'Yes.'

'Had he driven you home before?'

'Lots of times.'

'Where does he drop you?'

'Out front of the house.'

'And then he left?'

Josie seems less certain than before. 'We might have talked for a few minutes about acting,' she says. 'He's been helping me. Giving me advice.'

'What sort of advice?'

'Helping me choose monologues and polish my showreel. He used to be a famous actor.'

'He films you?'

'No. I mean, yes, but you make it sound . . .' She stops herself. 'He knows about editing and lighting.'

'Where did you film?'

'At the house.'

'Was Mrs Kemp-Lowe at home?'

Josie narrows her eyes. 'It was a monologue, not a sex scene.'

Keegan backs off. 'Where were you on Saturday and Sunday?'

'On a murder mystery weekend.'

'You'll have to explain that.'

'It was one of those role-playing weekends where guests dress up in period costumes and solve a murder. I work for a company called Murder Most Foul. They hire actors to play the characters and make it more authentic.'

'Why was your mobile turned off?'

'It was an Edwardian mystery. We all had to stay in character for the whole weekend, which meant no mobile phones or computers or technology of any kind. I was the killer. Eustace Bowe – an heiress with a dark secret. It was ever so much fun.' Josie suddenly stops herself again. 'I'm sorry. That's in very poor taste. I'm talking about a fake murder when you're dealing with the real thing.'

'When did you hear about the robbery?' asks Keegan.

'Not until Sunday afternoon when I turned on my phone. I had lots of missed calls and messages.' Josie switches tack. 'How is Daisy? Is someone looking after her? And poor Russell. He must be devastated. Was he hurt? I tried to call his number.'

'Let us ask the questions,' says Keegan.

'Oh, of course, I'm sorry. I talk a lot when I'm nervous. That's why I'm not very good at auditions. I go off script.'

'You're not reading from a script now, are you?'

'No. I didn't mean . . . It's a figure of speech.' She goes quiet.

Keegan reaches into a folder for an ink drawing of two rolling dice. Three sides of the cubes are visible, showing a combination of numbers.

'Ever seen a tattoo like this one?' he asks.

'No.'

'Has anyone approached you and asked about the family or the house?'

'No.'

'Has anyone ever visited while you've been babysitting or asked to come inside?'

'No.'

'Did you lock Daisy's bedroom door before you left last night?'

Josie frowns. 'How would she get to the bathroom?'

Keegan puts the drawing away and settles back in his chair. I have been quiet up until now. I clear my throat to attract his attention.

'Did you have something you wanted to say, PC McCarthy?'

'I wanted to ask Josie who she was talking to outside the station?'

Josie looks perplexed for a moment. 'Oh, that was my boyfriend.'

'You seemed to be arguing. I thought he was going to hit you.'

She scoffs. 'I'd like to see him try.'

'What's his name?' asks Keegan.

Josie stiffens. 'He's not involved in this.'

'Good. What's his name?'

'Hugo Desai. He's an actor. He was with me on the weekend. He played the gamekeeper, Tobias Croft, a ladies' man, who gets killed off in Act Two.'

'How?' I ask.

'With a pitchfork.' She smiles. 'I did enjoy that.'

# 18

When Daragh McCarthy thinks too hard his head begins to hurt. It's like he's trying to process too much information and his brain begins to splutter and backfire. Finbar, a natural mechanic, might say that his spark plugs needed cleaning or his timing was off, whereas Clifton would tell him to delete any unused files and run a spam filter.

Daragh doesn't understand engines or computers or smart-phones, any more than he knows how TV pictures are beamed around the world by satellite or how planes stay in the air or how the moon makes the tides go up and down.

His old man was the same. Victor McCarthy didn't believe in education, not in the book-reading sense. And while he didn't trust governments or banks, he believed that capitalism in its purest form was the most perfect economic model ever devised. It was faultless because anyone with the necessary readies could do whatever they wanted, whenever they wanted, however they wanted, to whoever they wanted, unless someone with more money chose to stop them. Rules and regulations and permits did not exist. Money didn't just talk – it kicked open doors and never shut up.

Not that Victor McCarthy ever had any money. He spent half his life in prison and the other half working out ways to get back inside. That was before dying of a heart attack at fifty-two, leaving a wife and four boys to navigate poverty. People still talk about him around the flower markets in

Spitalfields, calling him 'one of a kind', to which Daragh replies, 'Thank fuck for that.'

Their mother, Eileen, was a working-class saint, who cleaned houses, sewed clothes and took in washing to keep her sons fed and shod. All were born at St Bart's Hospital, which put them within earshot of St Mary-le-Bow Church in Cheapside. According to the legend, this made them true cockneys, but Daragh took no pride in the term. Too many posh wankers were putting on fake East End accents and pretending to be working class, thinking they were 'keeping it real'.

According to the oft-told story, Daragh came out of the womb wet and blue with fluid obstructing his lungs. The midwife smacked him in the arse and Daragh smacked her right back. Gave her a black eye. That's when his reputation for fighting began. Now he has a CV full of people that he's put into hospital or worse. Punching is easier than talking and much easier than thinking.

He has spent the morning seeking information about the Hatton Garden robbery. Looking under rocks and shaking trees. So far, he's managed to talk to Fat Tony Doherty, who was propping up the back bar of the Lord Nelson. Tony had been an expert safecracker in the days when breaking open a safe involved a delicate touch instead of a diamond-tipped drill and an ounce of nitro.

Calling him fat was ironic because Fat Tony was skinny as a rail. He once starved himself during a stint on remand and slipped through the bars of a holding cell beneath Marylebone Magistrates' Court. He joined a pool of prospective jurors and was almost made the foreman before a bailiff recognised his face.

Fat Tony couldn't help, so Daragh tracked down a rag trader called Sweatshop Ibrahim, whose sewing machines run around the clock, making knock-off fashions for market-stall traders at Petticoat Lane. From there, he visited Doris Holgate, a landlady in Peckham, who finds accommodation for girls just arrived from Eastern Europe. He found 'the Guvnor' Dickie Glover at his pigeon loft in Canning Town. Dickie was called 'the Guvnor' because he'd spent so much time in prison he basically ran the joint. Like the others, he couldn't shed any light on the jewellery robbery and home invasion.

After a pint and pork pie at the Morgan Arms, Daragh drops in to see Banjo Myers at his chopshop near Waterloo Station. Banjo deals in premium motors, stolen to order, that are dismantled and shipped overseas, mainly to Russia and the Middle East.

'Reckon it was the frogs,' says Banjo. 'They like the shiny stuff.'

'What frogs?'

'Can't give you any names. Just smells that way.'

'What way?'

'Garlicky.'

'You can't say somefing like that,' says Daragh. 'It's a bit racist.'

'How can something be a bit racist? It's either racist or it's not. And I love frog food. Maybe not the snails, but the other stuff, you know, only I wish they'd call a chicken a chicken. Nobody wants to eat coq.'

By mid-afternoon Daragh is none the wiser. The man he most wants to find is proving elusive. He knocks on the door of an ugly mock Tudor house in Romford. A woman answers, Omar Syed's new wife. She's pregnant and barely out of her teens and doesn't speak English but manages to communicate that her husband is at work.

*Which fuckin' work?* thinks Daragh. Omar is a pawnbroker, dry cleaner, loan shark and has two illegal gambling dens, known as spiels.

It's almost dark when he parks his Jag in a loading zone near Brick Lane and props a doctor's sign on the dashboard. Walking past shops full of colourful saris, black chadors, Halal meats, kosher pastries and other delicacies, he could be in Bangladesh or Mogadishu or Hackney or Lambeth. This is the face of Britain. Not good, or bad, just different.

Turning down an alley, he climbs a set of fire stairs to a small office where Syed has a signboard advertising himself as a financial advisor and moneylender. Nobody answers his knock. The blinds are closed, but Daragh can smell cigar smoke.

'I know you're in there, Syed. Open the door.'

Nothing.

Daragh steps back and aims a kick. The door bursts open.

Syed scrambles under his desk. 'Fuck me! You didn't have to do that.'

'You've been avoiding me.'

'That's not true. I had my aids turned off.' He points to his ears.

'What's that you're 'oldin'?' asks Daragh.

Reluctantly, Syed produces a golf club from behind his back.

'I didn't know you played golf. What's your 'andicap?'

'I'm not very good.'

'That's because you're fat.'

Daragh takes the putter from him and swishes it through the air.

'How can I help you, Mr McCarthy? You want a loan? A golf club membership? I know the chairman of the Hampton Club. I own the fucker. He can fix you up. No waiting lists. No joining fees.'

'I don't fink they want a member like me,' says Daragh, swishing the club like a sword. Several golf balls are nestled in a putting cup on the floor. Daragh picks up one of them and hands it to Syed.

'Hold that up for me. Bit 'igher. I don't wanna miss.'

'Please, Mr McCarthy, just tell me what you want.'

'The skinny. The drum. The dirt.'

'On what?'

'We've had a bit of fuckery at our building sites. Sabotage. Thievery. Workplace accidents.'

'I don't know anything about that.'

'What about that robbery in 'Atton Garden? The one with the fake bomb.'

'Haven't heard a thing. Not a dickie bird.'

'Oh, that's a shame. You were doing so well.'

Daragh takes a practice swing. 'Now 'old that ball steady. A bit 'igher. That's it.'

He swings the putter. Syed pulls his hand away, close to tears. 'On my mother's grave, I only know what I read in the papers.'

'Your mother ain't dead.'

'Yeah, but she's been poorly.'

'You're a bottom feeder, Syed. You filter the faeces. You must have 'eard somefing.'

'I can ask around. Come up with some names.'

'Give 'em to me now.'

Syed mumbles something. Daragh tells him to spit it out.

'Maybe Dave Hemsley.'

'Bzzzz! Roids is dead. Try again.'

'Larry Bulgin?'

'Bzzzz! Inside.'

Syed's whole body has started to shake. 'It could be foreigners. I heard about these Chechens who've been knocking off country houses.' He is about to say something else, but stops himself, swallowing the sentence.

Daragh raises the putter.

'It's nothing more than a whisper,' says Syed. 'There's a Bulgarian geezer who only works with his brothers or cousins. He's been making waves in South London.'

'What sort of waves?'

'He's pushed out Toothless and the Peckham Boys.'

'His name?'

'They call him the Wrestler.'

'What sort of bullshit name is that?'

'He was at the London Olympics. Fought for the bronze. Lost.'

'What's 'is game?'

'Insurance and security.'

'He breaks windows and fixes them?'

'Something like that, but on a bigger scale.'

'Thievery?'

'Like I said, whispers.'

'Where do I find this Wrestler?'

'No idea.'

The golf club swings through the air and shatters a standard lamp on the desk. Shards of glass rattle as they hit the wall. Syed screams and ducks. The next swing misses his head by an inch.

'He's got a warehouse somewhere out west. Hounslow way. And a house in South London.'

'Find 'im.'

'Then what?'

'Tell me.'

# 19

I feel self-conscious sitting at a desk in the incident room, surrounded by seasoned detectives, who all seem to know what they're doing. I'm the new face, the novelty, the work experience kid who either gets the coffee, or gets ignored, or both.

Right now, I'm typing up Josie Sheldon's witness statement. She is sitting next to the desk, correcting my spelling and enduring my two-fingered typing, which is painfully slow.

Josie's eyes are always shining, as though she's on the verge of crying. Maybe that's part of her training as an actor, being able to effortlessly conjure up emotion. She seemed genuinely shocked by Caitlin's death, but I don't know if that extends to sadness or grief. And during the interview I caught her sneaking glances at herself in the mirror, as though evaluating her performance. Maybe that's unfair.

I ask about her career and she says that most auditions are online over Zoom, or the casting agents just look at showreels.

'I'm better at face-to-face interviews. My personality shines through,' she says without any trace of modesty. 'And photographs seem to flatten my features because my face is so round and I have a small nose.' She turns her head from side to side, as though showing me the problem. I can't see any.

'I think you look very pretty,' I say.

She gives me a sideways look, as though I'm trying to pick her up.

After watching Josie sign and initial her statement, I escort her downstairs and wait for an Uber to arrive.

'How is Daisy?' she asks.

'OK, but I don't know if she fully realises what's happened.'

'Where is she now?'

'Her godmother is looking after her until Mr Kemp-Lowe is released from hospital.'

Her voice changes. 'Amber Culver?'

'You sound surprised.'

A lift of the shoulders. No words.

'Is she the wrong person to look after Daisy?' I ask.

'I didn't say that.'

'What then?'

Josie presses her lips together, as though internally debating how much to tell me.

'Caitlin had a fight with her a few weeks ago and they stopped talking to each other.'

'What did they fight about?'

'Me.'

'I don't understand.'

'Amber wanted to pick up Daisy after daycare and take her home and cook her meals. She didn't think Caitlin should employ me.'

'Was it something you did?'

'No! I barely know the woman. I think she was jealous.'

'Of you?'

'No, of Caitlin. She had everything that Amber didn't have – the lovely house, the handsome husband, the beautiful daughter . . . Amber missed out on that.'

'She got to be Daisy's godmother.'

Josie answers with a non-committal shrug.

'How did she and Russell get on?' I ask.

'He'd sometimes get annoyed when she visited the house or phoned Caitlin every day. He said he only married one woman, but finished up with two wives.'

That's pretty common, I think. Henry is often complaining about my girlfriends – saying they're too needy, or too bossy, or they drink too much and lead me astray. He likes some of them – the good-looking ones – but has trouble with loud, opinionated women. Then again, he has trouble with loud, opinionated men, so maybe it's not a gender thing.

'What do you think of Amber?' I ask.

'She's a bit weird.'

'In what way?'

'She's always telling Caitlin what to feed Daisy and how to dress her and what to let her watch on TV, but she tends to do it in a roundabout way, saying things like, "What made you choose that dress?" and "Who recommended that preschool?"'

Josie looks at her phone and curses, 'Bugger! My Uber driver just cancelled.'

'I'll drop you home?'

'That's OK. I can wait.'

'Honestly. It's easy to get a car.'

She waits while I sign out an area vehicle and collect it from the secure parking area at the rear of the station.

'You can sit up front,' I tell her.

She slides into the passenger seat, nervous about touching anything.

On the drive she becomes more talkative, telling me that she grew up in Liverpool and studied drama at school before working in local rep theatre. She came to London at the age of twenty, sure to be discovered. Expecting it. Still holding out hope.

'I've done some fringe stuff and a few small TV parts, and a bit of modelling. I was the Starburst girl in a TV commercial.'

'The sweets.'

Excitedly, 'Did you see it?'

'No.'

'Shame. My parents don't think acting is a proper job. They want me to come home and go to university, but all my friends are graduating and most of them are working in cafés or call centres. I'm only twenty-four. And a lot of actors don't get discovered until late. Look at Melissa McCarthy and Naomi Watts.'

We're stuck behind slow buses on Belsize Road that seem to shunt each other forward like the pendulums on a Newton's Cradle.

'Why would anyone hurt Caitlin?' she asks.

'Perhaps she saw their faces or they panicked.'

'Does her brother know?'

'Nobody can find him,' I say. 'He's living in America.'

Josie turns to face me. 'But he's in London.'

I take my eyes off the road. 'Are you sure?'

'He's been visiting the house.'

'Seeing Caitlin?'

'Yeah.'

'Since when?'

Josie does a mental calculation. 'A few months. Caitlin told me not to tell Russell. She wanted to keep it a secret.'

'Why?'

'I got the impression that Noah was *persona non grata* with the family, but Caitlin felt sorry for him.'

'Where is he now?'

'He lives on a narrowboat near Primrose Hill. I took Daisy to visit him.'

'Could you show me?'

Josie nods cautiously. 'Is he in trouble?'

'No, not necessarily, but he should have come forward. He must have heard the news about his sister.'

I turn right at the next intersection and double back, heading towards Regent's Park. Josie gives me directions, struggling to remember because she came on foot with Daisy. They stopped to feed the ducks and to listen to the lions roaring at London Zoo.

I pull over beside St Mark's Church and we descend steps to the canal, walking towards Camden Lock.

'We're getting closer, but they all look the same,' says Josie, studying the narrowboats. Some are colourfully painted and decorated with herb gardens and window boxes of flowers. Others are shuttered up for the winter, covered in tarpaulins with everything bolted down.

She stops and points. 'That one.'

'Are you sure?'

'Yes.'

# 20

Keegan has never liked visiting Westminster City Mortuary because it brings back memories of his police training. One of his instructors, a Geordie with a sick sense of humour decided to lock his trainees in the 'dirty-body room', which held the cadavers that had been discovered well after death. Decomposing. Putrefying.

The smell is something Keegan has never forgotten, nor the nickname 'Upchuck' that he carried for years afterwards.

Gerard Noonan is in his office. The pathologist is in his sixties with snow-white hair and skin so pale he must glow in the dark, which is why people call him 'The Albino' or 'The Count'. Keegan has always suspected that Noonan, unmarried and childless, had far better relationships with the dead than the living. The only sentient creatures he seems to relate to are the horses he owns and races, which are featured in photographs on his office walls.

'Did we have an appointment?' he asks.

'You promised me the results of the tox screen and swabs on Caitlin Kemp-Lowe.'

'I told you to call me.'

'Well, I'm here now.'

Noonan pulls a file from his drawer and begins reading aloud.

'White Caucasian female of medium build, weighing sixty-one kilos, dark wavy hair, dyed, shaped eyebrows and pubic hair. No tattoos. A vertical lower midline scar from a hysterectomy.'

'She couldn't have more children.'

'Not without a womb. Her medical records show she suffered from chronic endometriosis. That would explain the egg harvesting and IVF treatments. She must have struggled to fall pregnant.'

Noonan continues reading from the file. 'I found no evidence of sexual penetration. The anal, oral and vaginal swabs were negative for spermatozoa. Blood alcohol level: moderate. There were abrasions on her wrists where she fought against her bindings, which suggests she was alive when she was suffocated.'

'With the plastic bag?'

'Yes.' He turns the page. 'There were bruises on either side of her nostrils, which suggests someone pinched her nose closed, cutting off her oxygen supply. That could have been a punishment or a torture technique, but the bag was used to finish her off.'

'What makes you so sure?'

'When a plastic bag is placed over someone's head and sealed at the neck, there is only a limited amount of air available. Once the suffocation begins, the plastic is sucked against the mouth or nose. It takes about eight minutes to guarantee death. We found DNA on the inside of the bag. Saliva and skin cells. We also pulled a partial palmprint from the handle but latent prints left on soft plastics are less reliable because of the pliability and lack of surface texture.'

'It could still help us identify the killer.'

'Maybe, but the bag came from a local Italian restaurant. The partial print could belong to the delivery driver or someone who worked in the kitchen.'

Keegan makes a note. 'What about the semen stains?'

'They didn't come from Russell Kemp-Lowe. Wrong blood type.'

'Was Caitlin having an affair?'

'One possible explanation, but they were deposited recently.'

'Within days?'

'More like hours.'

Keegan is formulating his next question, when the pathologist gets to his feet and walks out of the door without any explanation.

The detective jogs to keep up with him. 'What's the rush?'

'I'm late for another post-mortem,' says Noonan. 'The dead don't have diaries, but they do keep appointments.' He talks as he walks. 'We also found older traces of semen on the front passenger seat of the Mercedes that did match Russell Kemp-Lowe.'

'He had sex in his car.'

'Or he banged one out, as they say.'

'What about forensics on the fake bomb?' he asks.

'Clever device,' says Noonan. 'The mercury tilt switch was homemade but would have been effective if the bomb had been real. Makes you wonder if they have experience.'

'A professional bombmaker?'

'I'd keep that between us.'

They have arrived at a post-mortem suite. Noonan shrugs off his coat and puts on dark green surgical scrubs. He begins washing his hands and arms with soap and running water. Keegan appreciates his thoroughness and wants to do the same. Still holding his wet arms aloft, the pathologist nudges a swing door with his hip, revealing a post-mortem suite and a naked body on a stainless-steel table. Two assistants are prepping the equipment. Keegan stops suddenly, getting a flashback of the dirty-body room.

'I'll be in touch,' he yells, letting the door swing closed.

Outside, on the street, he looks at his phone. There are five missed calls. Two are work related. The others are from his wife's solicitor, his bank manager and his mother. His heart is a pincushion.

The phone rings again. O'Neil's name on the screen.

'What is it, Sergeant?'

'The Kemp-Lowe jewellery store was robbed eighteen months ago. A couple came in posing as customers, asking to see the engagement rings. They spent about forty minutes trying on different jewellery. As they were leaving, two men burst into the store wearing balaclavas, and swinging baseball bats. One scooped up the rings and the other smashed up the display cases, taking what they could.'

'How much was taken?'

'Half a million in jewellery, although Kemp-Lowe has been accused of inflating the figure. His insurance company has refused to pay out. They're still in dispute.'

'Any arrests?'

'None, but I talked to the officer in charge. He got a whiff of an inside job.'

'Why?'

'The couple who were shopping for an engagement ring were already married, but not to each other.'

'Any links to the Kemp-Lowes?'

'The woman ran a mobile hairdressing business and had coloured Caitlin's hair. She'd visited their house.'

'Talk to her again. Lean harder.'

O'Neil again: 'Russell Kemp-Lowe was released from hospital two hours ago.'

'Where is he now?'

'Staying with his wife's parents. You want me to pick him up?'

'No, but get a forensic accountant to go over their books. Business and personal spending.'

'On the subject of money – we found a note in a drawer in the study. Caitlin's handwriting. It said: "Give her five thousand. Not a penny more. And this is the last time."'

'Who?'

'It doesn't say, but I did a quick check of their joint bank account. Five thousand pounds was transferred to an account at Barclays Bank in Liverpool.'

'Josie Sheldon moved to London from Liverpool.'

'An expensive babysitter.'

'Or something more.'

# 21

Edward McCarthy is sitting in his penthouse office, his feet propped on a chair, West London stretching out below him.

'He hasn't been back to the house,' says Clifton.

'What about other family?'

'He's Australian.'

'You make it sound like a disease.'

'Convicts, all of them. Maybe they put him in some sort of safe house.'

'That would suggest Russell needs protection. What about his daughter?'

'Staying with a friend of the family. Finbar is watching her place.'

'I hope he's discreet,' says McCarthy. 'If we're linked to this robbery, we'll have Old Bill crawling up our colons with grappling hooks.'

Clifton grimaces at the mental picture.

'What do we know about this Albanian geezer?' asks McCarthy.

'He's Bulgarian.'

'Close enough.'

'Daragh's Rosie is on maternity leave and has done a deep dive through the public records, looking for information.'

Rosie usually works as a school counsellor in Peckham, but she moonlights as the family's IT expert and part-time book-keeper. In between times, she writes letters for Daragh who, like Winnie the Pooh, gets bothered by long words.

'His real name is Dimitar Popov,' says Clifton. 'He's a former Olympic wrestler who came to London about three years ago.'

'Doing what?'

'That's not clear, but people are frightened of talking about him. How much do you know about Bulgaria?'

'Fuck all.'

'Basically, it's a failed state, run by corrupt politicians, bent coppers and criminal gangs. The big players are former spooks who control most of the transport, construction and energy, which is the lion's share of the economy. After the London Olympics, Popov joined the Bulgarian secret police. From there it was a hop, skip and jump into organised crime. Drugs. People-smuggling. Extortion.

'A few years back a crime-busting chief prosecutor in Sofia launched a crackdown and a court seized Popov's assets, his houses and his yacht. Two months later, the prosecutor survived a car bomb explosion that killed his wife and eight-year-old son. Popov fled the country and Britain offered him a safe haven on account of his Swiss bank accounts.'

'That'd be right,' says McCarthy. 'We've always been welcoming to oligarchs, despots and war criminals if they come with enough cash.'

His mobile is ringing. It's Finbar on speaker.

'I found Russell,' he says.

'Where?'

'He's taken his daughter to lunch at the Warwick Castle in Maida Vale. They arrived ten minutes ago.'

'Keep watching him. I'm on my way.'

Clifton drops McCarthy opposite Rembrandt Gardens in the heart of Little Venice – a neighbourhood of candy-coloured terraces, narrowboats, waterside cafés and gastropubs.

Buttoning his overcoat, McCarthy crosses a bridge, turning left into Warwick Place, passing Finbar, who is sitting on a bench, eating a paper cone full of chips. They don't make eye contact.

The pub has outside tables with green umbrellas, but it's too cold for al fresco dining today. McCarthy pushes through the polished wooden door and hangs his coat on a hook.

'We have space at the bar,' says a pink-haired waitress with a ring in her nose.

'I've just seen some friends. I might squeeze in with them.'

Russell and Daisy are at a corner booth. Daisy has a bowl of chips and a half-eaten burger in front of her. Russell has chosen a liquid diet – a double Scotch and pint of Guinness.

'Fancy running into you,' says McCarthy, putting his hands on the jeweller's shoulders. Russell tries to stand. McCarthy holds him down. 'Hello, Daisy. What are you drawing?'

'A unicorn.'

'It looks like a horse with a horn.'

'Yes, silly, that's a unicorn.'

'You-you-you can't be here,' stutters Russell. 'They could be watching.'

'Why would they be doing that?'

Incredulously, 'They're the police. They investigate crimes.'

'I haven't committed any. Have you?'

'No.'

'Then relax. Keep eating . . . or drinking.'

'I know you,' says Daisy. 'You were at the church.'

'Clever girl.'

McCarthy takes the bench seat opposite them. He has to avoid sitting on Hippo, who is propped up with a serviette tucked around his neck.

'Can I get you something?' asks the waitress.

'I'll have what she's having,' he says, pointing to Daisy's burger and chips.

'How would you like it cooked?'

'It's a burger, not filet mignon. Well done.'

'It's very big,' says Daisy. 'I couldn't finish mine.'

'That's because you left room for ice cream.'

She grins shyly and looks at her dad.

'Not yet,' he replies, glancing around the pub, looking for an escape.

'A word in your shell-like,' says McCarthy.

The two men get up from the booth and walk several paces to one end of the polished wooden bar, away from the beer taps. McCarthy adjusts the collar of Russell's shirt, which is folded the wrong way. He keeps touching the shirt. Running his fingers around the collar and down the sleeves, checking for a wire.

'Firstly, let me say how sorry I am about Caitlin. I only met her once or twice, but my Constance spoke very highly of her. They did some fundraising together. Do-gooder stuff.'

'Thank you,' says Russell, looking miserable.

'In the circumstances, I don't want to add to your problems, so I'll get to the point. Where are my fuckin' stones?'

Russell begins stammering. 'They're gone. We were cleaned out. Everything. The jewellery, the uncut diamonds, cash—'

'Who?'

'How would I know?'

'You must have some idea.'

'None. They came to the house. They held Caitlin hostage. They made me wear a bomb.' His voice begins breaking. 'I thought I was going to die.'

McCarthy pulls a clean handkerchief from his pocket and hands it to the jeweller, who mops his brow and blows his nose. He tries to return the handkerchief. McCarthy shakes his head.

'What did you tell the police was in the safe?'

'Not a word. I promise. Nothing about the stones.'

'Who *did* you tell?'

'Nobody. I swear.'

'Somebody knew they were there.'

'They didn't get it from me.'

'What about Caitlin? Did she know?'

Russell hesitates before shaking his head.

'I'm going to ask you again,' says McCarthy, his voice rumbling from deep in his chest. 'Did Caitlin know?'

'I-I-I might have told her, but she lets me handle that side of the business.'

'What side is that?'

'You know, the laundering and such.'

'Do I look like a fuckwit, Russell?'

'No.'

'Or maybe you think that you're some chess grandmaster, who can plot six moves ahead of everyone.'

'No.'

'Because I'm down eleven million quid and someone is trying to take control of my business.'

'I had nothing—'

'Don't interrupt me.'

'Sorry. I didn't mean—'

'You're doing it again.'

The jeweller keeps his mouth shut. McCarthy flexes his fingers, curling them into fists. He is staring at a point about two inches behind the bridge of the jeweller's nose.

'I'm sure you've heard the stories about me, Russell. Admittedly, most of them are apocryphal, but people tell them for a reason. For example, I've never fed anyone to the pigs. Can't see the point of ruining good bacon. And the idea of filling oil drums with concrete and dropping people into the North Sea seems like a lot of fuckin' effort. I prefer a wood-chipper because it's more environmentally friendly — for the garden, you know. Daragh is quite partial to hydraulic compactors — the sort they use to crush wrecked motors. Less mess, he says. He might have a point.'

Russell has gone pale and beads of sweat are forming on the end of his nose.

'Who took my stones?' asks McCarthy.

'I didn't see their faces. They wore masks.'

'Accents?'

'Foreign sounding.'

'Bulgarian?'

'Maybe.'

'Ever heard the name Dimitar Popov?'

'Never.'

'Daddy?' says a voice. Daisy tugs at Russell's sleeve. 'Can I have an ice cream now?'

'Yeah, sure. I'll see what flavours they have.'

Back at the table, a waitress is delivering McCarthy's burger and chips.

'I'll take that to go,' he says, handing her three fifty-quid notes. 'And I'm paying for everything.'

'This is too much.'

'Bring the kid some ice cream and keep the change.'

McCarthy walks out of the pub carrying a polystyrene box with the burger and chips. Clifton is parked at the end of the lane. McCarthy knocks on the car window. It glides down.

'Thought you might be hungry.'

'Thanks, Eddie.'

Finbar gets out of the passenger seat. 'What did he say?'

'It's what he didn't say,' says McCarthy, who has a very low tolerance for people he perceives as not respecting him. 'Arrange a meeting with Dimitar Popov.'

'What sort of meeting?' asks Clifton, suddenly animated.

'The normal sort – where people talk.'

'Yeah, it's better that way, although Daragh won't be happy.'

# 22

The narrowboat is tethered beside the towpath on Regent's Canal opposite Primrose Hill Primary School. Barely seven feet wide and fifty feet long, it has small round windows and brightly painted stern doors and a boxed herb garden on the cabin roof.

After Josie pointed out the boat, I drove her home to Kilburn and dropped her off a block away because she didn't want her neighbours seeing her get out of a police car. I returned the car to the nick and changed into my half blues. Now I'm back at the canal, standing on the towpath, studying the narrowboat.

I call out. Nobody answers.

I step on board, adjusting my balance as the boat moves beneath me. I don't trust watercraft, or maybe it's my own buoyancy that I doubt. I hated swimming lessons as a kid – the stench of the chlorine and the bellowed instructions, and the shivering walk to the changing rooms.

'They're not home,' says a voice from a nearby boat. An old guy is crouching on the deck, wielding a paintbrush. 'Saw 'em ride off on their bikes.'

'When?' I ask.

'Hour ago. Went back to work most likely. Sofia is Spanish. Very Mediterranean.'

'What does that mean?'

'They have siestas.' He winks licentiously.

'Where do they work?'

'At the markets. She's a painter. Sells her watercolours. Not bad, if you like that sort of thing. Tourists do.'

'I'm looking for Noah Kemp-Lowe.'

'The boyfriend. Nice chap. Quiet.'

I look along the towpath towards Camden, knowing it's not far. I grew up around here after my parents' divorce. My mother has a hair salon only a few blocks away. Immediately, I feel a pang of guilt because I haven't called her this week. I'm a terrible daughter.

I should tell DCI Keegan that Noah Kemp-Lowe is back in the country, but I want to be sure before I make the call. Noah must have seen the headlines about his sister's death, but he hasn't contacted his family or the police. He breached his parole conditions when he went overseas, which could explain his silence, or maybe he's involved. If I bring him to Keegan I could gain the kudos. He might let me join the task force. He said I had good instincts.

I follow the towpath beneath the arch of Gloucester Avenue Bridge and the railway tracks leading to Euston Station. The water ripples in the breeze, dotted with floating weeds and the occasional duck paddling between the boats.

The opening to Camden Lock appears suddenly, like I'm emerging from a tunnel. Buildings crowd the canal, warehouses and stables that once serviced the inland trade route. Now they're being used by artists, artisans and souvenir sellers. The markets are quieter so early in the week with fewer sightseers and shoppers. I pretend to browse, moving between the covered stalls, the cafés and food trucks. I focus on places that are selling paintings. Some of the artists have set up along the railing fence, creating an outdoor gallery.

I notice a young woman sitting on a wooden stool next to the fence. She's wearing paint-splattered jeans and a voluminous buttoned-up shirt that doesn't completely hide her pregnancy. An antique tiepin is holding the collar together and a baseball cap shields her eyes.

I pause and study her paintings, which are copies of famous images where the subjects have been replaced by monkeys. Waterhouse's Lady of Shalott is a chimpanzee, Whistler's Mother is a white-cheeked gibbon and the Mona Lisa is a Japanese macaque. I lean closer and notice the name 'Sofia' painted in the bottom-left corner.

'It's an allegory of our treatment of history,' she explains, looking up from a sketchpad. 'We humans think we are masters of this universe, but we're nothing more than highly developed apes.'

'Interesting.'

She laughs. 'People always say that when they don't understand.'

'Is Noah here?' I ask.

Her eyes narrow and she looks past me. I turn. A man is moving through the crowd, holding two iced coffees. She yells a warning. A heartbeat later, his hands release the cups and they explode as they hit the ground, spilling liquid across the concrete.

Noah runs, leaping over a child's stroller and swinging around a lamppost. I give chase, pulling out my mobile phone and calling for back-up.

'Suspect is a white male, dark hair, six feet, wearing a brown bomber jacket with a woollen hood, jeans and black trainers.'

Ahead of me, Noah is dodging pedestrians. He tips over a display of flowers, stumbling but scrambling to his feet. I take a short cut between stalls and narrow the distance between us, but it's difficult to talk and run at the same time. Noah has reached the towpath. He veers to the right and jumps onto the roof of a narrowboat. After two paces, he leaps to the next one, which is moored alongside. Running the length of that boat, ignoring the protests of the owner, he jumps onto another, which is motoring westward.

I look ahead along the towpath to a sloping ramp that leads to the bridge. If I can reach the ramp I can cut him off. I sprint alongside the moving boat, yelling at the skipper to stop. He's arguing with Noah, telling him to get off. He cuts the engine and steers towards the path. Giving myself a run-up, I leap onto the moving boat. At the same time, Noah jumps for the other side of the canal. His hands hit the stone wall and his elbows hook over the edge. He scrambles with his feet, but the bricks are slick with moss and lichen, making it hard to get any purchase with his trainers.

He's up, getting away.

I jump for the same wall, but don't have enough momentum. I slam into the bricks and feel my head crunch against stone before I hit the water, slipping beneath the surface. Cursing my stupidity.

The canal is less than six feet deep and I can touch the bottom. That's where I settle. Dazed. Sickened. I remember why I hated swimming lessons so much. It wasn't the cold or the chlorine or the bullying of the instructor. It was feeling exposed in that unflattering one-piece my mother insisted I wear.

From somewhere above me, a hand reaches out. Fingers touch my hair and then my collar. A fist closes around the fabric and I'm dragged up into the light and the air. An arm is hooked over my chest. Strong legs drag me towards a ramp where people are waiting to lift me out.

'Call an ambulance,' says Noah, breathlessly.

'It's coming,' says a voice in the crowd.

I feel my body being turned on its side. Fingers reach into my mouth, making sure my airways are clear. Filthy water is spilling out of my mouth and nose, coming in coughs and gobs. I try to say something.

'Stay still,' he says. 'You might be concussed.'

Sirens are sounding. Growing nearer. Noah looks over his shoulder. I reach out and grab his wrist. 'Don't go.'

'Who are you?'

'Police.'

He grimaces and sighs.

'Why did you run?' I ask.

'I thought you were someone else.'

138

'Who?'

'It doesn't matter.'

'You spent time in prison.'

'Yes.'

'And you breached your parole.'

At that moment Sofia pushes past onlookers and throws her arms around him, glaring at me, as if I'm to blame for his wet clothes and his ruined shoes.

'Don't tell her anything,' she says, adding several Spanish words, which are probably curses.

Noah speaks to her gently, asking her to get us something warm to drink. He glances at me. 'Hot chocolate?'

I nod.

Sofia gives me another glare as she leaves.

'Bit young for you, isn't she?' I ask.

'More grown-up than me.'

One of the onlookers has found two blankets. Noah wraps one of them around my shoulders and we sit close.

'Do you know about your sister?' I ask.

He nods.

'When did you last speak to her?'

'We don't talk.'

'You're lying.'

A wry smile. 'Did Daisy give me away?'

'No. It was Josie.'

There is a long silence. I spit out more canal water, feeling the oily filth clinging to my skin. Noah uses a corner of his blanket to wipe his face.

'Three, maybe four months ago, Caitlin contacted me.'

'Any particular reason?'

'She said she wanted to build bridges. Reunite the family.'

'What did your parents say?'

'She didn't tell them. I haven't spoken to either of them since before I went to prison. They made it abundantly clear that I wasn't part of the family.'

'You were written out of the will.'

'I don't want their money. I want to see them buried with their coffins full of gold and jewellery, just like the pharaohs in Egypt. I want to see how much good it does them in the next life.'

'You believe in Heaven?'

'Oh, they're not going to Heaven.'

'Where were you on Friday night?'

Noah looks at me incredulously. 'You don't think I had anything to do with . . . I mean, we had our differences, but I loved Caitlin. And I would never do anything to hurt Daisy.'

'You haven't told me where you were?'

'At an NA meeting. Narcotics Anonymous. My sponsor will confirm it. I've been clean for seven and a half years.'

'You remember your last fix?'

'So would you,' he says sadly.

I recall the story I read in the newspaper. How he injected his girlfriend and watched her dying of an overdose, unable to save her.

'What time was your meeting?'

'Eight-thirty.'

'When did it finish?'

'Around ten. Afterwards I met up with Sofia and had tapas in Greek Street.'

'Is she your only alibi?'

He doesn't answer.

'When did you last see Caitlin?'

'A week ago.'

'Are the police going to find your fingerprints in the house?'

He inhales slowly, filling his chest and letting the air leak out. 'I've been there.' His voice softens. 'What happened to her?'

'A home invasion. The gang was targeting the jewellery store. They held Caitlin hostage and forced Russell to open the safe.'

'But if they got what they wanted, why kill her?'

'Maybe Caitlin saw their faces or heard one of their names.'

'She would have cooperated. She's not reckless or careless.'

An ambulance has pulled up on the bridge overlooking the canal. Two paramedics jog along the towpath. The bigger of the two has one of those flawless black faces that make it impossible to estimate her age.

'How are you doing, darling?' she asks, setting down her first-aid backpack and sitting on the step next to me. 'Bit late in the season for a swim.'

'It wasn't planned.'

'Good.' She examines the bump on my head. 'God knows what's in that water. You'll need a tetanus shot and broad-spectrum antibiotics. And nobody is saving those clothes.'

I laugh, but it hurts. The other paramedic is examining Noah, who keeps saying he's fine.

Two uniformed police officers arrive. One of them I recognise from training at Hendon. As soon as he tells me his name, Bunbury, I remember he had a nickname, 'Cream Bun', which he hated. All of us seemed to have nicknames back then. I was 'Judi' after the actress Judi Dench, who played a character called Philomena in a film of the same name.

I explain the situation but stop short of calling Noah a murder suspect. Instead, I say that he may have important information.

'And he resisted arrest?' asks the other officer.

'It was a misunderstanding.'

'Did you announce yourself?' asks Bunbury.

'I didn't have time.'

'And he jumped into the canal to get away?'

'Not exactly. I fell into the canal and he saved me.'

They look at each other, clearly passing judgement or wondering if I'm concussed.

'What I'm saying is that he's an important witness. Call DCI Keegan. He'll send detectives.'

The paramedic interrupts, telling the constables to step back. She enjoys throwing her weight around.

'I hate cops,' she says, as she shines a pen torch into my eyes.

'I'm a police officer.'

'You might be one of the good ones.' She holds up three fingers, wanting me to count them. 'If you weren't, I'd be holding up the middle one.'

# 23

Henry brings a set of dry clothes to the hospital. We wait together for the results of my X-ray. A radiologist studies the images and gives me the all-clear. No fractures. Only bruises and my damaged pride.

'Why were you trying to arrest him?' asks Henry. 'You were off-duty.'

'It's complicated.'

'Imagine if I went off fighting fires on my day off . . . on my own.'

'It's not the same thing.'

'You're five foot five and weigh a hundred and twenty pounds.'

'And I can kick your arse,' I say, challenging him.

'How useful was your karate when you were drowning?' he asks, sarcastically.

'Fuck off!'

A nurse catches the final statement and looks embarrassed at overhearing us arguing. Henry smiles at her apologetically. She smiles back. I could lose him so easily to another woman, because he's funny and kind and handsome; and I am stubborn, selfish and single-minded, ergo, my father's daughter.

My phone is ruined. I keep pressing buttons, hoping the screen might light up, but nothing is going to save this handset.

'You can use my old one,' says Henry. 'And everything is backed-up on the cloud.'

*The mysterious cloud. What did we do before Internet storage?*

The nurse returns and gives me a tetanus booster and a prescription for antibiotics.

'Two detectives are waiting for you outside,' she says. 'One of 'em has a face like a dropped pie.'

That will be DS O'Neil.

'I thought we were going home,' says Henry.

'I won't be long.'

I don't know what I expect. Concern? Thanks? Credit? I don't expect a public dressing down.

'What in fuck's name were you doing,' says Keegan. It's not a question.

'I was following a lead.'

'How did you know Noah Kemp-Lowe was back in London?'

'Josie – the babysitter – let it slip.'

'And you didn't think to tell me?'

'I wanted to be sure.'

'Has he been in touch with Caitlin Kemp-Lowe?' asks O'Neil.

'She contacted him a few months ago.'

'You've spoken to him.'

'Briefly . . . beside the canal.'

'Was that before or after he rescued you from drowning?' asks O'Neil.

The sarcasm makes him look even uglier.

'Did you interview him under caution?' asks Keegan.

'I didn't think . . . I mean . . . it wasn't . . .'

'If you had told us we could have put him under surveillance. Instead, you went off half-cocked and tried to arrest him. You didn't wait for back-up. You didn't caution him. All you did was give him time to get a lawyer and rehearse his story.'

My cheeks are burning. 'I didn't know he was going to run.'

'That's what suspects do, Constable.'

'He has an alibi for Friday night.'

'That's also what suspects do – they lie.'

'I believe him,' I say.

'And I'm sure he'll find that very reassuring.' Keegan turns and stops at the door. 'I don't want to see your face again. You're not part of this investigation. Go back to arresting drunks and catching shoplifters.'

I will not give him the satisfaction of showing him tears or anger or frustration. 'Yes, sir,' I say, standing to attention and only crumbling after they've gone. Cursing them. Cursing myself.

Henry is waiting for me downstairs. 'Is everything OK?'

'Fine.'

'You look upset.'

'I'm not.'

The tears want to come, but I blink them away. As we leave through the automatic doors, I notice Noah Kemp-Lowe being put into a police car. He is wearing the same wet clothes, which will have dried by now.

A detective puts a hand on the back of his head, telling him to duck, as he slides into the back seat. The door closes and he looks out of the window, making eye contact. He raises his hands as if to wave or to show me the handcuffs.

# 24

It takes three hours to find a lawyer who can sit with Noah Kemp-Lowe during his interview. The duty solicitor is a rumpled-looking hack with cauliflower ears and a suit that he might have slept in. He introduces himself as Sherwin, which could be his first or last name. Keegan doesn't care.

'Am I under arrest?' asks Noah when the detectives enter the interview room.

Keegan and O'Neil take up chairs on the opposite side of the table. 'You face charges of resisting arrest and assaulting a police officer,' he says.

'She fell off a boat. I saved her.'

Keegan ignores him. 'When was the last time you spoke to your sister?'

'A week ago, maybe.'

'And before that?'

'I can't remember.'

'How often? Once a week? Twice a week?'

'I don't know.'

'How about eighteen times in the past month according to your phone records? What did you talk about?'

'Family stuff.'

'Elaborate.'

'Dad has dementia. Mum is struggling to look after him. We talked about putting him into a care home.'

'Who made contact first – you or your sister?'

'She did. She wanted to mend things . . . with my parents and me. Build bridges.'

'Did you visit your parents?'

'Caitlin was laying the groundwork. She saw I was clean. Drug free.'

'There's no such thing as a former drug addict,' says O'Neil.

'I'm a work in progress, I know that. But I'm in a good place. I have Sofia and a baby on the way.'

'That's going to be expensive. How are the finances?' asks Keegan.

'We get by.'

'Selling paintings to tourists?'

'I work at a restaurant.'

'Did you ask your sister for money?'

'No.'

'When was the last time you visited the house in Antrim Road?'

It's a loaded question, designed to trap him.

'I can't remember.'

'I'm sure you can.'

'I dropped around for coffee. I played in the garden with Daisy.'

'When?'

'A few weeks ago.'

'Did you go upstairs?'

'No.'

'Are you sure?'

Noah hesitates.

'Because if you did, and we find your fingerprints—'

'Wait! Daisy showed me her room . . . We played a board-game.'

'Maybe you were doing a recce of the house. Checking out the security system. What was your share of the robbery going to be? Or maybe you were getting a cut of the insurance money.'

'Don't answer that,' interjects Sherwin, who turns on Keegan. 'The scope of this interview appears to have changed. You arrested my client for allegedly resisting arrest and assaulting a police officer. Now you're accusing him of robbery and home invasion. I'm advising him to remain silent.'

'He doesn't have to say a word – but he is going to listen,' says Keegan, staring at Noah. 'Your sister is dead. Murdered. You failed to come forward. Why?'

'Don't answer that,' says Sherwin.

'I had nothing to do with the robbery,' says Noah.

'All the more reason to come forward,' says Keegan.

'I knew you'd make me a suspect.'

'Your silence did that.'

'I'd like to speak to my client alone,' says Sherwin, growing agitated.

Again, Keegan ignores him. 'Here's the thing, Noah. I don't care about the robbery or the insurance money. I care that a woman is dead and she doesn't have a voice. That's why I'm compiling a list of people who stood to gain from her death and you're at the very top of that list.'

'My family disinherited me.'

'That's a motive not an alibi,' says Keegan. He reaches into a folder that has been resting between his elbows and produces an envelope in a plastic sleeve. The embossed lettering says *Last Will and Testament*. 'We found this in the family safe – the one the thieves didn't touch.'

Noah remains silent.

'Do you know where that safe is?'

'No.'

A raised eyebrow. 'Are you sure?'

'What's this all about?'

'You're back in the good books, Noah. You and Caitlin inherit equal shares.'

'My father would never do that.'

'He has dementia. Caitlin has power of attorney.'

'She can't change his will. That's not allowed.' Noah stops suddenly, as though realising that he's said too much.

'How do you know she can't change his will?' asks Keegan. Noah remains silent.

'Did you and Caitlin discuss it?'

'No comment.'

'Did you ask her?'

'No comment.'

Keegan is enjoying this, watching each question land like a punch, jab, jab, jab, wearing him down.

'My client needs a break,' says Sherwin.

'He can have all night,' says Keegan, turning to O'Neil. 'Charge him with resisting arrest and breaching parole.'

'But Sofia . . . she's pregnant. Can I call her?'

'Lock him up.'

# 25

Daragh follows a waitress around a water fountain and through a jungle of potted palms beneath glowing glass balls suspended from the ceiling. Expensive restaurants make him nervous because too many things can confuse him. He could use the wrong spoon or the wrong glass, or spill food on the starched white tablecloths. And the menu is full of fancy dishes with poncy names. What the fuck is a ballotine of guinea fowl or a carpaccio of Bulgarian longline tuna?

The Tram Shed is a warehouse conversion near the old Battersea Power Station where the architects have retained the original exteriors of soot-blackened bricks and sandstone window frames, but refitted the interiors with glass and stainless steel and marble.

He approaches a table where a figure is seated, hunched over a platter of shucked oysters. Two men are standing watch on either side of him dressed in jeans and open-neck shirts that show off neck tattoos and heavy gold chains. One of them has white-blond hair that looks almost bleached. He steps forward and pushes Daragh against a pillar, patting him down, searching for weapons or a wire. He discovers Daragh's mobile phone and turns it off.

The man eating pauses and lifts his head, revealing a black patch covering his right eye with a strap running diagonally across his forehead. It makes him look like a pirate or a bit of a wanker.

'Why didn't your brother come?' asks the pirate.

'Which one?'

'The boss.'

'We 'ave no boss.'

'That's what the pigs said in *Animal Farm*.'

'The wha'?'

The pirate smiles and lifts another oyster to his lips, sucking it straight from the shell, letting it slide down his gullet. He wipes the brine from his chin. 'Which one are you?'

'Daragh. I didn't catch your name.'

'That's not important.'

'I got to call you somefing.'

'Sir.'

'Oh, I didn't realise I was meetin' a fuckin' lord. Sir Cyclops.'

'My name is Dimitar Popov.' He dabs at his lips with a serviette.

Daragh takes a chair and looks around. The ceiling fans spin gently at half speed, but nothing else is calm about the setting. More food is delivered to the table. A charcuterie board of cured meats and pâtés. Blinis with caviar. The blond minder takes a blini, swallowing without chewing – not a lover of fish eggs.

*He's a fuckin' food taster*, thinks Daragh. *What sort o' wanker—*

Popov interrupts his thoughts. 'You wanted a meeting.'

'We figured it was in both our interests.'

'How so?'

'To discuss business and establish boundaries.'

'I don't believe in boundaries.'

'To discuss the rules.'

'What rules?'

Daragh likes this cunt less and less. 'Somebody is fuckin' with our building sites. Vandalising machinery. Stealing equipment. Sabotaging whatnots.'

Popov continues eating.

'If this is a shakedown, tell us what you want. If we've done somefing to upset you, we can whatnot the situation. But the fuckery has to stop.'

'Or what?'

'Pardon?'

'What will you do?'

'You don't want to know.'

'Oh, but I do,' says Popov, leaning back in his chair, pushing his plate to the centre of the table. The black eyepatch has silver thread stitched around the edges; and the visible eye is pale and blue and glittering with pleasure.

'Tell me, Sir Cyclops, 'ow much do you know about my family?' asks Daragh.

'Enough.'

'People 'ave been trying to take us down for years. You're not the first. You won't be the last.'

Popov leans closer, fixing Daragh with his one good eye. He touches his eyepatch, flipping it upwards, revealing an empty socket surrounded by puckered skin that goes deep into his skull.

'Ask me how I lost it?' asks Popov.

Daragh doesn't respond, knowing he'll get the story anyway.

The Bulgarian picks up a knife and twirls the handle across his fingers before stabbing a piece of sliced salami and feeding it into his mouth with the tip of the blade.

'A man I respected, a business partner, accused me of betraying him. I promised him that I would cut out my eye before I ever did such a thing.' He holds the point of the knife against his cheek. 'My friend didn't believe me, so I showed him. I cut out my eye while he watched. Do you know what happened then?'

*You had your head examined*, thinks Daragh.

'I scooped out his eyes with a spoon.'

Popov flips the eyepatch back into place and licks the end of the blade.

Daragh thinks the story is probably bullshit but wouldn't put anything past this cunt. Under normal circumstances, he'd end this game of charades by giving this geezer a good kicking, but discretion is the better part of whatnot. And his two minders might have a say.

'If you won't talk to me, you can meet my bruver,' says Daragh.

'I thought you said that no one was the boss.'

'Yeah, well, he has more patience than me and he might understand your sick fuckin' sense of 'umour.'

Popov waves him away. 'I will decide the time and place. Now get lost. You're spoiling my appetite.'

# 26

Henry is under the shower, singing showtunes from *Hamilton*. I shout from the bedroom, but he doesn't hear me. I go into the bathroom, seeing his silhouette behind the steamy glass.

'Let's go to Paris.'

A soapy hand wipes a circle in the condensation. 'You mean, now?'

'Yeah.'

'I thought you had to stick around.'

'Not after yesterday. We can catch the Eurostar and be in Paris for dinner – that little restaurant on the Left Bank where you took me on our first weekend away.'

'I cancelled the Airbnb.'

'You can book another one. And I thought I might bring this.'

I'm holding up a piece of lingerie that Henry bought me for Valentine's Day. It's a silk teddy that I pretended to like but I've never worn.

He turns off the shower.

'You still have shampoo in your hair,' I say.

'Oh, right.'

He turns the water back on and I go to the bedroom to pack. We haven't been away for ages, unless you count going to Hertfordshire to visit Henry's parents, the vicar and the vicar's wife, who treat me like I'm the consolation prize after Henry divorced their favourite daughter-in-law. They'd love me more if I gave them a grandchild, of course, but I'm not getting pregnant to please his parents.

I go next door to our neighbour, Mrs Aintree, and ask her to keep an eye on the place while we're away. She's a one-woman neighbourhood watch scheme, who reports every suspicious car, domestic argument and dog fouling the footpath.

When I get back, Henry is on the phone to his ex-wife, Roxanne, explaining that he can't take Archie later in the week. She's angry, but I give Henry the look which says he cannot give in to her . . . not again.

Henry is holding firm. I can't hear her response, but his voice hardens. 'That's not fair, Roxy. And if you tell Archie this is my fault, I'll tell him you took the money that I put in his bank account. And don't tell me it was for child support. You've been paid.'

He hangs up and throws his phone on the bed next to his open suitcase.

'Everything OK?' I ask.

'Fine.'

I feel a stab of sadness because I want him to be happy. I finish packing. Four days, three nights, means I need three different dresses or my black jumpsuit, or I could wear my dressy jeans with a cashmere sweater and boots. This is Paris, so I want to look quite chic for those evening promenades, arm in arm, along the Seine.

I hold up the cashmere and notice a stain on the front. Bugger! I have a different colour, but it won't match my boots. While I'm searching for clean knickers I notice a pair of child-sized jeans on the floor. Daisy was wearing them when she came to our house but changed into a dress for the christening.

As I brush my fingers over the fabric, I experience a flashback of Daisy's face in the rear-view mirror. A barefoot child in pyjamas at three o'clock in the morning. I wonder how she is. Is someone looking after her?

# 27

Keegan pushes out his cheeks, expelling air. 'How much?'

'Half a million,' says O'Neil.

'A second mortgage on the house?'

'A third.'

'Is that even possible?'

'Yeah, if you have enough equity in the property. They took out a second mortgage during the Covid lockdowns; and another one in March. The same amount each time.'

The two men are sitting in Keegan's office, going over the results of a forensic audit into the Kemp-Lowe family's finances. Income. Debts. Cashflow. Investments. Assets.

O'Neil consults a tablet. 'Sales fell by eighty per cent during the pandemic, but turnover was back to pre-pandemic levels; and the wages and expenses have kept pace with inflation.'

'So why are they swimming in red ink?'

'Large sums of money were being withdrawn, listed as business loans but they don't tally with rent or other expenses. Meanwhile, our boy Russell has multiple accounts with online bookmakers and casinos.

'How much does he owe?'

'No idea, but two months ago he transferred fifty grand to a pawnbroker in Spitalfields, Omar Syed.'

'Should I know him?'

'He's an East End loan shark who runs illegal card games out of trucks that move their location every few days. I also talked to a croupier in the high-roller room at Les Ambassadeurs. He told me Russell Kemp-Lowe is a regular. Big spender. Big loser.'

'How much are we talking about?'

'Twenty grand a night. The club extended him credit but turned off the tap four months ago and demanded Russell settle his account. He threatened to sue, claiming the games were rigged. The case went to arbitration and they came up with a repayment plan.'

'Did his wife know?'

'She signed the papers for the second and third mortgages.'

'Get a handwriting expert to check her signatures. Russell could have forged them. And talk to these bookmakers and loan sharks. Find out how much money Kemp-Lowe owes.'

Keegan ponders this for a moment, revisiting his dislike for gambling. Debts and pending bankruptcy are motives for robbery, and Caitlin's life insurance policy could be a motive for murder. Yet Keegan can still picture Russell Kemp-Lowe wearing the bomb vest – the terror in his eyes and the puddle of urine around his chair. If he was acting – it was the performance of a lifetime.

The two detectives are crossing the incident room when Trisha Hobson intercepts them.

'You might want to see this, boss.'

'Can it wait for the briefing?'

'It's important.'

They gather at a desk where several large screens are arranged in a semicircle around a central console. Hobson takes a seat and calls up a file.

'We've been looking for anyone who visited the jewellery store in the weeks leading up to the robbery,' she explains, pressing play. The footage shows a dapper-looking man in a long black overcoat and a peaked cap. He walks into the jewellery store and peruses one of the display cases. Moments later, Russell Kemp-Lowe appears and they shake hands like old friends.

'That was taken eleven days before the robbery,' says Hobson. 'And this is three days later.'

The next clip shows the same man entering the store and again greeting Russell Kemp-Lowe. Both disappear into a rear office.

'Who is he?' asks Keegan.

Hobson toggles the footage frame-by-frame, stopping on the clearest image. The man in the overcoat is leaving the store. An assistant holds the door. The man turns and doffs his cap, lifting his chin, revealing his face.

'That's Clifton McCarthy,' says O'Neil. 'One of the McCarthy brothers.'

Another camera picks him up outside, walking along the street. A car pulls over at the next intersection – a dark-coloured Jaguar. Hobson zooms in on the driver and enhances the image.

'Daragh McCarthy,' says O'Neil.

'The vehicle is registered to Hope Island Developments, a construction company owned and run by Edward McCarthy,' says Hobson.

Keegan is staring at the screen, putting the pieces together. Edward McCarthy is a name he hasn't heard for years. He seems to belong to a previous century, when London's underbelly was inhabited by wideboys, geezers, spivs, pimps and strip-club owners.

'That family would steal the skin off your custard,' says O'Neil. 'Hijacking, extortion, VAT fraud.'

'That was thirty years ago,' says Keegan. 'What about since then?'

'Edward McCarthy made a killing during the Olympics, buying up land and flogging it for venues and the athletes' village. Now he calls himself a property developer, which is polishing the turd.'

'There's one more thing, sir,' says Hobson. 'The face recognition software came up with another match.' She points to the

158

screen. 'This was taken in the foyer of the Royal Free Hospital on Saturday afternoon.'

The footage shows a tall man with a beard and oiled scalp entering through automatic doors and walking across the foyer. He's dressed in a dark suit and white trainers. He changes direction and greets a young woman who is holding the hand of a little girl. They embrace. Touch cheeks. Smile.

'Finbar McCarthy,' says O'Neil.

Keegan is studying the vision. It takes him a moment to recognise the woman and child. A heartbeat later the penny drops. 'Shit!' he mutters, spinning away, and striding towards his office.

'Get me a warrant for Philomena McCarthy's arrest,' he yells. 'And another for her house, her car and her phone. And get her supervisor in here.'

O'Neil still hasn't caught up. 'What's wrong?'

'She's related,' says Keegan, not hiding his disgust.

'To Edward McCarthy?'

'A rat in the ranks.'

# 28

Our wheeled luggage rattles over the pavement on our way to Clapham Common Tube station. We pass people we know, neighbours and shopkeepers and nodding acquaintances. Outsiders think London is too big to have a sense of community, but everybody knows everybody in our street – the births, deaths, divorces and new arrivals. And most of the locals are generally friendly until they aren't, and then they become lifelong enemies over a noise complaint or a defecating dog or someone painting their front door the wrong colour. There is no feud like a neighbourhood one.

We catch the Northern Line to Leicester Square, before changing onto the Piccadilly Line for King's Cross St Pancras. Side by side, cases between our knees, we discuss Paris and the next four days. Henry has never been to the Louvre or seen the *Mona Lisa*.

'She's smaller than you think,' I say. 'And she isn't so much smiling as looking smug, like she knows something that you don't know.'

'A resting bitch face?'

'Or a silent fart.'

He laughs and shows me his phone. 'How about this? An erotic walking tour of Paris.'

'A porn tour?'

'It's not porn.' He reads from the website. 'It is "a guided tour of the Red Light District, hearing stories about the forbidden adventures, bizarre acts and the clandestine pleasures of monarchs, politicians, courtesans and statesmen".'

'You want to hear dirty stories?'

'Absolutely.'

We emerge into the bowels of St Pancras, following the signs to the Eurostar. Henry wants to get something to eat on the train. I pick up a newspaper. The front page has a photograph of Noah Kemp-Lowe and the headline: *Brother Held in Kemp-Lowe Murder Hunt.*

The younger brother of London jewellery heiress Caitlin Kemp-Lowe has been arrested by detectives investigating her murder.

Noah Kemp-Lowe, a convicted drug offender, was picked up at Camden Markets and held in custody overnight, accused of breaching parole and resisting arrest.

What? He didn't resist arrest.

According to family friends, Kemp-Lowe was estranged from his sister and family. Seven years ago he was found guilty of constructive manslaughter after supplying the drug cocktail that killed his girlfriend.

Henry joins me and we wait in line to go through passport control. Everything is done automatically these days with facial recognition machines. Henry is ahead of me. The gates open and he walks through and waits on the far side. I press my passport against the scanner and stand on the painted footprints, chin up, eyes to the camera.

Nothing happens. I try again. The people behind me are muttering.

'There's something wrong with the machine,' I say, swapping queues to use a different one. A man approaches. Overweight. Swaggering. He's wearing a Border Force uniform with insignia on the shoulders. He examines my passport. Holding it up.

Looking at my face and the photograph. Instinctively, I know something is wrong.

'This way,' he says, keeping the passport.

'But my husband is waiting for me.'

Henry has gone through to the bag-scanning area. I catch a glimpse of him talking with two Border Force officers. Arguing. One of them grabs his arm and twists it behind his back.

'Hey!' I shout, turning. My officer tries to stop me. Reacting spontaneously, I take his wrist and use my other arm to pivot up and over his elbow, forcing him to break his hold. He grunts in surprise as I use my momentum to drop him to the ground where I kneel on the corner of his shoulder, holding him down.

'You don't get to touch me,' I mutter.

'You're under arrest,' he says, breathing through his pain.

'Why?'

'Your name was flagged. The police are coming.'

Henry is being marched towards me. One of the escorting officers breaks away and reaches for the pistol on his right hip.

'This is all a mistake. I'm police,' I say, raising my hands. Moments later, I'm shoved against the wall and my wrists are cuffed.

The officer I took down gets up and rubs a graze on his elbow, complaining that I took him by surprise.

Henry is closer now. He yells out to me, but I can't hear the words.

I yell back, but the woman officer shoves me in the back. 'Keep walking.'

'What about our train?'

'You won't be going anywhere.'

'Why? What have we done?'

I'm pushed through double doors into a long corridor with an echoing concrete floor and neon strip-lights that blink on as we approach. A train rumbles in a tunnel above us or beside us. A keycard opens the door into a square room with a curved ceiling, a table and three chairs.

The woman holds out her hand. 'Your phone.'

I motion to the front pocket of my jeans. I can't reach it with my cuffed hands. She retrieves it with two fingers and puts it into a plastic evidence bag that is sealed and labelled.

'Why am I being treated like a criminal?'

She doesn't answer. The door closes behind her with a click.

'I'm a police officer,' I yell, imagining that she's still outside. 'I know my rights.'

The words bounce back at me.

# 29

The receptionist at Bayswater Spa is a short woman with a greying beehive hairdo. She hands Edward McCarthy and Daragh towels and locker keys.

'I won't need a towel,' says Daragh. 'I'm 'ere to observe.'

'Perverts aren't allowed,' she replies, her voice clackety and tough. 'Nobody gets into the steam room unless they're appropriately dressed.'

'I am dressed,' says Daragh. 'I don't wanna be undressed.'

'They're the rules.'

She hands them two giant-sized loofahs.

'What do we do with these?' asks Daragh.

'Use your imagination.'

'Or you could show me.'

Her smile fades. 'Inappropriate advances or suggestive remarks will be deemed as sexual harassment. Are you looking for trouble?'

'I apologise for my brother,' says McCarthy. 'He was kicked in the head by a horse when he was a baby.'

The woman's eyes soften. 'It must be a burden looking after him.'

Daragh doesn't pick up on the subtext. The receptionist points to a door. 'Mr Popov is waiting for you at the Russian steam room. Once you leave the changing area, you follow the signs.'

'I thought we were boycotting all things Russian,' mutters Daragh. 'On account of the whatsit in Ukraine.'

'This is a one-off,' says McCarthy, pushing through the swing doors.

Bayswater Spa has been around for a century and was members-only for most of that time, populated by politicians, toffs and European expats seeking a taste of home.

'Place could be full of pillow-biters,' says Daragh as he gets undressed. He has always been self-conscious about his square body and Popeye-sized forearms. Someone once told him that he had legs for arms and arms for legs and his arse was where his head should be. It was only mentioned the once.

Wrapping a towel around his waist, Daragh hitches it high, just below his nipples. McCarthy is more comfortable in his own pale skin. His chest is covered in curly grey hair that doesn't completely hide the vertical bypass scar down the centre of his ribcage.

Daragh takes a pistol from his bag and tucks it under his towel, making a gun-shaped bulge.

'That's pretty fuckin' obvious,' says McCarthy.

'Where else am I gonna put it − up my clacker?'

'You're not going to put it anywhere. No weapons allowed.'

'They could be armed to the teef. Perfect place for an ambush. They could cut us up and wash away the whatnot.'

'Nobody is getting cut up.'

Reluctantly, Daragh puts the pistol back in his bag, which he puts in the locker. They approach the steam room. A man is standing sentry. He has white-blond hair, and is dressed in faded jeans, a blazer and a polo shirt.

'He's Popov's food taster,' says Daragh. 'How come he gets to wear clothes?'

'You should ask him, but don't break anything.'

The sentry pats them both down. His jacket sleeve slides up his forearm, revealing a dice tattoo on his left wrist, just above a huge fuck-off Rolex that could be fake, but probably isn't.

He points to McCarthy. 'Only you.'

'Nah, we're both going in,' says Daragh.

The two men shirtfront each other. Daragh is a foot shorter and twice as menacing.

'It's OK,' says McCarthy. 'Stand down.'

'What if it's a whatnot?'

'You have my permission to rip his head off.'

A staring contest doesn't last long. The blond man blinks and looks away.

McCarthy enters a pine-scented room where geysers of steam billow from pipes creating indoor clouds that condense on the marble walls and ceiling. The wet heat scalds the inside of his lungs and perspiration prickles on his skin. Another cloud of steam balloons and dissipates, and he glimpses Dimitar Popov sitting on a marble bench. A loofah slaps against his nakedness, smearing soap over his chest and arms. He appears to be alone.

Popov acknowledges McCarthy and points at the bench opposite, before pouring a ladle of water over his head. He spits some of it away.

'You have ten minutes. Talk.'

McCarthy isn't accustomed to being given orders but cuts the younger man some slack. He's not a local. He doesn't know how things are done.

Taking a seat, he tries not to react when Popov raises his head showing his missing eye. Daragh had warned him.

The Bulgarian is in his early forties with a solid body, defying gravity everywhere except around his waist, where his flesh bulges above a forest of pubic hair.

'I wanted to introduce myself,' says McCarthy.

'I know who you are.'

'And establish a channel of communication. Set down some ground rules to avoid any misunderstandings.'

Popov wipes sweat from his eyes. 'We are most remembered for the rules we break.'

'Is that what you want – to be remembered?'

'No. I want to be feared. How about you?'

McCarthy is lost for words. He already has a bad feeling about this. He tries again.

'I am a property developer. I run a construction company. I sell building services. Scaffolding. Concreting. Security. I am not interested in your business and I want you to stay out of mine.'

The loofah slaps against Popov's skin. 'Is that what you came to tell me?'

'Somebody has been sabotaging equipment on my building sites and hijacking deliveries.'

'Accidents happen,' says Popov. 'I could help provide you with security.'

'Or you could leave us alone.'

Popov gives him a crooked smile. 'Since we are soon to be business partners, I think it best if I safeguard my interests.'

'What makes you think we're going to be business partners?'

'You need cash and I need somewhere to invest my money. You have employees, payrolls, turnover.'

'You want to launder money through Hope Island.'

'People use that term like it's a bad thing, but my mother was a cleaner and my grandmother, may she rest in peace.'

'I don't need a business partner.'

'Yet here you are.'

McCarthy can feel his blood heating up and not just because of the steam. He wants to launch himself across the space and slam Popov's head against the slick wall. He can hear the bones breaking and picture a smear of blood on the white tiles. Reaching into the bucket, he scoops a handful of water onto his face, washing the sweat from his eyes.

'There was a home invasion and a robbery a few days ago. A woman died.'

'Yeah, I read about that,' says Popov, leaning back and opening his legs. His penis hangs from a nest of pubic hair. A metal piercing glints in the pale light. Stainless steel through his foreskin.

167

'A friend of mine had certain items in the safe,' says McCarthy, looking away.

'What items?'

'Diamonds.'

'Your friend sounds very unlucky . . . or foolish . . . or old.'

McCarthy feels his hackles rise. 'If my friend's property were to be returned, I might be willing to overlook the vandalism and sabotage.'

'What if there were no diamonds in the safe?'

'I'd say you were lying.'

'How can I prove the non-existence of something?'

The Bulgarian wraps a towel around his waist. 'I need to cool off. You should too.'

He leads McCarthy out of the steam room and immediately steps into an icy plunge pool that shrinks his testicles to marbles. Two uniformed staff members are waiting nearby. Popov climbs onto one of the marble beds and a Slavic-looking man he calls Stefan begins kneading his neck and shoulders. The other masseuse is wearing a simple white smock dress. She's beautiful, with long dark hair and darker eyes.

'My name is Katya,' she says, smiling and pointing to the other bed.

'I'll pass,' says McCarthy.

She looks at Popov, unsure of what to do.

'Your loss,' says Popov. 'She can suck the colour out of a marble.'

McCarthy apologises to Katya as she leaves the room. Then he picks up a bottle of water and drinks deeply, trying to rehydrate. He wipes his mouth with the back of his hand, still feeling lightheaded.

Popov dismisses Stefan and sits up. Oil glistens on his arms and back.

'Now, let's discuss business.'

'We have no business.'

'You are bleeding money and the banks are breathing down

your neck – is that how you say it? How many more months can you hold them off?'

'For as long as it takes.'

'I am offering you a lifeline. Unlimited credit. And all I want in return is forty-nine per cent of Hope Island Developments.'

McCarthy laughs caustically.

Popov continues. 'Have you heard the term – the law of the jungle? People think it means unrestrained and ruthless competition; doing what is necessary to survive. But that's not true. There is a pecking order in the jungle. The strong devour the old and the weak and the young and the unprotected. You've been doing it for years, but now I'm taking over. I am offering you a one-time deal. After today, there will be no more talking.'

'This is not talking.'

Popov goes to a corner of the room and reaches into a bag. For a brief second, McCarthy pictures a gun appearing in his hand and Daragh being right all along. Instead, Popov is holding a mobile phone.

'Are you interested in family history?' he asks.

'Not particularly.'

'You should be. We are all products of those who came before us.' Popov is scrolling through something on screen. 'Your wife is very beautiful. Do you know where she is right now?'

'Keep my wife out of this.'

'She's having a coffee on the King's Road in Chelsea.'

Popov shows the phone to McCarthy. The real-time footage shows Constance at a table in a brightly lit restaurant, chatting to a friend. Someone is filming them from a nearby table. Snippets of their conversation can be heard.

'And what about your daughter, Philomena?'

Popov swipes his finger across the screen and the footage changes. Philomena and Henry are sitting on a train with suitcases between their knees.

Another swipe and the images show a woman wearing a headscarf entering the glass doors of the Oak Cancer Centre

169

in Sutton. Daragh's wife, Mary, steps aside to let a patient in a wheelchair pass ahead of her.

'Your sister-in-law,' says Popov, swiping the screen. 'And this is your neice.' Rosie is pushing a pram along a leaf-littered path between trees and gardens. 'Her younger brother, Jonathon, is a schoolteacher in Sevenoaks. Right now, he's teaching a biology class. Their middle sister, Adriana, is designing theatre sets in Birmingham. She's having an affair with the director, a married man. They use a little hotel in the Jewellery Quarter for their assignations – their love nest, is that how you say it?'

'Stop this,' says McCarthy, feeling hollowed out and disorientated.

Popov ignores him. 'Did you know your brother Clifton was gay? He has a boyfriend who works as a tour guide at the Tower of London. Why do they call them Beefeaters?'

Now the footage shows Clifton and Morris walking their dog, a Jack Russell called Luna, along the Thames Path near their house on the Isle of Dogs.

'I didn't come here to start a war,' says McCarthy.

'Oh, this isn't a war,' replies Popov. 'A war suggests a contest, a battle of one side against another. This one will be over before you leave this room. You see, Edward – I think I can call you that now – I have identified every member of your family. Your aunts and uncles, nieces and nephews, sons and daughters. Do you know how many I found? Thirty-one. I will kill your wife first. Then your brothers and their wives and children and grandchildren. When I finish, you will have no family, no legacy.'

McCarthy can feel his chest constrict and he wonders if his heart bypass might be failing. He glances towards the door.

Popov smiles. 'I am not here to talk or to negotiate. You will do as I say, or the killing begins.'

Again, he turns the phone to face McCarthy, who watches Constance at the restaurant, laughing with her friend. A noise distracts them – a crashing sound. She and her friend turn their heads. A figure is passing their table – a gloved hand reaches out, dropping something into her coffee. It happens so quickly McCarthy almost misses it.

'Have you heard of ricin?' asks Popov. 'It's a toxin that occurs naturally in castor beans. One milligram is enough. Your wife will start vomiting within the hour. Then comes the bloody diarrhoea. And within three days . . .' He makes a puffing sound.

McCarthy is so stunned he doesn't react. Everything has slowed down. He is still staring at the phone – at Constance – watching the restaurant return to normal. The women have picked up their conversation.

'Stop this,' he croaks, not recognising his own voice.

'You agree to my terms?'

'Yes.'

Popov presses a button on his phone. On screen, Constance reaches for her cappuccino and raises it to her lips. A waiter steps into frame and bumps her elbow. The coffee spills onto the white tablecloth. He apologises profusely, collecting the cup and saucer, insisting on bringing her another.

McCarthy breathes again. Quietly, he asks, 'What do I have to do?'

Popov puts the phone away. 'You will pay me two hundred thousand pounds.'

'A month?'

'A week.'

'That's ridiculous.'

'But not impossible. You have four days to make the first payment. In that time you will have your lawyers draw up plans to transfer forty-nine per cent ownership of Hope Island Developments to me. Not as a sale, but as a gift. And in return, I will pay the overdue interest on your loans. Your supply lines will open. Your building sites will be trouble free. And I will provide you with cash that you will run through your books.'

Dazed and dehydrated, McCarthy finds his feet and shuffles towards the door. He stops and turns.

'Why kill Caitlin?'

'Who?'

'The jeweller's wife. You didn't have to kill her.'

Popov wipes oil on his chest. 'I agree, that is a mystery.'

'What do you mean?'

'We left her alive.'

# 30

Without my phone, I don't know what time it is. Our train to Paris will have gone, putting paid to any romance or sightseeing or promenading along the Seine. Periodically, I cross the room and check the door, yelling questions that nobody answers. Clearly, I've been mistaken for someone else or my identity has been stolen or someone has labelled me a terrorist. Even as I consider these possibilities, I always come back to my father.

Ever since I joined the Met, I've known there could come a moment when our interests would collide. I won't call it our 'careers' because that gives legitimacy to what my father does. For ten years I convinced myself it didn't matter because I didn't talk to him or my uncles. I went to university and I joined the police, and I fought any attempt to label me as my father's daughter. And it would have stayed that way if I hadn't been getting married and if my father hadn't turned sixty and had a heart attack. Maybe I'm making excuses.

The door unlocks and DCI Keegan enters the room, along with his second-in-command, DS O'Neil, a man whose face puts the mug into smug.

'Is this really necessary?' I ask, turning to reveal my cuffed wrists.

Keegan ignores me. 'Caution her.'

O'Neil begins his spiel. 'Philomena Claire McCarthy, I am arresting you on suspicion of criminal conspiracy—'

'What conspiracy?'

'You do not have to say anything but it may harm your

defence if you do not mention when questioned something which you later rely on in court.'

Keegan is carrying a laptop and a manila folder. He takes a page from the folder.

'This is a warrant to search your house, your vehicles, and access your phones and computers.'

I've seen warrants before. I don't need to read this one.

'Where is Henry?' I ask.

'He's being interviewed.'

'We've done nothing wrong.'

'You were trying to leave the country.'

I look at him incredulously. 'We were going to Paris for a break. It was arranged weeks ago.'

'You booked the tickets this morning.'

'Yes, but I cancelled an earlier trip because you told me to.'

Keegan looks at me blankly and turns on a recording app on his phone, placing it carefully on the table between us. He asks for my full name and date of birth and address, all of which he knows.

'Can you confirm that you have been cautioned and that you understand what that means?'

'Yes.'

'You are entitled to free and independent legal advice either in person or by telephone at any stage. Do you wish to speak to a legal advisor or have one present during the interview?'

'Yes,' I say.

'Right. Good. Will it be a Police Federation solicitor or someone else? Perhaps your father has a lawyer on speed-dial. Would you like to call him?'

I'd like to wipe the smirk off Keegan's face, but the only name I can think of is David Helgarde, a criminal barrister, who works for Daddy. Giving his name would be tantamount to admitting that I'm on my father's payroll, which I'm not. It would also mean alerting my father to my arrest, something I'd rather avoid.

The detectives are waiting for my answer.

'Just get on with it,' I say.

'You're waiving your right to legal counsel?'

'I'm reserving the right.'

'Very well,' says Keegan. 'What were you doing in the vicinity of Antrim Road in the early hours of Saturday morning?'

'I was working. You know that.'

'Were you on an official call-out?'

'No. A food run.'

'You volunteered?'

'I drew the short straw.'

'Were there straws?'

'No. It's a turn of phrase.'

'And you saw a child standing in the middle of the road?'

'Yes.'

'But your colleague, PC Cooper, saw nothing.'

'I only glimpsed her for a moment.'

'You were asked to respond to a crime in progress at Hatton Garden. It was a high urgency call. You chose to ignore it.'

'My partner responded. I couldn't leave a child alone at that hour of the morning, it was cold . . . raining.'

'How did you know where she lived?'

'Daisy showed me. All of this is in my statement, sir.'

'You ignored orders and entered the property.'

'I was given permission.'

'Which was rescinded.'

'By then, I was already inside.'

'Bullshit!' mutters O'Neil.

'You deliberately disobeyed the order,' says Keegan.

'Daisy said she couldn't wake her mother. I thought she might be injured . . . bleeding. Daisy had blood on her pyjamas.'

'Upon finding her body, you failed to evacuate the premises. Instead, you searched the house and contaminated the crime scene.'

'I searched for other victims before securing the scene.'

Disdain swims in his eyes. 'When you joined the London Metropolitan Police, were you warned about associating with anyone who had a criminal history?'

'Yes.'

'You were told to declare any relationship with people who have been convicted of a crime, or are under investigation or awaiting trial, or who are the subject of criminal intelligence.'

'I'm aware of the rules.'

Here it is, I think. Finally, we're getting to the point.

'When did you last see your father?' asks Keegan.

'On Saturday at a christening. My cousin Rosie asked me to be a godparent.'

'When did you last talk to him?'

'Later that same day. He called me. He thought I was going to Paris.'

'What about your uncles?'

'At the christening.'

Keegan opens the folder and I glimpse photographs. In that moment, I realise my mistake, but it's too late. Keegan pushes an image across the table. I see myself hugging Uncle Finbar in the foyer of the Royal Free Hospital in Hampstead.

'I bumped into him. It wasn't planned. We only spoke for a few minutes.'

'For the record, I am showing Constable McCarthy a CCTV image taken three days ago. Can you identify anyone in this photograph?'

'Yes.'

'For the tape — what is his name?'

'Finbar McCarthy.'

'What relationship is he to you?'

'My uncle.'

'What was he doing at the hospital?'

'He said he was visiting a friend.'

'Who?'

'He didn't say.'

176

Keegan opens his laptop and turns the screen to face me. CCTV footage begins playing. A figure in a long black coat and flat cap is walking along a busy footpath. I can't see his face. On the far side of the road, I notice a red double-decker bus. Route number 8. It is somewhere in Central London.

The footage switches. The same man is leaving the jewellery store, taking off his cap to say goodbye.

'Do you recognise him?' asks Keegan.

'You know who it is.'

'Yes, but I'd like you to name him.'

'My uncle. Clifton McCarthy.'

The footage jumps ahead and shows Clifton outside the store, pulling on a pair of leather gloves, before glancing skywards as though checking for rain. After walking to the nearest inter-section, he gets into a car.

Keegan points to the driver. 'Who is that?'

'Daragh McCarthy.'

'Another uncle?'

'Yes.'

'Do your uncles have an interest in jewellery?'

I don't answer.

Keegan leans back and scratches at his navel through his shirt. The silence drags out.

'You have this all wrong,' I say. 'I found Daisy. I took her home. I discovered her mother's body.'

'Yes, you did. And I can't work out if you're a master crim-inal or dumber than a box of rocks.'

'I was doing my job.'

'At whose bidding?'

'I am not a bent copper.'

'I'm going to ask you outright, PC McCarthy. Were you part of the gang that killed Caitlin Kemp-Lowe and abducted her husband and robbed the Hatton Garden store?'

'No! Of course not.'

'Why did you ask to be involved in the investigation?'

'I told you — I want to be a detective.'

'You wanted to feed inside information to your father?'

'My father is a businessman. A property developer.'

Keegan's laugh bounces off the walls and my cheeks grow hot. 'Eddie McCarthy's stench is all over this . . . along with yours. You were responsible for the death of an innocent woman.'

'I want a lawyer,' I say.

'Thank God,' says O'Neil. 'I'm busting for a leak.'

Keegan pauses the recording and the two men get up, shrug on their jackets and turn for the door.

'Am I being charged?' I ask.

'You're being held for further questioning,' says Keegan, brushing lint from his sleeve.

'I want to see Henry.'

'No.'

'But I need to explain.'

The door has closed.

# 31

McCarthy stares out of the car window, looking at nothing but the images inside his head. One in particular – Constance raising the coffee cup to her lips, about to take a sip. He has no way of knowing if Popov was bluffing about the ricin, but he has to believe it was genuine.

'We should warn 'em,' says Daragh. 'Put 'em somewhere safe.'

'He'll know,' says McCarthy.

'If we do it in secret. Dead of night. Sneak 'em out.'

'He'll be watching.'

Daragh's knuckles whiten on the steering wheel. 'Does this cunt want a war?'

'Yes.'

'And people say I'm a psychopath.'

Daragh times his run through traffic lights, either holding back or speeding up to catch the amber. Each time, he checks the rear-view mirror, making sure they're not being followed.

McCarthy's phone rings. It's Constance.

'Hi, babe, where are you?' he asks, knowing full well.

'I've been having coffee with Anyo in Chelsea.'

'Say hello from me.'

'I will. Listen, I just bumped into someone who said he knew you.'

'Yeah, who was that?'

'Some foreign guy. He said you were going into business together.'

'Did he give his name?'

'No, but he was creepy, you know, the way he looked at me.'

'I want you to go home, babe.'

'But I still have shopping—'

'Another day. Just get home.'

'Is something wrong?'

'Nothing I can't handle. See you soon.'

As he hangs up, Daragh's phone chirrups on the hands-free. 'That's my Rosie,' he says. 'She never calls me at work.'

Her voice through the speaker. 'Hi, Dad, you busy?'

'Always time for you, girlie. All good?'

'Yeah, I think so. I was taking Victoria to the doctor.'

'She OK?'

'Good as gold. It was a regular two-month check-up. Anyway, I noticed a guy outside the surgery. He was sitting in a car, filming me.'

'Did you get the number plate?'

'Yeah. I took a picture.'

'Text it to me,' says Daragh, trying to sound relaxed.

'I think I might have seen him before,' says Rosie.

'Where?'

'I can't remember. At the supermarket, maybe, or outside of your place when I was visiting Mum. Maybe I'm being paranoid.'

'No. You're a good girl. Leave it with me.' He hangs up and mutters. 'We gotta get these fuckers.'

'All in good time,' says McCarthy, who puts in a call to Finbar at the garage.

'Family meeting.'

'Where?'

'At the Ten Bells in an hour.'

'Why the pub?'

'I fancy a drink. Make sure you're not followed.'

Daragh has steered them to the Embankment, heading towards Blackfriars. 'Why not meet at the office?'

'I don't trust anyone,' says McCarthy.

'You think it's bugged?'

'Maybe. I'm wondering how Popov managed to get all that information about us. Names. Addresses. Jobs. Appointments. He tracked our children and grandchildren.'

They have reached home territory. Spitalfields. The famous markets. People have been selling stuff here since the Great Fire of London. Ordinary folk, living ordinary lives, fighting, fucking, living and dying. McCarthy has spent all his life loving this place and hating it — wanting to escape the poverty and deprivation, but at the same time embracing the neighbours and friends and family that he grew up with. Mostly, he has an aversion to the mundane — the nine-to-five existence, Monday to Friday, going home to microwaved chicken Kiev and soggy oven chips in front of the TV watching *EastEnders* and *Coronation Street*. He remembers reading a quote by some guy with a gift for the gab: 'One crowded hour of a glorious life is worth more than an age without a name.' Words to live and die by.

Daragh parks two streets from the Ten Bells and they walk through the light rain. Pushing open a heavy door, they find a mixture of regulars and tourists in the main bar. McCarthy knows the publican, Big Dave, who once boxed bantamweight for the UK title.

'We need the upstairs room,' he says.

'You want drinks? Sandwiches?'

'A bottle of Jameson's and some privacy.'

Big Dave waves away his money. The room has two windows overlooking Christ Church and Fournier Street. A large snooker table is covered in a white sheet and chairs are arranged around the walls. McCarthy and Daragh have just settled when heavy boots clomp up the stairs. One set has thick rubber soles and are stained with vehicle grease. The others are oxblood Doc Martens with the classic yellow stitching.

Finbar and Clifton hang their overcoats on hooks and choose a seat. Knees spread. Drinks in hand.

McCarthy begins, giving them the long and short of his meeting with Popov. The brothers do lots of cursing and muttering between pouring and drinking.

'Who does this guy think he is?' asks Clifton.

'Oh, he knows exactly,' says McCarthy. 'He's the one with a gun pointed at our bollocks.'

'So what do we do?' asks Finbar.

'We give him what he wants?'

'Half the fuckin' business!'

'A downpayment. Two hundred thousand. And we set up meetings with lawyers to discuss a partnership.'

'You're letting him win,' says Daragh, incredulously.

'No. I'm letting him *think* he's won.'

'But the money—'

'Popov has been planning this for months. Stalking us. Learning stuff about our business, our movements, our supply lines, our contractors . . .'

'Our families,' says Finbar.

'A right slippery ballsack,' says Daragh.

'Indeed,' says McCarthy, who wonders if he should feel privileged that someone has gone to such trouble. 'We need time to undertake due diligence.'

'Due what?' asks Daragh.

'Time to research Popov and his operation. How many men does he have? Who's bankrolling him? How deep are their pockets? But in the meantime, we have to raise the two hundred grand in four days.'

'Bridging finance?'

'I want to avoid the banks.'

'You can't trust private equity,' says Clifton. 'They'll smell blood in the water.'

'We may need to raise it ourselves. Dip into savings. Sell some of our liquid assets.'

'Fuck-all left to sell,' says Clifton. 'We're leveraged to the eyeballs.'

'Do your best. The rest of you start searching for information on Popov. His connections. His associates. His past. Police files. Interpol reports. But do it quietly. Softly, softly, catchy gorilla.'

'I think it's monkey,' says Finbar.

'No, this guy is a fuckin' gorilla.' McCarthy turns to Daragh. 'We need reinforcements. Call Paddy Gallagher.'

'Yeah, OK, but Paddy is short-'anded. Three of his crew got nabbed by the 'ard-to-please money-robbing centre.' He means the tax office.

'What about Jimmy Webster?' asks Clifton.

'Suffered a stroke last Christmas,' says Daragh, 'Now he's in some 'ospice, dribbling into his pot of yoghurt.'

'Fergus Keeley?'

'Retired to the Costa del whatnot.'

'I heard he ran off with his Pilates teacher,' says Clifton.

'His what?' asks Daragh.

'It's like doing yoga on a bed.'

'Exercise lying down – I could 'andle that.'

They mention a few more names, but most are too long in the tooth or gone squeaky.

The men go quiet. Daragh's silence is different because McCarthy knows that he hates inaction or contemplation. He wants to fight back, but that's just what Popov expects.

McCarthy takes a sip of whiskey, swilling it around in his mouth. 'He said there were no loose diamonds in the safe.'

'Maybe Russell lied to you,' says Clifton.

'He wouldn't dare,' says Daragh.

'Yeah, but that's the problem with gambling addicts. They can't be trusted,' says Finbar.

'If he organised the robbery – how did he find Popov? It can't be a coincidence,' says McCarthy.

'What about Caitlin's brother?' asks Finbar. 'The filth picked him up yesterday and charged him with breaching his parole.'

'That means he's back inside,' says Clifton.

'Mixing with thieves and criminals,' says McCarthy. 'Maybe he made some friends in the big house.'

'You think he's part of this?'

'Up to his neck.'

McCarthy shares out the last of the Jameson, topping up the glasses, and wonders if he can hold the family together in the face of what's coming. Today he was bested by a younger man, who came better prepared and with greater intent. That had always been McCarthy's way – to speak softly yet carry a big stick. Now he is facing somebody who whispers and carries a grenade launcher.

Clearly, his hard-won respectability as a property developer had come at a cost. He had grown complacent and been blind to what was going on around him. Now a usurper wanted to take his crown and, like Popov said – there is no law in the jungle, no moral code. There is only survival.

McCarthy dons his overcoat and holds the door for the others. He puts a hand on Clifton's shoulder, signalling him to wait. When they're alone he hands him a piece of paper with a single name.

Clifton reads it. 'You gotta be jokin'.'

'In case of emergency, break glass.'

'And everything else.'

'Make the call.'

'And if they want to talk?'

'We talk.'

The men descend the stairs and say their goodbyes. McCarthy and Daragh share a large black umbrella on the walk back to the car. The lights flash. The doors unlock.

Daragh slips behind the wheel, while McCarthy shakes out the umbrella. It's then that he notices a soggy flyer tucked under the windscreen wiper. Hinging the wiper blade, he pulls it free. He's about to ball it in his fist and toss it away when something makes him pause. It's not a flyer, but a note.

The engine starts. He reads the four handwritten words.

*Tick, tock, tick tock!*

# 32

My holding cell was built in the nineteenth century and still has metal rings on the walls where prisoners were once shackled. It is six paces long and four paces wide, and reeks of a sulphurous odour that could be leaking from the bowels of the earth.

I have spent all night on a narrow bunk, dozing occasionally and being woken by the sound of people snoring, vomiting and complaining. It has given me time to marinate in a stew of suppositions and accusations, most of them involving my father and uncles. The CCTV footage of the jewellery store and at the hospital makes them all suspects. And as much as I want to blame Keegan, I can understand why he had me arrested. What I can't forgive is the manner of my arrest — my public humiliation and his treatment of Henry.

Breakfast has come and gone — a tray of cold scrambled eggs and soggy toast. And the court transfers have begun. The newly charged are being collected for their committal hearings and bail applications.

Four years into my police career and this is the second time I've been arrested. That must be some sort of record. Those senior officers who tried to stop me joining the Met must be gloating now. My application was rejected four times and I had to threaten legal action before they approved me for Hendon Police College. Every possible obstacle was put in my path, including an attempt to sabotage my final exams.

I swing my legs off the bench seat and sit up, leaning over my knees, staring at the concrete floor. It must be mid-morning by now. Where is Keegan? Where is my lawyer? Maybe they jumped the gun and arrested me too early, before they had linked me to the robbery and murder. Proximity and a surname aren't proof of guilt. My leaving the country for Paris must have forced Keegan's hand – and now he's scrambling to put a case together.

I've always known that my family was different but I didn't understand why until I was in secondary school. I was in Year 8 at St Ursula's, when our head teacher called a full school assembly and warned students about a local drug dealer who was operating near the school. We all knew who she meant – a young guy with hollow cheeks, who wore an overcoat even in the height of summer and used a young boy to run back and forth to where the drugs were stashed. I went home and told my parents about the assembly and the warnings.

A few days later, on my way home, I spotted Uncle Daragh talking to the dealer, radiating aggression like a pit bull terrier straining at a leash. I didn't see the drug dealer again, but afterwards, the head teacher asked me to deliver a letter to my father. It was sealed in an envelope but I steamed it open and discovered a thank-you card, unsigned.

This didn't mean that Daddy was welcome at the school. After an electrical fire gutted one of the old convent buildings, he offered to repair the damage, saying he'd do it 'at cost'. At first, the school seemed happy to take up the proposal, but then some of the parents complained and the diocese became involved. Daddy quietly withdrew the offer and nothing more was said.

Six months later, the chosen builder went bankrupt and took the school's money. The bishop came to my father and asked if he could finish the project, which he did, quietly, for no extra money. When the new building was opened by our local Member of Parliament, all the school dignitaries were on the stage – the governors and the representative councillors and the head of the P & F and famous alumni. During the speeches, they praised the architect and the project manager, and the patience shown by the students, but there was no mention of my father. He wasn't invited.

When I graduated, I carried the holy water to the altar at our graduation mass. When I curtsied in front of the bishop, he asked me my name.

'Philomena McCarthy,' I said. 'I think you know my father.'

Blood drained from his face and he dabbed at his brow with his colourful satin stole.

'How much did it cost you?' I asked Daddy afterwards.

'Nothing I couldn't afford,' he replied.

'Why did you do it?'

'Because you're my daughter and you love that school.'

I wanted to tell him that I didn't love it, not any more.

There were numerous other examples. People who crossed the road to avoid bumping into us when I was shopping with Daddy, or those who exchanged glances or whispered things behind his back. I saw them, even if he didn't.

Some of my friends thought my life was glamorous and violent, because they'd watched too many shows like *The Sopranos* and *The Wire*. They imagined it was all flash motors and fancy restaurants and holidays on the Costa del Crime. Either that or I was living in an Irvine Welsh novel – full of drug dealers, junkies and women turning tricks to feed their babies.

Yet in all of my childhood, nobody ever showed up at our house covered in blood and I didn't witness a crime or overhear anybody planning one. I didn't play with real guns (or fake ones) or have to move bags of cocaine off the breakfast table when I ate my Rice Krispies.

Often when children choose a career, they decide to follow in their parents' footsteps. Doctors beget doctors, lawyers beget lawyers, and builders beget builders. The same is true of criminals. When I was at Hendon we had a lecturer who said that two-thirds of all juvenile offenders came from 10 per cent of families. Keegan thinks I'm one of them – Edward McCarthy's daughter – but I'm nothing like my father.

The observation flap slides open. Someone is watching me. I resist the urge to raise my middle finger. After several seconds, the lock clicks and the door swings inwards. Keegan steps into the cell. He sniffs at the air, wrinkling his nose.

'I have talked to Assistant Commissioner Duckworth. You are suspended immediately and will be investigated by the department of professional standards.'

'On what charge?'

'You will be informed in writing of the charges against you.'

I have a sudden, overwhelming sense of déjà vu.

'Where's Henry?'

'He was released last night.' Keegan steps back, waiting for me to leave. 'I advise you to look for another career, Miss McCarthy, because this one is over.'

I am taken to the charge room and given my phone, belt, shoelaces and my suitcase, which is still packed for Paris. It will have been searched. They will have seen the lingerie and smirked, pawing it with their gloved hands, holding it up to the light. I will never wear it now. Poor Henry.

I'm signing for my things when I hear a door slam open and raised voices. A man is brought into the charge room by detectives. Russell Kemp-Lowe reeks of booze and is slurring insults.

'You'll be sorry for this. I'm going to destroy your careers. You fuckers won't get a job as crossing guards after I've finished.'

He notices me and stops in mid-rant, as though embarrassed by his appearance and his language. Once handsome, or almost so, his looks are fading, as alcohol, age and gravity take a toll, creating jowls and wrinkles and a double chin. Why has Keegan arrested him?

The charge sergeant notices me loitering and points to the door. 'You know the way.'

Outside, under a bruised sky, I turn on my phone. It pings with messages and voicemails from Henry, each more urgent than the last. I should call him. I should go home. But I don't want to have the conversation that's coming. He won't directly say, *I told you so*, but that will be the subtext. His parents, the vicar and the vicar's wife, had warned him not to marry me; and were horrified when Daddy walked me down the aisle – a gangster polluting their church and their godliness.

There is another text message – from Daddy. It says simply, *Give me a call*, followed by two x's and two o's. Kisses and hugs. Does he know I was arrested? He has spies everywhere, including in the Met.

The final message is from Jamie Pike. How did he get my number?

*Great seeing you again the other day. If you fancy a drink, I'm around the corner.*

My thumb hovers over the delete button, but I make a different choice. I send a message: *I'm at the Lion & Unicorn on Gaisford Street.*

The lunchtime rush has passed when I arrive. I don't know if Jamie will be joining me, but I order a bourbon and dry and swallow it in three gulps. I signal for another. At first, I feel self-conscious drinking alone, but soon I'm past caring.

Jamie arrives, dressed in baggy jeans that look a bit dated and a rumpled linen jacket that suits his just-out-of-bed hairstyle.

'Did you start without me?'

'Just a little,' I slur, letting him kiss my cheek, although he gets a little closer to my lips than I expect.

'What are we celebrating?'

'The end of my career.'

'That bad, eh? Well, I'd better catch up.' He signals the barman. 'I'll have what she's having.' Back to me. 'So, what happened?'

'I don't want to talk about it.'

'OK, let's talk about something else.'

Jamie seems to realise that I just need a drinking buddy, somebody who isn't part of my imperfect life: who doesn't know Henry, or his parents, or who isn't close to my family. We talk about childhood memories and favourite holidays and mutual friends and funny moments. The words aren't important, but the drinks keep coming.

At some point, I think I tell him what happened – letting the story spill out, littered with expletives and accusations and laced with self-pity. He listens, which is all I want.

I need the bathroom. I stumble as I get up and fall against him. He catches me. I'm drunk but fighting to appear sober. I tell him to order more drinks.

'I think you've had enough.'

'Don't tell me what to do.'

'Let's get out of here.'

'Where?'

'I'll order you a cab.'

'I'm too drunk to go home.'

'You could come back to mine. Sober up.'

We leave the pub. When did it get dark? I lean against him. We walk along leaf-covered footpaths, turning corners. The cold air is clearing my head a little but I'm seeing double of everything.

Jamie opens the door of a house and ushers me along a hallway towards the kitchen. We pass an empty living room.

'Where is all your furniture?' I slur.

'I only just moved in. I'll make you a coffee.'

'I think I need to lie down.'

I don't have a clear idea of what comes next. That's not quite true. I know exactly because it takes place in slow motion. I kiss him, or maybe he kisses me. It makes no difference. He carries me to his bed and lays me down and pulls the bedclothes over me. Do we kiss again? Does he push me away? Do I want to feel his weight between my thighs? Him inside me? I don't know the answers because he leaves me alone in the room and I fall into a drunken, dreamless sleep.

# 33

Russell Kemp-Lowe spends all night in a holding cell because his lawyer isn't available. Keegan doesn't mind the delay because it gives the jeweller a chance to sober up and worry about what comes next. Every hour will feed his doubts and erode his confidence.

A barrister arrives next morning, en route to the Old Bailey, wearing a black pencil skirt and fitted jacket. Simone Marnie KC has a clipped private-school accent and a ramrod-straight posture like she's balancing three books on her head.

She is allowed time to consult with her client before Keegan begins the interrogation. DS Trisha Hobson is second chair. In her forties, with a pageboy haircut streaked with grey, Hobson is an enigma around the station because nobody knows if she's gay or straight, married or single. Keegan has chosen her because she's a quick thinker and adept at stopping male egos from turning interviews into pissing contests.

'Can you state your full name and home address for the tape?' asks Keegan.

Kemp-Lowe looks at Marnie, waiting for instructions.

'It's your name, not a confession,' says Keegan.

The jeweller grudgingly complies.

'What did you and your wife argue about on the night she was murdered?'

The question surprises Kemp-Lowe. 'She accused me of flirting with a woman who came to our table.'

'Did you?'

'No. She was a customer. I was being polite.'

'Amber Culver told one of my constables that you were something of a player. What did she mean?'

'She's just jealous.'

'Of whom?'

'Amber and I used to go out. It was only a few dates, before I met Caitlin.'

'Was it a sexual relationship?'

Marnie interrupts. 'I fail to see what difference that makes.'

Keegan rephrases. 'Did Miss Culver introduce you to Caitlin?'

'I can't remember.'

'I'm sure you can,' says Keegan.

'If my client says he can't remember, that's his answer,' says Marnie.

'How did you meet Caitlin?'

'It was at an opening-night party in the West End.'

'Was Amber Culver there?'

'I don't know. Maybe.'

'We can ask her. I'm sure she remembers.'

'She might have been there.'

'You invited her?'

'Yes.'

'And she introduced you to Caitlin?'

'She may have done.'

'How did Amber Culver feel about being dumped for her best friend?'

'I didn't dump her. She was happy for Caitlin. She was maid of honour at our wedding and is Daisy's godmother, for God's sake.'

'Almost part of the family,' says Hobson sarcastically.

Keegan doesn't let up. 'On the night of the home invasion, you dropped the babysitter, Josie Sheldon, home. Is that correct?'

'Yes.'

'What time was that?'

'I told you the time.'

'You turned off your phone.'

'The battery was flat.'

'You must have had a charger in your car.'

'It was such a short trip.'

'How long does it take you to drive Josie home?'

'Fifteen minutes, give or take.'

'Miss Sheldon said you dropped her at home at around eleven, but according to the CCTV footage you didn't arrive back at the house until eleven-fifty. Where were you?'

'Josie must be mistaken.'

'We tracked her phone. Her version is correct.'

Kemp-Lowe glances at his barrister and then at Keegan. 'OK, yeah, we talked for a bit.'

'Where?'

'In the car.'

'What did you talk about?'

'Josie is a promising actress. She often asks me for advice.'

'Was she a good babysitter?'

'Caitlin thought so.'

'Is that why you gave her five thousand pounds?'

A different emotion flickers in the jeweller's eyes.

'Were you having a sexual relationship with Josie Sheldon?' asks Keegan.

Kemp-Lowe opens his mouth as if to answer but no words emerge.

'You see, Russell, our forensics lab identified traces of your semen on the passenger seat of your car.'

'Don't answer that,' says Marnie.

'No, no, it wasn't what you think,' says Kemp-Lowe, his voice rising.

'Was she blackmailing you?'

'No. No.'

'Did Caitlin find out?'

'No comment.'

194

Keegan glances at Hobson, encouraging her to take over.

'You and your wife had separate bedrooms, is that correct?'

'How is that relevant?' asks the barrister.

Hobson ignores her. 'How would you describe your marriage?'

'Good. Great. I mean, we had our ups and down,' says Kemp-Lowe.

'What downs?'

'The occasional disagreement. All couples have them. Even you, I daresay.'

'I'm not married,' says Hobson.

Kemp-Lowe points at Keegan. 'I meant him.'

The comment hits a nerve, which makes the jeweller smile.

'What did you argue about?' asks Hobson.

'The usual stuff.'

'Money?'

'Yes.'

'Did Caitlin know how much you owe to bookmakers and loan sharks?'

Kemp-Lowe doesn't answer. He stares past the detectives. The second hand slowly circles on the wall clock. The air conditioner hums.

Finally, he speaks. 'I no longer gamble.'

'Why?'

'Because it's an illness and I promised Caitlin I would stop.'

'What about your debts?'

'I negotiated a repayment plan.'

'The insurance money should help,' says Keegan.

It takes a moment for the barb to land. Marnie reacts first. 'If you have an allegation to put to my client, please do so. I have to be in court at ten o'clock.'

Keegan is still focused on the jeweller. 'Why did your wife buy two burner phones a month before the robbery?'

Kemp-Lowe looks at him blankly.

'We found the receipt in the pocket of an overcoat.'

'I have no idea what you're talking about.'

'What is your relationship with Edward McCarthy?'

A hesitation and a glance at Marnie. 'Mr McCarthy is a client of long standing. He buys jewellery; or has it appraised.'

'How did you meet him?'

'Caitlin met his wife at some charity event.'

'Do you know his brothers?'

'Two of them, I think. Daragh and Clifton.'

'Have they visited the store?'

'On occasions.'

'When did you last speak to any of the McCarthy brothers?'

'I would have to check my records.'

'We have. There are no records.'

'My phone.'

'Their names don't appear in your phone. How do you communicate with them?'

'They drop by.'

'Without an appointment?'

The barrister clears her throat. Before she can interrupt, Keegan spins a laptop to face Kemp-Lowe and presses play.

'I am showing Mr Kemp-Lowe security footage taken by a camera inside his store eleven days before the robbery. Can you identify that man?'

The jeweller doesn't answer.

'His name is Clifton McCarthy,' says Keegan. 'You're shaking his hand.'

'He was shopping for his wife.'

'Clifton McCarthy isn't married.'

'His girlfriend, then.'

'He's gay. Did he buy something?'

'He couldn't find anything he liked.'

The footage changes. 'This is Clifton McCarthy three days later.'

'Oh, now I remember, he gave me a watch to engrave.'

'We didn't find a receipt.'

'I must have forgotten to write it up.'

196

'Have you made an insurance claim for the robbery?'

Kemp-Lowe doesn't answer. Keegan produces the single-page document. 'You filed a claim within forty-eight hours.'

'If you say so.'

'I don't have to say so. It's here in black and white. And this isn't the first time your store has been targeted. Eighteen months ago, you were the victim of a smash-and-grab robbery. Men wearing balaclavas and swinging baseball bats. Your insurance company has refused to pay out and accused you of inflating the losses. They think it was an inside job.'

'That's ridiculous.'

'You see how it looks, don't you, Russell? You gambled your wife's fortune away and put her family business at risk. Then you helped her arrange a robbery to claim the insurance and pocket what was stolen, but something went wrong – Caitlin died – or maybe that was the plan all along. Get rid of the missus. Move on.'

Marnie interrupts, more forcefully this time. 'I can't decide if you are grasping at straws, detectives, or chasing shadows, or drawing a long bow? Maybe I should come up with my own analogy. I think you're flying a kite without a string and pretty soon you'll have no kite.'

Keegan ignores her. 'At the hospital, when I told you that Caitlin was dead, you kept saying that they promised. Who were you talking about?'

'The men who broke into the house. They said if I did as they asked, and opened the safe, nobody would get hurt.'

'Who promised you? Edward McCarthy? Clifton? Daragh?'

'No.'

'But you knew they were coming.'

'No.'

'I think you set this up – the home invasion, the robbery and the fake bomb – because you were drowning in debt and sleeping with the babysitter. Caitlin was part of the plan, until you decided to double-cross her.'

Unbidden, Simone Marnie gets slowly to her feet and smooths down the front of her skirt.

'This spiteful fishing expedition is over,' she says. 'My client was traumatised by this crime. He has lost his wife and spent time in hospital. He has cooperated fully with police, yet you insist on making these cruel and baseless allegations. I will be advising him to sue the London Metropolitan Police—'

She is interrupted by a knock. O'Neil enters and leans closer to Keegan, 'Sorry, guv, we have the warrants.'

'Home or business?'

'Both.'

'Two teams. We leave in twenty minutes.'

Keegan suspends the interview. Kemp-Lowe looks from face to face. 'Can I go home?'

'No,' says Keegan.

'But I've done nothing wrong.'

'We can hold you for twenty-four hours without charge and, as you've seen, we have very comfortable accommodation. Our executive suite. It has a bed and a toilet and a resident junkie who is going to shiver and puke all night. You're in my world now.'

# 34

There's a note on the pillow:

*Hope you slept well. There's coffee and milk in the kitchen. Sorry I couldn't stay. Work called. Jamie. xx*

I feel sick. My mouth dry. My head pounding. My fault. My stupidity. My kiss.

I tell myself nothing happened and nothing would have happened. I wouldn't have slept with him. I couldn't do that to Henry. Yes, I was drunk, but that's no excuse. If Henry said he had done something like that, I wouldn't have believed him, which is why I feel doubly disgusted and adulterous. I'm a hypocrite and a terrible wife.

In all the hours I spent talking to Jamie, I didn't once ask him about his job, or whether he had a girlfriend or, perish the thought, a wife. No, he wouldn't be living in a place like this if he was married. Maybe he's recently divorced or separated. That would explain the lack of furniture and home comforts.

I look around the darkened bedroom. There are hardly any clothes in the wardrobe. There's no TV. It's like he doesn't live here at all. Maybe it's a bolthole, and his main place is out of town.

My phone battery is almost dead. If I call Henry it will probably cut out half way through my explanation, my excuse, my lies. Will the police have told him that I've been released? I hope not.

I visit the bathroom, splash water on my face and straighten my hair. I look awful. No wonder Jamie didn't want to sleep with me. That's unfair. I should give him credit for not taking advantage of me. A lot of men would have jumped at the chance and put a notch on their bedpost. Me? A notch. I could puke.

I still have the suitcase I packed for Paris, but I don't want to shower here because it would mean taking off my clothes and for some reason that makes last night even worse. Instead, I rub deodorant under my arms, brush my hair and put on a clean blouse. Eschewing the coffee, I let myself out of the flat and walk several blocks before I call an Uber.

Today is Wednesday. No, Thursday. Get a grip, Philomena. More importantly, get a story. What am I going to say to Henry?

The car drops me outside the house. Henry opens the front door before I can find my keys. He pulls me into his arms, hugging me tightly, not letting go.

'Thank God,' he says, speaking in a rush. 'I've been calling the police. Nobody would talk to me. Is that allowed? Can they just disappear people?'

'No, and I'm fine,' I say.

'Why didn't you call?'

'My phone died.'

It's not a complete lie. I expect to be consumed by guilt or to blurt out the truth or for Henry to see straight through me. Feeling normal doesn't even enter my calculations.

Henry is still holding me. 'They questioned me for hours,' he says. 'They asked me why we were going to Paris . . . and about that jewellery robbery.'

'They made a mistake,' I say.

'But they had photographs of your uncles. CCTV footage.'

'What did you tell them?'

'Nothing. I don't know anything.'

'I'll explain,' I say. 'Let me get inside.'

He steps back and I feel the warmth of home. Familiar rooms. My own stuff.

We're in the kitchen. He's waiting for me to make everything clear to him, but all I want to do is shower and change my clothes and forget.

I have never regarded myself as a risk-taker or someone who gets a thrill from living close to the edge. Once or twice at university, I had one-night stands. It seemed natural then. Hooking up. This is different. I kissed someone who wasn't my husband. I offered myself. What if Jamie had said yes? Could I have lied about that and kept it a secret? The first lie is the hardest, they say. The second and third and fourth get easier until lying becomes second nature and begins to slowly erode the thing you love.

I shower and change into comfort clothes – track pants and a sweatshirt. And go to the kitchen where Henry has made me comfort food – toasted sandwiches. I feel better once I've eaten, but no less guilty. I tell him about my arrest and interrogation, everything except meeting up with Jamie Pike.

'Is your father involved in this?' he asks.

'I don't know.'

'But you're going to ask him?'

'Yes.'

'Maybe you should stay out of it.'

I don't like his tone. It's OK for me to find fault with my family, but I don't want Henry passing judgement. I don't criticise his father for being a Bible-thumping, Brexit-supporting xenophobe, while his mother is an interfering, small-minded snob.

None of this is said out loud because I'm too exhausted to start a fight. I go to the bedroom, draw the curtains and lie down, trying to still my mind, to rest, to sleep, to forget. When I wake I realise that I'm not alone. Henry is standing at the window, peering through the curtains, looking down at the street.

'What is it?'

He doesn't answer. I join him at the window and notice an expensive car parked opposite, heavily tinted, a figure just visible behind the wheel.

'How long has it been there?' I ask.

'Almost two hours.'

'What time is it?'

'Three o'clock.'

I've been asleep for hours.

'Maybe he's waiting for someone,' he says.

I wonder if the police could be watching the house. If so, they're making it obvious. And the Met doesn't do stakeouts in luxury cars.

'Do you have your phone?' I ask. 'Take a photograph.'

'Are they watching us?'

'I don't know.'

I begin getting changed into my running gear, leggings and a sweatshirt, and lace up my trainers.

'Where are you going?'

'For a run.'

'Now?'

'I want to see if the car follows me.'

'You want me to come?'

'Sure.'

Two minutes later, we leave the house, pausing on the front steps to stretch and loosen up. I look past Henry, studying the car more closely. As we begin to jog along Marney Road, towards Clapham Common, I purposely cross the road and pass close to the Mercedes-AMG.

The rear door opens, triggering the interior light. A woman is sitting in the back seat. I catch the briefest glimpse of her as I pass by, but her voice follows me.

'Philomena McCarthy?'

I stop and turn.

She steps from the car, dressed in a trench coat, cinched with a belt. Her dark hair is pulled back and held in place with a tortoiseshell hairclip. Taking off her sunglasses, she spins them in her hand.

The driver hasn't moved.

'And you must be Henry,' she says, smiling.

'Have we met?' he asks.

'No, not officially.' She extends her hand. 'My name is Jordan Koenig. I am the director of intelligence at the National Crime Agency. I was hoping we could talk, Philomena.'

My mind is in turmoil. 'Do I need a lawyer?'

'Heavens, no!' She laughs. 'I would have called you in advance, but your phone wasn't turned on and I didn't want to create a record of our meeting.'

'That sounds ominous.'

'Merely a precaution. You're not in any trouble – not from me.' She turns to Henry. 'Would you mind if I borrowed your wife for the next hour? I want to discuss her future.' She points to the open car door.

'Where am I going?' I ask.

'For a drive.'

'Can Henry come with me?'

She tilts her head to one side. 'No.'

'How do we know you're from the NCA?' says Henry.

She gives him a tired smile and flips open a leather holder with a warrant card.

For some reason, curiosity perhaps, or desperation, or residual guilt, I slip onto the back seat. Leather. Expensive. I can only see the driver's eyes in the rear mirror.

'Are you sure?' asks Henry, speaking through the open door.

'I'll be fine. You make dinner.'

'I'll open a bottle of wine.'

'Not for me.' *I'm never drinking again.*

The engine starts and the car pulls away, leaving him standing on the footpath. Jordan Koenig is typing a text message. I feel underdressed. She's wearing a beige trench coat, tailored black trousers and a beautifully pressed white blouse. In profile, her face looks like something from an Italian religious painting with every feature slightly exaggerated, her mouth, her nose, her eyes.

'Do you have your phone?' she asks.

'No.'

'Good.'

'Why the secrecy?'

'I want to discuss certain things that are best kept off the record. If asked, I will deny this meeting ever took place.'

'Am I to do the same?'

'Preferably yes.'

'But Henry is a witness.'

'I'm sure you can persuade him to forget what he's seen.'

The car is ghosting through the streets of South London, floating over potholes. Finbar could tell me why the ride is so smooth, because of certain struts or double wishbone suspension.

'What do you know about the NCA?' she asks.

'You investigate corruption and organised crime.'

'Among other things. Human trafficking. Gun running. Cybercrime. Mostly across borders. We look at the bigger picture,' Koenig explains. 'Usually we work closely with the police, particularly the organised crime units and Serious Fraud Squad.'

*Is this a job interview?* I wonder. Surely not. A director of the NCA wouldn't waste her time with a lowly police constable, particularly one who has been suspended. She has the power to summon chief constables and make politicians squirm.

'Do you enjoy your job?' she asks.

'Yes.'

'You have had some difficulties.'

'Nothing I can't handle. Is that what this is about?'

'No.'

She crosses her legs and turns to face me. Her eyes spark with intensity. 'How much do you know about your father's criminal activities?'

My stomach flips over. 'Is that why I'm here?'

'Answer the question.'

'He has never been convicted.'

'A badge of honour,' she says, with the barest hint of sarcasm.

The Mercedes pulls up outside a mansion block on Cheyne Walk, opposite Chelsea Embankment Gardens.

'Come inside,' she says. 'I want to show you something.'

The driver has opened my door. I'm ushered up the steps through a large painted door into a wood-panelled entrance hall. She climbs a curving staircase to an apartment on the second floor. We enter a large room lined with books and furnished with expensive sofas and armchairs. Koenig takes off her coat.

'Tea?'

'No, thank you.'

A tray has been set out with cups and saucers. She was confident I'd come.

Koenig boils the kettle in the kitchen and returns with a teapot with a knitted cover. Meanwhile, I wander around the room, studying the paintings, which are mostly turbulent seascapes. Is that a Turner?

Having poured herself a cup of tea and added one lump of sugar, she walks to a large antique desk near the window, where she takes a folder from a drawer. Opens the cover. Reads.

'Philomena Claire McCarthy. Born 12 November 1993 in London. Parents Edward McCarthy and Rosina Anne DeMarco. Attended primary school in East London. Graduated from St Ursula's Catholic School in Greenwich in 2012. Studied politics and history at Leeds University, earning a first-class degree. Spent a year working as a volunteer for the Svalbard Global Seed Vault on the Norwegian island of Spitsbergen, where they seek to preserve plant seeds in case of large-scale crises or disasters. You suffer from hay fever, and don't like the smell of fish. You have a black belt in karate. You are obsessed with all things Japanese but have never been there. And your oldest friend Sara runs a language school in Hammersmith and is very active on Tinder.'

'You forgot my tattoos?' I say, flippantly.

Koenig consults the file. 'Two of them, both rather small. Left ankle and right shoulder blade.'

I feel myself growing hot and the room shrinking. I have an urgent desire to use the bathroom, and a greater one to leave quickly before I learn any more about this woman or myself.

Koenig takes a seat opposite me. She folds her feet under her like a cat finding somewhere comfortable to curl up. Light from the window emphasises the length of her eyelashes.

'Your career is now hanging from a thread, Philomena. But I have the power to resurrect it. I can make your troubles go away.'

'How?'

'I am in the middle of a rather delicate investigation and you can be of assistance. Your father and your uncles are believed to have paid a million pounds in bribes to public servants and elected officials of two London councils to secure planning approval for a development on Hope Island. They are also suspected of having compromised at least one government minister, two police officers and a handful of senior public servants.'

'If you know all this—'

'I know a great deal, but your father is not my interest. I don't care what Edward McCarthy does. I can live with criminals who know they are criminals. What I can't abide are public servants and elected officials who swear an oath to uphold the law and do exactly the opposite.'

She seems to swallow her anger and take a breath to settle herself. More gently now. 'I need your help.'

'How?'

'I want you to plant listening devices in your father's house and his office, and hide tracking devices in his vehicles.'

'You want me to betray him?'

'I want you to prove that you're not your father's daughter.'

'I'm my own person.'

'Then it shouldn't be a problem.'

She crosses the room and opens the same drawer, retrieving a small silver case with a hinged lid. Returning to the sofa, she flips a latch and takes out five electronic devices. Holding one on the end of her finger, she says, 'This is a GPS tracker that can be slipped into the pocket of a jacket or the tongue of a shoe. Preferably, it should be placed in the lining so it can't be easily dislodged or discovered.'

She points to two of the remaining items, small black squares that are just over an inch long and as thin as credit cards. 'These are voice-activated recording devices. Each of them weighs less than half an ounce and can record continuously for fifty hours.'

'You need a warrant.'

'The surveillance has been approved.'

She chooses another device shaped like a button. 'This is a magnetised tracker that can easily adhere to any metal surface, such as the wheel arch of a car, or a bumper bar or beneath the dashboard.'

'Why not just bug his phones?'

'Your father doesn't use a landline and swaps his phone out every few days. Most of the time, he calls people when he's walking in the garden.'

'I can't change that.'

'True, but you can get closer than we can.'

Koenig points to the final device, a USB stick. 'It contains a program that can harvest and transmit information from a computer or any device connected to the same network. It takes about sixty seconds to load.'

'I won't do it.'

'That's your choice, but take them with you.'

'I won't change my mind.'

'Yes, but you'll think about it,' she says, handing me the small silver case. Smiling. 'If you're anything like me, your career is important to you. It might even define who you are.'

'No.'

That same smile. 'Let's get you home.'

I'm still holding the case. 'How do I contact you?'

'You don't. I'll be in touch.'

# 35

Keegan is tucking into a chicken korma and pilau rice, which is the first thing he's eaten all day. He should be losing weight since his wife left him, but the curries and kebabs are adding unwanted pounds.

O'Neil knocks. 'There's a woman downstairs asking to see you.'

'Who is she?'

'Amber Culver.'

Keegan puts a cardboard lid on the foil container and wraps up his naan bread, knowing it will be cold by the time he returns. His hands are sticky. He squeezes hand sanitiser from a pump pack and dry washes them, working the disinfectant between his fingers.

Amber Culver gets to her feet when he enters the waiting room. She looks different than she did at the hospital. Her hair is no longer tied back and she's wearing tailored slacks and a lightweight sweater with the barest hint of make-up around her eyes.

The detective nods and motions to a seat. 'You wanted to see me, Mrs Culver.'

'Miss. I'm not married.'

She presses her hands between her thighs, leaning forward. 'It's about Caitlin . . . Mrs Kemp-Lowe. I think she knew.'

'Knew what?'

'About the robbery.'

Keegan tries not to react. 'What makes you say that?'

'Something she said to me.' Amber fills her lungs, exhaling slowly, unsure of what to do with her hands. 'She knew about Russell's gambling and the debts. She confronted him and he promised it wouldn't happen again. He was always apologising for something – usually an affair.'

'He was unfaithful?'

She nods nervously.

'With you?'

'No, of course not,' she snorts. 'But Russell can be a real charmer. Women are drawn to him and he enjoys their company. Caitlin knew that when they married but she was blind to his faults.'

'Why do you think that is?'

Amber opens her hands, as though the answer should be obvious. 'Love.'

When was love ever enough, thinks Keegan, remembering the vows that he and Veronica delivered on their wedding day, looking into each other's eyes.

'What makes you think she knew about the robbery?' he asks.

Amber has two vertical lines above her nose that crease when she concentrates. 'It was during the summer. We were having coffee after a yoga class and she told me about Russell's gambling debts. She said a robbery would solve all their problems – because of the insurance – but she said it in a joking way, you know.'

Keegan doesn't answer. After a long pause, Amber continues. 'We began having a little fun, making a plan, plotting . . .'

'Plotting?'

'It was an intellectual exercise. We were plotting the perfect crime.'

'There's no such thing,' says Keegan. 'Because if it was perfect, we wouldn't even know a crime had taken place.'

Amber looks past him towards the main door of the station. 'I'm probably wasting your time. I'm sorry. Forget everything I said.'

'No. Stay. Please,' says the detective. He collects a cup of water from a cooler and hands it to Amber. She sips from the cup, choosing words carefully.

'Caitlin said it happened all the time. People staged break-ins or faked robberies. She said it was a win–win because they would get to keep the jewellery and claim the insurance.'

'She said that?'

'Yes. But I didn't think she was serious. We were joking. It was a game.'

Keegan's silence seems to rattle her.

'I asked her about the previous robbery, the smash and grab. You know about that?'

Keegan nods.

'I asked her if that was an insurance job.'

'What did she say?'

'She gave me a funny look and laughed, but she didn't say no.'

Keegan runs his fingers through his hair, which feels oily and unwashed, even though he shampooed it this morning.

'This perfect crime you were planning – how was it going to play out?'

'Caitlin suggested a home invasion. A gang could hold her hostage and force Russell to open the shop and the safe. "He's an actor – he'd be very good," she said.'

'What gang?' asks Keegan.

'That's what I asked her. She said she'd have to find one. I asked her how. I mean, you can't just order a gang on Amazon.' She looks at Keegan to see if he agrees.

'And what did Caitlin say?'

'She said that Noah would know someone.'

'Her brother?'

'She said Noah had met lots of criminals in jail and they would have connections, you know. I must have looked shocked because Caitlin started laughing and said she was joking and that I was gullible.'

'Why didn't you mention this earlier?' asks Keegan.

'I should have, but I was in shock. And Caitlin can't have organised the robbery.'

'Why do you say that?'

'Because somebody killed her. That can't have been part of the plan.'

Keegan leans back in his chair, mentally threading the facts together, like beads being dropped onto a string. The burner phones, the McCarthy brothers, the insurance claim, the debts.

'Did Russell Kemp-Lowe know about the plan?' he asks.

'He must have known. I mean, he's claiming the insurance.'

'Did he tell you that?'

'No, but he is, isn't he?' There is a beat of silence and Amber's face slowly hardens. 'Daisy deserves better.'

'Better than what?'

'Parents who are criminals.'

# 36

My father lives in a house on the banks of the River Darent, a chalk stream that flows for twenty-one miles through the Kent countryside before becoming a tidal estuary in Dartford where it joins the River Thames. When I say house, I mean ancestral pile, although none of his ancestors had a pot to piss in. Most were hod-carriers and dustmen.

When I pull up at the electronic gates, there is a security guard seated on a fold-up chair. He is dressed in black with a tattooed neck and a Dobermann sleeping at his feet. The dog wakes and wags his tail when I lean out of the car window and say hello.

'Careful, miss. He's a killer,' says the guard.

'Only in the looks department,' I say.

The guard doesn't understand because he's less intelligent than the dog. He asks to see my identification.

'I'm Edward McCarthy's daughter.'

'Can you prove that, miss?'

I skip the formalities and punch four digits into the console. I know the code because I have a good memory for such things and I have watched my father use the console.

Pulling inside, I navigate the single-lane asphalt drive, moving in and out of the shade. A gardener is repairing sections of damaged turf and another is on a ride-on mower, leaving perfect lines on the lawn. The whitewashed seventeenth-century manor house has nine chimneys and a porte cochère partially covered by ivy. The lawns slope down to the river, past a pond, croquet green, swimming pool and summer house.

Daddy loves telling stories about sharing a bedroom with his brothers when they were growing up in a two-up, two-down terrace on the Isle of Dogs with an outside privy and a coin-operated gas meter and metal bars on every window. That version of Edward McCarthy no longer exists. It was bulldozed in the 1980s, along with the terrace, when the Isle of Dogs became a gentrified playground for the loadsamoney generation.

Constance opens the door as my finger hovers over the bell.

'How did you get in the gate?' she asks.

'I had the code.'

'What about the guard?'

'Next to useless.'

As always, she looks immaculate, her make-up perfectly applied, and the clothes casual yet expensive. She brushes her cheeks against mine and trails her hand down my arm, loosely holding my wrist like we're girlfriends.

'Where is he?' I ask.

'Edward?'

'Who else?'

'He's on his way home. Is everything all right?'

'Yes.'

She can tell something is wrong but doesn't press me. Instead, she offers to take my jacket. I'm about to give it to her when I remember the listening devices and trackers are in the pocket. I had no intention of bringing them, but now they're weighing me down.

'How is he?' I ask.

'Distracted,' says Constance. 'I know something is bothering him, but he never confides in me.'

'Why do you need a security guard?'

'I find it best not to ask.'

Everything about Constance is serene, like a duck floating

on a pond, but I always suspect that beneath the surface she's paddling like crazy.

She fills the kettle and collects cups. I notice a gold bracelet, inlaid with diamond chips, slide down her wrist.

'That looks new . . . and expensive.'

'Edward surprised me with it. Isn't it lovely?'

'Any particular reason?'

'No. A jealous wife might think he was having an affair.' She laughs.

'When did he give it to you?'

'Last Sunday.' She rattles off the choices of tea.

'English breakfast,' I say, looking past her. 'I'll just borrow your loo.'

I cross the entrance hall and follow a corridor past the sitting room and bathroom. I slip into the library. Bookshelves reach to the ceiling and line every wall except for where the bay window has created a reading nook with a cushioned bench seat. Opposite the window, a large mahogany writing desk faces the view. It has drawers on either side and an inlay of green leather set into the wood. Elsewhere in the room are two chesterfield sofas that flank a coffee table with a chessboard set up midgame. Daddy and Uncle Clifton play each other – one move per day – sent by text message.

The room smells of paper and leather and wood polish. This is where the men retire to after dinner to smoke and to drink from Daddy's collection of single malts.

Reaching into my jacket, I feel the listening devices with my fingertips. I take one out and examine the small thin square. It would be so easy to slip it between the pages of a book, most of which are war histories and biographies of generals and statesmen.

I sit at the desk where a computer has a darkened screen. I press the space bar. The screen lights up, asking for a password. I try a few obvious ones – names and birthdays – but the screen shakes with every incorrect guess.

I open a drawer. There are letters and financial statements.

Paper clips, rubber bands, nail files, batteries, a cigar cutter, an old wristwatch . . . I look for a password written down on a piece of paper, or the edge of the blotter.

When I came here, I was so sure that I wouldn't do this, but I think of the ways my father has betrayed and deceived me – his lies and excuses, my arrest and suspension. Just because someone is family doesn't mean they avoid accountability. If he robbed the jewellery store and murdered Caitlin Kemp-Lowe he deserves to be caught and punished.

I take out a listening device and slip it between two books, *Lincoln* by Gore Vidal and *SAS Rogue Heroes* by Ben Macintyre. There is a USB slot at the back of the computer. I could plug in the flash drive that Koenig gave me.

I have it in my fingers when the front door opens and I hear Daddy's voice calling out, sounding like a character from *Mad Men*, expecting his dutiful wife to greet him with his pipe and slippers.

In a panic, I try to put the USB stick away, but it slips from my fingers and bounces off the edge of the desk, dropping between the drawers and the wall. On my hands and knees, I feel blindly for the device.

'Is Philomena here?' asks Daddy.

'She's gone to the bathroom,' says Constance. They're in the entrance hallway. They can see the bathroom door, which I stupidly left open.

Daddy calls out my name. I touch the USB with my fingertips but only push it further away. It's in an awkward place, below the drawers, and the desk is too heavy for me to move quickly or quietly.

I hear his footsteps. I crawl out, bashing my head before scrambling into his swivel chair. Daddy steps into the library and takes in the scene. The desk. The glowing computer screen.

'What are you doing?' he asks.

'I'm looking for a book for Archie. Henry's little boy. I remember we had all my old childhood books.'

'They're in the attic.'

'Oh.'

He glances at the computer screen.

'I wanted to look up the name of an author,' I say.

'What book?'

'*Charlotte's Web.*'

'E. B. White.'

'Is that a man or a woman?'

'A man. Why aren't you in Paris?'

'Something came up.'

'Work related?'

'Yes.'

I study his face, wondering if he can spot my lies. More importantly, can I spot his?

Constance calls from the kitchen. 'I've made tea.'

'Would you mind if we talked alone?' I ask.

'Are you in trouble?'

'We both are.'

'Well, let's take a walk. I think better when I'm moving.'

Constance is annoyed at being abandoned, but quickly shrugs it off. Nothing seems to dent her sunny disposition and I wonder if she is one of those modern-day Stepford Wives who pop Prozac like Smarties and smile like a gameshow hostess.

Daddy ushers me out of the house and we walk along a crushed gravel path that circles the pond. He is rugged up in a scarf and a flat cap and a Barbour jacket, looking every inch the country gentleman, inspecting his estate. A gardener is pushing a wheelbarrow. He pauses and they discuss the apple trees and when they should prune the rose garden.

'I saw Uncle Finbar at the hospital the other day,' I say. 'He said he was visiting a friend.'

'Is that so?'

'How long has he known Russell Kemp-Lowe?'

'You'll have to ask him.'

'Do you know him?'

'I've done some business with Russell over the years.'

'What sort of business?'

'Buying and selling jewellery.'

'Is that where you got the gold bracelet? Constance showed it to me.'

'No. Another shop.'

'Did you rob that one too?'

There is a beat of silence that stretches out, filled with the sound of birds and insects and the lawnmower. We are opposite the pond, which is dotted with floating leaves.

'Is that why you're here?' he asks.

'Did you kill Caitlin Kemp-Lowe?'

'I had nothing to do with the robbery or Caitlin's death.'

I want to believe him, but I've seen the CCTV footage.

'Why did Uncle Clifton visit the jewellery store twice in the days leading up to the robbery?'

Daddy leans down and deadheads a rosebush. 'Are you wearing a wire?'

'Why?'

'I want to know if I'm talking to my daughter or a police officer.'

'You're afraid of incriminating yourself.'

'I want to know whose side you're on.'

'My side. The right side. The only side that matters.'

He smiles sadly and I feel an irrational anger. I take off my jacket and hand it to him and begin unbuttoning my shirt.

'What are you doing?'

'I'm showing you.'

My blouse is off. The cold hits my bare skin. A gardener has stopped working and is staring at me from the far side of the pond. I toss the blouse at Daddy, kick off my shoes and unbutton the front of my jeans, pushing them over my hips. My knickers threaten to come with them.

'No! Please, don't—'

'Satisfied?'

217

I'm wearing only a bra and knickers and must look ridiculous with my jeans around my ankles.

'Cover yourself. Please?' He looks ready to cry.

I pull up my jeans and hold the blouse against my chest. He slips the jacket over my bare shoulders. If he reached into the pockets, he would find the listening devices. I'm not good at this – the secrecy and lies.

We're close to the garage, which was originally a stable block and blacksmith's forge. Now it houses Daddy's cars, which include a Range Rover, a red Jag, a Bentley and a beaten-up Land Rover held together by mud and rust.

A small kitchen area has been built behind a wall of tools. It has an electric kettle, a bar fridge and an overly large TV, where Daddy watches football matches and secretly smokes cigars.

Taking off his coat, he hangs it on a hook behind the door. Then he fills the electric kettle, setting out two mugs. I finish buttoning my blouse and jeans. While he's distracted, I slip a tracking device into the inside pocket of his jacket, deep into the corner of the fabric.

'This'll warm you up,' he says, putting the mug of tea in front of me.

We sit side by side in silence, gazing out of a window across the garden. A crow lands on a thin branch, flapping and cawing. Maybe it's a raven. I can't tell the difference. Either way, it sounds mournful and lost.

'Whoever robbed the jewellery store, stole from me,' he says.

'Care to explain?'

'There was something in the safe that was taken. I won't go into the details.'

'Because it was illegal?'

He doesn't reply.

'You were laundering money?'

'Please, Philomena, for your sake and mine.'

'No, you don't get to fob me off like that. I just spent a night in a police cell because of you. They think I was involved in the robbery. I've been suspended. They're kicking me off the force.'

'Why?'

'Because I found the little girl, Daisy. And because I'm your daughter. And because they have CCTV footage of Clifton and Daragh visiting the jewellery store. And Finbar at the hospital. They're piecing it together.'

'They're wrong.'

'What was in the safe?'

'I can't tell you.' His face crinkles into something resembling sympathy. 'I'm trying to shield you.'

'Liar! You're protecting yourself.'

'Somebody has been targeting Hope Island – sabotaging equipment, hijacking deliveries, cancelling orders . . .'

'What does that have to do with the robbery?'

'It's another shot across the bow.'

'Give me a name.'

'I don't want you involved.'

'I'm *already* involved.'

'I'm sorry.'

That's not good enough. I want to punch his chest, pinch his skin and twist his earlobe. I want to make him talk.

His phone is ringing. 'Don't answer that,' I say.

He lifts the phone to his ear and then looks out of the window. A convoy of police cars is flashing between the trees, windscreens reflecting in the patches of sunshine. The vehicles cross the small bridge and approach the house.

Daddy looks at me, asking an unspoken question.

'They're not with me,' I say, and in the same breath, 'I can't be found here.'

Instantly, he understands. 'Come with me.'

He leads me past the cars into a rear room of the stables. This was once the old blacksmith's forge and still has a brick firepit and two large iron anvils.

'Do you remember I told you about the history of this house?' he says, pushing a wooden crate to one side.

'You said it was built by a smuggler.'

'He died one of the richest men in England.'

'Something to aspire to.'

My sarcasm doesn't touch him.

'He owned properties right across south-east England, which he used to smuggle goods that he brought ashore at Seasalter, on the Kentish coast. He built rooms and tunnels to move the contraband.'

He opens a wooden trapdoor and I peer into the darkness below. A wooden ladder is leaning against the opening.

'You want me to go down there?'

'Unless you have a better idea.'

'Is it safe?'

'It's lasted this long.' I begin to climb down. 'Just don't touch any of the beams.'

'Who's going to let me out?'

'You can open it from the inside. But wait until they've gone.'

I descend the ladder until my foot touches the dirt floor, which is solid and dry. I glance up and see my father's face. He suddenly looks old and sad and tired, like an animal being led into a knacker's yard.

My Fiat is parked beside the house. The police will trace it to me but I can make an excuse for that. If Keegan finds me here, it will confirm everything that he suspects – that I'm part of this.

The trapdoor closes. I'm breathing in darkness and cool, damp air. I hear Daddy kicking straw and dirt across the trap-door, to hide the evidence. Taking out my phone, I turn on the torch app. The room is about fifteen feet square with a compacted earth floor and beams holding up the roof. It is empty except for several old drums, crumbling to rust, and a packing crate with jagged spars of wood.

My phone has no bars because I'm too far below ground. The police won't be able to trace me if they try searching for the signal. I examine the subterranean room, which narrows at one end, leading to a tunnel that I won't risk exploring. I sit on a packing crate, steadying my heartbeat, and turn off the torch to save my phone battery. The darkness is absolute. I can picture what's going on above my head. The police search. Furniture being moved. Drawers opened. Books feathered. Carpets peeled back.

I was five years old when the police first raided our house. They came before dawn, when I was still in bed. Armed officers swarmed through the front door, going from room to room. They made my mother and me wait in the kitchen. I sat on her lap, still dressed in my pyjamas.

'The police have lost something,' she said.

'But why are they looking here?'

'Because they've looked everywhere else.'

Later, after the police had gone, I went to my bedroom. Toys and books and clothes were dumped in a huge pile. Posters had been ripped from the wall and a hinge was broken on my rocking horse.

That might have been the beginning of the end of my parents' marriage. My mother could accept a lot of things, but not being treated like a criminal and having her belongings ransacked. Six months later, my uncles went to prison.

Now Constance is experiencing the same thing. Her life is being picked apart, opened, examined and swabbed. Her phone will be confiscated, as well as her laptop and tablet. Forensic officers will be checking the sinks and washing machine, looking for any fibres or particles that match the crime scene.

Maybe this search will end another marriage. Would I be disappointed? I used to hate Constance – no, hate is too strong a word – I disliked her because she wasn't my mother and she was closer in age to me than to Daddy. But I've seen how she dotes on him and looks after him and I admire her for that.

Time passes and I begin growing cold. I hear footsteps above me. Male voices. They're searching the garage.

'Hey, this kettle is still warm,' says one of them. 'Two mugs.'

'There were three mugs inside,' says his partner.

Dust falls from the ceiling as they walk across the hidden trapdoor. I try to blink it away, holding back a sneeze.

'You see those motors,' says the first officer. 'Who says crime doesn't pay?'

'And what about the wife. I bet she goes off like a bottle rocket.'

'I'd light her fuse.'

They sound like they're directly above me.

'What are we looking for?' asks one of them.

'Secret rooms. Tunnels. The boss says old places like this are full of them.'

One of them taps his foot, creating a hollow echo. Dust falls into my eyes.

'There's something under here.'

'Here, help me lift this.'

I don't wait. I head for the narrow entrance on the far side of the room. Feeling blindly, I bump my head on the ceiling but try not to make a sound.

Holding my hands out, I touch the walls on either side of me as I move into the tunnel.

The trapdoor opens and a beam of light searches the subterranean room.

'It's empty.'

'Go down and have a look.'

'I'm not going down there. It could be boobytrapped.'

'OK, I'll go.'

I hear the ladder creak under his weight. I'm thirty feet into the tunnel, moving further away. I wait until I can't hear their voices before I risk turning on my phone's torch. The brick walls glisten with water, which has pooled at the curved bottom of the tunnel, creating puddles that come up to my ankles, soaking my shoes.

Occasionally I come to a junction where the tunnel branches off in several directions or widens to create a room. I choose the larger of the tunnels and press on, unsure of where I'm going. It could lead to a dead end or the tunnel could collapse on top of me. At least there are no spiders or cobwebs. The bats must have scared away the spiders. What scared away the bats?

My shoulder brushes a wall, which crumbles and splashes. I trip over something partially submerged. An old lantern. This tunnel was built two centuries ago. What were they smuggling? Weapons? Alcohol? Tobacco?

The police won't try to search it without the proper equipment. They'll need torches, ropes, cameras and an engineering report. This gives me time, but only if there's some way out at the other end.

Slowly, almost imperceptibly, the tunnel has begun to slope downwards. I can feel the pressure on my calf muscles and the water has drained away. My phone is almost out of battery. If it dies, I could be lost in the darkness, unable to find my way back. Maybe I should turn around now. I could surrender and accept the consequences. Every choice I've made – including hiding down here – has compounded my problems.

I feel a slight change in the temperature and taste fresher air. The tunnel has begun to climb again and the darkness slowly softens until I see a faint glow, diffused by greenery. The tunnel entrance has a barred metal gate. For a moment I worry that it's padlocked, but the hinges are so corroded by rust that I kick it down and climb out, using vines and tree roots as handholds. I'm on the banks of the River Darent, a yard above the water level. Scrambling higher, I hear the sound of cars on a nearby road. Immediately, I turn off my phone, not wanting the handset to be traced.

I weave through the trees where dead leaves soften my steps

and water squelches in my shoes. The road is ahead of me. I can flag down a car. I'm about to step out when something makes me stop and I press myself against the trunk of a tree. Moments later, three police cars sweep past me. My father is in the back seat of the second car. Head back, chin up, he is staring into the distance, as though trying to see his future.

# 37

Keegan lets his eyes scan the shelves in McCarthy's library, reading the titles. Most are books he has never read by authors he doesn't recognise. The search warrant gives him the right to confiscate computers, phones, files and photographs, but he doesn't expect to find any incriminating evidence. McCarthy is far too clever to make a mistake like that. He's old school with nothing written down or spoken over the phone. Messages are delivered in person or using coded language, where something as simple as a takeaway order or a discussion about the weekend football could have an entirely different meaning.

McCarthy is being taken to Kentish Town police station. His wife has been allowed to stay in the house and remain in the kitchen, where she's sitting at the island bench. Keegan expected her to complain, but instead she offered to make everybody tea or coffee and to 'open a packet of biscuits'.

'We're not invited guests,' he says.

'Yes, but you're in my house and I want to be polite.'

Her accent is unexpected. She sounds like a minor royal or someone who works for *Tatler* or *Vogue*. She's flicking through a magazine now, waiting for the police to finish.

'Please make a note of everything you take,' she says. 'And be sure to bring it back.'

Something topples and breaks upstairs. 'I do hope that's not the Ming. It will cost you a year's salary.'

Keegan notices the Fiat parked in the turning circle outside. It looks out of place.

'Who owns the car?'

'My stepdaughter,' says Constance. 'She dropped it round a few days ago. Edward offered to have the tyres changed. One of her uncles runs a garage.'

'Finbar.'

'You seem to know a lot about this family.'

'Not by choice. Where was your husband last Friday night?'

'At a dinner in London.'

'Can anyone confirm that?'

'There were three hundred people there. I'm sure one of them will remember us.' She is being facetious but smiling sweetly.

Keegan runs his finger along the island bench.

'Calacatta Vagli marble,' says Constance, as though he wants to ask about the stone. 'I can get you a quote from the supplier.'

He gives her a pained smile. 'What's it like being married to Edward McCarthy?'

'Rather nice. Have you seen my wardrobe?'

'I thought you'd have a little more pride in your family name than to get mixed up with someone like him.'

'What do you know about my family?' She doesn't wait for him to answer. 'My maiden name is Hawkins. I'm a descendant of Sir John Hawkins, a sixteenth-century slave trader who profited from human misery. Robbing natives. Enslaving them. Sleeping with their women. Giving them diseases. After that, his sons and grandsons began pissing away his fortune. So, when it comes to *my* family, detective, I feel nothing but contempt.'

Keegan can't match her gaze and steps out of the kitchen. Officers are carrying boxes to a waiting van. His phone buzzes. Gerard Noonan is calling from the Met's Forensic Science Laboratory in Lambeth.

226

'We have some more results on the crime scene samples. Some of the fingerprints are linked.'

Keegan looks at the time. 'Give me an hour.'

A sleeting rain is falling diagonally, smiting his cheeks, but Keegan doesn't have an umbrella. Instead, he pulls up his collar and puts his head down as he walks briskly along Lambeth Road.

Shaking out his coat in the foyer, he flashes his warrant card. A receptionist looks at his shoes and the mess he's made on the floor.

'It's still raining outside,' he says, stating the obvious. 'But it's easing off.'

She calls upstairs and then summons a cleaner to the foyer.

Noonan meets Keegan at the lifts and holds open a door as they pass through the digital and electronics section, where phones and computers are repaired and hard drives are uploaded to recover hidden, damaged or lost data. The department used to take up two rooms but now has an entire floor, he explains, dedicated to unlocking smart devices and deciphering encryptions. More controversially, they have twenty million faces in the biometric database – images that can be trawled using facial recognition software to identify witnesses and suspects.

Noonan is dressed like a public servant today, in a suit and business shirt with a royal blue tie. After navigating another corridor, they arrive at an open-plan office, where the pathologist has a desk near the window and a potted palm that leans towards the natural light.

Noonan taps at the computer keyboard.

'As expected, the semen stains found upstairs in the main bedroom aren't a match for Russell Kemp-Lowe. Based on the degradation markers, the samples were left within a few hours of Caitlin's death.'

'What about DNA?'

'Nothing on the database, but we're still checking hair samples and skin cells found on the bedspread and towels in the ensuite bathroom. The blood on the girl's pyjamas came from her mother. Caitlin was most likely struck across the face, which caused a nosebleed. The bruising is showing up post-mortem.'

'You mentioned fingerprints.'

'Three of the unidentified prints are from the same individual. One was pulled on a windowsill in the main bedroom, another in an upstairs bathroom and a third on the edge of the packing tape that covered Caitlin Kemp-Lowe's mouth.'

'It has to be one of the intruders,' says Keegan. 'He must have taken off his gloves.'

'Careless.' Noonan consults the screen. 'We haven't traced the partial print we found on the plastic bag used to suffocate the victim. We know it came from a local restaurant but the print doesn't match anyone in the kitchen or the delivery driver or the babysitter. Then we have a few anomalies. The safe upstairs had no prints on the handle.'

'Why is that odd?'

'A smooth metal surface is the perfect medium to preserve a fingerprint.'

'It was wiped clean?'

'That would be my opinion.'

'I want you to test the contents of the safe. Run any prints through the database again.'

'Any particular reason?'

'Edward McCarthy and his brothers are now our prime suspects. Their phones and computers are on their way.'

'Now there's a name I haven't heard in a while.'

'Write it down so you don't forget.'

# 38

'Are you going to tell me what happened?' asks Henry, who has been following me through the house as I shower, change and put my muddy clothes in the washing machine. 'Where is your car?'

'I had to leave it behind.'

'Why?'

'The police arrived. I had to hide.'

'Isn't that what guilty people do?'

I don't answer. Instead, I start sorting laundry, which has been drying on the radiators. Henry helps, but we have a different method for folding socks. I roll each pair together and tuck one inside the other, creating a ball that 'smiles' at me. Henry ties his socks like odd pieces of string, which looks untidy and takes up more space. He doesn't agree, of course, and if we start arguing over socks we know that our marriage is doomed.

'What did your father say?'

'He denied everything.'

'Do you believe him?'

'I want to.'

'What are you going to do?'

'I'm going to clear my name.'

'How?'

'I don't know yet.'

Henry waits, expecting more, but I have nothing to add. We have had this conversation before and it always ends in an argument. He doesn't like me being a police officer. Then again, I feel the same way about his firefighting. Every time he leaves for a shift, I silently whisper, 'Come home to me.'

Henry was there when Grenfell Tower burned in 2017 and seventy-two people died and a similar number were injured. When he arrived, there were people trapped on the twenty-third floor. Wearing breathing apparatus, he and his crew fought their way up the crowded stairwell, stepping over the bodies of the dead. By the time he reached the ninth floor, they had lost all visibility and the heat was rising, but still they continued, up and up through the blackness. Finally, unable to tell what floor they had reached and with their oxygen running out, they were forced to turn back, still hearing the screams from above them. Henry carried an unconscious woman down the stairs, but she was dead when they reached the ground.

There were still people trapped inside, talking to friends and families on their phones. Onlookers begged Henry to go back in and that's what he did. He grabbed another oxygen tank and returned to the stairwell, searching floor by floor. Four times he went inside the blazing tower block and carried someone out alive, but he still felt it wasn't enough.

I have never asked him to give up his job. And in return, I expect him to respect my choices and put up with my baggage – the internal politics, misogyny, sexism, 5 a.m. search warrants, paperwork, unpaid overtime, assaults and abuse. This is not a competition. We're a team.

The front doorbell plays the *William Tell Overture*. Henry has hooked it up to the Wi-Fi system and changes the chime whenever he gets bored. Amber Culver is standing on the doorstep.

'How did you get my address?' I ask.

'Daisy remembered it. I'm sorry. I know I shouldn't bother you.'

The little girl steps from behind her, smiling shyly, still holding her stuffed hippo.

'I'm not involved in the investigation and I can't talk to you about the case,' I say.

'I understand, but I need your advice.'

Henry appears on the landing, shouting, 'Who is it?'

'Visitors. Put the kettle on.'

Hot water is poured over tea leaves and Daisy nibbles at a Jammie Dodger, starting at the edges and moving towards the strawberry-flavoured heart.

'Can we talk privately?' Amber nods towards Daisy.

Henry steps in and takes Daisy's hand. 'C'mon, Bug, let's see if there's something on TV.'

'Hippo likes watching *Bluey*,' she says.

'What's *Bluey*?'

'Only the best TV show in the whole world.'

'Well, we definitely need to see that.'

I'm alone with Amber, who cradles a mug in two hands, blowing on the surface of her tea.

'Are they going to charge Russell?' she asks.

'I don't know.'

'He knew about the robbery, they both did. I've told DCI Keegan.'

'What did you tell him?'

'I said Caitlin talked about staging a home invasion and claiming the insurance. I thought she was joking. Fantasising about committing the perfect crime, but DCI Keegan is right and there are no perfect crimes. Someone always gets hurt.'

I stop her and tell her to go back to the beginning. She tells me about the coffee morning and the light-hearted conversation about solving Caitlin's money woes.

'Everything she talked about came true,' says Amber.

'How would she know how to hire a gang?'

'Noah helped her. He must know people . . . criminals . . .'

'Why would she plan a robbery that led to her death?'

'Something must have gone wrong. If I'd known, I would

have stopped her. Bankruptcy was better than risking her future. And Daisy was in the house. What were they thinking – putting her at risk like that?'

Her voice shakes with anger. She apologises, smiling weakly. 'Do you have children?'

'Not yet. Henry has a little boy.'

'I always wanted a family. I thought my husband wanted one too, but he changed his mind. That's why we broke up.' She looks into her mug as though studying the tea leaves. 'You want to know what's funny? My husband has met someone else – younger, of course – and guess what?'

*I think I know where this is going.*

'She's pregnant,' says Amber. 'He's posting all these pictures on social media, showing her growing bump and the ultrasound images and updates on how they're decorating the baby's room.'

'That's cruel,' I say.

'I'm happy for him. I am, really. I think he always wanted kids, secretly, but not with me.'

She blinks and smiles and lets out a small sigh.

'Why are you here?' I ask.

'If Russell helped organise the robbery the police are going to charge him and Daisy will be alone. Losing one parent is bad enough, but losing two doesn't bear thinking about.'

# 39

Edward McCarthy is waiting for the interview to begin. It is not a new experience. He was first picked up by the police at the age of ten, accused of stealing milk money from a neighbour's doorstep. The second time he allegedly trespassed in the same neighbour's yard, when he climbed over the back fence to give food and water to a dog that had been chained up for days. His subsequent run-ins with the police were less altruistic. In his late teens he began buying old tat at car-boot sales and repurposing it as memorabilia from TV shows like *EastEnders* and *Doctor Who*. Hats, helmets, scarves, vases and pint glasses were given a back story, along with a fake certificate of authenticity and the forged signatures of the actors. Would-be buyers were told the 'souvenirs' came from one of McCarthy's uncles who worked in the props department of the BBC.

People tend to romanticise the past, calling it the 'good old days', and McCarthy can understand why. Things were simpler back then. He didn't want to be rich or to drive a fancy motor. He wanted enough cash in his pocket for a few pints at his local, and to take his girlfriend to the Odeon, and to buy her a cone of chips afterwards.

Policing was also simpler. Blunter. More direct. Interviews were brief, aggressive affairs, often punctuated by a punch or a slap or the bruising of knuckles. Nowadays the police use something called the **PEACE** method: Planning, engaging, accounting for events, closure and evaluation. There's an acronym for everything and most of them are insanely irrelevant, thinks McCarthy.

He is alone in the interview room with his barrister, David Helgarde, who looks like an undertaker in a black suit and a white court tunic shirt.

'Where are the boys?' asks McCarthy.

'Finbar and Daragh are being held at Paddington Green. They can't find Clifton.'

'He's out of the country.'

'Business or pleasure?'

'A bit of both.'

'I got an odd message on my phone just before I arrived,' says the barrister. 'I didn't recognise the number. Apparently, I'm to show it to you.'

He holds out his mobile. The photograph on the screen is of Philomena opening the door of her house to a woman and child. 'According to the time code it was taken thirty minutes ago,' says Helgarde. And there's a message underneath: *Shakespeare. Henry VI Part Two.*

'I looked it up,' says Helgarde, reading a quote: *Seal up your lips and give no words but mum: The business asketh silent secrecy.* 'Someone wants you to keep quiet.'

'I know who it is.'

The door opens. DCI Keegan enters carrying a folder and a laptop computer. He's with a second detective, who is heavyset with a flushed face. McCarthy recognises him. Remembers his name. O'Neil. A puffed-up plod. Stupidity combined with arrogance.

Keegan begins by asking for McCarthy's name, age and address. The housekeeping. Every police interview is a strange piece of performance art where the roles are clearly defined. There are the interviewing officers, the lawyers and the suspects. Sometimes, there is even an audience, watching from behind mirrored glass or on a video feed.

Different versions of the same event are presented and challenged, torn apart and reconstructed. Allegations are made and refuted. Questions are answered or parried. The guilty dissemble to obscure or mask the truth and the innocent try desperately to prove their virtuousness.

'Do you know a man called Russell Kemp-Lowe?' asks Keegan.

'Yes.'

'What is your relationship with him?'

'We do business occasionally.'

'What sort of business?'

'I buy jewellery for my lovely wife, or get it cleaned.'

'What about Caitlin Kemp-Lowe – did you know her?'

'We've met. She and my wife are on several committees together. Charitable pursuits.'

'When did you last see her?'

'On the night she died.'

The air seems to leave the room, as though inhaled completely and waiting for someone to exhale.

'You saw her on the night she died?' asks Keegan, unable to hide his shock.

'Yes. She came to our table.'

'What table?'

'At the charity dinner. Constance and I were at the Banking Hall. Is that what this is about? Poor Caitlin's death. She and Russell were at the dinner.'

The answer has blind-sided Keegan, who seems angry that nobody has established this fact before now.

'What time did you leave the dinner?' he asks.

'Constance was one of the organisers. She wanted to stay until the bitter end.'

'Was it bitter?'

'The speeches were interminable. Do-gooders do like congratulating themselves.'

'And afterwards?'

'We drove home.'

'Any witnesses?'

'You could check all your fancy traffic cameras along the route.'

Keegan studies his notes, taking a moment to collect his thoughts. 'When did you last speak to Noah Kemp-Lowe?'

'Who?'

'Caitlin's younger brother.'

This is what McCarthy has been waiting for – a chance to hear how much the police know and if they can help him fill in the blanks.

Helgarde touches McCarthy's forearm. McCarthy ignores him. 'Never met the guy.'

'Never?' asks Keegan.

'Don't answer that,' says Helgarde.

McCarthy corrects himself. 'I don't recall.'

'We're going to search your phone records and computers; check your movements against those of Noah, until we find a link.'

'Knock yourself out.'

'I think Noah contacted you or one of your brothers and asked you to rob the jewellery store.'

'No comment.'

'He was acting on the instructions of his sister.'

This is more information than McCarthy had hoped to learn.

Keegan turns the laptop to face him and plays the CCTV footage of Clifton visiting the jewellery store. 'What was he doing?'

'Buying jewellery, perhaps. He likes expensive watches.'

'Does he buy them for his boyfriend?' asks O'Neil, smirking.

'I'm sure he does,' says McCarthy, refusing to take the bait.

'There's no record of any purchase,' says Keegan.

'Maybe he didn't find anything he liked.'

'Clifton McCarthy took a flight from Heathrow to Dublin on Wednesday. He checked into three different hotels but stayed at none of them.'

'He's a fussy bugger.'

'What is he doing in Ireland?'

'Catching up with old friends. He's partial to a pint of Guinness.'

'When is he due back?'

'Day or two.'

'Do you have a phone number for him?'

'No.'

Keegan doesn't seem to appreciate the flippancy of his answers. He changes direction. 'Did you encourage your daughter to join the Met?'

'I advised her against it,' says McCarthy. 'I told her the police were a bunch of bumbling idiots, present company included.'

Keegan ignores the insult. 'I think you wanted someone on the inside.'

'I already have people on the inside.'

'Are you admitting to bribing police?'

'No. I'm admitting to having friends who are coppers. Most of them are pretty friendless. You look like you need one.'

The fat detective chuckles and Keegan shoots him a look.

'What was her job on the night of the robbery? Monitoring the police radios? Acting as lookout? Keeping the little girl out of the way?'

'I had nothing to do with the robbery and neither did Philomena.'

'Did you tell your daughter to spy for you?'

'I don't find it easy to tell my daughter anything.'

'She's headstrong.'

'One word for it.'

'Is she on your payroll?'

'Last I heard she was on yours.'

'Not any longer.'

'Oh, that's right. You suspended her for doing her job. Typical of your lot. She's decent, thoughtful, intelligent and honest as a mirror but you lot can't handle that. And when you eventually realise that I didn't rob the jewellery store and I didn't murder Caitlin, you might even get your heads out of your arses and discover that someone is trying to pin this crime on me and my family.'

'Give me a name. I'll check it out.'

'I can't do that.'

'Why? Because of some bullshit code of silence? Honour among thieves?'

McCarthy doesn't respond.

'Please show me your wrists,' asks Keegan.

McCarthy pulls up his sleeves like he's a magician proving there is nothing hidden inside.

'Do any of your brothers have tattoos?' asks Keegan.

'Finbar likes to get inked.'

'Have you ever seen a tattoo like this?'

Keegan pushes a drawing across the table. It shows two tumbling dice. McCarthy recognises it immediately. The man who stood guard outside the steam room when he met with Popov had the same tattoo.

This is McCarthy's chance. He could tell Keegan about Dimitar Popov, the vandalism and the hijacks and the attempt on his wife's life, but then he remembers the photograph on Helgarde's phone and the warning.

The detectives are waiting.

'I'm afraid I can't help you,' says McCarthy. 'But I'll ask around.'

A knock on the door. A uniformed constable enters and whispers something into Keegan's ear. Muffled words. Nods. The interview is suspended.

Outside the interview suite, Keegan takes a call from Noonan.

'You wanted me to test the contents of the safe. I found a

238

thumbprint on an envelope that held a will signed by Caitlin Kemp-Lowe's father. The print belonged to the babysitter.'

Keegan's head is spinning. Josie Sheldon got into the safe. How? What isn't he seeing?

He turns to O'Neil. 'Get me Josie Sheldon's phone records.'

# 40

'Visitor!' yells a prison guard, rapping twice on the cell door. Noah Kemp-Lowe is startled by the sound. His first thought is of Sofía, whom he hasn't seen since his arrest. And their only phone call was cut off after ten minutes before he could say that he loved her and that he was sorry.

It's not visiting hours for partners or family. Who else could it be? What if it's a trap? Three days back in prison and he's already been warned to keep his mouth shut. He was in a food queue, pushing his tray along the shelf, collecting mashed potato, mixed veg and some mystery meat, when an inmate poked a fork into his side, leaning close, whispering with a foul breath, 'Next time it's a shank and I take out a kidney.'

Noah had looked for the nearest guard, who was leaning on a pillar staring at his fingernails as though considering a manicure. Since then, Noah has avoided quiet corners of the exercise yard and bottlenecks on the landings.

A different guard escorts him from his cell and down the stairs. Instead of going to the visitor room, he is taken to a cell on H-wing where DCI Keegan is waiting, standing beneath a small square window that only provides a glimpse of blue sky. He tells Noah to sit and remains standing.

'Do you know a man called Edward McCarthy?' he asks.
'No.'
'Daragh McCarthy. Clifton McCarthy. Finbar McCarthy.'
'Who are they?'

'I know you helped set up the robbery. Caitlin asked you to find someone.'

'I want my lawyer.'

Keegan turns and slowly pulls back a chair, which scrapes across the concrete floor. He sits astride the chair, leaning on the backrest, resting his chin on his forearms. He stares at Noah, until the younger man grows uncomfortable.

'I'm trying to work out your angle.'

'I don't have an angle.'

'Sure, you do. You agreed to help your sister find a gang to rob the jewellery store, and in return she promised to have you written back into your father's will. Fifty–fifty.'

'You can't prove that.'

'You wanted to make sure that Caitlin kept her end of the bargain, so you asked Josie Sheldon to open the safe upstairs. It can't have been hard to guess the combination. Daisy's birthday. Either that, or you watched Caitlin open it earlier and memorised the combination.'

Noah can't meet his gaze and stares at the floor. Keegan continues. 'We found Josie Sheldon's thumbprint on an envelope that contained your father's will. She also took a photograph with her phone and she texted it to you on the night that Caitlin died. She deleted the image immediately afterwards, but we have the tools that can retrieve data from devices even when people think it's been overwritten or purged. Pictures. Texts. Files.'

Keegan swipes his phone and holds up the screen. The image shows a page of a last will and testament.

'Your father divided his estate equally between you and Caitlin. Only now that she's dead, you stand to inherit everything. That's a strong motive for murder.'

Noah tries to protest, but the words get trapped in his throat and emerge as a moan.

Keegan continues. 'Armed robbery and accessory to murder. You'll be old and grey before you leave this place.'

'I didn't kill her. I loved her.'

The detective gets to his feet, preparing to leave. 'I hope it was worth it.'

'Help me,' whispers Noah.

'Only you can do that.'

Noah reaches out and grabs Keegan's arm. The DCI softens his tone.

'When is the baby due?'

'January.'

'A boy or a girl?'

'A boy.'

'You were probably hoping to be at the birth. Nothing beats that. Now you're wondering if Sofia will bother hanging around. Maybe she'll go home to Spain. And you'll never see them again.'

'What do you want?' asks Noah, defeated.

'Your help. Caitlin asked you to find someone to rob the jewellery store. All I need from you is a name.'

Noah is silent.

'We will find the link. We'll trace your movements and put you in the same place at the same time. After that, you'll have nothing to trade. There won't be a plea bargain. You'll be an accomplice to a home invasion, a robbery and a murder.'

'I didn't hire them,' whispers Noah. 'I gave Caitlin a name and a phone number, that's all.'

'Who?'

'Someone I met when I was inside.'

'I need a name.'

Noah shakes his head. 'They can reach me anywhere.'

'Have you been threatened?'

He nods.

'What if I had you transferred? Category D. Minimum security. You'll be able to work outside the prison during the day and see Sofia and the baby.'

'They'll find me. Even worse, they'll find her.'

Keegan seems to ponder this. 'I'll talk to the Protected Persons Service.'

'Witness protection?'

'It doesn't have to be in Britain. We could resettle you in Spain or Argentina.'

Noah studies Keegan's face, wanting to believe him.

'But you would have to testify and tell everything in open court.'

'I want a deal in writing.'

'It doesn't work like that.'

Noah gets to his feet and crosses the room, banging on the door, yelling, 'I want to go back to my cell.'

Keegan follows him, resting his hand against the door. 'Let me make some calls.'

'What do I do in the meantime?'

'Stay safe.'


Keegan leaves the reception area and crosses the prison access road, through the ornamental metal gates to a parking area where O'Neil is waiting. Sliding into the passenger seat, he looks back at the Victorian facade of HMP Wormwood Scrubs, the twin brick towers on either side of a large arched door.

Taking a bottle of sanitiser from his jacket pocket, he works the gel into every crack and cuticle of his fingers and hands. He offers the gel to O'Neil, who shakes his head.

'I don't think it's McCarthy,' says Keegan, as though answering a question that he hasn't been asked.

'But the CCTV . . . ?'

'He's involved somehow, but not in the robbery.'

'We'll have to let him go,' says O'Neil, bitterness in his tone.

Keegan, as an afterthought. 'Release them together.'

'What do you mean?'

'Russell Kemp-Lowe and McCarthy. I want to see what happens.'

# 41

My phone is vibrating. I glance at the screen and my hearts sinks. I don't want to talk to Jamie Pike. I don't want to think about the drunken kiss. My tongue. His mouth. My hips. His groin. Ugh!

'What is it?' I hiss.

'Hello to you too,' he says, laughing.

'Why are you calling me?'

'I wanted to make sure you got home OK.'

'I'm fine. Please don't call me again.'

'Is something wrong?'

'Yes, I'm married. And you're trouble.'

'Hey, I didn't do anything wrong. You invited me for a drink, remember?'

'That was a mistake. Delete my number.'

I hang up. Henry chooses that moment to walk into the kitchen. 'Who was that?'

'A wrong number.'

'You're all flushed.'

'No, I'm not!' I snap, touching my cheek. 'It was nobody.'

He raises his hands. 'OK. Nobody. Message received.'

My phone vibrates again. I snatch it off the benchtop, fearing it might be Jamie.

It's Constance, speaking in a rush. 'Have you heard from Edward? The police won't tell me anything. Is that allowed? We're not Russia or China. We don't hold people in secret. Can you find him?'

'I've been suspended.'

'But you have contacts. Friends? Colleagues?'

*Most of whom are trying to forget I exist.*

'Have you tried his lawyer?' I ask.

'Helgarde isn't answering.'

'They could be together,' I say, trying to sound reassuring. 'But don't keep calling the police. It will only make things worse.'

'They searched the house,' she says, her voice breaking. 'They went through my things . . . very personal and sensitive items in my bedroom drawer.'

*More information than I need.*

'And they took my phone. How am I supposed to contact people?'

'You have a landline.'

'But I don't have anyone's number.'

*Is that a first-world problem or a digital-age problem?*

'They broke things,' she continues.

'Which can be fixed.'

'Why are you defending them?'

'I'm not. But this is how investigations work. Police gather evidence.'

'But we've done nothing wrong. Edward was with me all night. He can't have robbed the jewellery store. And what do I tell the others? I've had Mary and Poppy on the phone. They haven't heard from Daragh or Finbar.'

'Tell them not to worry.'

'That's not good enough. The detective asked about your car. I lied for you.'

'Shh,' I say, harshly, aware the police might be listening. 'I'll make some calls, OK?'

'Promise me.'

'Yes.'

'Say the words.'

'I promise.'

I end the call and grab my jacket from the coat hook near the front door, along with Henry's car keys.

'Where are you going?' he asks.

'To get some answers.'

'Maybe you should stay out of it.'

Spinning around, I kiss him hard on the lips, telling him to stay safe at work. And before he can close his arms, I'm out of the door and down the steps, getting into his car, which smells of old rugby socks and Lynx deodorant and the jelly tots he snacks on when he's driving.

Jordan Koenig of the NCA didn't give me her contact number or email. The last thing she said was that she'd be in touch. That's not good enough. I did as she asked and planted a listening device and a tracker.

I call the general number for the National Crime Agency and ask a receptionist to patch me through to Jordan Koenig's office.

'What is the reason for your call?' she asks.

'I'm assisting in an investigation.'

'And your name?'

'I'd rather not say.'

'I can't put you through unless I know your name.'

'Tell her it's Philomena McCarthy.'

'Pardon?'

'Philomena McCarthy.'

'Did you say *her*? Jordan Koenig is a man, not a woman.'

There is a long silence. I can hear myself breathing into my handset. The receptionist asks me again, the nature of my call.

'It doesn't matter,' I say, hanging up.

I go back over our first meeting. The woman flashed a warrant card in a leather wallet. I didn't look at it closely, but it looked genuine. It had her photograph and rank. She knew where I lived and about my schooling and my hobbies . . . my tattoos for God's sake.

I type the name Jordan Koenig into a search engine and the

first hit is for the NCA website. There is a page dedicated to the senior leadership team, but it doesn't include photographs. Next, I call up a story about Koenig attending an international security conference in Madrid. There is a photograph. The face that stares back at me is a man, in his late fifties with dark-rimmed glasses and short-cropped grey hair.

Trance-like, I steer Henry's car along Marney Road, heading north across the Thames into Chelsea where I slowly circle the streets, trying to remember the address, but all the mansion blocks look the same. Just when I think it's pointless, I come to a block that is more familiar than the others. The window boxes are bright with winter pansies of blue, mauve and pink. Opposite is a communal garden with an iron railing fence.

The building has an old-fashioned doorbell, with a button for each apartment. Koenig took me to the first floor, but I don't know the number. At that moment, the door opens and a cleaner appears. She's dressed in a blue smock apron and carrying a bag of rubbish to the bins, which are in an alcove beneath the front steps. Her long skirt is tucked into her belt to stop it dragging on the ground. I catch the heavy door before it closes.

She turns. 'Can I help you?'

'I'm visiting Jordan.'

'Who?'

'Jordan Koenig. She lives on the first floor.' I motion to the window above my head.

'That apartment belongs to Nigel,' she says.

'Nigel?'

'Nigel Aitkin – the actor. He's in Morocco filming.'

'When did he leave?'

'Two weeks ago.'

Her trolley is parked in the wood-panelled entrance hall. I look up to the stairwell.

'You clean for him?' I ask.

She nods.

'I work for the police. I think someone borrowed Nigel's apartment. If I could just look inside . . .'

'You can't do that.'

'It will only take a minute.'

'You're not in uniform.'

'Not today. Are these the keys?' A set is hanging on the handle of the trolley.

I take them and jog up the stairs. She protests and follows but more slowly. By the time she reaches the landing, I've unlocked the door and stepped inside the darkened apartment. The heavy curtains are drawn and dustsheets are draped over some of the furniture. I recognise the sofa and the paintings and the ornate desk.

'You can't be in here,' says the cleaner.

Ignoring her, I cross the drawing room to the desk and open the drawers, which are empty.

I was here. I sat on that sofa. She offered me tea. She gave me the silver case.

'I met a woman here,' I say. 'She said her name was Jordan Koenig. She was in her mid-forties, tall and slim and well dressed.'

'Is she an actress?'

'I hope not,' I mutter.

'You must have the wrong building.'

'No. This is it. Who else has a key?'

'Nigel, of course, and his sister who lives in Manchester, and I have mine.'

'Does Nigel ever rent the place out or allow friends to stay?'

'Never.'

I walk into the kitchen and find the teapot and teacups. The cleaner is growing more agitated. I apologise for upsetting her and make my way downstairs and outside where the day seems different. Darker. Colder.

The sense of betrayal is something I can taste and it makes me want to spit. I believed this woman. She offered me a job with the NCA – thirty pieces of silver to spy on my father. And I did as she asked because I wanted to think the worst of him. I hate him for what he's done to this family and I hate myself for not believing him and I grieve for what we had and what we've lost.

# 42

The door unlocks automatically. McCarthy gets to his feet, bracing his hands against the cell wall.

'Turn around,' says an officer, who snaps handcuffs around his wrists.

'Where am I going?'

'You're being released.'

Boots echo along the corridor. 'Give yer old lady one for me,' yells a voice from a neighbouring cell. Another shouts, 'Tell Stacey I'm sorry.'

They reach the charge room. 'Sit there,' says the officer, shoving him towards a bench seat. McCarthy does as he's instructed. He doesn't hold a grudge against the officer, who is only doing his job. His animosity is not personal – it is cultural – a mentality created by decades of feeling under threat from hostile forces. This attitude is not taught or written down or codified. It emerges from the work, as police come to see the world as a profoundly dangerous place and the only way to survive is to dominate the people they are supposed to protect.

'What about my brothers?' McCarthy asks, only to be ignored.

He doesn't want to be released if Finbar and Daragh are still in custody. They have already sacrificed enough for him. Along with Clifton, they spent a decade in prison, enduring the shitty food and violence and boredom, while McCarthy got to sleep in his own bed, eat at nice restaurants and raise his daughter.

Since then, McCarthy had strived to repay their loyalty and sacrifice by making them richer than any of them could ever have dreamed. Now an outsider is trying to take it all away from them; a brutal psychopath, who is willing to poison McCarthy's wife and stalk his only child.

McCarthy looks up when Russell Kemp-Lowe is led into the charge room.

'What's he doing here?' he asks, sensing a trap.

Kemp-Lowe is told to sit. The jeweller hesitates, eyes wide, wanting to run. They're together, sitting as far apart as physically possible without falling off the bench.

'I didn't tell them anything,' mutters Russell.

'Shut up!' whispers McCarthy.

'I swear. Nothing.'

'Shut the fuck up!'

McCarthy considers the situation. This is either a mistake, or Keegan is playing mind games. There is a CCTV camera in the corner of the ceiling. He can smell the sweat and body odour coming off the jeweller, whose knee is bouncing up and down.

The officers are going about their work, seeming to ignore them. McCarthy shuffles along the bench, closer to Kemp-Lowe.

'Don't hurt me.'

'I'm not touching you,' whispers McCarthy. 'I'm going to ask you some questions. If the answer is yes, I want you to tap your right foot. If the answer is no, tap your left foot. If you don't know, do nothing. Understand?'

Kemp-Lowe nods. 'Right for yes, left for no.'

'I met a guy the other day, a one-eyed geezer, who calls himself the Wrestler. You know him?'

Kemp-Lowe looks at him blankly and taps his left foot.

'He's Bulgarian. Mad as a March hare. I think he robbed your store and murdered your wife. Did you know he was coming?'

Another tap. Same foot.

'What about Caitlin?'

Nothing.

'What about her brother, Noah? Is he involved?'

Kemp-Lowe doesn't react.

'Did you tell either of them about the diamonds?'

Right foot.

'Noah?'

Left foot.

'Caitlin?'

Right foot.

McCarthy's name is called. He stands and goes to the counter where his handcuffs are removed and he's given a plastic Ziploc bag containing his watch, belt, shoelaces and mobile phone.

As he leaves the charge room he glances back towards Russell, who is staring at the floor, unsure of what comes next. That's the problem with being alive. You have to keep thinking of what to do.

He may not have planned the robbery, but his gambling debts were most likely the catalyst. Was it a coincidence that Caitlin found Popov or did the Wrestler learn about the diamond investments and money-laundering some other way?

Knowing the answer won't change the past, but it could change the future.

# 43

Detective Sergeant O'Neil knocks on Keegan's open door. He pauses as though waiting for permission to enter. Keegan waves him in.

'We've had a call from a jeweller in Chelsea,' says O'Neil. 'Someone is trying to flog a single earring, a diamond cluster. It could be the one Caitlin Kemp-Lowe was wearing on the night she died.'

'Who?'

'Some young guy. The jeweller tried to keep him talking, but he got spooked and took off.'

'CCTV?'

'I've sent a car to pick it up.'

'No. I want to talk to the jeweller.'

Keegan grabs his coat. He wants to be out of the office, doing something active. The daily grind of a murder investigation is more bearable if the task force keeps moving, gathering information, chipping away at the problem. Sometimes it feels like they're building the mountain even as they're climbing it, never able to see further than the rock face.

The jewellery store is in Duke of York Square just off King's Road, in an area crowded with shoppers, sightseers and tourists. The manager is in his forties wearing Italian loafers without socks and a three-piece suit that is a size too small with no pockets to ruin the lines. His name is Arnoldo, his accent is Italian and he has a moustache that curls like a bass clef on each of his cheeks.

'Didn't you think it was odd that he only had one earring?' asks Keegan.

'He told me that his mother had lost the other one. I took one look and I knew it was special.'

'How?'

Arnoldo opens a hardcover book full of photographs of jewellery. 'Have you heard of Harry Winston?'

'No.'

'He is a famous jewellery designer. Legendary. Dead now.' He points to a photograph of similar-looking earrings. 'This is one of his designs.'

'Expensive?'

'That depends on what you regard as being expensive.'

'Did this boy know it was valuable?'

'I don't think so. He said the earrings were a wedding present, but his parents had divorced.' Arnoldo opens a laptop on his desk. 'This is from our CCTV feed.'

The footage shows a young man entering the store. He looks like a bicycle courier in Lycra leggings and a top. He removes his bike helmet and browses at the display cases.

'Had you ever seen him before?' asks Keegan.

'Earlier. Outside. He was walking back and forth, talking to someone on his phone. When he came inside, I knew he wasn't a buyer.'

The CCTV footage shows the cyclist moving around the store. He has an angular face and sinewy body, with shoulder-length hair pulled back into a ponytail. Eventually, he approaches a shop assistant. Arnoldo is summoned. The cyclist shows him the earring. Arnoldo displays it on a square of silken cloth, using an eyeglass and a bright light to examine the piece.

'I told him the earring was very distinctive,' says Arnoldo. 'I said I would have to check a catalogue to get a price. That's when I went to the office and phoned the police.'

'You did the right thing.'

The footage shows Arnoldo leaving the counter and returning again.

'I offered him a thousand pounds, but said I needed permission from my boss before I handed over any cash. If he could wait fifteen minutes. He said he'd take five hundred if I gave him the money straight away. I said I couldn't do that and suggested he leave the earring and come back, but he got anxious and left.'

'On foot?'

'On his bike. I asked my assistant to follow him.'

'I couldn't keep up,' says his colleague. 'He was up out of the saddle, pedalling hard.'

Something about that phrase triggers a memory for Keegan. Someone else had used it recently. It was in a statement. Philomena McCarthy had mentioned a cyclist coming out of a side road on the night she found the little girl.

He thanks the manager and leaves the store, radioing control. 'I need an address for Philomena McCarthy.'

Moments later, the answer: 'Marney Road, Clapham Common.'

He turns to the driver. 'Let's go.'

# 44

Whenever I park Henry's car in Marney Road, I avoid the trees because he complains about the fruiting balls and fallen leaves that collect in the air vents. He takes better care of his car than I do mine. He likes machines and gadgets – the way they automatically respond when he turns the key or presses a button. Machines don't have moods or sad days or 'that time of the month' (my words, not his). He's not uncaring or indifferent. Quite the opposite. He's extra nice to me when I'm cramping and feeling rotten. He just likes certainty rather than disorder or moodiness.

I'm almost at the front door when I hear the short burst of a police siren. The patrol car pulls over and DCI Keegan steps out, joining me on the steps.

'Can I come in?'

'You've already searched the place.'

'I have a question.'

'And I have a lawyer.'

The stand-off lasts several seconds. 'What is your question?' I ask.

'When you found Daisy Kemp-Lowe, you said you saw a cyclist.'

'He came out of a side street. I almost ran him over.'

'What street?'

'England's Lane, across Haverstock Hill and into Parkhill Road.'

'Did you see what he looked like?'

'He was travelling too quickly.'

'What about his clothes?'

'One of those Lycra cycling suits. Mainly black and white. Why?'

'Did it look like this?' asks Keegan, showing me his phone.

The CCTV footage shows a cyclist entering a jewellery shop and taking off his helmet. I recognise him, but not from that night. Instead, I picture him standing outside Kentish Town police station talking to Josie Sheldon.

'That's her boyfriend,' I say.

'Whose boyfriend?'

'The babysitter.'

Keegan doesn't reply. He's already moving, down the steps, heading towards the police car. I follow him, asking questions.

'What's he done? Why was he at a jewellery store?'

'He was trying to sell the missing earring.'

The details topple like dominoes, one into the other, a chain reaction of revelations and recriminations. Josie's boyfriend was at the house that night. He was there when Caitlin Kemp-Lowe took off her earrings. He was there when she died.

I chase after Keegan, open the rear door of the police car and get inside.

He turns. 'Get out!'

'No.'

'I could have you arrested.'

'You won't. I'm an important witness.'

'You don't even know where I'm going.'

'Josie Sheldon's place.'

Keegan sighs in frustration and signals the driver to carry on. On the journey he asks me about Josie and the man I saw outside the nick. They were arguing at first, but then they kissed.

Thirty minutes later, we reach Kilburn. I used to come here a lot as a teenager, watching dodgy pub bands in dodgy pubs.

By then I was living in Camden with my mother, who was working six days a week because she refused to accept a penny in child support from my father. The wages of sin.

Kilburn has changed since then. It's now a mix of upmarket and down-at-heel, renovated and unrenovated, middle class and working class. One patch of the High Street has fashion boutiques, specialist grocers and patisserie cafés, while a block further on you'll find burger bars, kebab shops and bookmakers.

Josie Sheldon lives near the eastern boundary in a four-storey house with a loft conversion. Music is blaring from inside. Techno. The beat rattles the windows.

Two other police cars pull up. Four detectives. Keegan tells me to stay in the car, but I'm already on the footpath. I hang back at the front gate.

He knocks. After a long wait, a young woman opens the door. She's wearing a pyjama top and a pair of cotton briefs. A tattoo peeps from beneath the waistband. She looks at his warrant card.

'I'm looking for Hugo Desai and Josie Sheldon,' he says.

'They're upstairs.'

She doesn't move.

'Perhaps you could get them,' says Keegan.

She sighs and pouts and pirouettes, flouncing down the hallway to the stairs, where she yells, 'Hugo? Josie? The cops are here.'

There is a bumping sound and a mumbled reply, although it's hard to hear anything over the music. The girl returns and leans against the wall, picking at her nail polish.

'Can we wait inside?' asks Keegan, shouting to be heard.

'The place is a mess,' she replies, with a patronising smile. 'We had a few people over last night.'

Keegan looks past her, along the hallway. There are empty bottles and cans, overflowing ashtrays and grease-stained pizza boxes on a table. A pair of bare feet stick out from a blanket on a sofa.

'What did the neighbours say?' he asks.

'That is our neighbour,' she says casually. 'He came around to complain and stayed.'

Minutes tick by. I can see Keegan growing annoyed. Josie Sheldon appears, hungover and pale, with her hair newly brushed.

'Where is your boyfriend?' asks Keegan.

'Who?'

'Hugo Desai.'

'Oh, he left early.'

Keegan motions to the bicycle chained to the railing fence outside. 'Is that his?'

'He took the train.'

'Where did he go?'

'To his job?'

'I thought he was an actor.'

'He also works as a barista.'

The music stops at the end of a track. In the brief respite, I hear the sound of something falling upstairs. Keegan hears it too.

'Around the back,' he yells, pushing past Josie, heading for the stairs.

As he reaches for the banister, I see a figure flash past the kitchen window, dropping from an upper floor into the rear garden. By the time I reach the kitchen I see Hugo Desai belly-rolling over the rear fence into the neighbouring garden. Keegan does the same with none of the athleticism or grace.

Other detectives are following, but I return outside, looking for a way to cut Hugo off. I run along the street until I find a path that traverses two houses, emerging on a different road. Hugo and Keegan are eighty yards ahead of me. Hugo is wearing track pants and sweatshirt and trainers. He sprints along a road and jumps a low hedge as he turns the next corner. Keegan is losing ground.

Giving chase, I reach the intersection and notice a work crew digging up one side of the road. A mound of red clay and broken tarmac flanks a ditch where new pipes are stacked, end-to-end, ready to be laid. Keegan yells and one of the workers tries to tackle Hugo, but the whippet-like young man sidesteps him easily. A second road worker crouches like a rugby player, going in for the tackle, but Hugo switches direction and leaps the mound of clay. Keegan does the same but misjudges the width of the trench. Gravity does the rest and he crashes into the muddy hole.

Hugo pauses to watch or gloat and I'm on him, kicking his legs out and swinging him over my hip, dropping him face down to the road. I kneel on his neck and twist his arm behind his back.

'Move and I'll break it,' I say calmly.

He stays quiet.

The workmen help Keegan out of the trench. He is covered in foul-smelling mud that clings to his clothes and skin. Spitting out a gob of filthy water, he wipes his eyes and holds his arms away from his body, as though frightened of touching himself.

'I told you to stay in the car,' he says.

'I made a citizen's arrest.'

Other detectives arrive. One of them handcuffs Hugo and reads him his rights.

Keegan is walking gingerly along the road, towards the police cars, but nobody will take him home until he's hosed down.

'Where are you going?' I ask.

'To get a hot shower.'

# 45

McCarthy steps out of Kentish Town police station and buttons up his overcoat, raising his face to the sky, searching for the sun behind the clouds. He whistles to a passing cab, a sound so piercing that every head turns towards him. The cab does a U-turn. McCarthy gets inside.

'Canning Town. The Hope Island site.'

The Indian driver has colourful decorations across the dashboard made from tinsel, beads and tassels. At the centre is a photograph of Ganesha, the elephant-headed god, who brings good luck.

McCarthy lowers a window, wanting to feel the air, but there's nothing particularly clean or invigorating about what he's breathing. Two hundred years of industrialisation have left a permanent haze across London, a cataract that steals distance and blurs the edges of buildings.

He turns on his phone, which pings with messages. Finbar and Daragh have been released. He sends them each a coded text, wanting a meeting. He chooses the site office at Hope Island because the workmen will have gone home by now and the place will be quiet.

After paying the driver, he crosses the road, expecting to find security guards at the entrance to the construction site. Instead, the gates are open. He walks unchallenged onto the site, heading for the portacabin office, which is made of prefabricated wood and metal. The muddy road is lined with shipping containers full of equipment and building supplies, alongside earth-moving machinery and pyramids of concrete pipes.

When he reaches the portacabin, he finds the door open and the office empty. Trashed. The place smells of piss and vomit and faeces, and the floor is littered with used needles, scorched foil, bloody tourniquets and putrid bottles of bong water.

He phones the foreman, Mohsin Ali. He answers, somewhere noisy, shouting to be heard. 'Mr McCarthy, I've been trying to reach you.'

'I'm on site. There's nobody here.'

Mohsin is on a train platform. He goes somewhere quieter. McCarthy waits.

'I left you messages,' says the foreman.

'I was indisposed. What happened?'

'The men weren't paid.'

'What do you mean?'

'No wages.'

'The payments are automatic.'

'They didn't arrive and some slick bird showed up and said the banks had shut you down. Said you were bankrupt. She told everyone to go home. I tried to call you. Left messages. I couldn't get hold of you or Clifton.'

McCarthy checks his messages. He has at least five from Mohsin and others from contractors, tradesmen and union delegates.

'I had a mutiny on my hands. It was all I could do to stop 'em looting the place,' says Mohsin.

McCarthy can't understand what happened. Clifton handles the payroll and there should be plenty of money to cover wages up until Christmas. Either someone has drained the account or the bank has withheld the payments deliberately.

'I'll sort it out,' he says.

'When?' asks Mohsin. 'My guys have mortgages to pay and mouths to feed.'

'By Monday. You have my word.'

Finbar is first to arrive. He's carrying two six-packs of beer, a bottle of whisky and a Sainsbury's bag full of snacks. He looks at the devastation. 'What the fuck happened?'

'The workers weren't paid and walked off. Junkies or squatters did the rest.'

'Are we short?'

'No. This is bank fuckery. We had enough to get us through until Christmas.'

McCarthy is still checking his messages. He has two missed calls from Carmichael at the bank. One of them is a voicemail. On speaker:

*Mr McCarthy. You're not answering my emails or my calls. The loan department is pressing me for a decision on the partnership offer. If you refuse to accept the deal, we will have no choice but to recall your loans. I need a decision by tomorrow morning. Either you pay your arrears, accept the offer, or we call in an administrator.*

'We missed the deadline,' says Finbar.

McCarthy doesn't respond. Clearly, this whole shitshow had been orchestrated – the arrests, the non-payment of wages, the walkout. Somebody knew the brothers couldn't respond if they were banged up.

Daragh is the last to arrive, already in a foul mood because of the prison stink on his clothes. Plonking himself down in a swivel chair, he opens a can of bitter and swallows it without pausing.

'We were better off 'ijacking trucks and flogging merch,' he says. 'You can't trust bankers. Bunch of James Blunts.'

McCarthy doesn't disagree.

'We've been set up,' he says. 'This is down to Popov and the banks. Maybe the police are part of it too.'

'Are we bankrupt?' asks Daragh.

'No. We're illiquid.'

'I dunno what that means.'

'It's like owning a Rolls-Royce but not having the readies to fill the tank,' says Finbar. 'Where is Clifton? Shouldn't he be here?'

'He's running errands,' says McCarthy. 'Out of the country.'

'Strange fuckin' time to be away,' says Daragh. 'I fought he was looking for a bridging whatnot.'

'Nobody wants to lend to us,' says McCarthy.

'We're like lepers,' says Finbar.

'Man-U fans,' says Daragh.

McCarthy has been jotting numbers on a piece of paper, calculating how much money they need to cover wages for the month. It's close to three hundred thousand. Added to what he promised Popov, that's half a million.

'We need to raise the money ourselves,' he says. 'I know you have nest eggs. Rainy-day money. Well, it's raining now and I wouldn't ask if it wasn't urgent.'

Daragh speaks first. 'I got an offset account and I can take a mortgage 'oliday.'

'And I can borrow on the house, but not by Monday,' says Finbar. 'I got a couple of cars in the workshop that I can flog on the weekend. That might get us sixty.'

'I want you to sell my cars,' says McCarthy.

'Not the Jag,' says Daragh, in disbelief.

'The Jag. The Range Rover. The Bentley.'

'What are you gonna drive?'

'Constance has a car.'

'A fuckin' Prius.'

He turns to Finbar. 'Contact everyone who owes us. Don't take no for an answer.'

'You want me to squeeze 'em?' asks Daragh.

'Till they squeak.'

If his calculations are correct, McCarthy can get to half a mill, but not by Monday.

'Maybe we could rob a bank,' says Daragh.

'Banks don't hold that sort of cash any more,' says Finbar.

'What about an armoured truck? The gee-gees are racing at Kempton Park on Saturday.'

'We're not robbing a bank or an armoured truck,' says McCarthy. 'We don't do that shit any more. We're businessmen.'

'Yeah, we keep telling people that, but nobody believes us,' says Daragh.

'The filth should be looking at Popov and his goons. Not us,' says Finbar. 'Why not give 'em a name?'

'Because we don't grass people up,' says Daragh. 'We fuck 'em up. Ain't that right, Eddie?'

McCarthy has a thought. 'When I met with Popov, there was a blond guy with a Rolex.'

'Popov's food taster,' says Daragh. 'What about 'im?'

'He had a tattoo on his forearm. The police showed me a drawing of the same tattoo.'

'Yeah, me too,' says Finbar.

'Get me his name,' says McCarthy. 'Find out everything you can about him, but do it quietly, OK?' He's looking at Daragh. 'No squeezing.'

Daragh leans closer. 'You got a plan.'

'Half a plan.'

A rumbling sound interrupts them, a truck engine, getting closer. When it hits the perimeter fence it doesn't stop. The brothers run outside as the cement truck rolls past them in first gear, headlights blazing, nobody at the wheel. Ahead, directly in its path, is a metal cage housing gas cylinders and hazardous liquids for the construction site. High above the cage is a jib crane that reaches into the night sky alongside a partially built skyscraper.

McCarthy is moving, running. He leaps onto the side-step of the truck and pulls himself up, using the wing mirror as a handhold. A brick has been taped to the accelerator and a rope is wrapped around the steering wheel, holding it steady. He tries the door. Locked.

'Don't risk it,' yells Daragh.

McCarthy jumps off the running board, and searches for something to smash the window. He picks up a metal bar from a pile of scrap and returns to the truck, which is rolling through puddles, relentlessly rumbling forward. Two empty drums disappear under the wheels and emerge crushed.

The metal bar bounces off the window. He tries again, harder this time. The glass shatters and punches inwards. He clears the frame and unlocks the door, pulling it open. He's behind the wheel, reaching for the ignition, but the key has been snapped off. He pumps at the brakes. Nothing.

Daragh and Finbar are screaming at him, telling him to jump, picturing the explosion and a fireball engulfing the half-finished building, bringing down the crane like a demolished chimney, collapsing in on itself.

McCarthy presses the clutch and takes the truck out of gear, before trying the handbrake. Nothing. He bends and reaches into the footwell. The rope is wrapped around the brake pedal and looped twice through the spokes of the steering wheel. Twisting his body at an odd angle, feeling his back spasm, he gets both hands to the brake and pulls the rope free.

Wrenching the wheel sideways, he changes the truck's direction. The front bumper clips the metal cage, crushing one corner. Canisters topple from the shelves, bouncing and clanging as they collide, but there's no explosion, no fire. Ten yards further on, the truck hits a concrete pillar, one of the foundations, and the entire building vibrates like a struck tuning fork.

Daragh and Finbar wrench open the door. McCarthy is sitting in the driver's seat, slumped forward over the steering wheel.

'You are a mad cunt,' says Daragh. 'The whole place could have gone up.'

'My back,' moans McCarthy, bent over.

'Yeah, we had your back,' says Finbar.

'No. I can't move.'

'You wanna see a doctor?'

'Nah. Get me home.'

# 46

Keegan has showered and changed, having scrubbed at his skin until it feels raw and painful to touch. Now back at Kentish Town police station, he ignores the smirks and muted laughter of colleagues. Someone has pinned a photograph to a white-board. It shows him being dragged out of the trench, covered in mud, looking like a morose Terracotta Warrior.

Hugo Desai is in Interview Room 1. He has the same duty solicitor that looked after Noah Kemp-Lowe. Sherwin is wearing an identical rumpled suit and sauce-stained tie. Maybe he only has one of everything.

'My client wishes to cooperate fully and to make amends,' he says in a nasally voice, his head full of cold.

'Amends for what?' asks Keegan.

'Running from the police. He has offered to have your clothes dry-cleaned.'

'They're being burned.'

Sherwin looks at Hugo. 'He will replace them.'

'That won't be necessary. Your client seemed rather reluctant to give police his fingerprints and DNA, which are required by law upon arrest. Any particular reason?'

'He was confused and upset,' says Sherwin. 'It wasn't an act of defiance.'

'Where's Josie?' asks Hugo. 'Can I talk to her?'

'No,' says Keegan.

'But I need to speak to her . . . to explain.'

Hugo looks at his solicitor, hoping for help, but Sherwin doesn't respond.

'We ran your name through the police national computer,' says Keegan. 'You have a bit of a history, Hugo. Vandalism. Trespass. Criminal damage.'

'Youthful indiscretions,' says Sherwin. 'Climate activism. Anti-war protests. No convictions were recorded.'

Keegan takes a small, sealed plastic evidence bag from his pocket. Inside is the single lotus-cluster earring that the police retrieved from Hugo Desai's bedroom, hidden in his girlfriend's jewellery box. Keegan holds it up to the light.

'Who does it belong to?' he asks.

'That woman who got killed.'

'Caitlin Kemp-Lowe?'

'Yeah. She gave the earring to Josie.'

'Why would she give Josie a single earring?'

'As a present.'

'One earring?'

'Yeah, I know it's weird but we figured it was probably fake, you know.'

'Which is why you wanted to have it valued?'

'Yeah.' He looks from face to face, desperate to be believed.

Keegan to Sherwin. 'You said your client was going to co-operate.'

The solicitor leans close to Hugo and whispers in his ear.

Hugo looks affronted. 'I am. It's the truth.'

'How often had you been to the house in Antrim Road?' asks Keegan.

'Once or twice when Josie was babysitting.'

'What about the last time Josie worked there?'

'No.'

'So, we're not going to find your semen on the bedspread, or on Caitlin Kemp-Lowe's dressing gown?'

Hugo pauses and lowers his eyes. Thinking. 'We did it on

the bed. Just the once. No harm meant.'

'When you say you did it . . . ?'

'Bumped uglies. Did the dirty. Hid the sausage . . . Josie gets off on that sort of thing.'

'Having sex in someone else's bed?'

Hugo grins. 'Yeah.'

'So just to be clear, you were at the house on the night that Caitlin Kemp-Lowe was murdered?'

'No. No. Yeah. I mean, for a bit. I dropped round to see Josie.'

'What time did you arrive?'

'About eight.'

'How did you get inside the house without the security cameras picking you up?'

'I came through the rear gate. Josie knows where they keep the key.'

'Where was Daisy?'

'Asleep. I'm not a pervert. I wouldn't do it with a kid around.'

'What time did you leave the house?' asks Keegan.

'About ten o'clock.'

'Where did you go?'

'Home.'

'Can anyone vouch for that?'

'Not until Josie got home.'

'Two police officers saw you riding your bike away from Antrim Road at three o'clock in the morning. They almost ran you down.'

'They're mistaken.'

'Is that what Josie is going to tell us?'

'Yeah.'

'You seem very confident that she'll lie for you.' Keegan leans closer. 'I think you were in the house when Russell and Caitlin Kemp-Lowe came home that night. They were early. Unexpected.'

'No.'

'You were trapped there when Josie was driven home by Russell Kemp-Lowe.'

'No.'

'Where were you hiding, Hugo?'

'Nowhere.'

Keegan turns off the tape and gets to his feet, motioning for DS Hobson to follow him.

'Is that it?' asks Hugo, looking from face to face.

'We're going next door to talk to Josie,' says Keegan. 'We'll see if your stories match. I don't expect they will. And if I find out you're lying, I'll charge you with obstructing police, robbery, handling stolen goods, and being an accessory to murder.'

'I didn't kill anyone,' says Hugo, whose cockiness has evaporated.

Sherwin has already turned on his phone to check his messages.

Interview Room 2 is painted in the same pastel shades, with a similar table and chairs, as well as a large display mirror that hides a viewing room and cameras.

Josie gets to her feet when Keegan enters with Hobson. Her voice rises an octave.

'Please don't tell my parents I'm here. My father thinks anyone who is arrested must have done something wrong. They're guilty until proven innocent.'

'Sounds like my father,' says Hobson.

'Mine is the chairman of the local Conservative Association.'

'Mine voted for Brexit.'

'What is this – a competition?' says Keegan.

He takes a seat. 'Do you want a lawyer present?'

Josie shakes her head.

For the tape: 'The suspect has waived her right to legal representation but can change her mind at any time.'

The word 'suspect' makes Josie flinch. 'Where is Hugo?'

'Next door. He says that Caitlin gave you the earring as a gift.'

'Yes.'

'Why didn't you mention it in your earlier statement?'

'It slipped my mind.'

'Did Hugo ever come to the house when you were baby-sitting?'

'Caitlin didn't allow that.'

'That's not answering my question.'

She pauses. 'What did Hugo tell you?'

'I'm asking you.'

There is a long silence. Keegan decides to press her. 'Let me tell you how forensic science places someone at a crime scene. It could be their fingerprints, or saliva, or skin cells, or semen . . .'

Josie tugs at the sleeves of her sweatshirt. A bra strap appears, white against her skin.

'For instance, we found an envelope inside a locked safe and your thumbprint was on the flap. We also found a deleted photograph on your phone of a document that was stored in that safe. Care to explain?'

'I didn't take anything.'

'That wasn't my question.'

She pauses, looking more and more like a trapped rat scur-rying between the corners of a room. Keegan feels sorry for her, an unusual feeling. Normally, he is quite ruthless when he's holding a winning hand.

'I know you sent the image to Noah Kemp-Lowe,' he says. 'My question is why?'

'He asked me to.'

'You broke into a safe because you were asked?'

'No. It's not what you think . . . I mean.'

'How did you get the combination?'

'He gave it to me.'

'Noah Kemp-Lowe?'

'Yes.'

'Why?'

'He said his father was leaving everything to Caitlin, but she'd promised to have him included in the will. He didn't trust Caitlin to keep her end of the bargain.'

'What was his end of the bargain?'

'I don't know.'

Keegan has a mocking laugh.

'I'm telling you the truth,' says Josie. 'Noah wanted me to open the safe and take a photograph of the will. He gave me two hundred quid.'

'You're a right little grifter, aren't you?' says Hobson.

'I don't know what that means.'

'A petty criminal. A chancer.'

Josie doesn't respond but looks miserable.

Keegan leans closer. 'You're in pretty deep, Josie. Way over your head. A woman is dead and you were involved.'

'No! No!'

'Was your boyfriend at the house that Friday evening?'

'Yes, but Hugo had nothing to do with what happened. He did nothing wrong.'

'When did he arrive?'

'After I put Daisy to bed I opened the rear gate.'

'You knew about the cameras?'

She nods, looking wretched.

'What did you do?'

'We ordered a pizza and watched some TV.'

'Is that all?'

Her face twists into a grimace. 'We had sex.'

'Where?'

'In the main bedroom.'

'You wore Caitlin's dressing gown?'

'Yes.' Josie is looking at her hands and her feet, anywhere but at the detectives. 'I don't want Hugo getting into trouble.'

'He's a grown man. He can look after himself.'

Her voice wavers. 'We were in the bedroom, fooling around, when I heard their voices and the key in the door. Hugo wanted to climb out of the window, but he couldn't get it open. I told him to hide.'

'Where?'

'He tried the walk-in wardrobe, but I knew Caitlin would come upstairs to get changed. I pushed him into another bedroom. I thought if I could distract them, keep them busy, he could sneak out.'

'Why not just tell them?'

'We'd been caught before. Hugo drank some of Russell's Scotch and watered it down. He also took a leather jacket.'

'Stole it?'

'Borrowed it. It was returned. I didn't know about the security cameras – not then. They saw Hugo coming and going and told me it could never happen again.'

'What happened when you went downstairs?'

'I could tell that Caitlin and Russell had been arguing. They weren't talking. Caitlin went straight upstairs to change. Russell said he'd take me home. I tried to delay things – offering to make them a hot chocolate, or herbal tea, but he was in a hurry to leave.'

'Did you go back upstairs?'

'No.'

'You left Hugo?'

'I didn't know what else to do. I thought he could sneak out after Caitlin had gone to bed.'

'Is that what happened?'

Josie nods without conviction, squeezing her hands between her thighs, rocking back and forth.

'How did he get out?'

'I don't know.'

'He didn't tell you?'

'No.'

Keegan pictures the scene – Caitlin taking off her cocktail dress and her jewellery. Putting on her nightdress. She used make-up wipes to clean her face and brushed her teeth. She pulled down the bedspread. She did everything you'd expect of someone getting ready for bed. Meanwhile, Russell drove Josie home.

'Is that why you kept Mr Kemp-Lowe talking when he reached your place?'

'I wanted to give Caitlin time to fall asleep and for Hugo to escape.'

'Listen to me, Josie. I want you to understand what I'm saying. You're in a lot of trouble.'

'But I did nothing wrong.'

'Caitlin didn't give you that earring.'

'She did.'

'No. You told us she came home and went straight upstairs. By the time she took off her jewellery, you'd gone. She had no opportunity to give you a gift. And why give you one earring and not the other? No jury is going to believe your story – not when you've been sleeping with her husband.'

The shock registers on Josie's face.

'We know about the five thousand pounds that was paid into your account. And we found traces of Russell Kemp-Lowe's semen on the front seat of his car.'

Josie lowers her eyes, unable to look at him.

'Were you having an affair with Russell Kemp-Lowe?' asks Keegan.

'It wasn't sex,' she says defensively. 'No kissing or other stuff. He said he could help my career. He had contacts in TV and film.'

'And he wanted something in return,' says Hobson.

Josie nods. 'Hugo said it was an opportunity. He told me exactly what to say and do – how to get him off, you know.' She raises a hand and waggles her fingers.

'You blackmailed him.'

'No. It wasn't like that. He helped me.'

'He paid you five thousand pounds to keep quiet.'

'That was Hugo's idea. I didn't . . . I shouldn't . . .' She goes quiet.

'Did his wife know?'

'She thought the money was to pay off my credit card,' says Josie.

'How did Hugo get the earring?'

'He said it was lying on the floor and he picked it up. It was a stupid, spur of the moment thing.'

'He was there during the home invasion?'

'Yes.'

'Did he see them . . . hear them?'

'He heard their voices. I wanted him to go to the police, I begged him, but he said that you wouldn't believe him – not with his history.'

'How did he get out of the house?'

'When it was quiet, he crept downstairs. The men had gone. He opened the patio doors and picked up his bike and rode home. I was beside myself, worrying about him.'

'He must have seen Caitlin Kemp-Lowe.'

'She was tied to a chair. He tried to help her, but she told him to leave. She said he was ruining everything.'

'Those words?'

'Yes.'

Keegan looks at Hobson, aware of the subtext.

'Why didn't he call the police?'

'Because he was trespassing and because he was scared. That's why he ran. We left London the next morning.'

'And pretended nothing had happened.'

'We didn't know . . . we didn't . . .'

Her voice breaks and her shoulders shake. Like a good actress, she is crying on cue.

# 47

Constance answers the intercom.

'It's me,' I say.

'And who is me?' she asks, knowing full well because she can see me on the camera.

I smile through gritted teeth. 'Philomena. I've come to pick up my car.'

The electronic gates begin to open. The cab driver who drove me from Dartford Station has been hanging around, hoping for a return fare. Now he waves goodbye and I enter the gates, following the driveway on foot. My car is still parked in the turning circle, next to the waterless fountain, which is dotted with fallen leaves.

Constance greets me at the door. Her cheek brushes mine. I smell her perfume and notice the worry lines forming around her eyes. Maybe she's finally starting to look her age, even if that age is ridiculously young. Am I betraying the sisterhood by having that thought? I can never tell.

'Is Daddy home?'

'He's in bed. He hurt his back.'

'Where? Did the police—?'

'He was getting out of a truck, according to Daragh. The boys brought him home and carried him upstairs. I've dosed him up on painkillers and given him a hot-water bottle.'

'What about a doctor?'

'He doesn't want one.'

'Can I talk to him?'

'If he's awake, but please don't upset him.'

For a moment I think her perfect veneer is going to crack because she's close to tears.

'Is something wrong?' I ask.

'Edward won't talk to me but I know something is wrong. The boys took his cars. The red Jag and the Bentley. I think they're going to sell them.'

'Why?'

'For money, obviously, but I don't know the reason.'

I climb the stairs and cross the first landing, knocking softly, knuckles on wood. He answers. The darkened room is dominated by a king-sized four-poster bed. Daddy is propped up on three pillows, wearing a dressing gown and slippers. He smiles through the pain or the drugs.

The dark shadows beneath his eyes have a permanency that I don't remember, and the wrinkles that are etched across his forehead seem deeper and more enduring.

'Hey, how are you?' I ask.

'I'm crocked. Damn back. It's given me gyp since I was your age.'

'How did it happen?'

'Carelessness.'

'Can I get you something? A cup of tea? A sandwich?'

'Morphine. Opiates. Heroin.'

'You'd never use heroin.'

'No, but I fancy trying it at least once before I die.'

'Really?'

'Just to see what all the fuss is about. I figure I'll wait until I'm close to the end, when it doesn't matter, and I'll give it a whirl.'

'I should try it too,' I say.

'Over my dead body.'

He laughs and it hurts. Serves him right. 'How are Daragh and Finbar?' I ask.

'Happy to be home.'

'Are you going to tell me about your relationship with Russell Kemp-Lowe?'

'You don't need to know that.'

'You said there were people who wanted to hurt you. Who are they?'

'Outsiders. Interlopers.'

'Are they following me?'

I see a spark in his eyes. 'Have you seen someone?'

'When I left the christening, there was someone in a car taking photographs of me.'

'Did you get the number?'

'No.'

'If you see them again, call me.'

I don't tell him about the mysterious Jordan Koenig with the fake address and warrant card because that would mean revealing details about what she asked me to do. Instead, I climb onto the bed and lie next to him, tucking my head against his shoulder, putting one arm across his chest, listening to his heartbeat. I remember doing this as a little girl, when he'd read me bedtime stories. He was good at accents and painting word pictures that took me from Beatrix Potter to Harry Potter and beyond. Even when I learned to read, I used to beg him to tell me one of his own stories. I wanted to hear how he met my mother and how they fell in love and how I was almost born in the back of a car because my head suddenly popped out when they were ten minutes from the hospital.

When I hear his breathing change and I know he's asleep, I creep out of the bedroom and down the stairs. Constance is somewhere in the house, perhaps in the kitchen. I head directly to the library, which looks different today. Everything is slightly out of place. Books and photographs and paintings have been moved during the search. Daddy's computer has been taken.

Scanning the shelves, I find the Gore Vidal novel and Ben Macintyre history of the SAS. The listening device has gone. I feather the pages, wondering if I could have placed it inside, but it's not here. I crouch and crawl beneath the desk, feeling for the USB stick that I dropped and left behind. Growing more desperate, I try to lift the desk, which is way too heavy. Bracing my legs, I slide it sideways, moving it half an inch away from the wall. I do it again and again, edging the desk across the floor. Now I have enough room to lie down and reach beneath the drawers. There's nothing there.

My heart sinks. The police must have found the devices. Either that, or my father did. I don't know what's worse. Will he blame me or assume that Keegan tried to bug his house?

'What are you doing?' asks Constance, standing in the doorway.

'I was looking for my car keys. I thought I left them here. They must be in the garage.'

'You've moved the desk.'

'I couldn't find them,' I say, as though it should be obvious.

'I've made a pot of tea.'

'Let me check the garage first.'

I step around her and out of the front door, walking quickly across the soft grass, remembering the last time I was here when I stripped off my clothes to make a point. I'm sure that story has been swapped among the gardeners.

Reaching the garage, I enter the side door. Two of Daddy's cars have gone, leaving only oil stains on the polished concrete. Sold. Is he having cashflow problems? Is that why he was doing deals with Russell Kemp-Lowe?

Daddy's oilskin jacket is hanging on the hook beside the door. I search the pockets, once, twice, but the tracker has gone.

As a child, I remember watching an old Disney animated movie called *Fantasia* that dated from the 1940s. One scene, in particular, disturbed me. Mickey Mouse plays a magician's apprentice, who steals his master's magic hat and casts a spell to make a broom do his chores. But the spell goes wrong and he raises a million brooms from the dead, causing an apocalyptic flood and tornado that nearly sucks Mickey into oblivion. I feel like that now. As though I've conjured up a million brooms, all marching towards me, carrying buckets of water that will drown me.

As I walk slowly back to the house, I call PC Rowan Cooper's mobile number. Coop answers in a hurried whisper. 'I'm not supposed to be talking to you.'

'What have they told you?'

'That you're under investigation for the jewellery robbery and the murder of that woman.'

'You were there, Coop. You know that's not true.'

He doesn't answer.

'Where are you now?' I ask.

'At work.'

'I need a favour.'

'No, no, I can't, Philomena. Don't ask me.'

'I haven't told you what it is.'

'I don't care. I've been interviewed twice by detectives and once by the DPS. They're out to get you, kid. They're not going to give up.'

'I know.'

There is a long pause. I can hear Coop breathing into his phone. Finally, he breaks. 'What is it?'

'I'm going to send you a photograph of a car – a dark-coloured Mercedes-AMG, top of the range, that was parked outside my house a few days ago. You'll be able to see the number plate. Can you trace it for me?'

'You know I can't do that.'

'I have reason to believe the car and the occupants were involved in the Hatton Garden robbery and the home invasion.'

'Tell the task force.'

'I will, but I need to be sure. Please, Coop.'

'OK, but if I do this, you'll owe me a favour,' he says.

'Anything.'

'Lose my number.'

# 48

Hugo Desai has spent the night in a police cell and is now eating his breakfast – a bacon and egg roll from a local café. He uses both hands, sucking brown sauce and runny yolk from his fingers.

Keegan is watching through the mirrored glass of the interview suite. You can tell a lot about a suspect by the way he eats and sleeps. The guilty snooze peacefully and tuck into their food with gusto because they have less to worry about; while the innocent toss and turn and lose their appetites because they have more to lose.

The idea that someone is innocent until proven guilty is one of the great myths that people hold to be true. It is supposed to be the golden thread that runs through the entire legal system – the foundation of a fair trial and safeguarding of human rights. In reality, the police operate on a presumption of guilt rather than one of innocence. From the moment they identify a prime suspect, every resource is focused on proving guilt, not innocence.

Keegan isn't a neutral observer or a disinterested party. He has a stake in solving this crime. It will further his career and reassure the community that the police are keeping the streets safe.

Hugo licks his fingers and wipes them with a paper serviette. Keegan can feel his skin crawling. He enters the interview room with DS Hobson and the duty solicitor.

'Did you sleep well, Hugo?' asks Sherwin.

'They kept the lights on all night.'

'A security precaution,' says Keegan.

'And the place stank.'

'I'll book you a room at the Savoy next time.'

Keegan turns on the recording equipment and announces those present.

'Before we begin, is there anything you'd like to add to what you told us yesterday?' he asks.

'Nope.'

'Your girlfriend, Josie Sheldon, says you were hiding upstairs when the couple came home from the charity dinner.'

'She's wrong.'

'And that you didn't return home until three in the morning.'

'No.'

'You're saying that Josie is lying?'

'She's mistaken.'

'About which bit?'

'All of it.'

Keegan sighs and leans back in his chair, studying Hugo and letting the silence weigh on his shoulders.

'You have a mobile phone.'

'Yeah. So?'

'The police can track phones using mobile towers. We triangulate the signals and can narrow down the location of a handset to within ten or fifteen yards. We have tracked your phone. We know you were at the house that night. We know what time you arrived and what time you left. And your phone says you were still at Antrim Road until three o'clock in the morning.'

A knock on the door interrupts the interview. A detective constable enters carrying a note, handing it to the DCI. Keegan reads the page, studying it for a moment before thanking her. The note is placed on the table and smoothed beneath his palms.

'The fingerprints you gave us yesterday – we've found a

match for them in an upstairs bathroom and on the window-sill in the main bedroom.'

'Like I said, me and Josie got a little frisky.'

'She said that you tried to get out of the window when the couple came home.'

'Nah. I wanted some fresh air.'

'When we found Caitlin Kemp-Lowe, she was tied to a chair and her mouth was taped, but you know that already.'

'No way, José.'

'You didn't see her?'

'Nope.'

'You didn't touch the packing tape that covered her mouth?'

Hugo's smugness evaporates.

Keegan holds up his thumb like an artist gauging proportions. 'That's all it takes, Hugo. One thumbprint. And it puts you in the kitchen with the murder victim.'

'No, no, no. I didn't hurt her.'

Sherwin interrupts. 'I'd like to consult with my client privately.'

'When he answers the question,' says Keegan.

Hugo's face twists through a range of emotions, before he gives a defeated sigh. 'OK, I was there, but I didn't kill her. She was alive when I left the house.'

'I think you'd better start at the beginning,' says Keegan. 'But do yourself a favour, Hugo, stop pissing on my leg. We know you killed Caitlin Kemp-Lowe. We just need to know why.'

'That's bullshit! I never touched her.'

'Clearly, you did.'

'OK. This is the truth, I swear. We were upstairs, me and Josie, when they came home. I tried to find a way out, but the windows were locked. Josie told me to hide. She went down-stairs and was gonna keep them busy in the kitchen, while I snuck out, but the old lady came straight up to the bedroom.'

'Caitlin Kemp-Lowe?'

'Yeah.'

'You saw her?'

'I heard her. She checked on Daisy and then went to the bedroom, but she left the door open and I couldn't risk sneaking past.'

'Where were you?'

'In the room opposite, hiding beneath a bed. I heard Josie leave with the sleazebag.'

'You pimped out your girlfriend so you could blackmail Russell Kemp-Lowe.'

'Once, OK? I wanted to go back for more but Josie felt sorry for the sleaze.'

'You heard Josie leave and then?'

'I waited, but Caitlin didn't go to bed. I heard her brushing her teeth and getting changed, but she didn't turn out the light, so I knew she was still awake. I waited and waited. Then I heard scuffling downstairs and Russell was yelling and Caitlin came out of the bedroom and told them to be quiet or they'd wake Daisy.'

'She didn't scream or try to call the police?'

'Nah.'

'Did she know they were coming?'

Hugo shrugs. 'I dunno.'

'You heard their voices?' asks Keegan.

'Yeah.'

'Did they have accents?'

'Russian maybe, or Hungarian. I looked over the banister and saw two of them.'

'What were they wearing?'

'Khaki trousers, black jackets. One of them had a gun tucked into his belt.'

'What sort of gun?'

'A pistol.'

'What about faces?'

'They were wearing masks – a zombie and the Joker. It was like something out of a horror movie.'

'What about your phone? You could have called the police.'

'I left it downstairs.'

'What happened then?'

'The little girl woke up. She almost saw me, but I think she was half asleep. She went down the stairs and frightened the shit out of them because the missus was yelling at them not to hurt her.'

'Caitlin Kemp-Lowe?'

'Yeah. I think they hit her because she cried out and called one of them a brute. I knew I had to get out of the house so I started trying all the other windows in the bedroom and bathroom. That's when two of them came upstairs – the Joker and the zombie. The zombie took Daisy back to bed and the Joker came into the bathroom because he needed to piss. I was standing in the tub, behind the shower screen. I could smell him, you know, his piss. He was standing in front of the mirror and he pulled up his mask.'

'You saw his face?'

'His reflection.'

'Describe him.'

'Your age, maybe. Dark hair, curly, turning grey.'

'How tall?'

'My height.'

'Eye colour?'

'He only had one of 'em.'

'What?'

'He had this eyepatch like a pirate, you know.' Hugo covers his right eye.

'Are you taking the mickey?'

'No. I swear. He was this close – from me to you. I was scared shitless. Trying not to breathe. If he'd seen me, I'd be dead. You don't mess with a one-eyed man.'

'What happened then?' asks Keegan.

'Both of them went back downstairs and I hid in the bedroom until I heard them leaving the house. Even after that, I waited until I was sure they were gone before I went downstairs.'

'When did you steal the earring?'

'It was on the floor of the main bedroom. I was going to put it back, but it sort of found its way into my pocket.'

Keegan doesn't react. 'How did you get out of the house?'

'Through the back door.'

'Through the kitchen?'

Hugo nods.

'You saw Mrs Kemp-Lowe?'

Hugo looks at Sherwin and back at the detectives. Sighs. Speaks.

'She was sitting in a chair, tied up, with tape over her mouth. She was shaking her head, trying to talk, so I took off the tape and she hissed at me to leave her alone. It was like I was doing something wrong. I thought maybe the men were coming back, so I scarpered. Got the fuck out of Dodge.'

'You left her there?'

'It's what she wanted.'

'You could have saved her,' says Keegan, his face full of contempt.

'She didn't *want* me to save her.'

'You could have called the police. You could have untied her.'

'I panicked.'

'You were frightened of a woman tied to a chair?'

'It wasn't like that.'

Hugo looks at Trisha Hobson, caring more about her opinion, perhaps because she's a woman and he doesn't want her thinking him a coward, but the sergeant gives him no comfort.

'I think you're still lying to us, Hugo,' says Keegan. 'I think you got trapped in the house, you stole the earring and came downstairs. You found Caitlin Kemp-Lowe in the kitchen and realised that she could identify you. That's when you panicked and put a plastic bag over her head and suffocated her.'

'What? What bag?'

'You killed her and ran away.'

Hugo rocks back and forth in his seat. 'That's bullshit! She was alive, I swear. She didn't *want* to be helped.'

Keegan and Hobson are alone in the interview room. The tapes and cameras are turned off. Hugo Desai is back in a holding cell.

O'Neil enters, grinning. 'You nailed the bastard. I'm buying the first round.'

'Bit early for the pub,' says Hobson.

'Oh, come on, let's celebrate. It's not every day you catch a killer.'

'We're not charging him,' says Keegan.

'What? Why?'

'Because I don't know if he killed her.'

'But his dabs are all over the gag. He had the motive and the opportunity and he lies every time he opens his mouth.'

Keegan doesn't answer. He's exhausted and wants to go back to his office and close the door and lower the blinds. Some people recharge by being around other people, feeding off their energy. Keegan is an introvert and needs quiet.

Maybe O'Neil is right and the murder is solved, but would the killer really be stupid enough to flog the earring? Hugo admitted touching the packing tape on Caitlin's mouth, but looked surprised when Keegan mentioned the plastic bag.

When Daisy left the house, she couldn't wake her mother. She said the bag was covering Caitlin's head. A five-year-old witness is unreliable, but she wouldn't make up a story like that. When PC McCarthy broke down the front door and entered the kitchen, there was no plastic bag.

When there is too much detail, it can be hard to see what's missing.

# 49

The media conference is scheduled for ten o'clock on Monday morning. Keegan is wearing his best suit and a shirt that took him fifteen minutes to iron because he's out of practice. Veronica did that sort of thing when they were still together, which could be another reason why she left him.

Keegan had often argued with her that there were 'men's chores' and 'women's chores' and that the demarcation lines added to their joint productivity. *Did he really say that? What a tool.* Veronica had disagreed, quite rightly, because her chores involved hours of laundry, cleaning, ironing, vacuuming and cooking, while he occasionally mowed the lawn, cleaned the gutters and took out the bins.

Arguments like this embarrass him now, particularly his excuses, which bordered on gaslighting, like when he tried to claim that picking up a takeaway curry counted as cooking, and that his doing the laundry might 'mess up' Veronica's system. Now it's too late to say he's sorry because she won't return his calls and she doesn't want him back.

Keegan is waiting for Assistant Commissioner Duckworth to arrive at Kentish Town police station. When his car pulls up outside, he opens the door and Duckworth emerges wearing his dress uniform, with every button and medal polished, and his name stitched into the fabric.

'Sorry I'm late, Brendan,' says Duckworth in a booming show of bonhomie. 'I lost track of time on my training run.'

'Training, sir?'

'I have a half marathon at the end of the month. Along the Thames to Hampton Court. Lovely course.'

He has the physique of a runner, thinks Keegan, like one of those Kenyan or Ethiopian athletes, who seem to float across the ground, ignoring gravity.

'They're waiting,' says Keegan, holding open the door. 'Would you like to take the lead?'

'No, I'll introduce you and let you do the talking.'

Reporters, photographers and camera operators have filled the conference room. Every lens and light is focused on the lectern and the large white screen, which displays the coat of arms of the Metropolitan Police Service.

Duckworth strides onto the stage. Keegan almost misses the last step and stumbles. He corrects himself but hears the laughter.

'Good morning and thank you for taking the time to attend this briefing,' says Duckworth. 'I am the assistant commissioner in charge of specialist operations and I am joined by DCI Brendan Keegan, who is the senior investigating officer running the task force.

'It has now been nine days since the murder of Caitlin Kemp-Lowe and the abduction of her husband. Let me first offer my heartfelt condolences to the family and friends of Mrs Kemp-Lowe and reassure them that solving this murder and robbery is a top priority.

'Brendan will brief you shortly, but first let me say that I'm aware of the media interest in this tragedy. I have seen the commentary and the criticisms of the investigation and Brendan will address those concerns today.'

Duckworth steps back and Keegan walks to the microphone. He also offers his condolences to the family, but his remarks sound nowhere near as polished or sincere.

'I'll begin by taking you through a timeline of events,' he says, hearing someone groaning. 'Some of this information has already been made public, but we are constantly adding to the

289

picture, filling in the blanks. At approximately eleven p.m. a week last Friday, three, possibly four masked men forced their way into a house in Antrim Road, Belsize Park, North London. The intruders were armed and wearing masks and dark clothing.

'At home at the time was Caitlin Kemp-Lowe, aged forty-five, her daughter, aged five, and her husband, Russell Kemp-Lowe, aged forty-eight. The intruders struck when Mr Kemp-Lowe was returning to the house, having dropped off his daughter's babysitter. The men forced their way into the house and held the couple hostage for nearly three hours.

'Shortly after two o'clock on Saturday morning, Russell Kemp-Lowe was taken in this van to his jewellery shop in Hatton Garden.' A CCTV still is projected onto the screen behind him. 'He last saw his wife tied to a chair in the couple's kitchen. He was told that if he cooperated, his family would be released unharmed.

'When the van arrived at Hatton Garden, Mr Kemp-Lowe was forced to open the jewellery store and the safe. Afterwards, he was made to put on a vest, which was wired to look like an improvised explosive device. The attackers left him in the store with a tilt switch on his lap.'

Not a single reporter is taking notes because Keegan has told them nothing they don't already know. He describes how the couple's daughter was found wandering the streets of Belsize Park and how Caitlin Kemp-Lowe was found dead in the kitchen of the house.

'How did she die?' asks a reporter.

'We're not revealing those details.' Keegan continues: 'We have more than forty detectives working for the task force and they have so far reviewed a thousand hours of CCTV and dashcam footage. We have door-knocked three hundred premises and taken more than a hundred statements. Every reasonable line of inquiry has been followed and we continue to ask for the public's help in identifying the perpetrators.'

A different reporter shouts, 'Who did you arrest yesterday?'

'A North London man is assisting us.'

'Is he part of the gang?'

'I cannot comment.'

'Why did you arrest Edward McCarthy?'

'Mr McCarthy and Russell Kemp-Lowe are known to each other. They attended the same charity dinner on the Friday evening.'

This triggers a barrage of fresh questions. 'Is he a suspect?' 'Did he kill Caitlin?' 'Why did you let him go?'

The noise level in the room rises. The reporters were expecting more – a new lead or revelation. Duckworth covers the microphone with his hand and whispers to Keegan, 'Give them something.'

'I want to keep my powder dry.'

'Until it blows up in your face.'

Keegan is torn between following orders and protecting Hugo Desai's identity. He turns back to the microphone. 'In the past twenty-four hours we have interviewed an eyewitness to the home invasion. He has given us a description of one of the intruders and we are seeking the public's help in identifying a man with a black cloth patch covering his right eye.'

'Like a pirate?' asks a reporter.

'That's correct.'

An image flashes onto the screen behind Keegan. It shows an artist's impression of a one-eyed man. The slide changes.

'We are also seeking the public's help to identify a member of the gang with this tattoo of rolling dice on his right wrist or lower forearm,' says Keegan. 'We believe these men may have Russian or Baltic accents.'

'They're foreigners?' asks a reporter, seeking clarification.

Duckworth interrupts. 'We are not ruling anyone in or out, but the gang responsible for this crime is likely to have deep ties with London's criminal underworld.'

'Someone like Edward McCarthy?' yells a reporter.

'Who is this witness?' asks another. 'Was he in the house?'

'I think that's enough,' says Duckworth, abruptly ending the briefing, ignoring further questions.

When he gets off the stage he spins and confronts Keegan. 'What was that bullshit about Russians?'

'Foreign accents were heard, sir.'

'Edward McCarthy is in this up to his neck.'

'There are links, but we have no firm—'

'How do you know McCarthy didn't hire this gang?'

'I haven't ruled that out, sir.'

'What about this witness? Is he one of them?'

'His fingerprints were found on the packing tape used to cover the victim's mouth, but I'm not convinced he killed her.'

'You keep making excuses for people,' says Duckworth. 'Next, you'll be giving McCarthy a character reference.'

'I'm keeping an open mind, sir.'

'Well, the trouble with an open mind, Brendan, is that people keep dropping rubbish into it.'

The two men are chest to chest.

Duckworth whispers harshly, 'Edward McCarthy is a blight on this city. He is a scum-sucking bottom-feeding parasite who pollutes everything he touches. He is not a man of the people or Robin-fucking-Hood. He is a pariah. And now, after forty years, we're *this* close to taking him down.' He holds up his thumb and forefinger. 'Don't fuck it up.'

# 50

Given three guesses and a phone-a-friend, Edward McCarthy would struggle to find Bulgaria on a map. He knows it's probably one of those Balkan countries, like the 'Stans' that used to be part of the Soviet Union. Violent, lawless places, full of men with bushy moustaches and fur hats.

Popov calls himself 'the Wrestler' – a name that is meant to intimidate people, but the whole vibe of wrestling has homo-erotic overtones. Half-naked men, covered in oil, grappling on the floor – *You got to ask yourself*, thinks McCarthy.

It's nothing like the pro-wrestling that he used to watch as a kid when his dad took him to the Embassy in Catford and Fairfield Halls in Croydon. Showmen like Big Daddy and Giant Haystacks would hurl their bodies around the ring, shaking dust from the rafters. He knew it was make-believe, but he still booed the 'heel' and cheered the 'face'.

Clifton has been out of contact for five days. Off the radar. Silent. He'll be using burner phones, turning off the handset to stop his movements being traced, but he promised to call regularly. McCarthy won't panic just yet, but he's running out of time.

Sitting in the penthouse office, oblivious to the view, he waits for a phone call from Popov. Two hundred thousand pounds is sitting in a sports bag beneath his desk. Another three hundred thousand has gone to cover the payroll. Raising the money had meant emptying accounts, selling cars, calling in loans and pooling their emergency funds. And in seven days, according to Popov's timetable, he will have to find another two hundred gees.

His phone pings. The message gives him instructions on where to deliver the money. He's doing it himself because he can't trust Daragh, who only has two settings – he goes nuclear or he goes home.

The location is a dilapidated pier in Greenwich, on the south bank of the river, just west of the Thames Barrier, the giant movable dam that keeps London safe from storm surges and king tides.

Finbar drives one of the garage cars. They chat casually on the journey, pointing out landmarks and reminiscing about teenage years full of mixtapes, pub lock-ins, punk rock and Thatcherism.

They park on the nearest road to the pier, beneath a billboard that shows a woman screaming at a padlocked door. The banner reads: *Escape Room. Find the Clues or Die.*

Finbar studies the poster, scratching his head.

'People pay to get locked in a room,' explains McCarthy.

'Why?'

'So they can figure out how to escape.'

'That's the dumbest thing I've ever heard.'

'Maybe it's a millennial thing.'

McCarthy opens the boot of the car and collects the sports bag. Tucking it under his arm, he walks along the riverfront path. Joggers ghost past him, wearing expensive running shoes that barely make a sound on the concrete.

Alone on the pier, he waits for Popov. Light rain is falling and the river is a brown colour, moving sluggishly through the silver barriers. A boat appears. Shaped like an arrowhead, it does a long sweeping turn before decelerating and pulling alongside the pier. A blond-haired man leaps from the bow and expertly loops and knots a mooring line. Popov emerges from the cabin. The deckhand helps him up the ladder. It's the same man who stood guard outside the steam room – the Diceman.

McCarthy points to him. 'You can stay on the boat. I talk to Popov alone, or I walk away.'

Popov nods in agreement and the blond stays on board.

McCarthy drops the bag at his feet. 'Your money.'

'Keep it,' says Popov, hitching up his trousers and sniffing at the air as if smelling something unpleasant on the breeze. 'The deal has changed.'

McCarthy is robbed of speech. This cunt has no idea how hard they worked to raise that cash. Then again, maybe he does.

'I want seventy-five per cent,' says Popov.

'That's not going to happen.'

'You have no choice. Your banks are putting your companies into administration. Next come the receivers. Hope Island will be sold off. Your houses. Your assets. Everything will go. You'll be declared bankrupt and that pretty wife of yours will leave you for someone younger and richer.

'On the other hand, you could sign over control to me and I will pay your loans and your outstanding debts and provide an overdraft facility. You will be a junior partner, but still a partner.'

'No.'

'Is that your final word?'

'It's my *only* word.' McCarthy swallows the ball of phlegm in the back of his throat before he speaks again, his eyes twitching. 'The police have an eyewitness to the home invasion and the Hatton Garden robbery. They've released an identikit picture of a one-eyed man. They're also looking for someone with a dice tattoo. Sound familiar?'

Popov shrugs dismissively. 'Eyewitnesses are unreliable.'

'You were sloppy and unprofessional.'

'Yet here we are.'

McCarthy takes a deep breath and shuts his eyes, silently counting down from ten. 'You're not the first, you know. People have spent years trying to steal or destroy what I've built.

Chancers, cheats and conmen and even the occasional psychopath with delusions of grandeur.'

'I'm different.'

'I don't think so.'

'I understand power. It doesn't come from having deeper pockets, or bigger guns, or more ammunition. It comes from being willing to do what the other person won't. You have boundaries and rules. I have none. You have lines you won't cross. I have none. I will kill women, children, babies and family pets. I will destroy everything you love. Your family, your friends, their families and their friends. That's the difference between you and me.

'But I'm not a complete monster. I will leave your daughter alive. Philomena. An uncommon beauty. She could have been a model. Not on the catwalk maybe, but she'd look good draped over the bonnet of a shiny new motor at a trade show or bent over my bed.'

McCarthy's hands curl into fists and a red mist blurs his vision. He wants to crush Popov's windpipe. He wants to reach into his chest and rip out his heart.

'Either that, or I could use her to keep up morale. That's the thing about crack whores – once you get them hooked they'll fuck a shitty stick to get one more puff of the pipe.'

McCarthy launches himself but Popov is prepared. A knife drops from his coat sleeve, into his fingers, a six-inch double-sided blade. It looks like a magic trick, but instead of a rabbit pulled from a hat, he has produced a lethal weapon.

At the last moment, McCarthy manages to pull away, as the knife slices through the air, inches from his face. Rearing backwards, he stumbles and rights himself, breathing hard.

Popov grins, holding the knife out, crouched, ready for his next move.

'You said unarmed,' says McCarthy, breathing heavily.

'I lied.' Popov twirls the blade over his knuckles. 'It is called a Brannik Youth Knife. In World War Two the Nazis had their

Hitler Youth, but in Bulgaria we had the Brannik, our "guardians". Anyone who joined was given a knife like this one. Made in Germany. Aluminium hilt. Black strap. Finger guard.' He points to an enamelled letter B inset into the grip. 'It belonged to my father and should be in a museum, but I keep it with me. I am nostalgic, you see. I miss the old days.'

He holds out the blade, as if offering the weapon for inspection, but McCarthy knows it will be snatched away.

'Did you have something else you wanted to say?' asks Popov.

McCarthy is silent.

'Good. Then it's decided. You have forty-eight hours in which to transfer seventy-five per cent of your businesses to me. The banks will hold off until then. My lawyers will be in touch.'

# 51

Keegan is lying in a bath with a cold flannel over his face, enduring a migraine. Pain is jackhammering into the right side of his forehead, as though a gremlin were trapped inside his skull trying to break free.

His childhood had been punctuated by headaches such as these, which were normally triggered by excitement or expectation. So much so, that he can't remember a single birthday, or school excursion, or concert, or sporting final, that hadn't been curtailed, or postponed, or cancelled. Back then, he would try to fight through the pain, telling himself it wasn't that bad, until he finished up vomiting in a bathroom, or on the bus, or on the football field.

Keegan had felt this one coming at the media conference and the aftermath. It started as a dull buzzing behind his eyes and a sensitivity to light and a coppery taste in his mouth. Now, lying in the bath, he goes over what Duckworth said to him. His message had been clear. Edward McCarthy was to remain a suspect and all roads had to lead to him.

He'd told reporters that he had a witness to the home invasion, although he didn't release the name. It was more information than he'd wanted to reveal, but Duckworth had forced his hand.

The doorbell sounds. He ignores the summons. It rings again, more insistently. It could be important. No, work would have called him. It's probably some canvasser or charity collector. He sinks lower in the water. Now someone has a finger on the bell, holding it down, ringing it constantly.

Cursing, he gets out of the bath and pulls on a dressing gown, padding along the hallway to the front door, leaving wet footprints on the floorboards. There is a shadow behind the glass.

Philomena McCarthy is on his doorstep. Jeans. Jumper. Raindrops clinging to her hair.

She begins to apologise.

'How did you get this address?' he asks, angrily.

'I'd rather not say, sir.'

'You can't be here. I could have you arrested.'

'I have information about my father,' she blurts.

Keegan pauses. He is damp beneath the dressing gown, growing cold, his head still pounding. He opens the door and Philomena McCarthy follows him along the hallway to a kitchen, where dirty dishes are piled in the sink and on the benches.

'Wait here,' he says, before going to get dressed. It takes him a while because the pain makes it hard to focus. When he returns to the kitchen, the dishwasher is packed and humming. She hands him a cup of tea.

'I see you've made yourself at home.'

Philomena ignores the comment. 'Are you running an under-cover operation against my father?'

'You can't expect me to answer that.'

'Last Friday I was approached by a woman who claimed to work for the National Crime Agency. She said her name was Jordan Koenig.'

'Jordan Koenig is a man.'

'I know that now,' says Philomena. 'This woman said the NCA was investigating my father and that I could save my career if I cooperated and agreed to plant listening devices in his house and car.'

'Did you?'

'Yes.'

'Who was she?'

'That's what I'm trying to find out.'

Keegan takes a seat, his head still pounding. 'Why should I believe you?'

'I have proof.'

Philomena shows him a photograph of the dark-coloured Mercedes that Henry took from their bedroom window.

'This was her car. I checked the plates. They belong to a completely different vehicle, registered to an address in Birmingham.'

Keegan narrows his eyes. 'Did you ask someone to access the DVLA database?'

Philomena seems to realise her mistake and switches tack. Reaching into her satchel, she pulls out a small silver case with the remaining listening device and tracker. Keegan examines the technology. It is cutting edge and not police issue.

'Start at the beginning,' he says.

Philomena tells him how she was picked up and taken to the address in Chelsea by a well-dressed middle-aged woman who knew all about her, right down to her hobbies and oldest friends. She claimed to be running an undercover operation targeting public servants and politicians who took bribes from her father.

'You said you planted two of the devices. Where?'

'One in the library and another in the pocket of his oilskin jacket in his garage. But they've gone. I went back and checked. I thought you might have found them during your search.'

Keegan shakes his head.

'I think my father is in trouble. Someone is trying to set him up.'

'Nobody faked the CCTV footage of his brothers visiting the jewellery store.'

'They had nothing to do with the robbery.'

'Let me guess. You asked them and they denied it?'

She ignores his sarcasm. 'My father said he was a victim. He had something stolen from the safe.'

'What?'

'He wouldn't tell me.'

'And that's why he remains a suspect.'

'He didn't kill Caitlin.'

Keegan doesn't have the energy to argue. He also remembers his interview with Hugo Desai, who said the gang had foreign accents. Russell Kemp-Lowe had said the same thing. He presses his palms over his eyes, watching white spots dance behind his closed lids.

'Go home, Miss McCarthy!'

'You know I'm right,' she says. 'Whatever you might think of my father, he's not a stupid man. If he was going to rob the store, he wouldn't send his brothers to be filmed entering the place only days before the robbery. And you've checked my phone records, my browsing history, my movements – you know I'm not involved.'

Keegan doesn't know what he believes, but he desperately wants to lie down. He stands but loses his balance, reaching for the kitchen bench.

'What's wrong?' she asks.

'A migraine.'

Philomena is holding his forearm. She leads him into the sitting room, to the sofa. Keegan mumbles in protest, embarrassed, but she orders him to lie down and puts a pillow under his head. His eyes are closed. Her hands are stroking his forehead. She finds a point at the top of his left ear, and gently presses it with her finger, holding it there. The relief is almost instantaneous. Then she takes his right hand and locates a point in the valley between the base of his thumb and index finger, pressing it firmly, again easing his pain.

'How?' he mumbles.

'Acupressure,' she says softly. 'I was taught how to do it by a Chinese doctor.'

'Why?'

'My mother gets migraines.'

Her face is close to his. He can feel her breath on his eyelids and her fingers on his face. He breathes. He relaxes. He sleeps.

# 52

My class of little dragons looks so cute in their karate gear, the white trousers and belted white coats. I teach them one morning a week when I'm not working the early shift. I also share an adult class with another instructor, two evenings a week.

With the young ones, it is all about having fun – jumping and sliding and rolling, blocking fake blows and kicking at the padded mats. Occasionally, I let them spar, but there's no head contact and they're more likely to get hurt tripping over.

I was nine when I went to my first karate class. I had badgered my parents for weeks because my best friend Jacinta had signed up to attend. Jacinta had blonde hair and blue eyes and could do back-flips and had twelve different Barbie dolls. I was infatuated by her, maybe in love. Sadly, she dropped out of karate after three weeks, but I kept going to the classes because I liked my new friends.

Later, as a teenager and a young woman, I could see the benefits of being able to defend myself. I could block a punch and take a fall; but more importantly, I could read a situation and stay cool under pressure.

When the class is over, I wait for the last little dragon to be picked up by her mum, before getting changed into a tartan skirt, black tights, Doc Martens and a sweater. I have three missed messages. I don't recognise the number. The mobile rings again.

'Hello?' says a small voice. 'It's me.'

'Daisy? How did you get this number?'

'It was in Auntie Amber's phone.'

I can hear her holding back tears. 'Is everything OK?'

'I lost Hippo.'

Her favourite toy. Her security. Her best friend.

'Where did you last see him?' I ask.

'At the supermarket. Auntie Amber said he must have dropped out of the trolley, but I think it was taken by the bad man.'

'Did you see the bad man?'

'No.'

'Where is Amber?'

'She's with Daddy.'

'Where's Daddy?'

'In bed.'

'Whose bed?'

'Auntie Amber wouldn't let him drive because he was too drunk.'

I try not to jump to conclusions, but I don't like the mental image.

'Has that happened before?'

Daisy makes a non-committal sound. 'Can you find Hippo?'

'Oh, sweetheart, that's not possible.'

'But you find things.'

'I don't look for toys.'

'It's Hippo. He can't sleep without me. He gets scared.'

I can picture Daisy, red-eyed, holding the phone with both hands.

'Do you know the name of the supermarket?'

'No.'

'Let me speak to Amber.'

Daisy is carrying the phone. I wait, trying not to think about Russell Kemp-Lowe and Amber Culver sleeping together. Maybe there is an innocent explanation. Amber is Caitlin's best friend and Daisy's godmother. She isn't a beauty, like Caitlin, but grief can do strange things to people, either bind them together or push them apart.

I hear Daisy knock on a door.

'Not now,' says a male voice.

'But I need Amber,' says Daisy.

'Watch TV.'

'Philomena needs to speak to her.'

'Who?'

'The police lady.'

Muffled voices. Russell Kemp-Lowe takes the phone. 'Who is this?'

'PC McCarthy.'

'Why are you calling my daughter?'

'She called me. She's upset about losing Hippo.'

'That damn toy,' he mutters. 'Listen, I'm sorry. I don't know how she got this phone.'

'Is Amber there?'

'No. She's gone out.'

'You're staying with her?'

'No.' There is a long pause. 'I drank too much. She wouldn't let me drive.'

'No taxis? Ubers?'

'I have every right to stay here.'

'Why?'

Russell stops himself. The silence stretches out, vibrating like a struck bell.

'You know my father,' I say.

'Who's that?'

'Edward McCarthy.'

'He told me you'd joined the police. He was very proud of you.'

'Really?'

'Yes.'

'The police think he robbed your store.'

'I have no idea who robbed me, but I can assure you that it wasn't your father or your uncles.'

'Did you tell the police that?'

'Yes.'

I want more from him. I want some details that I can take to Keegan but there's nothing the jeweller can offer me.

'Where did Daisy lose Hippo?'

'We were shopping yesterday. She must have dropped it.'

'Maybe I can help.'

'No! It's not your concern.' His reaction is too harsh. His voice softens. 'It was at a supermarket on Edgware Road. We didn't realise it was missing until we were almost home. I went back to look but couldn't find him.'

I jot down the details. 'Let me see what I can do.'

# 53

'One hippo is not like all the others,' says Henry, who is leaning over my shoulder as I search the internet. 'You're not going to fool her.'

'I'm not trying to fool her. I'm trying to cheer her up.'

I'm searching online gift stores and toy websites. Who knew that hippos came in so many shapes, colours and sizes — woven, knitted, patchwork, plush, tartan, dressed and undressed, mouth open or mouth closed?

The screen refreshes. I point. 'There it is!'

Henry leans closer. 'Are you sure? That looks more like a donkey than a hippopotamus.'

'It's the one,' I say, making a note of the name. 'They have them at Hamleys.'

He looks at the price. 'Is it stuffed with drugs?'

Ignoring him, I call the store and ask a shop assistant to put the toy aside, specifying the colour. Then I grab my car keys and turn to Henry. 'Are you coming?'

'Me?'

'I need someone to drop me off and circle the block.'

'A road trip,' he replies, slipping on his shoes. 'Only if I can drive.'

My Fiat is across the road. Henry presses the fob but no lights flash and there isn't the dull clunk of the internal locks disengaging.

'You must have left it unlocked,' says Henry.

'I'm normally pretty careful.'

I search the car, checking the boot and the back seat and the glove compartment. Nothing is missing. We don't live in a dangerous neighbourhood, but I take precautions, leaving nothing inside that might attract a thief.

I crouch near the driver's door and examine the seal where the window meets the frame. There is a small scratch in the paintwork near the rubber. I remember once seeing Uncle Finbar break into a car, how he slid a long metal rod down the side of the window and triggered the internal door mechanism.

This could be evidence of a break-in, or proof of my paranoia, but too much has happened in the past ten days that I can't explain. Henry shares none of my disquiet as he gets behind the wheel and starts the engine.

We drive towards Central London, crossing the Albert Bridge as the sun makes an appearance, shining on the river, which is dotted with rowers skimming across the surface. North through Fulham and Chelsea and Knightsbridge, we pass Harrods and Hyde Park Corner, following Piccadilly to the famous Eros fountain. Henry complains about the congestion charge, but we rarely drive into the West End.

After turning left into Regent Street, he drops me over the road from Hamleys and I wait for a walk sign. Entering the famous toy store, I am transported back to my childhood when every Christmas we made the pilgrimage to see Santa Claus and I told him I'd been a good girl and didn't deserve a lump of coal, but instead wanted something far too expensive, or grown-up, or inappropriate for my age. Eventually, something suitable was discovered in the seven floors of toys, games, puzzles and dolls.

Daisy is young enough to embrace magic and fairy tales, but I doubt if she'll believe that Hippo has been found. The new one is too brightly coloured and unchewed and unstained.

'Where to now?' asks Henry when I'm back in the car.

'Let's go to the supermarket. I want to make sure Hippo is lost.'

We follow Oxford Street as far as Marble Arch and then turn

north along Edgware Road and through Paddington towards Maida Vale. The Aldi supermarket is north of St Mary's church-yard, guarded by large London plane trees. Many of the leaves have fallen, filling the gutters and covering the footpath, softening the sound of my Doc Martens.

The supermarket is bright and clean, smelling of freshly baked bread. Most of the checkout counters are self-service, with cameras watching the customers. I talk to a woman collecting baskets and ask her what happens to lost property.

'If it's an umbrella, you won't find it,' she says. 'They never get handed in.'

'It's a child's toy.'

She gives me a look of sympathy and directions to the rear of the store where I find a shop assistant in a blue tunic.

'I'm sure I looked for that already,' she says, when I describe Hippo.

'Can you look again? Please?'

She disappears through swinging plastic doors. Meanwhile, I walk along the aisles, searching the shelves in case a shopper has tucked Hippo between cans or boxed goods. Henry has decided to shop for dinner. It's his turn to cook tonight.

As I reach the end of an aisle, I get a sense that I'm being watched, but there is nobody behind me except an elderly woman with a pull-along trolley and two teenage girls looking at the chocolate bars and energy drinks. I study the front windows and the road outside. A bus passes. The occupants are oblivious to their surroundings, plugged into earbuds or tapping at their phones.

The shop assistant returns. 'Nothing,' she says. 'You could check the bins out back, but I wouldn't recommend it – not without a tetanus booster.'

I thank her and meet Henry at the checkout.

'It was always a long shot,' he says, scanning and packing groceries. I help him carry the bags to the car. As we're loading the boot, I glance over my shoulder.

'What's wrong?' he asks.

'I keep thinking someone is following me.'

'Who?'

'I don't know. It's just a feeling.'

I collect the toy from the back seat. 'I'm going to give this to Daisy. It's not far from here.'

'I'll drive you.'

'No. I can walk. You go. I'll be home for dinner.'

He gives me a peck on the lips and squeezes my bum, which should annoy me, but never does. After he's gone, I walk along Edgware Road towards Kilburn, past shops and Tudor-style apartment blocks. At Sutherland Avenue, I turn left and kick at the fallen leaves. At the next intersection, I get the same feeling of eyes upon me. It is a crawling sensation across the back of my neck or an unseen weight on my skin. I spin around. The footpath behind me is empty. Nobody is watching from a window or a parked car. No eyes. No footsteps. No shadows.

When I reach the next corner, I scurry forward and duck through a gate into a small front garden, crouching behind the hedge. It reminds me of Daisy's hiding place on the night I found her.

As I wait, I grow self-conscious. I'm a grown woman hiding behind a hedge. I'm a police officer, or I *was* one. At any moment I expect the owner of the house to look out of the window, or come out of the door, and I'll have to explain what I'm doing.

I see a shadow on the footpath, behind the foliage. The figure stops, as though searching for me. I straighten and step out. Drawing my fists across each other, I brace my legs in a classic karate stance.

'Why are you following me?'

The figure turns. I'm shocked. Jamie Pike is equally surprised, but this morphs into lightness.

'Hello,' he says, smiling. 'Fancy bumping into you.'

'You were following me. Don't even try to deny it.'

He takes a step back, keeping his distance. 'I can explain.'

'I'm listening.'

'I saw you with your husband . . . at the supermarket. I didn't want to interrupt, so I waited until you were alone.'

'Don't bullshit me. Did you break into my car?'

'What?'

'Who do you work for?'

'Nobody.'

'Jordan Koenig?'

'Who?'

'The police?'

Jamie laughs nervously. 'I thought *you* worked for the police.'

The details fall into place. 'We didn't accidentally bump into each other the other day. You were following me. Why?'

'To catch up.'

I rock onto my back leg and kick out with the front leg, snapping my right boot into his stomach. He doubles over, gasping for breath.

'You don't have to . . . I'm no threat.'

The next kick connects with his jaw, splitting his bottom lip. He stumbles backwards, sitting on a low stone wall.

'I'm sorry,' he says, raising his hands in surrender. 'Your father.'

'What about him?'

'He wanted me to keep an eye on you.'

'You're terrified of my father. He caught you with your hands inside my knickers and threatened to cut them off if you ever touched me again.'

'That was a long time ago,' says Jamie, spitting blood onto the cement.

My anger is leaking away, along with the adrenaline. 'You work for him?'

He nods.

'Since when?'

'I came out of the army four years ago and was struggling

to find a job. I read a profile in one of the Sunday mags about Edward McCarthy and the Hope Island development. I thought maybe he could use someone like me.'

'A soldier?'

'A telecommunications engineer.'

'And now you're spying on people.'

'I'm keeping you safe.'

'How is that going?'

He grimaces and touches his bloody lip.

'Did you break into my car?'

'What?'

'You heard me.'

'No.'

'How long have you been following me?'

'Since that first day – outside your nick.'

'You tricked me into having a drink.'

'You invited me, remember?'

'You lied to me about everything.'

'Not everything. We only talked about you.'

He's right. I was so bound up in my own self-pity that I didn't ask him about his job, or his family or if he had a girl-friend or a wife. That's still no excuse for him stalking me and betraying my trust. I told him personal things. My secrets.

Jamie is pressing a handkerchief to his bleeding lip. 'I meant no harm, Phil. And I didn't regard it as work.'

'What sort of creep accepts money to stalk a woman?'

'It wasn't like that. I enjoyed getting to know you again.'

'Making me look like a fool.'

'No.'

'Embarrassing me.'

'I never intended that. Your father was worried about you.'

'And he can fuck off as well.'

Jamie gets to his feet and steps closer.

'Stay away from me,' I hiss. 'If I ever see you again, I'll kick your teeth in.'

# 54

Keegan is asleep when a phone begins ringing in his dream. He picks it up but nobody answers. It is still ringing. His mobile. His eyes open and he recognises his surroundings. His migraine has gone, leaving behind an echo of the pain and a general fogginess that narrows his field of vision and slows his reactions.

At that moment the doorbell sounds. He's caught between what to answer first. He chooses the phone.

'Been trying to reach you, boss,' says O'Neil. 'There's been an accident. Hugo Desai is dead.'

'But he's in custody.'

'He was released two hours ago.'

'On whose orders?'

'Assistant Commissioner Duckworth said he was baiting a trap. He wanted us to follow the kid. Said he'd lead us straight to McCarthy.'

'What happened?'

'A hit and run in St John's Wood. Desai was knocked off his bike.'

'Witnesses?'

'Plenty. The driver took off.'

'We get the plate?'

'Car was stolen nine days ago.'

'Shit!'

The doorbell sounds again.

'That'll be Hobson,' says O'Neil. 'I've sent a car.'

'Tell her to give me five minutes.'

He dresses in his light grey suit and the same shirt he ironed for the media conference. The tie is hanging around his neck when he emerges from the house.

DS Hobson opens the door of the unmarked police car.

'On blues, sir?'

'Yes.'

She triggers the siren and they weave through traffic, accelerating between lights and bottlenecks, as vehicles pull aside. Pedestrians stop and stare at them as they pass. Keegan notices a young man in a suit and slicked-back hair, who raises his hand in a one-finger salute. *What have we done to deserve such anger?* he wonders. *The police didn't steal his girlfriend, or scratch his car, or jump the queue at the Post Office.*

'Turn off the siren,' says Keegan.

'Sir?'

'Please.'

Wellington Road has been sealed off and officers are redirecting traffic into the side streets. There is an ambulance and a fire engine and an accident investigator, taking measurements and photographs.

A forensic tent has been erected over two of the northern lanes. Keegan ducks under the police tape and walks towards the tent. The twisted frame of a bicycle is twenty yards along the road and a bike helmet is lying in the gutter like an upturned tortoise. Both are marked with evidence flags. Further on, a white hatchback car straddles two lanes, pointing south.

O'Neil emerges from a nearby BP service station, eating a bag of crisps. He licks at his fingers and crumples the packet into his pocket.

'You're sure it's him?' asks Keegan.

'Yeah.'

'What happened?'

'I can show you.' O'Neil takes out his phone. 'The service station has a CCTV camera in the forecourt.' He turns the screen to Keegan and presses play. The footage shows the petrol pumps and several motorists filling up their vehicles. The northbound lanes of Wellington Road are visible in the background.

Hugo Desai walks from the shop. He's wearing black and white cycling clothes and carrying his bike helmet. He tucks his purchases into a backpack and hooks the bag over his shoulder, before walking his bicycle to the road. Pausing to clip on his helmet, he props one foot on the pedal and pushes off, swinging onto the bike's narrow saddle, before looking both ways as he steers onto the road. He is almost out of frame when a dark silver-coloured car appears, travelling at speed. It swerves at the last moment. There is no sound to the footage, but the collision has a sickening finality. Desai is thrown onto the bonnet of the car and then into the air where he somersaults and crashes to the asphalt, rolling once before he comes to rest on his stomach.

'This is from a different camera,' says O'Neil, pointing to a house opposite.

The new angle shows Desai lying on the road, clearly dead, when a second car, the white hatchback under brakes, slides into his body and rolls over him.

'A young mum was driving the hatchback,' says O'Neil, taking back his phone. 'She had a toddler with her. The paramedics took them to hospital as a precaution.'

'And the first car?'

'Kept going. A silver-grey Audi RS3 stolen from an address in Surrey. Cloned plates. The tracker was removed.'

Keegan takes a moment to weigh up the information, but he knows this wasn't an accident. Hugo Desai became a target the moment that Keegan publicised the existence of an eyewitness. He wanted to keep it secret, but let Duckworth bully him.

'You said you were tailing him.'

'Two unmarked cars. One stayed to render assistance. The other pursued the Audi but disengaged when the suspect vehicle

314

clocked ninety in a thirty zone. We couldn't get a chopper in the air in time.'

'Roadblocks?'

'On the major streets, but nothing yet.'

The two men are staring at the blood smear on the road.

'I notified Commissioner Duckworth,' says O'Neil. 'He said it was your decision to release Hugo Desai.'

Keegan gawps. 'That's bullshit.'

'Yeah, I know, but he's already made a public statement expressing support for you, praising your running of the task force, blah, blah.'

'I'm being hung out to dry.'

'I'd say fucked up the arse, but yeah, something like that.'

Keegan tries not to contemplate his faltering career. Whoever killed Hugo Desai was frightened of the evidence he could give at any future trial. The one-eyed man is in the frame.

'Where is Daisy Kemp-Lowe?' he asks.

O'Neil looks at him blankly. 'She'll be with her father or her aunt.'

'She needs protection. Get a car on her.'

# 55

How did Jamie Pike follow me so easily? Clearly my father fed him information: my home address and workplace. Jamie denied breaking into my car. Then again, I wouldn't believe a word that came out of his mouth.

I take off my jacket and check the pockets, feeling along the edges of the lining and the collar. My phone! Jamie could have downloaded a tracking app when I stayed overnight at his place.

Ahead of me, Russell Kemp-Lowe's Mercedes is parked outside Amber Culver's mansion block. Given the number of leaves on the windscreen and bonnet, it hasn't been moved since yesterday.

I ring the intercom. Amber answers, sounding surprised, and even a little fearful.

'It's not a good time,' she whispers.

The door lock triggers and I cross the foyer, passing the stairs, reaching her garden flat. The door opens a crack, but Amber doesn't invite me inside.

'Is he still drunk?' I ask.

'No, but he insists on spending time with Daisy.'

'Do you want me to get rid of him?'

She glances over her shoulder. 'Not if it causes trouble. I don't want to upset Daisy.'

At that moment I hear him calling for her. He appears behind her, his once handsome face pale, blotchy and hungover. 'I told you to leave us alone.'

'I'm not here as a police officer.'

'I don't care. You can piss off.'

He fills the door frame, stepping closer, trying to intimidate me with his size. Instinctively, my karate brain kicks in and I look to defend, identifying which hand he favours and how I can take him down.

'Maybe you should go,' says Amber, pushing Russell inside.

'You heard her,' he says.

'I need to speak to Miss Culver privately.'

'Anything you say to her, you say to me.'

'No. Go back inside or I will sit you on your arse.'

I curl my hands into fists and pass them across my chest, dropping into a karate pose, rocking on my toes.

'Please, Russell, go back inside,' she pleads. Her hand is resting on his chest. 'I'll be two minutes.'

He steps back. She whispers to me. 'I'll meet you somewhere else. There's a café at Paddington Rec, near the pavilion.'

'Bring Daisy.'

'I wouldn't leave her here.'

# 56

McCarthy is upstairs in the Ten Bells, halfway through a pint of Guinness. Foam clings to the glass as he drinks, smudging the world beyond. He has voicemail messages. He presses play.

*I've been made,* says Jamie Pike. *Philomena caught me following her and threatened to knock my teeth out. I've had to back off for now. You might get some incoming fire – she was pretty pissed.*

Beep! Carmichael at the bank:

*Edward, I hope you're not avoiding my calls. We have now begun formal proceedings to put Hope Island Developments into administration. An independent administrator will appoint an insolvency practitioner, who will restructure your business. The aim is to either return it to profitability or effect a sale to pay off existing debts. You are obliged to cooperate fully, which means handing over all relevant documents, files, contracts and invoices . . .*

Beep! His site foreman, Mohsin Ali:

*Mr McCarthy, I can get the workers back on site by midweek. And I've pushed delivery of the metal girders back until the eighth. It's gonna slow us down but it can't be helped.*

Beep! Constance:

*Hi, sweetheart. I told Tilda that we'd give some money towards the orphanage she supports in East Timor. I have no idea where East Timor is, but she says it's a very good cause and they need to fix the roof. When I looked in our account there was insufficient funds and the overdraft is maxed out . . .*

Beep! Daragh:

*I'm runnin' late. The North Circular is chock-a-block. I got a fix on the Wrestler's 'ome address. He's renting a posh pile on Putney 'Eath, out of the way, behind walls. Might go back tonight, have a little nose-around.*

Beep!

There are no more messages. Nothing from Clifton. If something has gone wrong, McCarthy needs to know now because he has no more cards to play. Maybe Popov discovered Clifton was travelling and decided to intervene. That's how it will happen – he'll pick them off, one by one.

Taking another sip of beer, he glances out of the window. Two tramps are pushing the same shopping trolley along the footpath, arm in arm. Maybe they're a couple. Spend long enough living in London and nothing surprises you. Only last week he came across a woman screaming in the street, yelling up at a woman in an upstairs window, telling her to send her husband out.

'He's not coming out,' she replied. 'I married him and he's mine.'

The woman on the street lifted her top, showing her breasts, yelling, 'Well, he paid for these, and I'm keeping them.'

Another time, he saw a naked man mowing his lawn with a sock on his dick; and a swan sitting on a driver's lap as they drove across Tower Bridge. You can love or hate this city, but you cannot be ambivalent.

McCarthy has met with Helgarde, instructing him to transfer ownership of 75 per cent of Hope Island Developments. The barrister recommended a corporate lawyer who is drawing up the papers with the final percentage withheld until the signing.

Big Dave appears from downstairs with another pint. McCarthy orders the fish and chips because Constance won't let him eat fried food at home – not since his heart surgery. Normally, he tries to do the right thing – taking statins and aspirin and walking ten thousand steps a day according to the tracker on his wrist. But he also cheats on the steps by shaking his hand up and down like he's having the world's longest wank.

Philomena hasn't called. She's going to be seriously pissed off about Jamie Pike, but he only did it to keep her safe. She won't see it that way, of course. She'll threaten to have him charged with stalking and quote all the laws he's broken. Sometimes she can sound like she's swallowed the police handbook the way she burps out statutes and regulations.

Then again, he's reasonably sure that Philomena planted two bugs at the house – one in the library and another in his oilskin jacket. It was a pretty amateurish effort and she should have realised that he had the place swept regularly. Saying that, if it hadn't been for the police raid, he might not have discovered the devices for another week, which could have added to his problems.

Ever since Philomena had become a police officer, McCarthy had studiously avoided discussing business around her. For a decade, it hadn't been an issue because she refused to speak to him after he divorced her mother. Their reconciliation had been long overdue – at his sixtieth birthday party and her marriage to Henry – and he loved having her back in his life, but it had created complications.

Finding the bugs and the USB stick was a case in point. If only she'd come to him first. No, that's not right. She did ask, but he denied everything and fobbed her off.

They live on different sides of the law. Her side is black and white, while his is every colour and shade imaginable. He is *not* the father that she wanted him to be, which is both tragic and freeing because all parents disappoint their children, even if it's just by growing old.

# 57

The pavilion at Paddington Recreation Ground has a café with large windows that overlook a courtyard which is furnished with wagon-wheel tables, bench seats and enormous potted plants. Daisy waves from the gate and comes running towards me, throwing her arms around my waist.

She spies the polished paper bag and peers inside. The bag drops away and she's holding the toy.

'You found him,' she squeals. Then it registers. 'This isn't my Hippo.'

'I know, but it's the best I could do.'

She holds the toy at arm's length, as though trying to decide how to react. For a moment, I think she's going to cry. A tear hangs from her eyelid, ready to fall, but she brushes it away with the back of her hand and then licks the dampness with her tongue.

She tucks the toy under one arm and then the other, as though trying it on for size.

'You should give him a name,' I say.

'He has a name. Hippo.'

'That works for me.'

Amber has been hanging back. She seems tired, with bruised-looking eyes and dry patches of skin on her forehead. She's wearing an oversized sweater and exercise gear – leggings and a Lycra top.

We choose a table outside, where it's colder but we can watch

Daisy playing on the slides and climbing frame. She has found another little girl, about her age, and the two of them are deep in discussion.

'Are you sleeping with Russell?' I ask.

She looks shocked. 'No!'

'He's sleeping in your bed.'

'Who told you that?'

'Daisy.'

'Russell slept on the couch. He came into my bedroom in the morning. I was up and dressed by then. I had a medical appointment.'

'Is everything OK?'

'I've been diagnosed with cervical cancer. I'm going to need surgery.'

'I'm sorry to hear that.'

Daisy stumbles as she gets off a swing and falls to her knees. Amber instinctively reaches out, as though she can catch her from here. Daisy gets up and brushes dirt from her stockinged knees and continues to play.

'Why did Russell say he had every right to be at your flat?'

'He doesn't.'

'OK, but why did he say it?'

'Caitlin bought it for me.'

'Why?'

'I needed somewhere to live . . . after the divorce.'

'That's very generous.'

'She was like that. We've been best friends since we were twelve. Through thick and thin. I'm Daisy's godmother and her guardian.'

'Guardian?'

'In Caitlin's will. If something ever happened to her and Russell, she wanted me to raise Daisy.' Amber pauses and bites her bottom lip. 'If it weren't for the cancer I'd apply for custody now.'

'But Russell is still her father.'

'And he's partly to blame for this – his gambling and woman-ising. Caitlin should have divorced him years ago, but she kept forgiving him. Why do women let love turn them into door-mats?'

'Not all of us,' I say. 'And even if Russell was involved in the robbery, the family will decide who gets custody of Daisy.'

'What if Russell goes to prison?'

'There's Noah.'

'A junkie!'

'He's clean now.'

'He's in prison.'

'He'll be out soon.'

Amber's features have hardened, but her eyes shine with tears. 'I don't expect it matters because they won't let me look after a child. Not with the cancer.'

'How bad is the prognosis?'

'Stage two, maybe three. The surgeon says I have a fifty per cent chance of surviving the next five years.'

I can almost see her doing the maths in her head. Daisy will be ten or eleven. Too young to lose someone else. I want to say something reassuring but can't think of the words.

Daisy appears at Amber's side. Breathless. Excited. 'Can I have an ice cream?'

'It's too cold for ice cream,' says Amber. 'How about a hot chocolate?'

'With two marshmallows?'

'Of course. You stay here with Philomena.'

Amber goes to the café. I take Daisy back to the swings.

'Can you push me?' she asks. 'Please? Please?'

'OK, but let me mind Hippo.'

I lift her onto the swing and tell her to hold on tight, as I drag the swing backwards and let go.

'Higher . . . higher,' she sings, her little legs kicking at the air and her bobbed hair lifting up and down.

Across the playground, past the garden, I notice two men

entering the park on foot. They're both clean-shaven, wearing trousers, leather jackets and open-neck shirts. One looks Nordic and the other swarthy and dark-skinned. They check out the café and the tables before scanning the playground.

The blond one seems to focus on me. He lifts the latch on the childproof gate. A ball rolls towards his feet. He picks it up and hands it to a little boy, without smiling or making eye contact.

I feel a familiar sense of alarm, the fight-or-flight response. They're closer now. One tall, one short. The dark-haired one has his right hand inside his coat.

'Are you Philomena McCarthy?' asks the Nord.

'That's right.'

'You have to come with us.' He's smiling, showing off his polished white teeth.

'Who are you?'

'Police.'

'Am I being arrested?'

'No, it's for your protection, miss.'

It might be the old-fashioned use of 'miss' or the weight-room bulk of his upper body, but this doesn't feel right.

'Why do I need protection?'

'We're following orders.'

'Can I see a warrant card?'

The two men exchange a look, which tells me everything I need to know.

Amber arrives with three hot chocolates in a cardboard tray. She's holding her phone. 'Russell just called. The police are at the house.'

'That's why we're here,' says the blond man.

'Why? Has something happened?' she asks.

'Nothing to worry about.' He addresses me. 'Get the little girl off the swing.'

'Who is your boss?' I ask, as Daisy swings away from me.

'The usual one,' says the Nord.

'DCI Fraser?'

'Yeah.'

Wrong answer. The short one steps closer and partly opens his jacket, revealing a pistol holstered under his right armpit. It is not a police-issue firearm.

I turn back to the swings and continue pushing Daisy, trying to calculate my next move. I could take one of them – shatter his kneecap with a kick – but if they're both armed, this could escalate. Bystanders could get hurt. Mothers and children.

'Get her off the swing,' says the Nord, more urgently.

'I'm coming too,' says Amber.

'No, not you.'

Her eyes cloud with confusion.

'It's all right. I'll look after Daisy,' I say. 'Tell Russell that he'll have to take her to the zoo another day.'

'The zoo?'

'Yes.'

She blinks at me. Her mouth opens, but she's wise enough to stay silent.

'Time to go,' I say to Daisy.

'But my hot chocolate.'

'We'll bring it with us.'

I take two hot chocolates from Amber's tray and give one to Daisy, before taking her other hand and leading her out of the playground, along the asphalt path towards a pay-and-display parking area. One of the men is ahead of us, the other behind. Two teenage boys in hoodies appear from the trees, kicking a can between themselves. They want the path. The two men refuse to move. The boys pick up the can and step onto the grass.

'Oh, your shoelace is undone,' I say, bending to tie Daisy's laces, placing my hot chocolate on the ground.

'Come on, come on, stop wasting time,' says the Nord.

I'm on my haunches. I tie the laces using double bows. The dark-haired one steps closer, hissing at me to stand up. I explode off my legs, karate chopping him in the throat with a swinging right hand. He rocks back on his heels and then drops to his knees, fighting for air, losing. He won't breathe again.

'Run, Daisy run!' I yell, pushing her past me. 'Find Amber! Go! Go!'

The Nord reaches for her, but I bodycheck him and throw the hot chocolate into his face. He dodges my follow-up punch and lands one of his own, knocking me backwards. I glimpse Daisy running along the path, showing off the pink soles of her sneakers. A woman appears, pushing a pram, but Daisy doesn't stop.

The Nord has his forearm around my neck, across my throat, leveraged with his other elbow. A chokehold. I use both hands to pull at his arm, trying to create space to breathe, but he's strong and he's in deep, firmly against my throat, cutting off my air. I don't have much time.

I take my right hand away and punch him in the balls, feeling him flinch. His grip loosens. He tries to recover, but I drive my head backwards into his chin and lift my shoulders, leveraging his forearm away from my throat.

I roll away and bounce to my feet. He reaches for his gun, but I spin into a leg kick, knocking him backwards, and then I run, in the opposite direction, trying to lead him away. I reach the parking area and the access ramp and then the road outside the park. I look for a car to wave down. Any car.

A red hatchback is coming towards me. I step into the middle of the road and hold up my arms, but it swerves around me. The side mirror almost clips my hip as it passes.

There is a van on the corner. The driver is wearing sunglasses. I bash on the side window, yelling at him to help me. He turns to me, surprised, unsure of what to do.

'Please. Help me,' I say, trying the door again.

He presses a button and the locks pop open. I climb into the passenger seat, telling him to drive. He turns the key and pulls away, accelerating down the narrow road, which has cars parked on either side.

I look in the side mirror and see the Nord standing in the middle of the road, hands on hips, smiling. I don't understand. I glance at the driver, who is staring straight ahead. His left hand is on the steering wheel. His right hand is holding a sawn-off shotgun across his lap, the barrel pointed at me.

I reach for the door. Locked.

'It's too late,' he says, in a foreign accent. 'We have a saying in my country – there's no point putting on a hood after it has rained.' He lifts the gun. 'Phone.'

I hand it over. He tosses it out his open window.

'Who are you?' I ask.

He takes off his sunglasses. He only has one eye.

'They call me the Wrestler.'

# 58

Keegan is in the incident room, looking at the CCTV footage. The grainy images are from a street camera that covers the eastern entrance of the Paddington Recreation Ground. They show Philomena McCarthy coming out of the gates and running along the footpath. She steps onto the road and tries to wave down a passing car, a red hatchback, which swerves around her.

She then runs to a van parked on the corner in a loading zone. She bashes her hand against the side window. The door opens and she gets inside. The van drives away, taking the next right turn. The man chasing her gets into a different car, a grey BMW 1 series with cloned plates.

'The van was reported stolen ten days ago by a dry-cleaning company in Croydon,' says DS Baxter.

'Was it waiting for her?' asks Hobson. 'I mean, she seemed to get in willingly.'

'Maybe she knew the driver,' says Baxter.

Keegan rewinds the footage and plays it again, unsure if Philomena was abducted or rescued by the van. 'What does Amber Culver have to say?'

'She and McCarthy arranged to meet at the park because Philomena had bought a toy for Daisy,' says Hobson.

'Who chose the meeting place?'

'Culver. They arrived separately. They were in the playground when two men showed up, claiming to be police officers. McCarthy asked to see their warrant cards. She must have known something was wrong. She told Amber that Russell Kemp-Lowe could take Daisy to the zoo another day, but they hadn't discussed going to the zoo.'

'It was a secret warning.'

'That's what I figure, sir. As they were leaving the park, McCarthy took down one of the men. Crushed his windpipe with a karate chop. She told Daisy to run.'

Keegan whistles through his teeth. Philomena McCarthy keeps surprising him.

'What do we know about the attackers?'

'No names yet. We're checking the dead guy's prints and DNA. According to Noonan, he's most likely East European because his dental work had full metal crowns with acrylic facings.'

Keegan watches the footage again. Philomena leaves the park and looks up and down the road before trying to flag down a driver. At one point she slows and looks over her shoulder, as though waiting for her pursuer. She was trying to lead him away.

This morning, he had two witnesses to a home invasion and was on the verge of cracking this case. Now one of them is dead and the other is in hiding – and she's only five years old. Her evidence is next to useless without corroboration.

'How do we handle this?' asks Baxter.

'Put out a missing person's report on Philomena McCarthy and find me that van.'

His phone is ringing. O'Neil.

'Amber Culver and Daisy are at the safe house.'

'Were you followed?'

'No, boss, but Russell Kemp-Lowe is demanding to see his daughter. He's asking why he's being kept away.'

'Because I don't trust the bastard,' says Keegan, rubbing his temples. The dull buzz of the migraine is returning. 'Did Daisy recognise the men in the park?'

'No, but it must mean we're getting close,' says O'Neil, ever the optimist.

*Or we've missed our chance*, thinks Keegan. He blows air from his cheeks. 'Tell the team leaders I want a briefing in my office at six.'

After hanging up, he scans the whiteboard that covers one entire wall of the incident room. A picture of Caitlin Kemp-Lowe is in the centre of the board with radiating lines that connect her to others through phone calls, meetings and family relationships. Along the bottom are four photographs – Edward, Daragh, Finbar and Clifton McCarthy – not the ones he wants to charge, but he has no other names or faces. He has a one-eyed man and a dice tattoo and a series of stolen cars and vans.

Confirmation bias is something that Keegan has always tried to avoid as a detective – the tendency to process information in a way that confirms preconceptions and beliefs. These are career criminals. It's easy to see them being behind the robbery, but sometimes the obvious answer is the wrong one.

Philomena McCarthy said her father was a victim of the crime but couldn't give him any details. Everybody wants to keep their secrets.

He turns to Baxter. 'Get me Philomena McCarthy's husband.'

'On the phone?'

'No. I want him here. Tell him his wife is missing.'

# 59

Every time the van takes a corner, my body shifts and I roll against the wheel arch. I'm in the back now, with plastic zip-ties on my hands and feet. I can smell engine oil and road dirt, as well as something else like dry-cleaning chemicals. My cheek is grazed on a nylon rug. I turn my head. The Nord is sitting with his back to the rear doors, knees spread, a gun resting lazily in his left hand, looking at me with contempt.

I push myself into a sitting position. He points the gun at my chest.

'Is that really necessary?' I ask.

'You killed my friend.'

'He was kidnapping a child.'

'Maybe he was trying to take you.'

'Well, he should have introduced himself properly and bought me flowers.'

'You think you're funny.'

I shrug and stretch out my legs, trying to get comfortable.

'What was that thing you did to him?' he asks.

'You mean the throat punch?'

'He couldn't breathe.'

'I must have crushed his windpipe.'

'It was a sucker punch.'

'Yes, but who was the sucker?'

The van takes another corner and I have to brace myself to stop from sliding sideways.

'Where are we going?'

No answer.

'So, tell me about the Wrestler. Strange name. His parents must have been sadists or comedians.'

'He used to wrestle.'

'That makes it rather generic. It's like calling your dog, "Dog".'

Defiantly, 'He almost won a medal at your Olympics.'

'My Olympics. You mean, London? Greco-Roman wrestling. The ancient Greeks used to wrestle in the nude. Are you a wrestler?'

He raises the butt of the gun, wanting to wipe the smile from my face. There it is. The tattoo of the dice on his wrist. He was at the house the night Caitlin died.

I cringe, waiting for the blow, but he stops himself. He's clearly under instructions not to hurt me. I stay quiet, closing my eyes, feeling the wheels bump over a grate and take another corner. There are questions to answer. They knew my name, which means my father is involved. He said someone was targeting him. That makes me a hostage or a bargaining chip. The fact that I'm alive means I have some value to them. This is to my advantage. It gives me time.

The van has stopped. A bag is pulled over my head. The doors open and I'm dragged along the tray and slung over someone's shoulder like a rolled-up carpet. Momentarily, I am in the fresh air, before we're inside again.

My head bangs against the man's back as I'm carried along a passageway into a room, where I'm flipped onto a bed. He pulls the sack from my head. My eyes take a moment to adjust. I'm in some sort of warehouse or factory, and this is a storage room with with brick and plasterboard walls. Metal beams supporting the roof and a single skylight. The final streaks of daylight are visible through a small window, above head-height, where raindrops are beaded on the dusty pane of glass.

Elsewhere in the room, there is a table, two chairs, a tray of bottled water and a bucket with a sealable lid. My toilet.

The Nord rolls me over and cuts the plastic ties on my wrists and ankles. I rub at the chafed skin, trying to restore the blood flow.

'Grab hold of the frame,' he says, pointing to the metal headboard.

I reach above my head and grip the pole. Packing tape rips from a spool and wraps around my wrists.

'You don't have to do this,' I say, as he rips another piece of tape, covering my mouth, preventing any further conversation.

Satisfied with his efforts, he sits on the edge of the bed and looks at me. His eyes travel up my body, from my knees to the hem of my tartan skirt, to my sweater, my neck, my face. He places his hand on my thigh and slides it higher, grinning at me as he reaches the edge of my skirt.

My eyes are pleading with him. I rock my head and kick with my knees, but he forces them apart and his hands slip further up my leg.

'Leave her alone,' says a voice. The older man, the Wrestler, is standing in the doorway. This time he's wearing a black curved patch over his right eye.

'I'm just having a bit of fun,' says the Nord, who is worming a finger inside my knickers. The hatred in my eyes seems to excite him.

A moment later, he is flung backwards and pinned against the brick wall, a forearm across his throat.

'I said leave her alone,' says the Wrestler. 'We don't bruise the fruit, understand?'

He releases his hold. The Nord rubs his neck.

Both men leave and I'm alone in the room, still feeling where his hands touched me, and swallowing the vomit that rises in my throat and fills my mouth behind the plastic tape, leaving me with the aftertaste of bile and defeat.

# 60

'Do you know anyone who might have a grudge against your wife or might want to cause her harm?' asks Keegan.

Henry Chapman shakes his head. 'Nobody. Everybody loves Phil. Although your lot seems to have it in for her.'

'By my lot, you mean the police?'

'Yeah.'

Keegan ignores the comment. They're sitting in his office with the door closed.

Henry is wearing the uniform of a London firefighter, the dark blue trousers and zip-up jacket with a Fire Brigade insignia stitched onto the right sleeve and the letters LFB on the left breast pocket. He is a big man with a tangle of brown hair and the physique of someone accustomed to putting his body on the line on a sporting field or when fighting fires.

Keegan points a remote at a TV screen and presses play, showing Henry the CCTV footage from outside Paddington Rec.

'Do you recognise the men?'

'No, who are they?'

'We believe they were involved in a home invasion and robbery.'

'The jewellery shop?'

'What did your wife tell you about that?'

'She found the little girl and took her home; and you accused her of being involved.'

Again, Keegan disregards the gibe. 'The van was stolen ten days ago. Could she have known the driver?'

'What are you suggesting?'

'We're trying to understand what happened.'

'Clearly, she was abducted.'

'Yes, but there's also the issue of the dead guy. Your wife crushed a man's windpipe. A witness said it was a single blow to the throat.'

Henry looks shocked. 'She must have been provoked. She wouldn't otherwise. Phil knows when to pull a punch and when not to.'

'Meaning?'

'She's a karate black belt. The guy was either armed or she was outnumbered, or both.'

'That explains a few things.'

Henry points to the screen. 'You have the number plate. You can trace the van.'

'Like I said, it was stolen.'

'Yes, but you have traffic cameras and helicopters and satellites.'

'You watch too many TV shows,' says Keegan. 'Could your wife's father be involved in her abduction?'

Henry looks at him incredulously. 'Why would he take his own daughter?'

'Did she express any concerns for her safety? Odd phone calls. People following her.'

'We were in the supermarket today and she thought someone was watching her, but we didn't see anyone.' Henry perks up. 'And we found her car unlocked this morning. Nothing was taken or damaged.'

'Where is the car now?'

'Outside our house.'

Keegan picks up a phone and makes a call, asking forensics to fingerprint and swab the car for clues.

Afterwards, he leans back in his chair, studying Henry. 'Do you get on with your father-in-law?'

'I barely know him.'

'He came to the wedding?'

'Phil hadn't talked to him in years, but they reconciled.'

'Any particular reason?'

'They're family. She's an only child.'

'Does Philomena involve herself in her father's business interests?'

'No.'

'Protecting your wife's reputation is noble, but that's not going to help us find her. Do you know the whereabouts of Clifton McCarthy?'

'No.'

'Do you know why he visited the Kemp-Lowe jewellery store twice in the days before the robbery?'

'No.'

'Philomena must have said something to you.'

'She said they were being set up.'

'Yet she planted a listening device and a tracker at her father's house. Hardly a vote of confidence.'

Henry looks surprised, as if it's news to him. He opens his mouth to protest, but stops himself, as though robbed of words.

The detective rubs at his eyes, feeling the rawness. 'I have put out a missing person's report on your wife and posted Philomena's image at ports and train stations and transport hubs. We have foot and vehicle patrols looking for the van, but London is a big city. What we need is something that can narrow the search – a name, an address, a connection – but I'd be wary about involving your father-in-law.'

'Why?'

'He'll go to war and Philomena will be the first casualty.'

'You don't know that.'

'Think about it, Henry. She was likely taken because she's Edward McCarthy's daughter. You say she's not involved, but she clearly must be – accidentally, inadvertently, innocently, it doesn't matter.'

'So, what am I supposed to do?'

'Go home and stay close to the phone. I'll have a detective spend the night in case her kidnappers call.'

'How do I know I can trust you?'

'You don't, Henry, but right now you're sitting on a white picket fence, unsure whether to side with the police or Edward McCarthy. Do that for long enough and people will start to think you're not there for the view. You're enjoying the fence-post.'

# 61

Near midnight. A lone circle of light shines on a desk. Edward McCarthy is staring at spreadsheets and cashflow charts, trying to fathom numbers that seem to float and merge or disappear before his eyes. This would normally be Clifton's purview, but his brother is still MIA.

A knock on the door. Constance in her nightgown. The light behind her creates a silhouette.

'Are you coming to bed?' she asks — a question, not an invitation.

'Won't be long.'

'I'll be asleep.'

'I'll try not to wake you.'

He can't see her face in the shadows. She takes two steps into the library.

'What's wrong?'

'Nothing.'

'The cars have gone and the overdraft has been fully drawn. Are we in trouble?'

'We have a cashflow problem.'

'It's more than that. You don't have to protect me.'

McCarthy pushes back his chair and rises, walking to the sofa, patting the spot next to him. Constance sits close enough for their thighs to touch. His arm slips around her waist.

'Do you like your life?'

'What sort of question is that?'

'This house. The cars. The social engagements . . .'

'Of course.'

'How would you feel if you lost it all?'

She shrugs his arm aside and turns to face him. 'You mean, if we were poor?'

'Yes.'

'I've been poor before.'

'A long time ago.'

'I wouldn't care,' she says. 'I know your brothers call me "the duchess", but I grew up in a semi-detached house in Croydon and went to the local comprehensive. We didn't have cleaners or gardeners or drivers.'

'And then you married me—'

'Which I didn't do for the money, if that's what you're thinking.'

'I wanted to give you a comfortable life – and now I'm not sure if I can do that.'

'Are you going to prison?'

'No.'

'So, whatever happens we'll be together?'

'Yes. If that's what you want.'

'That's what I want. And that's all I need.' She puts her arms around him, burying her face in his neck. 'Sell my jewellery. Sell this house. Sell the paintings. I don't care. It's only money. If we're poor, we're poor.'

Outside the dogs begin barking. They both look to the darkened window, where the curtains are drawn.

'A fox?' she says.

'No,' says McCarthy, getting to his feet and turning off the lamp. Edging closer to the window, he opens the curtain a crack. He can see the turning circle and the fountain and the gravel driveway leading to the garage where the dogs are kennelled. They're still barking.

'Someone is out there,' he whispers.

'We have guards on the front gate.'

'Gone. I couldn't afford to keep paying them. Go upstairs. You know where to hide.'

'Call the police.'

'Upstairs. Now.'

She does as he asks. McCarthy goes to the drinks cabinet, where he lifts out a tray and then presses a button that reveals a secret drawer. Inside is a pistol and an ammunition clip. He slides the two together and ratchets the slide, putting a bullet into the chamber.

He goes back to the window, crouching beneath the sill, studying the grounds. A security light on a motion sensor is triggered near the old stable building. It illuminates the croquet lawn and one edge of the pond. A dark figure emerges from a corner of the building and heads towards the house in a low crouching run.

There are three entrances to the ground floor – one through the laundry, another the sunroom and the main door beneath the porte cochère. Moving through the darkened house, McCarthy stops and listens. Old houses like this creak and groan as the temperature changes or when the wind blows or when people move around, but he knows these sounds.

He hears a rattle. The laundry. Feeling his way along the corridor, he enters the kitchen and flattens himself against the wall behind the door. Something bumps and a voice curses.

The door begins to open. A dark-clad figure steps into the kitchen. He bends and rubs at his shin, or maybe he's reaching for a gun in an ankle holster.

McCarthy places the barrel of the pistol against the intruder's head. The man straightens, raising his arms.

'How many of you are there?' asks McCarthy.

'Just me. Do I get a hug?'

'A what?'

'A hug, you dopey bastard.'

Clifton pulls off his beanie, making his hair stick up like he's been electrocuted. He gives McCarthy a lopsided grin.

'You're a dickhead! I almost shot you!'

'I'd rather you not.'

'Why were you sneaking in like that?'

'I thought you'd be asleep and I was trying to shake a tail.'

McCarthy has turned on the light. Clifton takes a chair, smoothing down his hair. His black jeans are covered in mud and he has cobwebs clinging to the shoulders of his jacket.

'I came through the tunnel. Someone was watching the front gate.'

'It's either the police or Popov's men. Why didn't you call me?'

'Because these fuckers knew more about my movements than my gastroenterologist. I wasn't taking any chances.' He looks around the kitchen. 'Is this place clean?'

'It was swept two days ago. Tell me about the tail.'

'Someone made me at the airport in Belfast – a geezer I'd seen earlier in the day. I waited airside until the flight left and then caught a cab to Belfast Docks. I took the ferry to Glasgow and a train to Edinburgh. Instead of flying south, I came by rail because I could watch anybody getting on and off the train. When I reached London, I caught the Tube and two cabs, and then came in using the tunnel because I saw someone parked up opposite the gate, hiding in the trees.'

A soft voice calls from the top of the stairs. Constance. 'Is everything OK?'

'Fine,' says McCarthy.

'Who are you talking to?'

'Clifton.'

She emerges into the kitchen, wearing a dressing gown over her nightdress. 'Hello, duchess,' he says.

Ignoring the nickname, she hugs him.

'Wow, you *did* miss me,' says Clifton, grinning sheepishly.

'You look exhausted,' says Constance.

'I've been travelling for twenty-four hours.'

'Can I get you something to eat?'

'A drink and a shower and a pillow.'

'I'll make up a bed in the spare room. Top of the stairs. Second door on the right. I'm going to retire for the evening. Good night.'

She kisses McCarthy on the cheek and leaves the two brothers. McCarthy takes Clifton to the library and returns the pistol to its hiding pace. He pours each of them a drink. The two men sit on the chesterfield sofas in the semi-darkness. Drinks in hand. Swallowing, not sipping.

'Tell me you have good news,' says McCarthy.

'You have a white knight with a black heart.'

'I can live with that.'

# 62

I have spent hours unable to sleep because the mattress is too thin and the room is too cold and the tape across my mouth makes it difficult to breathe. My nose runs when the temperature falls, but I can't blow it.

As a child, I was prone to throat and ear infections that went straight to my sinuses. Numerous specialists examined me, and each seemed to have an alternative theory, or wanted to perform a different procedure to 'improve drainage'. That was until an old guy, who looked like Einstein's less crazy-haired brother, told me to snort warm salted water up my nose. It was horrible, but it worked.

I don't know what time it is, but I can see the night sky through the high window. There are no stars visible, but this is London. I doze and wake to the sound of the door opening. The one-eyed man enters, carrying a brown paper bag, stained with grease, and two large takeaway coffees.

He is wearing the convex black eyepatch, held in place by an elastic strap that runs diagonally across his forehead. He looks at me, as though expecting me to talk, but then realises that I'm bound and gagged. Smiling apologetically, he takes a knife from a weathered scabbard strapped to his ankle and slices away the tape from my wrists and feet. Gingerly, I peel the gag from my lips, feeling the sting.

'Did you sleep well?'

'No.'

'That's unfortunate.'

'I stayed awake in case one of you tried to rape me.'

'My colleague has been disciplined. No harm will come to you when you're in my care – not unless your father refuses to cooperate.'

'What has this got to do with him?'

'We are soon to be business partners.'

'I doubt that.'

'It has been agreed. He is giving me a controlling stake in Hope Island Developments and I am to pay his debts, his outstanding loans and guarantee the future of the project.'

'Why kidnap me?'

'You are my insurance.'

'That would suggest that he hasn't agreed.'

'I would hate for him to renege on his promise. After all, a man's word is his bond.'

'I'm a police officer.'

'I know who you are.'

'The entire Metropolitan Police will be looking for me. You won't be going into business. You'll be going to jail.'

'My understanding is that you're a disgraced police officer. Under investigation.'

He motions to the chair and pushes a coffee towards me. A smaller bag contains pods of milk and sachets of sugar.

'I hope you're not a vegetarian,' he says, unpacking two bacon and egg rolls, wrapped in white paper.

'A pescatarian.'

'What's that?'

'A failed vegetarian.' I take the roll from him because I need to eat and to keep my strength up if I'm going to escape.

'First, I must put this on you,' he says, holding up a collar with a small black box attached. 'It is used to train dogs not to bark and do as they're told.'

'You want me to wear a *dog* collar?'

'It is for your safety as well as mine. Otherwise, you go back on the bed.'

He steps behind me and places the collar around my neck, doing up the buckle. The box is beneath my chin, against my larynx. He tightens it another notch and slides his fingers between my skin and the collar, making sure it fits snugly. Then he adds a small padlock to make sure it can't be easily removed.

Retaking his seat, he takes a bite of his bacon roll. Brown sauce drips down his chin. He looks for a serviette but can't find one in the bag. Cursing, he crushes the bag and hurls it across the room. 'Can't they get anything right?'

His anger is so sudden and explosive, I automatically recoil. Seeing my reaction, he stops and settles himself.

'I'm sorry, but small things irritate me more than they should.'

'There is a term for that,' I say. 'Intermittent explosive disorder.'

'How do you know that?'

'It runs in my family.'

'Your father?'

'Why do you assume it's him?'

The man finds me amusing, which is irritating, but the more I can learn, the more I can use.

'Do you mind if I ask you a question?' he asks.

'As long as I can ask you one.'

'What did your father say when you became a police officer?'

'I didn't tell him. We weren't speaking back then.'

'You were estranged?'

'For ten years.'

'Why?'

'That's a second question.'

'Humour me.'

'Because he divorced my mother and ran off with a younger woman, and because I know what he does for a living.'

'And now?'

'We agree to disagree.'

'You are the white crow.'

I wait for an explanation.

'In Bulgaria we do not use the term "black sheep" to describe someone who brings shame upon a family or who refuses to conform. We call them a white crow because they are outsiders. Misfits.'

'I hardly think I'm the misfit.'

'But you *are* different, Philomena. Have you ever seen a white crow?'

'No.'

'It has a genetic abnormality or a mutation, which causes its feathers to grow white instead of black. Such birds struggle to survive in the wild because they are picked on by the other crows and are more visible to predators.'

'If we're done talking about birds, it's my turn to ask a question. What's your name?'

'Dimitar Popov.'

'Are you going to kill me, Dimitar?'

'It won't come that.'

'I have seen your face. I can identify you.'

'You will be silent.'

'How can you be sure?'

'I know things about you, Philomena. Where you live. The car you drive. The route you take when you go for a morning run, or when you walk to the train station. I know about your husband and his little boy, Archie.'

I remember my meeting with Jordan Koenig and the file she had on me. She knew about my background, my mother, my friends. That sort of research takes time and money. This isn't some random, opportunistic shake-down. It has taken months, possibly years, to plan.

'Information is currency, Philomena. And success comes from knowing what motivates people, what they desire, what they fear.'

'What motivates me?'

'Right now, the desire to escape. You are weighing up whether to attack me or to disable me, but you have ascertained that there is at least one person on the other side of that door, perhaps more, and that we are being watched.' He motions to a corner of the ceiling where a small bulbous camera is bolted to the wall.

'You seem to be enjoying this.'

'That's because your father is a worthy adversary. He is the bull. I am the matador. Have you ever seen a bullfight?'

'No.'

He clears the table and leans forward, explaining a fight, using milk pods and sugar sachets to tell his story.

'After the bull enters the ring, the toreros on horseback and the picadors on foot taunt the beast, sticking banderillas, coloured spears, into his neck. Finally, the matador takes to the ring with his cape and swords. What follows is a beautiful dance full of thrusts and parries and pirouettes, until the *coup de grâce* is delivered painlessly, a blade driven between the shoulder blades to the beast's heart.'

'Sounds barbaric.'

'It is a ballet of death. Fought with honour and skill.'

'Is that why you robbed the jewellery store, to weaken my father?'

'Yes. We had been following him and his brothers for months, learning their routines, their contacts. How they laundered money. How they won tenders. How they bribed officials and influenced planning meetings. I was looking for a weakness. Then, completely by chance, somebody approached an acquaintance of mine, seeking to set up a robbery.'

'Was it Russell Kemp-Lowe?'

'A buffoon.'

'Caitlin?'

'You have exhausted your questions.' His one good eye is dancing with amusement. I wonder if it has become more expressive since he lost the other one and it now does twice the work.

347

'Just one more,' I say. 'Why kill her?'

'She was alive when the last of my men left the house.'

'Perhaps he lied to you.'

'You could ask him yourself, but you put him in the morgue.'

There is a knock on the door. A woman appears. She is dressed in jeans rather than a business suit, but I recognise her immediately.

'Well, if it isn't Jordan Koenig, but maybe you're someone new today,' I say.

'Nice to see you again,' she says, coolly, handing Popov a newspaper. *The Times*. He checks the date on the front page and gives it to me.

'Would you like to say something to your father?' he asks, framing me with his phone camera. I raise the paper beneath my chin.

'Hi, Daddy, don't give them anything. They'll kill me anyway.'

Popov lowers the phone, his face ripening and his one good eye bulging.

'I will give you one more chance.'

'Not necessary.'

I launch myself across the table. The newspaper conceals my first punch, which hits him in the stomach, toppling him backwards off his chair.

The woman reaches for the gun tucked in the back of her jeans, but I pivot on my right foot and kick her in the head. She is unconscious before she hits the floor. I pull the gun from her belt and step over the Wrestler, who is gasping for breath. I take the phone from his hand and head for the door.

It opens into the corner of a warehouse, which is filled with enormous storage shelves, row after row, that reach as high as the ceiling. Some of the shelves are empty except for bare wooden pallets, while others have boxes or shrink-wrapped pallets with labels and numbers. I look down one row and see light leaking through the edges of a roller door. A smaller door is inside the larger one. I start to run, hoping I can reach the door before I'm intercepted. Speed and surprise are my only advantages. As I run, I punch the emergency number into the phone. It rings. A voice answers.

'Officer in trouble. Warrant number: two, five, niner—'

The electric shock fells me like someone has swung an axe into the back of my knees. My muscles spasm and my teeth vibrate and my brain feels like a peanut being shaken in a jar. I'm writhing on the filthy floor, clutching at the collar. I desperately try to pull the electrodes away from my neck. I try to crawl, but the charge hits me again and again.

I don't remember what happens next. Maybe I black out or hit my head. When I become aware of my surroundings, I see Popov standing over me, filming me on his phone. I'm lying in a puddle of my own urine.

He presses send.

# 63

The McCarthy brothers have taken over the upstairs room of the Ten Bells before opening time. Outside, a street-cleaning machine is scrubbing the gutters, picking up leaves and litter. Commuters are walking to work under umbrellas, a conga line of the besuited and smartly dressed, who have places to be and people to meet.

The boys greet Clifton like he's woken from a coma or returned after a long sea voyage. They posture and piss-take and punch arms. It's like watching wolves or wild dogs, greeting a member of the pack.

They settle and Daragh pours himself a Scotch because it's never too early to have a snifter. Clifton is happy with a take-away coffee and Finbar loads up a plate from a breakfast buffet that Big Dave has brought up from the kitchen – bacon, eggs, beans, mushrooms and grilled tomatoes.

'You 'ad us worried,' says Daragh. 'We almost sent out a search whatnot.'

'I was just being careful,' says Clifton, spooning sugar into his coffee.

'How did it go?' asks Finbar.

'We got what we needed, but it's going to cost us,' says McCarthy.

'How much?' asks Daragh.

'Twenty-five per cent.'

Daragh whistles through his teeth.

'For that we get immediate funds, an overdraft facility, and help with our current cashflow problems.'

'What about boots on the ground?'

'That, too.'

'How many?'

'Enough.'

'When?'

'They're on their way.'

Daragh raises an eyebrow to McCarthy. 'Are you OK with this, Eddie?'

McCarthy is staring at a damp patch on the ceiling that has started to bubble beneath the plaster. 'Better the devil you know.'

'You say that now, but when the devil is outsourcing he goes straight to Belfast. He's got 'em on speed-dial. It's a local fuckin' call.'

'What would you have me do?'

The boys fall silent.

McCarthy's phone is vibrating in his pocket. His right-hand slides inside and turns it to silent without looking at the screen. Moments later, there's a knock on the door. Big Dave enters.

'Sorry to bother you, Mr McCarthy, but there's a geezer downstairs says he knows you.'

'I said no interruptions.'

'Yeah, but he says he's family. Your son-in-law.'

'Henry Chapman.'

'That's him.'

The brothers look at each other. 'How did he know we were here?' asks Finbar.

'Constance must have told him.'

'You told her we were meeting in a pub? That's brave.'

'Send him up,' says McCarthy, and then to the boys, 'Not a word in front of him.'

Minutes later, Henry appears. He's wearing a bomber jacket

with a fur-lined collar and a woollen beanie pulled down low on his forehead. He nods to the brothers, takes off his hat, holds it in his hands.

'I'm sorry to bother you, Mr McCarthy.'

'Why so formal? It's always been Eddie. Come in, sit down.'

'I think I've made a mistake,' says Henry. 'It's about Phil. I know I should have told you sooner, but the police said it would make things worse and I didn't know what to do. But then I went home and I couldn't sleep . . .'

'OK, slow down,' says McCarthy. 'Clifton, get him a coffee.'

Henry takes a chair. Cup in both hands.

'What about Phil?' asks McCarthy.

'She's gone.'

'She left you?'

'No. Gone. Taken. She was at Paddington Rec with that little girl – the one she rescued. Two men came to the park, claiming to be police officers. Phil must have known. She managed to save Daisy, but then they took her.'

'These two men – who were they?'

'I don't know. She killed one of them, but there was a third guy waiting in a van.'

McCarthy is leaning forwards with his fists clenched, as though he wants to beat the answers out of Henry because they're not coming quickly enough.

'What about this van?'

'It was stolen.'

'Who was driving?'

'I don't know.'

'What did the police tell you?'

'They said not to tell you, because you'd go to war and get her killed. They told me to go home and wait by the phone in case the kidnappers called, but nobody did. I had a detective watching me all night. This morning, I snuck out and came looking for you. I had to leave my phone behind.'

McCarthy's mobile is vibrating again. An unknown number.

A message with a video file attached. Normally, he wouldn't open anything from a strange number, but it could be Philomena.

He opens the attachment. Philomena is writhing on the floor, her eyes bulging, as she clutches at a collar buckled around her neck, in a world of pain. She stops moving and a newspaper is tossed onto her prone body. Proof of life.

Words appear on the screen.

*Tick, tock, tick tock! I have your white crow.*

# 64

Keegan steps outside and double locks his front door before walking along the weed-fringed path, slick with moss and soggy leaves. His squat, grey pebble-dash bungalow is the same as every other bungalow in the street with the same slate roof and the same net curtains and the same square garden. A little shabbier than others, maybe. A little less loved.

A light rain is falling, beading the shoulders of his woollen coat. His umbrella pops open and he steps out of the gate, noticing a black Rover parked opposite. A rear window glides down. Assistant Commissioner Duckworth raises his hand. 'Brendan. If I might have a word . . .'

Keegan crosses the road. The driver of the car, a uniformed constable, gets out and opens the rear door.

Duckworth tells the officer to make himself scarce.

'I don't have an umbrella, sir.'

'Take mine,' says Keegan, handing it over.

They watch as the officer walks along the footpath, unsure of how much distance to give them. Even with the windows cracked open, the car feels humid and close because the men are wearing too many clothes and Duckworth's aftershave has a cloying intensity.

'Unfortunate incident, yesterday,' he says. 'A setback.'

Keegan doesn't answer.

'Cycling is a dangerous pastime in this city. Seven people were killed last year. Ten the year before.'

'We both know it wasn't an accident,' says Keegan.

'Do we? I'd rather not prejudice the inquest.'

The comment triggers a mental image of Hugo Desai, lying on the road after being crushed beneath the wheels of two cars.

'I wanted to make sure we were on the same page with this,' says Duckworth. 'There will be an internal investigation, of course. I think it's important that we agree on the facts.'

'Yes, sir,' says Keegan.

'What are your thoughts?' asks Duckworth.

'My thoughts are that Hugo Desai should never have been released from custody. He was a suspect and an important witness, who could have helped identify one of the attackers.'

'Oh, yes, the mysterious one-eyed man. Sounds rather fanciful, like he made it up to divert our attention.'

'Are you suggesting—?'

'You said he was a suspect,' says Duckworth. 'His death could have saved us the expense of a trial.'

'You want me to pin the murder on Hugo Desai.'

'It's your investigation. You're calling the shots.'

Keegan's voice hardens. 'I will tell any future inquiry that you ordered Hugo Desai's release from custody and asked my detectives to follow him.'

Duckworth matches his intensity. 'I have already briefed the commissioner and told him it was your decision. I counselled you against it, but you insisted that your mobile surveillance operation would keep the boy safe.'

'There are witnesses,' Keegan mutters. 'You briefed O'Neil.'

'And I've told him that the instructions came directly from you. I was merely passing on your orders. It will be your word against mine and we both know how that ends. Right now, you have me as a friend, Brendan; you don't want me as an enemy.'

The stench of the aftershave is making Keegan nauseous.

Duckworth continues. 'You will be disciplined, of course, and the coroner may have criticisms, but I will have your back and this setback to your career will only be temporary.'

'If that's all, sir.' Keegan opens the car door, wanting to escape before he does something he might regret. The driver returns with the umbrella.

Standing on the footpath, Keegan watches the Rover pull away and looks at the drops of rain falling from the edge of the brolly, adding to the water trickling along the gutter and swirling down a drain, much like his career.

# 65

McCarthy has rarely used the front door of a police station. In the past he has been escorted through the custody entrance or made to navigate the 'walk of shame' with a coat covering his head, as photographers and TV cameras recorded the moment.

Shaking raindrops from his overcoat, he addresses a uniformed officer seated behind a Perspex screen, tapping at a keyboard. He gets no response. He knocks on the screen.

'How can I help you, sir?' asks the station officer, without looking up.

'I'm here to see Detective Chief Inspector Keegan.'

'What is the nature of your business?'

'I want to know what he's doing to find my daughter.'

Now their eyes meet and suspicion flows both ways. A phone call is made. McCarthy is shown to a waiting area with plastic chairs, an empty water cooler and posters on the wall advertising community policing and neighbourhood watch programmes.

After twenty minutes he goes back to the front desk.

'DCI Keegan is not at the station,' says the sergeant.

'Why didn't you tell me that?'

'You didn't ask.'

'Get him on the phone.'

'You can't order me around,' says the sergeant. 'Now take a seat over there and I'll try to establish his whereabouts.'

*Why do the police talk like that?* wonders McCarthy. They ponce-up their language or talk like robots. Fights are 'physical altercations', people are 'intoxicated' not drunk, they are 'apprehended' not caught, and bodies are 'deceased' not dead.

More time passes. McCarthy phones Daragh, who is checking out Popov's house in South London. He sends McCarthy a photograph of a whitewashed, two-storey house with a walled garden.

'It backs on to Putney 'Eath,' says Daragh. 'Posh-looking pile with iron gates, four guards and security cameras.'

'Make sure nobody sees you.'

'I'm just a geezer walkin' me dog.'

Daragh has a Jack Russell that thinks it's a pit bull and is always picking fights with bigger dogs, like its owner. 'Your Philomena could be in there,' he says. 'Behind one of them windows.'

'We don't move until we're sure.'

McCarthy ends the call and sends a message to Finbar, who is searching for a safe house where they can take the families. Clifton is with the lawyers, drawing up the contracts.

DCI Keegan comes through the automatic doors, shaking out his umbrella. The desk sergeant gives him a nod.

'I'm sorry to keep you waiting, Mr McCarthy. If you'll follow me.'

The detective's office smells like a recently cleaned urinal. Keegan squirts sanitiser on his hands and rubs them together, adding to the stink. He offers some to McCarthy, who declines.

'What are you doing to find my daughter?'

'She was last seen getting into a white van in Carlton Vale, near the northern entrance to Paddington Rec. She appeared to get in the van willingly. Maybe she knew the driver.'

'You know that's bullshit.'

'We have circulated her description and put a watch on all ports, airports, train stations, bus terminals.'

'What about tracing her phone?'

'It was discarded at the scene.'

'The van?'

'We know it travelled through Chiswick on the M4 and took one of the Heathrow Airport exits. After that, it disappeared, but we have number plate recognition software searching the live feeds from traffic cameras and CCTV.'

McCarthy is silent, unsure of how much he can share, or whom he can trust.

'She killed a man,' says Keegan. 'She'll have to explain that when she shows up.'

'She was being abducted.'

'Who by?'

McCarthy doesn't respond.

'I thought so,' says Keegan. 'You're here to complain, not to cooperate. You are worried that sharing information might implicate you in a crime and you'd rather risk your daughter's life than expose yourself.'

'That's not the reason.'

'OK. Explain it to me.'

'You wouldn't understand.'

'Oh, I understand. There is an old Sicilian proverb: "Cu è surdu, orbu e taci, campa cent'anni 'mpaci." He who is deaf, blind and silent lives a thousand years in peace. That's you, Mr McCarthy. And it's going to be very peaceful without your daughter.'

McCarthy lunges across the desk, reaching for Keegan, but the detective kicks back his chair, rolling out of reach. Papers and photographs and a laptop clatter to the floor. A coffee cup topples over. Liquid leaks onto loose pages.

Keegan snaps his wrist, lengthening an extendable baton, holding it ready, raised. McCarthy is sprawled across the desk, empty-handed, embarrassed. Pushing himself upright, he stands and steps back. One side of his shirt has pulled out of his trousers. 'If you want to charge me with assault, I understand.'

'I think I do,' says Keegan.

'I need twenty-four hours. After that, I'll hand myself in.'

Keegan nods and retracts the baton, putting it into his drawer.

'I will give you a name,' says McCarthy. 'Dimitar Popov. He's a Bulgarian national, a degenerate piece of filth, who is threatening my family and trying to take control of my businesses.'

'How?'

'Extortion. Blackmail. Intimidation. And now, abduction.'

'Excuse me if I find that amusing.'

'Yuck it up all you want,' says McCarthy. 'But he's going to kill Philomena if I don't do as he says.'

'Did he murder Caitlin Kemp-Lowe?'

'He denies it.'

'But he robbed the store?'

'Yes.'

'What was in the safe that belonged to you?'

'Diamonds. Purchased legitimately.'

'With undeclared funds. You were laundering money.'

McCarthy doesn't answer.

'What makes you believe he has your daughter?' says Keegan.

McCarthy takes out his mobile phone and turns it to face the detective, pressing play, showing the footage of Philomena curled up on a concrete floor, writhing in pain, clawing at the collar around her neck. 'That's today's newspaper.'

'Let me have your phone,' says Keegan. 'We have digital forensic experts who can trace the message.'

'There's no time. I have less than twelve hours to hand over control of my companies. They'll keep her alive until then.'

Keegan's tongue flicks nervously into each corner of his mouth.

'Make a statement. Tell us everything you can about Popov. I can have a task force—'

'You're not listening to me. There is *no* time.'

'Well, what do you expect me to do?'

'When I find her, I might need your help.'

Keegan looks at him disbelievingly. 'You want the police to provide you with back-up?'

'I prefer to call it logistical support.'

'No. You will provide me with any information and the police will handle her recovery.'

McCarthy's voice drops to a whisper. 'I know what that means. You will run it up your chain of command and ask for permission to requisition firearms officers, vehicles and weapons. And they will request schematics of the buildings and will evacuate anyone living or working nearby. They will set up a surveillance operation and cut the power and the gas and the phone services. And by that time my daughter will be dead.'

The two men eyeball each other.

'Do you have children?' McCarthy asks.

'A little boy.'

'If it were your son and you knew where he was being held, and you knew that every wasted minute could put him in greater danger, what would you do?'

'It's not my son and I'm not in your line of work.'

'Spoken like a true public servant.'

# 66

Same bed. Same room. Hands taped. Mouth gagged. Collar in place. My skirt is damp and my nostrils twitch when I catch a of whiff of myself. I didn't know what to expect from the collar. I thought I could ride out the pain, but it dropped me like a taser barb.

Another jet is passing overhead. I must be somewhere beneath a flight path because they're coming regularly. Popov sounded European, Romanian or Bulgarian or one of the old satellite states. If he wanted to kill me, he would have done it by now. I still have some value as leverage. That's why he wanted the proof-of-life video.

My emergency call was brief but might allow the police to triangulate the signal and pinpoint my location. Apart from that, I've done everything wrong. I've provoked rather than pacified, antagonised instead of appeased. From now on they will be more careful and less likely to drop their guard.

Hours have passed since then. In that time, I've put more of the pieces together. My father told me the truth about the robbery. He wasn't responsible for Caitlin's death. And he couldn't tell me the reason because he knew that I'd take it to my superiors. It was my duty. I swore an oath to uphold the law, which I learned by heart when I graduated from Hendon.

**I do solemnly and sincerely declare and affirm that I will well and truly serve the Queen [it was still a Queen then] in the**

office of constable with fairness, integrity, diligence and impartiality, upholding fundamental human rights, and according equal respect to all people; and that I will, to the best of my power, cause the peace to be kept and preserved and prevent all offences against people and property . . .

I have tried to live up to those words, but my family has made that difficult. My father had me followed by my ex-boyfriend. That alone should be enough to guarantee I never speak to him again. But then I think of the devices that I planted in his house. I put my career ahead of family, which is what I swore to do when I joined the police, but that doesn't make it any easier.

I force myself to think of something else. The robbery and the murder. Popov said that Caitlin was alive when the last of his men left the house in Antrim Road. That means someone else was there or arrived afterwards. It can't have been a coincidence.

Noah Kemp-Lowe knew about his sister's plan. She had promised to change their parents' will to give him his share of the family fortune, which he'd been denied because of his drug convictions.

Who else stood to gain from Caitlin's death? Her husband would have collected on her life insurance and inherited her assets, the house and the jewellery store. He'd be free to remarry. Maybe Josie Sheldon. His muse. A young actress besotted by an older man.

No, there is something I'm missing, a detail that explains Caitlin's death. I go back to the beginning, to Daisy standing barefoot on a rainy night in London. She couldn't wake her mother, which means Caitlin was dead when Daisy left the house. Popov said his men had gone. Could someone else have been in the house?

Russell Kemp-Lowe was with Popov at the jewellery store. Noah claimed he didn't care about his inheritance, but clearly that isn't true. He told police he was with Sofia – a weak alibi that can't be independently verified – but killing his sister is a huge leap. Who else knew about the robbery? And then it comes to me: the answer and the reason.

# 67

The brothers regroup upstairs at the Ten Bells. The mood is sombre, yet there is a strange energy in the room, a mix of expectation, testosterone and cortisol. McCarthy wonders if it was like this for Daragh when he was waiting on a troop ship in the South Atlantic, preparing to go ashore on the Falklands. The questions. The doubts. The introspection.

Daragh wasn't even nineteen when he sailed for the Malvinas, tasked with liberating a rock in the South Atlantic. They gave him a send-off in this very pub and everybody came by to wish him well and tell him to put those 'Argies' in their place. When he came home, three months later, he never talked about that war, and as far as McCarthy knew, he had never attended a military reunion or marched on Remembrance Day. That part of his life is a closed book and Daragh doesn't open books unless they have pictures.

'We've identified three possible locations,' says Clifton. 'The house on Putney Heath, a warehouse near Heathrow and a block of flats in Brixton. That's where most of Popov's crew are living.'

'How many?' asks McCarthy.

'Fifteen, maybe more. Four guard the house and there are six at the factory. Coming and going. Working shifts.'

'What about Popov?'

'Stays mainly at the 'ouse,' says Daragh. 'I saw 'im walking 'is dogs earlier, big fuckers. A Dobermann and a Rottie. They all piss on the same tree. I could 'ave taken 'im out easy-peasy, but it would have been messy. I don't like killing dogs.'

'Looking at the hostage video, Phil is probably at the warehouse,' says Finbar.

'Close doesn't get you a cigar,' says McCarthy. 'We don't move until we know.'

They all nod in agreement.

Clifton speaks next. 'I know how Popov got his intel on the family. A senior manager at Revenue and Customs has just been sacked for accessing private data for payment. She was feeding information to two private dicks, outa-towners. One an ex-cop, the other a convicted hacker.'

'They should have known better,' says Finbar.

'Yeah, that's what I'm gonna tell 'em,' says Daragh, rubbing his right fist.

'Where are we with the safe house?' asks McCarthy.

'I found us a hotel in Wembley,' says Finbar. 'It's being refurbished but doesn't open for another fortnight. I can get everyone in, but there won't be any mod cons, and we'll have to bring our own linen.'

'OK, we do this quietly. Nobody changes their routines. They leave work, or school, or the gym, everything as usual, but along the way they take a detour. They change trains and buses and cabs. Nobody goes directly to the safe house. Understand?'

'We should be there to make sure,' says Daragh.

'No, we're going to rely on Mary and Poppy and Constance to do what has to be done.'

'What if they refuse?'

'They won't – not after they see the video of Philomena.'

Henry has been sitting in the corner, listening to all this. He hasn't said much since he saw the video of Philomena, writhing on the ground, clutching at the collar around her neck. He hasn't gone home since then, insisting on being a part of the planning. For McCarthy, he's just another person he has to keep safe.

Big Dave knocks. Head around the door. 'Got a Jamie Pike downstairs.'

'Let him come up.'

Moments later, Jamie enters breathlessly. 'I think I've found her.'

Every head in the room turns towards him.

'I tagged her. I mean, it didn't work at first, but then it did.'

'You're babbling,' says McCarthy.

Jamie starts again. 'I put a tracking device in Phil's Doc Martens, under the laces. It was almost invisible unless you looked closely. But when I tested it afterwards, it didn't pick up a signal. Loose connection maybe. Then, an hour ago, it began pinging my phone. Phil must have accidentally bumped it.'

'Could have been when she got zapped,' says Finbar, thinking out loud.

Henry interrupts. 'What do you mean, tagged her?'

The others go quiet. Henry is on his feet. Fists bunched. Face twisted. 'Were you following my wife? Did you break into her car?'

'Jamie was under orders,' says McCarthy.

'Whose orders?'

'Mine.'

Henry is chest to chest with Jamie. McCarthy steps between them. 'Stand down, fireboy.'

Henry turns on him. 'This is your fault. Phil was taken because of you. Every time she tries to do the right thing and to live a normal life, you keep getting in the way. She's right. You're a poison.'

The punch comes from low down, below Henry's eyeline. It sinks deep into his abdomen because he has no time to tense his muscles or brace himself. His eyes go wide and his mouth opens and closes, as he collapses into McCarthy's arms.

'You hit me,' he groans, almost in disbelief.

'And I'll hit you again, if you don't behave.' McCarthy helps him to a chair. 'When this is over, you can take your best shot at me, but right now, sit down and shut the fuck up.'

McCarthy turns to Jamie. 'Where is she?'

Jamie opens his phone. 'Right now, the tracker puts her in Hounslow, out towards Heathrow. See that blue dot?'

The screen shows a satellite view of West London. McCarthy is staring at the blue dot, as though wanting to be sure.

'That's the warehouse,' says Clifton, noting the location.

'You want us to go and get 'er?' asks Daragh.

'Not without a plan,' says McCarthy. 'We have to isolate as many as we can or draw them away.'

'Divide and whatnot,' says Daragh.

'A diversion,' echoes Henry, who is breathing normally again. 'I can get us in there.'

'How?' asks McCarthy.

'Firefighters have unlimited powers of entry. We can knock down doors and ask questions later.'

'We could set up a practice run,' says Finbar.

McCarthy shakes his head. 'This is something we only fuck up once.'

# 68

Keegan has a task force briefing at Kentish Town police station. Senior detectives only. The atmosphere has changed because they have a new focus for the investigation.

'Dimitar Popov is a Bulgarian national and a former member of the secret police,' says Baxter. 'Interpol has linked him to one of the organised crime groups operating out of Sofia, specialising in people trafficking and property fraud.'

'Any outstanding arrest warrants?'

'None, although he's suspected of a fatal car bombing that targeted a chief prosecutor who was investigating his activities. A woman and child died. The prosecutor's wife and daughter.'

'Why hasn't Popov been extradited?'

'Lack of evidence.'

'Maybe he's being protected,' says O'Neil. 'Or he could be an informant.'

Baxter throws an image onto a screen. 'Interpol sent this through.'

The photograph shows a square-headed man with short-cropped hair and heavy eyebrows. However, his most notable feature is what's missing – his right eye.

Baxter continues. 'He entered Britain three years ago on a Tier 1 Entrepreneur visa. To qualify he invested half a million pounds into a construction business in South London. The visa has been renewed twice. His business partner is another Bulgarian, Damyan Georgiev, who they call "the Swede" because he has blond hair. Georgiev has British citizenship. He was charged with attempted murder after a business dispute eight years ago but escaped prosecution when two witnesses changed their stories. And how's this: he has a tattoo of rolling dice on his wrist.'

'Got an address?' asks Keegan.

'He has an office in South London, but it looks abandoned or disused.'

'You said Popov bought into a construction business.'

'On paper maybe, but that's the thing with these entrepreneur visas, they're easy to game. The same half a million gets churned through accounts, and applicants only have to provide a business plan, or proof of a sale. There's no follow-up.'

Keegan turns to O'Neil. 'I want warrants for Popov's house, his car and his phone.'

'Easier said than done. Popov has no fixed address and puts nothing under his own name. He's not on the electoral roll and he hasn't applied for a driver's licence.'

'What about tax returns?'

'Hasn't lodged any in three years. Keeps applying for extensions. We have a name for his lawyer and his accountant. We're making approaches.'

'He's gonna know we're coming,' says Baxter.

'He knows already,' says Keegan. 'That's why Hugo Desai is dead.'

A knock on the door. A detective constable. 'Sorry to interrupt, boss, but control said it was important.'

Keegan motions him in.

'It's about Philomena McCarthy. Earlier today, emergency services received a call from someone claiming to be a police officer in trouble. It was a woman's voice. She began quoting her warrant card but was cut off. They only got three of the six digits before the phone went dead. There is a recording.'

The officer plays it back on speaker, turning up the volume.

*'Caller, you're through to the Metropolitan Police?'*

(A woman panting.) *'Officer in trouble. Warrant number: two, five, niner—'*

The caller cries out in pain and the phone falls and bounces off a hard surface before going dead.

'Why am I learning about this now?' asks Keegan.

'The call came from an unregistered handset. They thought it was a hoax.'

'Those numbers match McCarthy's warrant card,' says Hobson.

'They're trying to triangulate a signal,' adds the DC.

Keegan doesn't answer, but he feels a dull hollow emptiness in his chest. He accused Philomena of being part of the conspiracy and having blood on her hands, but now she's in trouble and trying to lead police to her.

'Forget about the robbery and Caitlin Kemp-Lowe,' he says. 'I want every resource focused on finding Philomena McCarthy.'

The detectives file out and Keegan follows them to the incident room. He stands in front of the whiteboards, studying the photographs, timelines and phone wheels. Thousands of pieces of information have been processed. Hundreds of hours of work. Overtime and expenses. All of it had been aimed at the wrong targets. He is to blame. He chose what aspects of the crime were salient. He prioritised the lines of inquiry and what to concentrate upon. Now he knows the truth but lacks the evidence to arrest Dimitar Popov and Damyan Georgiev because one witness is dead and another is a child.

A thought occurs to him. He goes to a computer and logs into the database, typing in Damyan Georgiev's name and calling up his previous arrests, convictions, sentences and remands. He cross-checks these details against Noah Kemp-Lowe, looking for a link between them.

The information leaps off the screen. Both men were remanded to the same prison after Noah was charged with drug offences. Keegan types a second search, this time of prison records. Picking up the phone, he calls HMP Wormwood Scrubs and asks for the governor.

Patched through. Static on the line. Skipping pleasantries. 'I'm requesting that Noah Kemp-Lowe be separated from the general prison population because of fears for his safety. I'm sending you the paperwork now.'

'I haven't had any reports of threats,' says the governor.

'He made them to me when I interviewed him.'

'Why didn't you inform my staff?'

'New information has verified his concerns.'

There is a silence and Keegan knows that he's treading on toes. Prison governors have a degree of independence and autonomy that leads some to treat the inmates as their subjects and their jail as a personal fiefdom.

'I'd like to talk to Noah Kemp-Lowe on a secure line,' says Keegan. 'Nothing recorded.'

'That's against protocol.'

Keegan quotes Rule 39, where certain communications with inmates are privileged and protected if they are for a legal or humanitarian reason. The governor grudgingly agrees and Keegan waits in his office.

Ten minutes later, his phone rings.

'Hello?' says Noah.

'This is DCI Keegan. Are you alone?'

'Yes.'

'I can have you transferred within the hour to a Category D prison near London where you will serve the remainder of your sentence. You will be able to work outside the prison, participate in community activities, and gain a temporary licence to spend nights away.'

Noah begins to speak, but Keegan cuts him off.

'I will also arrange for your partner to be relocated to the nearest village and be given protection, until such time as you are released. Then, I would suggest, you return to America or go to Spain or Argentina, somewhere well away from here.'

'Will you put that in writing?' asks Noah.

'Yes, but only if you answer a question. Who did you contact when Caitlin asked for someone who could stage a home invasion and rob the jewellery store?'

He waits, breathing into the phone.

'I am going to say a name,' says Keegan. 'If I'm right, you hang up immediately. If I'm wrong, you stay on the line. Either way, you'll be transferred within the hour.'

Noah's silence is acceptance.

'Damyan Georgiev.'

There is a beat of dead air before Noah hangs up.

# 69

The private bank is in Mayfair, a Georgian building with a wedding-cake facade that seems to glow in the descending darkness. Most of the staff have gone home, but the windows are illuminated on the lower floors.

McCarthy and Helgarde meet on the footpath outside at six o'clock. The barrister is carrying a briefcase and a grim expression. No handshakes.

'I thought you were supposed to be semi-retired,' says the lawyer.

'I'm a masochist.'

'You should have said earlier. I can give you the name of a wonderful woman. Very good with a whip and paddles. Never leaves a mark.'

'Is that a personal recommendation?'

'From a friend – a judge who swears by her. Says she looks like Margaret Thatcher.'

'You private-school boys are all sick fucks.'

'Yet we run the country.'

Pushing through a revolving door, they enter a foyer with chequerboard marble flooring and potted palms. A young man is waiting with a handwritten message for Helgarde. The barrister reads the note and screws up the paper.

'The boardroom is ready. It has been swept.'

'And no weapons?'

'Everyone will be scanned before entering.' Helgarde raises

the briefcase. 'I did as you asked and drew up the documents, but I don't understand.'

'The less you know the better.'

'Plausible deniability?'

'You can't pick a dog turd up by the clean end.'

The two men cross the foyer and pass through a metal detector before climbing the stairs to the first floor. They are met by George Carmichael, who throws out his arms. 'Welcome, welcome, gentlemen. An auspicious day, yes?'

The banker is dressed in his customary three-piece suit, pinstriped, with a crimson handkerchief in the jacket pocket. Two paces behind, his lapdog, Aaron Morby, is making himself seem smaller. McCarthy hasn't seen either of them since they met in the conference room at Hope Island and they suggested he sell half his business to a mysterious suitor.

'Well, we got here in the end,' says Carmichael, rubbing his hands together as though warming them on a fire. 'Although I must say I was surprised to hear you'd agreed to seventy-five per cent.'

'Mr Popov made a compelling business case,' says McCarthy, who removes his coat and hands it to Carmichael, treating him like the cloakroom attendant.

'You're a little early,' says the banker. 'We could have a drink in my office. Champagne? Whisky?'

'I'd like to check out the meeting room,' says McCarthy. 'And then I have to make a few calls.'

'Of course. This way.'

He is taken along a corridor through double doors, into a high-ceilinged room dominated by a rectangular rosewood table polished to a brilliant sheen. Three tall windows show the darkness outside. The chairs are all carved and upholstered with leather seats. Two fountain pens – Montblanc, inlaid with mother-of-pearl – are resting on matching blotters. McCarthy unscrews the lid from one of the pens and practises his signature on a blotter.

375

He walks to the windows and looks at the Regency row houses opposite.

'Are these shutters going to remain open?' he asks.

'Unless you wish them closed,' says Carmichael.

'No. I like the view. And now, if you'll excuse me . . .'

He waits until Helgarde and the bankers have left the room before taking out his phone. Speed-dials.

'How is the weather?' he asks.

'Clear,' says Daragh.

'You want me to sit anywhere in particular?'

'Won't matter. Just don't get in the way.'

'You heard from Mary?'

'Everyone is safe.'

'What about Clifton and Finbar?'

'They're ready.'

'Tell them seven o'clock. No sooner. No later.'

'They're gonna need help.'

'I can't promise them a cavalry.'

McCarthy hangs up and types a text message to DCI Keegan. An address of a warehouse in West London and a simple message: *You have until 7.*

# 70

Daragh is sitting in darkness on a chair facing the window, far enough back to be completely in shadow. He has watched the moon come up, rising above the trees and the rooftops. At times like this, he wishes he still smoked, but he can't help but wonder if Mary's cancer is down to his past pack-a-day habit that dated from his teens. The tumour is in her breast, not her lungs, but even so . . .

Resting on a tripod near the window is an L115A3 Long Range Rifle, bolt-action, chambered with 8.59-mm shells and kitted with a Schmidt & Bender scope. It was the same weapon he used in the Falklands more than thirty years ago, when he could hit a target more than 1,300 yards away, seeing only a puff of red mist before the enemy fell.

Next to him is a bottle of water and an open box of Cheerios, which he eats dry by the handful. Daragh doesn't cope well with boredom. It is one of the reasons he hated the army. He didn't mind the training and the camaraderie, but soldiering involved too much waiting around, scratching your bollocks.

Every fifteen minutes, his watch vibrates and he gets up and walks the length of the room, loosening the tension in his limbs. The apartment is tastefully furnished. The owners were happy to relocate for the evening when he told them about the gas leak and the risk of an explosion. Daragh had been suitably attired in coveralls and carrying a toolbox. He said that Westminster Council would cover the expense of their hotel bill for the evening.

Dropping to his stomach, he does twenty push-ups, but struggles through the last five. He's grown soft . . . and old. That's why this Bulgarian cunt is trying to take away their hard-earned. An outa-towner, who knows nothing, but thinks he knows everything.

Flexing his fingers, he goes back to his chair and looks through the window. On the far side of the road, on the second floor, Eddie is sitting in a chair at a conference table. His calmness is remarkable. If one of Daragh's tin lids had been kidnapped he'd have torn a hole in time to get them back. He would have raged and fought and wreaked havoc indiscriminately, but Eddie isn't like that. He's a thoughtful man. A planner. Even so, this has aged his brother. Maybe it is time they all retired, but the McCarthy brothers can't just sail off into the sunset. Geezers like them don't play golf, or garden, or race pigeons, or sail boats for that matter. Then again, if they stepped away, they wouldn't have to deal with the bent cozzers and straight cozzers and treacherous bankers and vicious cunts like Popov who don't know their place. Daragh could spend more time with Mary and the kids and little Victoria, the newest member of the family.

When Daragh was in prison, he promised himself he'd never go back inside. That's when he learned that the system hates someone like him – an honest tealeaf with no airs or graces or delusions of whatnot. Not like the company bosses and CEOs and accountants who hide wealth and evade taxes and screw the workers. They're the real criminals, which is why Daragh used to enjoy hijacking their trucks and flogging their merch. It wasn't some steal-from-the-rich-give-to-the-poor Robin Hood-type shit. He's not that generous – but he believes in fairness and family and keeping his loved ones safe.

Six miles west, at a fire brigade training centre in Park Royal, Finbar McCarthy is doing up the Velcro straps on a padded bunker jacket.

'How do you move in this kit?' he says, swinging his arms.

'It's fire retardant,' says Henry. 'And you get used to the weight.' He hands him a yellow helmet, with a retractable face mask.

Clifton and Jamie Pike are lacing up their boots, clipping gloves to their belts. There are also three Irishmen, whom Finbar calls 'bogmen' but not in a mean way. He likes the Irish because they enjoy a drink and good craic, but this lot has barely said a word. They wanted to wear ski masks instead of helmets, but Clifton told them they weren't bombing a bus off the Falls Road.

Henry has given them a crash course in firefighting, showing them around an appliance known as a pump ladder, which has a dual cabin, a water tank, portable generator, floodlights, chemical suits and breathing apparatus.

'Can I drive?' asks Jamie, eyeing the rig.

'No,' says Henry.

'Oh, come on. I've always wanted to—'

'I'm driving.'

They climb on board. Clifton and Finbar ride up front with Henry, the bogmen are in back with Jamie. Henry drives them south towards Acton and then takes Gunnersbury Lane, until they reach the M4. Further west, he takes the Sutton Lane exit and then Staines Road. It's just gone six and already the air is heavy with smoke and sulphur. Families are on their way to firework displays and lightshows, and the first of the bonfires have started burning in fields and parks.

Turning into the back streets, they pass higgledy-piggledy houses with net curtains, cars out front and barking dogs, spooked by the early fireworks. Henry pulls over under a small stand of trees, waiting for the signal. A couple is walking their two dogs. Poodles. Yappy things clipped to look like toys. The man looks up at the pump ladder and says, 'Aw right?'

'Yeah,' says Henry.

'What are you doing out here?'

'Bonfire watch.'

379

'Must be a busy night for you.'

'Yeah.'

'I got a brother-in-law who's a firefighter. Works at Heathrow. Does fuck all most of the time. I mean, how often are there fires at Heathrow? You might know him.'

'No,' says Henry.

'I haven't told you his name.'

Finbar leans over Henry. 'My friend is too polite to say it, sir, but he wants you to fuck off.'

The bogmen finally find something funny.

A double-decker bus trundles past Daragh's window. The people on the upper deck are almost at his eye level. The bus pauses at traffic lights. He can't see the first-floor windows opposite. This might be a flaw in their plan. The lights change and the bus moves on.

Below him, a large black motor pulls up. It's like one of those cars you see carrying the lord mayor or the royals. Two other motors are close behind. The doors open in unison and four men get out. They stand on the footpath, forming a guard of honour.

Popov exits the larger motor, accompanied by a tall, thin woman who straightens her skirt and touches her hair. She hooks her arm into his and they enter the bank.

Daragh turns on his phone and types a message, getting all poetic.

*The fuckery begins . . .*

# 71

Keegan has been made to wait outside Duckworth's office at New Scotland Yard. The corridor smells like a proper workplace, rather than a police station. No puke or vomit or sweat. People look happy. Some of them are laughing. Different world.

'He'll see you now,' says an assistant.

Keegan knocks and enters. Duckworth is standing at his desk, packing a briefcase. He's dressed in black tie.

'Make it quick, Brendan. I'm off to the opera. The wife is a patron. Can't stand it myself.'

'What are you seeing?'

'*Madama Butterfly*. A tragedy in every way.' He puts on his jacket.

'We have a location for Philomena McCarthy,' says Keegan. 'A warehouse in Hounslow. I'd like to brief a tactical response team.'

'Where did you come by this information?'

'Constable McCarthy made an emergency call early this morning but was cut off before she could give her location. Since then, I have received confirmation.'

'From her father?'

Keegan doesn't reply.

'You referred to her as Constable McCarthy, but she no longer works for the Metropolitan Police.'

'She's technically still an officer.'

'Suspended, facing disciplinary action.'

'She was abducted yesterday. I can show you the footage of the incident.'

'I've seen the footage.'

'Her father received a hostage video.'

'From whom?'

'We believe a Bulgarian national called Dimitar Popov is trying to take over McCarthy's East End development. He has made threats to the McCarthy family.'

Duckworth's lips curl into a smile. 'How ironic.'

'As I said, we have a location. I want a tactical response team to—'

Duckworth raises his hand, signalling Keegan to stop. 'What you're telling me is that Edward McCarthy is involved in a turf war with a rival gangster and he wants our help to win that war.'

'No, that's not—'

'Did he ask for your assistance?'

Keegan is quiet.

Duckworth continues. 'Did I ever tell you about my first year as a detective, Brendan?'

'No, sir.'

'I investigated a VAT fraud worth more than two million quid. Clifton McCarthy was facing ten years in prison, but two days before the trial, my main witness disappeared. Sixteen hours later, he walked into a police station three hundred miles away, pale and shaken and suffering complete memory loss. The case collapsed. McCarthy walked free.'

'I'm not defending the family, sir. I'm trying to save a young woman.'

'Is she involved?'

'I don't believe so.'

'Well, collateral damage is unfortunate but sometimes unavoidable. If something happens to her, we will bring the weight of the law down on those responsible, but I'm not going to authorise a tactical response team to do Edward McCarthy's dirty work.' Duckworth looks at his phone. 'I really do have to go. Was there anything else?'

Keegan is still standing, feeling numb. He is ushered to the door by a hand resting in the small of his back.

'And Brendan,' says Duckworth, 'if I'm ever asked about this meeting, I will say that you came here to request additional assets for your investigation into the murder of Caitlin Kemp-Lowe. Anything beyond that, I will deny.'

Keegan walks out of the office and the building and along the Thames Embankment. He can't remember if he drove a car to the Yard or was dropped off. Around him, people are heading home from work or out for the evening. There are tourists taking photographs of Westminster Bridge and the Houses of Parliament.

Edward McCarthy thinks the police are coming to help him rescue his daughter. That's not going to happen. What is the point of being a police officer if he can't do this? If his soon to be ex-wife Veronica could see him now, she'd be scathing about his passivity and ineptitude.

*You couldn't find water if you fell out of a boat*, she'd say.

Well, he's in the water now. Drowning.

# 72

Popov's voice booms along the corridor, jovial and buffoonish, sounding like a first-time father celebrating his new baby. He enters the room, carrying a bottle of champagne.

'Eddie! Sorry to keep you waiting. London traffic, eh? Quicker to walk.'

He is dressed in an expensive suit that doesn't fit him properly and a new eyepatch made of red velvet that matches the pocket square in his jacket. *Maybe he wears this one for special occasions or with formal attire*, thinks McCarthy. He's brought two male lawyers along, as well as a woman whom McCarthy recognises. Charlotte Farley. She had been with Carmichael when they floated the idea of selling half of Hope Island.

'I believe you know Charlotte,' says Popov.

Charlotte Farley holds out her hand. 'It's nice to see you again, Edward.'

Even with heavy make-up, she can't hide the swelling on one side of her face.

'That's a nasty bruise,' comments McCarthy. 'Did you run into a door or into my daughter?'

The woman stops smiling and withdraws her hand. Meanwhile, Popov is circling the room, introducing himself and repeating people's names, making friends. His two lawyers look like they're representing a defendant not a businessman. Both have remained near the door, as though hoping to escape quickly once the signatures are dry.

'You have the contracts?' asks Popov.

'You have the money?' counters McCarthy.

'Of course.'

Charlotte Farley produces her iPad. 'I'll be completing the transfers.'

'Where is the money coming from?' asks McCarthy.

She smiles, bemused. 'I don't imagine that's a question you ask very often.'

'Money is money,' says Popov.

McCarthy: 'Is that one of your Bulgarian sayings?'

'No, but I do have one that you might like: "You are permitted in times of great danger, to walk with the devil until you have crossed the bridge." I am that devil and today you cross the bridge.'

Popov is about to sit down when he pauses and glances at the window. He moves both blotters, sliding them down the table.

Finally he settles, with his lawyers on either side of him. Charlotte Farley remains standing, looking over his shoulder. McCarthy takes a seat directly opposite, next to Helgarde, who opens his briefcase. He takes out a contract bound in red ribbon, which he hands to McCarthy, who passes it on to Popov, who relays it to his lawyers, who read silently.

Minutes pass. The only sound is turning pages and the hum of the air conditioner.

'How is my daughter?' asks McCarthy.

'She was perfectly happy last time I saw her,' says Popov. 'We had breakfast together. I told her that she'd be home for supper.'

The lawyers turn another page. They look at each other.

'What's wrong?' asks Popov.

'It's only twenty-five per cent,' says one of them.

'We agreed on seventy-five.'

'Keep reading,' says McCarthy.

More pages are turned. The older lawyer turns to Popov. 'This is already signed.' He points to the signatures. 'You're not the buyer.'

McCarthy interrupts. 'Oh, I didn't tell you. I have new business partners. They only wanted twenty-five per cent.'

Popov's face gurns through emotions, moving from anger to rage to apoplexy. 'I want the room,' he rumbles.

Charlotte Farley puts a hand on his shoulder. He brushes it away.

'Get out,' says Popov. 'Everybody. Except you.' He is pointing at McCarthy.

Helgarde leans closer. 'I don't think you should agree.'

'It's fine,' says McCarthy.

The lawyers and the bankers leave the room. McCarthy and Popov are alone.

'If it makes you feel any better, it was a difficult decision,' says McCarthy, walking to the window, looking down at the street where luxury cars are parked nose to tail. Drivers are waiting. Minders. Bodyguards.

'Who are they?' asks Popov.

'Red Hand Limited. An interesting enterprise,' says McCarthy. 'They don't seem to make anything or own anything, but they do have a workforce. Contractors. Have you heard of the Real IRA? It was a paramilitary group that split from the Provisional IRA after the Good Friday Agreement was signed in 1998. These were hardcore nationalists who didn't want to give up the fight for a united Ireland. Most of them put down their weapons more than a decade ago, but some of them didn't believe in ceasefires or sharing peace.

'Now, to be honest, I don't like getting into bed with people like that, but it's like you said, "In times of great danger, you're allowed to walk with the devil until you cross the bridge."'

Popov explodes to his feet, screaming, 'She's dead! Hear me. Dead!'

He takes out his phone, but suddenly stops. A small red beam of light has flashed into his left eye and across his eyepatch and then to his forehead. He freezes. Eyes wide. Understanding the significance.

Stepping closer, McCarthy points his finger at Popov's chest. The red dot moves and comes to rest above the Bulgarian's heart. When he moves his finger, the dot follows, down to Popov's groin and up again to his neck and across his cheek and back to his forehead.

'Where would you like the bullet to enter?' asks McCarthy.

'Killing me won't save her,' says Popov, less belligerent than before.

The red dot is now dancing on the Bulgarian's face, like a bouncing dot on a music score.

'Oh, I'm not going to kill you,' says McCarthy. 'I leave that to others. Some of my employees are downstairs now, getting acquainted with your entourage.'

He motions out of the window where Popov's car is surrounded by dark-clad figures. His driver and bodyguards are holding their hands aloft.

'You can't save her,' says Popov, frozen in place by the red dot. 'If they don't hear from me in the next twenty minutes, she's dead.'

# 73

My eyelids are sticky and glued shut. I want to reach up and peel them open, but my hands are taped to the frame of the bed and my bruised body is stiff with the cold. The adrenaline that imbued me yesterday has evaporated, leaving exhaustion and a growing sense of despair.

Shadows move. Shapes against the light. A figure leans over me and whispers my name. 'Philomena.'

My eyes finally open. I watch the ritual. The heated spoon. The plunger pulled back. The needle filling. The Nord taps it with his fingernail. He examines my forearm, searching for a vein. Finds the spot. I feel the prick and a drop of my blood mixes with the potion that is injected into my bloodstream. Moments later, a wave of euphoria washes over me, ringing in my ears, numbing my face, my lips, my tongue.

He peels the tape covering my mouth. 'What did you give me?' I murmur.

'You're riding the dragon now,' he says.

'Mmm.'

As if by magic, my vision clears and I can see every rivet in the metal beams and every corrugation and cobweb on the roof. I can feel my skin breathing. I can see the tiny wrinkles around his cruel eyes and every different shade of blue in his irises. I am warm inside, soft but firm, loving but dangerous. All of the best feelings in the world are wrapped up into one

– love, laughter, fireworks, spring rain, mown grass, babies, rainbows, waterfalls . . .

'Can you scratch my nose?' I ask.

'No.'

'Please. It's itchy.'

He cuts the tape away from the frame of the bed, but my wrists are still bound. I rub at my nose. It is still itchy. I rub again. I want to scratch. I want something sharp to claw at my skin, which is suddenly crawling with insects that swarm into my mouth and nose and ears. I want the love to come back. I want the love to keep chasing me. I want to taste it in my mouth and draw it into my lungs. But it's gone now, replaced by nausea and fear.

The Nord is running his hands up my leg and over my hip. 'Are you ready to have some fun?'

'No.'

'I can make you feel good.'

'Please, no.'

I'm sobbing and shaking. My body vibrating. My feet are free. My clothes are coming off. He is lying next to me. I hear a knock on the door. A voice. 'He told you to leave her alone.'

'Yeah, well, he's not here, is he? And she's enjoying it, aren't you?'

I struggle to find my voice because the vomit rises into my mouth and a scream fills my ears. I push him away and cover myself, finding the words.

'Touch me again and I'll kill you.'

# 74

Henry parks the pump ladder between two factories on an industrial estate, in a CCTV blackspot, out of sight of nearby houses and businesses.

'Wait here,' he says, setting off on foot, carrying a plastic jerry can. Finbar goes with him, breathing hard, sweating in the uniform. Soon, Clifton and the bogmen are silhouettes in the distance, lost in the shadows.

Pausing at the edge of a building, Henry studies the entrance to the warehouse, which has a large metal roller door with a smaller door inserted. The eastern end of the building is made of red brick with windows on each floor. The western end has brick on the lower level and metal at the top with no windows. There are security lights above the doors and more along the sides, burning brightly in the darkness. Two dark-coloured four-wheel drives are parked out front. A Land Cruiser and a Range Rover.

The nearest business, beyond a metal spiked fence, is a logistics company with freight trucks parked in a loading area. On the opposite side is a scrap-metal yard where wrecked vehicles are jumbled on top of each other like carcasses at an abattoir.

'That door is a choke point,' says Finbar. 'We can't storm it without taking casualties. We need to draw them out.'

At that moment, a man emerges from the office. Sucking on a vape, he emits a cloud of water vapour that disperses in the light breeze. He scratches his balls and looks at his phone. Henry signals to Finbar and they move again, crouching low, staying out of sight. They follow a wire fence until they reach the western end of the warehouse. Another business, directly behind, is leasing construction equipment. Backhoes, trenchers, pavers, forklifts, compactors, tractors and bulldozers.

The warehouse wall is now above them. Four large industrial bins are nearby, waiting to be collected. Henry peers into one of them, which is full of papers and broken-down boxes. He looks up and studies the eaves.

'Here, help me with this.'

The wheels are rusty and the bin has to be manhandled into place, against the wall of the warehouse. Opening the jerry can, Henry pours petrol into the skip, the fumes catching in the back of his throat.

'It will take about fifteen minutes for the fire to spread into the roof and fill the warehouse with smoke.'

'Are you sure about this? Phil is inside.'

'We have breathing equipment. They don't.'

'We're not firemen.'

'I am. I'll find her.'

He tells Finbar to go back to the others. When he's out of sight, he takes a lighter from his pocket and snaps it open, hesitating as the flame dances from his fingers. There is one weakness in his plan. He doesn't know what's inside the warehouse – what flammables and combustibles. Chemicals. Gas bottles. Plastics. Synthetics. Toxins. Any number of silent, unknown killers.

When he drops the flame there is a whooshing sound as the accelerant ignites and begins to feed on the paper and cardboard. The flames rise quickly, licking against the walls, trying to climb. Henry retraces his steps, along the wire fence and between the factories.

When he reaches the truck, he can already see an orange glow above the nearest rooftop. He looks at his watch. 'OK, in ten minutes we turn on the siren and arrive like this is a normal job. We hook up the hoses, we fight the fire and we search the building.'

'How do we do that?' asks Jamie.

'Just follow my lead.'

Keegan uses his satnav to find the address and pulls over when he's ten minutes away, walking the final quarter mile. As he turns into the industrial estate, he notices a fire truck parked under the trees. Four men are standing next to the appliance. Firefighters.

In the distance he can hear fireworks exploding and see a colourful cascade of light dripping from the sky above bonfires. Guy Fawkes night. Never let anyone tell you that Protestants don't hold a grudge.

He approaches the truck and clears his throat. 'Are you guys on a job?'

Four heads turn. Four hands. Four guns. All pointing at his head.

'Police,' he says, feebly. His hands are held high. He's holding his warrant card.

'Fuck me, you scared us,' says Clifton.

Keegan recognises him. 'Your brother gave me this address. He wanted me to help.'

Clifton McCarthy looks past him. 'Where are the others?'

'It's just me.'

Before Keegan can explain, Finbar arrives back at the pump ladder, followed by Henry Chapman. In the darkness, in their uniforms, it's hard to recognise faces, but the voices are unmistakable.

'Are you armed?' asks Finbar.

'No.'

'Well, take this.'

He hands Keegan a pistol.

'I don't think that's a good idea.'

'You could wait until they're shooting at you.'

Keegan takes the pistol, weighing it in his hands, wondering if he should wipe it down with a disinfectant cloth. Then he considers how many laws have been broken with this weapon; how many laws he's breaking. He can feel his heartbeat in his teeth.

Then he notices the orange glow appearing above the nearest rooftop. 'It that a fire?'

'Yeah, but don't worry, we're firefighters,' says Henry. 'Climb on board and hang on.'

'Are we using the siren?' asks Jamie.

'Oh, yeah.'

And the sound cuts through the night.

# 75

McCarthy and Popov are still standing at the window. Popov is too scared to move because the red dot is fixed on his forehead. Instead, he stares at his reflection in the glass, knowing that that somewhere behind that dark square, in the building opposite, a figure is sitting at a window, looking down the scope of a rifle.

'That's my brother, Daragh,' says McCarthy. 'You've met him. Daragh used to be a sniper in the army. Fought in the Falklands. He can stare down that scope for hours, finger on the trigger, never losing focus. If you try to duck, or move, you won't have time to realise that you're dead.'

'What happens next?' asks Popov.

'We wait.'

'They're expecting me to call. If they don't hear from me, they'll kill her.'

'You said they'd kill her anyway.'

'I can call them off.'

'I don't trust you.'

'But if they kill her—'

'I'll kill you.'

'You're starting a war.'

'That's exactly what I said when I met you in the steam room and you told me that a war suggested a contest, a battle of one side against another. You threatened to kill every member of my family – my nieces, nephews, aunts, uncles, sons and daughters. Innocent people, good people, people whose only mistake was to have some connection to me.

'Daragh's wife has been sick. Breast cancer. Stage four. Chances are she's going to die, but she's fighting to watch her first grandbaby grow up. You want to take that away from Daragh, from Mary, from that newborn baby.'

'We can come to a deal.'

'No. That time has passed.'

'I know where they are.'

'No, you don't.'

'The hotel in North London. You think I wouldn't have you followed?'

'I knew you would. That's why they were intercepted en route and taken somewhere else. All of our families are safe. Meanwhile, my new business partners are outside your gaffe on Putney Heath and the boarding house you rent in Brixton and at the warehouse where you're holding Philomena.

'When we first met, I was at a disadvantage, because I didn't know much about you, but it's different now.' McCarthy glances at his watch. 'Your dogs will be going for a walk about now. Big fuckers. Must be a handful. Who takes them when you're not home?'

Popov doesn't answer.

'It's not your wife. She's in Greece on the island of Evia where you have a holiday house.'

'My housekeeper. She's not involved in any of this.'

'She's a very attractive dog-walker. Over-qualified, I'd say. And I can't see her washing and ironing in that wardrobe.'

Popov doesn't answer.

There's a knock on the door. McCarthy looks at Popov, and points to the window. The red dot doesn't move. He answers the door.

Helgarde: 'Is everything all right?'

'Hunky-dory.'

'Charlotte Farley wants to consult with Mr Popov.'

'We're still talking.'
'And the others are wondering if they might go home.'
'Sure.'
'Are you staying?'
'For a while.'
'What's going on?'
'The endgame.'

# 76

I'm vomiting so hard I feel as though my stomach lining is coming out through my mouth along with my other organs. I can picture my insides slithering onto the floor in a hot, pink mess.

'How much did you give her?' asks someone.

'A baby dose.'

'Well, she's going to aspirate on her own vomit.'

'Aspir-what?'

'Choke on her own vomit. Help me roll her over.'

'Fuck that! I've got to wash my clothes.'

I threw up all over the Nord. Serves him right.

Someone turns me on my side so I can throw up in a bucket. My entire body spasms as I dry-retch. I feel a pain in my chest. Maybe this is a heart attack.

'Here, drink this,' says one of them, putting a bottle to my lips, but the water runs over the side of my face. I keep sucking at the wrong time. Eventually it goes down the wrong way and I cough, spurting water out of my nose.

'Can you smell that?' asks a voice.

'What?'

'Smoke.'

'It's bonfire night.'

'No. Look at the ceiling.'

There is a cracking sound of wood breaking or a window shattering somewhere in the building, and then a siren.

'Shit! The police.'

'No, that's a fire engine.'

'But they'll be coming.'

'Go outside. I'll get the extinguisher.'

Having vomited, I feel better. Without raising my head from the bucket, I know that I'm alone. Sitting up, I glance at the ceiling where smoke is blurring the beams, billowing downwards.

# 77

The pump ladder pulls up and Henry cuts the siren. He jumps down from the cab and immediately begins yelling instructions. The bogmen are surprisingly capable of following orders, unrolling hoses and running them across the asphalt parking area to a hydrant. Henry attaches the hose, turning on the water, which spews out in a glistening silver arc.

The warehouse door opens and two men emerge with weight-room physiques and short-cropped hair. Heavy coats. Arms away from their bodies. Something beneath. Weapons, maybe.

'What is the problem?' asks one of them, in a heavy accent.

'Fire,' says Clifton. 'Who called it in?'

The men look at each other.

'We got a triple-nine call. Did you report the fire?'

More blank looks. Another two men emerge from inside wearing similar clothes or camouflage gear. One is holding a cloth supermarket bag, hand hidden inside. Definitely a weapon.

Jamie Pike arrives at a jog. 'The south-western corner is alight. Looks like it's in the roof.'

'OK, focus on the water on the upper floor, aim at the rafters, or above the flames,' says Henry, who turns back to the four men. 'What's in the warehouse?'

'Huh?'

'Flammables? Combustibles? Gas bottles? Chemicals? I need to know.'

'Fuck knows,' says the older man.

'What are you doing here?'

'Working.'

'Doing what?'

'None of your business.'

'Well, you need to evacuate. Everybody out.'

'That won't happen,' says the man they saw vaping earlier. He's standing King Charles style, hands behind his back, like he's keeping something out of sight. 'You put the fire out. We'll take care of anyone inside.'

'No. You evacuate the building,' says Henry.

'There's nobody else,' says the man.

'I don't believe you,' says Henry. They're face to face. Chest to chest.

Clifton and Finbar have taken axes from the side of the truck. At that moment, a skylight shatters with a popping sound and flames leap out of the opening, sending sparks and smoke high into the air.

One of the men is looking closely at Finbar. 'I know you?' he says, more a statement than a question.

'I don't think so.'

The guy is clicking his fingers, trying to remember. It's like he's growing balls in front of their eyes. His colleague still has his hand in the shopping bag.

'Could have been when I was shagging your mother,' says Finbar.

It takes a moment for the insult to register. The hand emerges, holding a sub-machine gun. It doesn't reach hip-height before Clifton swings an axe into his midriff, felling him like a tree. His gun falls and skitters across the cement. Finbar punches his axe-handle into the other shooter's face, breaking teeth and bones.

The two other men start firing. Bullets ricochet off the pump ladder and the asphalt. The bogmen are up for a fight, crouching and firing, covering one another as they move across the compound. Jamie is with them, acting like he's in some Hollywood movie. Clifton screams at him to get down.

Henry only has eyes for the fire. The flames have reached the middle section of the warehouse where dark black smoke billows from the skylights. He yells at Clifton and Finbar to take the hose, which is writhing across the ground, spraying water indiscriminately. They wrestle with the hose, pinning it down with the weight of their bodies before directing the spray.

'Aim it into the rafters,' yells Henry, who has taken a breathing apparatus from the truck. He slings an oxygen tank over his shoulders and fastens the straps, before checking the gauge and the cylinder connection valve.

Keegan is next to him. 'You want me to come with?'

'No.' Henry throws him the keys. 'I want you to drive.'

'Where?'

He points at the warehouse. 'Straight through that wall.'

Keegan gets behind the wheel and turns the ignition. Henry is on the running board next to his window.

'It's a normal manual transmission. You don't need to double clutch,' he shouts, above the gunfire. A bullet punches through the windscreen and hits the passenger seat headrest.

The pump ladder jerks forward and picks up speed. More bullets are pinging off the metal.

'Put on your seatbelt,' says Henry. 'Head directly for that window. Don't miss. Either side and you'll bring the whole place down. Faster.'

'What about you?' yells Keegan.

'I'll be fine.'

The rig is forty yards from the wall, accelerating. Henry jumps at the last moment, tumbling over the ground and bouncing to his feet. The truck slams into the warehouse, punching through the bricks, creating a cloud of dust and falling debris. It looks to be wedged inside, but Keegan puts it into reverse and begins pulling out, revving the engine hard as the wheels spin and gain traction on the rubble.

He creates a gap for Henry, who slips between the appliance

and the wall. He squirts the bypass valve to check his air and slips the harness over his head, fixing the full-face mask in place. Air hisses into his ears and he turns on the torch, moving into the darkness.

# 78

Smoke has filled the room and I can no longer see the rafters or the window on the wall. Something shatters above me. The skylight. Glass rains down, making plink-plink sounds when it hits the concrete floor.

I heard a fire siren earlier. They must be outside. I need to signal them or to find a way out of this room.

Quickly, pulling on my clothes, I crawl across the floor, staying beneath the smoke, flinching as broken glass digs into my palms and knees. I put my hand against the door but can't feel any heat. The handle is warm but not hot. It's not locked. I slip outside into the belly of the warehouse where half the roof is alight. Flames sweep back and forth in waves of red and orange. A funnel of water arcs above the fire, evaporating into steam before it hits the ground.

Blinded by smoke, I put my right hand on the nearest shelf and use it to direct me towards the roller doors. Something falls from above, a burning box that sends a shower of sparks into my face and hair.

There are popping sounds coming from nearby. It could be gunfire. I can see random holes in the roller door and small shafts of light. The flames sweep across the ceiling again, creating a whooshing noise like a strong wind, sucking oxygen from the air. I'm trying not to breathe, but every so often I'm forced to inhale. The smoke goes deep into my lungs, making me cough and suck in more poison.

Suddenly, my collar triggers and my brain explodes in pain. I claw at the padlocked collar, trying to rip it off, but it triggers again and I'm rolling on the floor, moaning and crying.

I'm barely aware of the pain stopping. I'm lying on my back, looking up at a world on fire. I turn my head and see a light moving towards me, a figure, a one-eyed monster, an astronaut walking on the moon, a lantern fish deep in the ocean lighting its own way.

Strong arms embrace me and hold me tightly. Something presses over my face and I taste air. It hisses in my ears. Henry's voice, soft in my ears.

'Count between each breath. Inhale, two, three, exhale, two, three, inhale, two, three, exhale, two, three.'

My head clears. I have air. I'm breathing. I'm alive. He takes the mask away and fills his lungs, but I want to rip it back. He needs it too. I fight the urge, but reach for it anyway, pleading for air. He straps the mask over my head and corrects the seal.

I point to the dog collar around my neck but he has no way of cutting it off. Instead, he picks me up like a rag doll and carries me down towards the roller doors. Shelves are starting to topple behind us and flames are falling from the sky, singeing my hair and my clothes.

Henry stumbles and I cling to him. I'm too heavy. He needs oxygen. I want to give him the mask, but he ignores my hands. We've reached the large roller door. Bullets have penetrated the metal, creating jagged exit holes. Henry puts me down and presses his lips to one of the holes, trying to suck air from outside. I tap on the side of his helmet, pointing to the mask. We share again. I count the seconds between breaths.

Through the smoke, I see a fuse box. Beneath that is a door-post. The doorpost has a photoelectric switch. I crawl towards it, reach up and press the button. Metal groans, gears engage, the door begins to rise.

I have no idea what's waiting outside. I don't care. I'd rather die out there than spend another moment in this inferno. Henry goes first. There's just enough room for him to belly crawl to the other side. He holds up the door, waiting for me, but the collar triggers again. I'm rolling and thrashing on the ground.

'Where do you think you're going?' says a voice. The Nord. The Diceman. He is silhouetted against the flames.

Henry grabs my hand and tries to pull me through the gap but the Nord has one of my legs. I'm caught in the middle, trying to hold the collar away from my neck. The Nord is on his knees, coughing, still clinging to my right leg. I kick with my left, connecting with something soft like his stomach or his groin. Groaning, he lets go.

I'm free, being dragged under the door. Henry picks me up and carries me with whatever strength he has left. Stumbling and running and stumbling.

Firemen are rushing towards us. Only they're not firemen. Clifton and Finbar are lifting me.

'You got her. You fucking got her,' says Jamie Pike, slapping Henry on the back. Someone is pouring a bottle of water into my eyes. They're doing the same for Henry.

He looks up at me and smiles, and then I see blood blossom on the front of his uniform and hear the sound of the bullet as it exits his body and passes close by my head. Moments later, blood leaks from the edge of his mouth and he drops to his knees and then onto his face, and I scream until there is no sound left in my body.

# 79

McCarthy is sitting at the table, cradling his phone, wanting it to ring and at the same time dreading the sound. He'd rather it remain silent forever than to hear that he'd lost her.

'Can I sit down?' asks Popov.

'No.'

'I'm getting cramp in my legs.'

'I don't care.'

'I don't believe your brother will shoot me. You need me as leverage.'

McCarthy gets to his feet and walks to Popov. The red dot is now resting above the Bulgarian's heart, near his pocket square. McCarthy touches it with his forefinger and drags the dot higher, across Popov's neck and left cheek, until it comes to rest on his ear. McCarthy moves his hand away. The dot remains. He turns to the window. Nods.

The bullet shatters a pane of glass and slams into the wall beside Popov's head. His hand shoots up and he feels for his missing ear as blood spills down his neck.

He curses McCarthy and pleads, 'What can I do to stop this?'

'Nothing. Both of us have to wait.'

A knock on the door. McCarthy answers. Helgarde again.

'What was that?' he asks.

'Nothing to worry about.'

He looks across the room. Popov is holding the velvet handkerchief to the side of his head.

'Should I call a doctor?'

'No. I thought you'd gone home.'

'I promised Carmichael that I'd lock up.'

'I can do that. You go.'

The door closes.

McCarthy's phone buzzes on the table, bouncing on the smooth cherry wood. He collects it and presses receive. Listens.

'We have her,' says Clifton. 'She's safe.'

'Unhurt?'

'Bumps and bruises. A few burns.'

'What about the others?'

'One man down.'

'One of the bogmen?'

'No.'

'Jamie?'

'No.'

McCarthy's heart sinks.

'We took out Damyan Georgiev, but not before he gut-shot Henry. It looks bad.'

McCarthy is gripping the phone so tightly it might crumble to dust in his fist. 'Where's Phil? Can I talk to her?'

'She went in the ambulance.'

There are sirens in the background. 'I got to go. The filth are coming. The bogmen have taken off, but DCI Keegan insisted we stick around.'

'He showed up?'

'On his own. The fuckers wouldn't back him up.'

'That lad is full of surprises.'

Popov has been listening to half the conversation, but it's enough for him to know that his last card has been played. He drops to the ground and a bullet smashes into the wall where his head used to be. Then he dashes for the door, bouncing off the walls as he runs down the hallway and the stairs.

McCarthy doesn't bother giving chase. He stays in the conference room, looking out of the window, as Popov emerges from

407

the building and turns along the road. Four men surround him. Not his disloyal retainers, who are long gone.

Another phone call. It's Daragh, from the opposite side of the street. 'Am I right in thinking—'

'She's safe.'

'And the others?'

'Henry is on his way to hospital.'

Below them, more of the bogmen are marching Popov to the larger of the two cars.

'What do we do with 'im?' asks Daragh.

'Take him to the police.'

'Why?'

'After tonight, Keegan is going to need a win.'

# 80

Each time the ambulance slows at an intersection or for traffic, the siren becomes louder, as though the sound is catching up and chasing us again. Two paramedics are leaning over Henry, talking to him.

'Don't go to sleep, Henry.'

'Stay with us, Henry.'

'Keep your eyes open. That's it.'

At the same time, they're talking to each other.

'Blood pressure is falling.'

'Pulse is weak.'

'Prep another bag.'

I want to hold Henry's hand. I want to put my arms around him. I want to reach into the hole in his chest and stop the bleeding with my fist.

At Hillingdon Hospital, the rear doors swing open and trolley wheels unfold and rattle across the pavement, carrying Henry through the entrance. Doctors take over, pushing him towards a lift. A surgical team is waiting upstairs. I try to squeeze in, but one of them blocks me.

'You can't come with us. Find a doctor.'

I catch sight of my reflection in the closing doors. I have panda eyes and singed hair and my clothes are torn and bloody. I can taste soot and grit between my teeth that no amount of water has washed away.

A nurse takes me by the hand.

'You can't help him any more.'

In the hours that follow, I am joined by the family. Aunties. Uncles. Cousins. Nieces. Nephews. There aren't enough seats in the patient lounge, so some are perched on windowsills or sitting on the floor or spilling out into the corridor. Daragh brings Mary, who is barely out of hospital, her head wrapped in a scarf to hide her hair loss.

'You didn't have to come,' I say, feeling her fragile arms around me.

'Where else would I be?' she replies.

Not everyone is here. Clifton and Finbar are 'helping police with their inquiries', and nobody has seen my father since he walked out of the private bank. Four bodies were found at the warehouse, killed by bullets or burned to death. Two men were wounded and taken to hospital under armed guard.

Constance has brought me a change of outfit and a nurse has told me I can use the staff showers. I put my scorched and bloody clothes into a plastic bag, knowing the police will want them. Naked in front of a mirror, I look at my reflection. The hair on one side of my head has been singed off, along with my left eyebrow. Antiseptic cream is slathered on my burns.

Edging under the warm spray, I curl up on the floor of the cubicle, sobbing loudly because nobody is around to hear me. I pray, which is a rarity. I haven't been to Mass since I left home at eighteen. Under my mother's roof it had been mandatory. Mass every Sunday. Confession once a month. Saying grace before every meal.

There's a knock on the door. 'Are you all right?' asks Constance.

'Fine.'

'Do you need anything?'

'No.'

410

She leaves and I turn off the shower and I dress in her clothes, which are more expensive than anything in my wardrobe. I put more cream on my burns and take another painkiller.

I don't want to go back to the lounge. There are too many people. Yes, they're family and they love me, but I want to fall apart without anyone watching.

I think about sneaking away, going somewhere quiet, but what if Henry wakes up or the surgeon wants to talk to me? As I leave the bathroom, I turn away from the lounge. I'm almost at the lift doors, when I notice someone standing at a window, staring into the dark square.

Daragh turns. Our eyes meet. He takes a step towards me, but stops just out of reach, as though seeking permission. Almost unconsciously, I take a step towards him and his arms fold around me and I'm sobbing into his shirt, telling him about the bullet that tore through Henry's chest and how much blood he lost and how many organs must have been in the way.

'Where's Daddy?' I ask.

Daragh shrugs. 'Eddie blames 'imself, but it weren't 'is fault.'

'Yes, it was.'

'No, girlie.'

'He should have called the police.'

'He did. They didn't want to 'elp you.'

'What?'

'Eddie asked for back-up, but none of the bastards showed up except for Keegan. I guess we had 'im figured all wrong.'

'But I was a hostage?'

'They didn't care. Nobody else was coming to save you except us. And that was down to Eddie and to your man, 'Enry. He was fuckin' amazing. You should 'ear Finbar and Clifton talkin' about what he did – the way he charged into that building and carried you out through the flames and the smoke. He's a fuckin' 'ero.' Daragh is getting teary-eyed and has to stop himself.

'I'm going to lose him.'

'Don't say that. 'Enry is a fighter. It's in 'is nature.'

I push him away, wiping my eyes. I can't find a tissue. He has a clean handkerchief. Of course he does. He's a man of a previous generation. Not a gentleman thief exactly. Less John Robie – Cary Grant – in *To Catch a Thief* and more Charlie Croker – Michael Caine – in *The Italian Job*.

Daragh tells me what happened at the bank and how he and Daddy handled Popov while the others came for me.

'How did you get the money?' I ask.

'That's not your problem, girlie, but whatever 'appens, Eddie is gonna look after the family.'

'He had me followed.'

'Jamie enjoyed that too much.'

'He's an arsehole.'

'He's very fond of you.'

Further along the grey corridor, Constance appears. She's looking for me. How does she walk in those heels?

'The surgeon wants to see you.'

The doctor is in his early fifties with short-spiky hair, a down-turned mouth and whitened teeth that show when he smiles. Is that a good sign – the smiling?

'Let me explain what we had to do,' he says, sitting opposite me in a quiet corner. 'The bullet went through Henry's stomach, kidney, liver and part of his lower lung.' He points to the entry and exit wounds, using his body as a model. 'During surgery, he lost twenty-five units of blood – twice what his body can hold. We had three surgeons, two anaesthetists, their nurses and registrars working in shifts, as well as porters running units of blood from the haematology department to the theatre. I guess what I'm trying to say is that this was a team effort.'

*But did the team win?*

'We spent the first two hours trying to control his bleeding and administering adrenaline to stop Henry slipping into cardiac arrest. Enormous doses – ten times what we'd usually give someone. We were ventilating his lungs and administering new blood and trying to repair the damage. The bullet destroyed one kidney and effectively cut Henry's stomach in half. We had a vascular surgeon and a urologist, working together to stop the bleeding.'

'Is he going to . . . will he . . . ?' The question keeps getting caught in my throat.

'He survived surgery, that's step one. There's still a long way to go, but we're lucky to have a patient as strong as Henry. He's one tough cookie.'

'Can I see him?'

'He's in an induced coma and will be for the next few days.'

'I can sit with him . . . talk to him . . .'

The surgeon nods. 'We're moving him to the ICU. I'll have someone let you know when he's there.'

# 81

Assistant Commissioner Duckworth strides onto the stage and seems to grow in stature under the TV lights. He is in full dress uniform again, with all his medals, braids and ribbons on display. Keegan follows him into the spotlight, more circumspect, dressed in a crumpled suit and a hastily knotted tie that is too short on his chest.

Duckworth waits for the assembled media to settle before clearing his throat.

'Thank you for coming. I am going to read from a prepared statement and then take questions. First, I shall address the shooting incident at Fairway Trading Estate in West London, which resulted in the deaths of four men, and the wounding of three others. At this stage, the investigation is ongoing, which means limited information will be released today.

'What I can tell you is the following. Two days ago, a twenty-nine-year-old London police officer was abducted from a street in Maida Vale, London, by a gang that police believe was responsible for the home invasion and robbery that led to the death of Caitlin Kemp-Lowe.

'We are not releasing that officer's name, but I can tell you that she was protecting the life of a five-year-old girl, who was a witness to the home invasion. Earlier that same day, another important eyewitness, Hugo Desai, was run down and killed in a hit-and-run on Wellington Road in St John's Wood.

That suspect vehicle, which had been stolen, was subsequently found burned out in a layby in Hertfordshire.

'At approximately seven forty-five yesterday morning, emergency services received a nine-nine-nine call from the missing officer, but she was cut off before she could give her location. By triangulating the signal, police established her whereabouts. She was being held at a warehouse on the Fairway Trading Estate in Hounslow.

'Detective Chief Inspector Brendan Keegan, the officer in charge of the task force, planned and led a rescue operation that involved Specialist Firearms Command, armed response teams and other branches of the emergency services, including the London Fire Brigade.'

Keegan is at the side of the stage, shifting uncomfortably in his chair, feeling the weight of eyes upon him. Is anyone going to believe this complete crock of shit?

Twelve hours ago, Duckworth had been spitting with rage and rattling off all the laws that Keegan had broken or disobeyed. His career was over. He faced arrest and imprisonment and public disgrace. That was until Keegan produced the recording of their previous conversation in Duckworth's office. An app on his phone had captured the assistant commissioner describing the fate of a young police officer as 'collateral damage'.

Now, Duckworth was painting a different picture of last night's events, doing what he does best – covering his arse. Credit where it's due, thinks Keegan, it's an award-winning performance, a monologue for the ages, with just the right mix of gravitas, emotion and pride.

'In a daring and dangerous operation, DCI Keegan and his team came under sustained gunfire in the most trying of circumstances. I'm sure you have all seen the footage of the burning warehouse.

'Four suspected gang members were killed in the rescue operation and another two were wounded, suffering gunshot or blunt-force injuries. They are currently in hospital, under armed guard. The alleged ringleader of the gang, a Bulgarian national, has been charged with murder, armed robbery and abduction. More charges are pending.

'As for the young officer who they abducted, she was rescued from the warehouse, suffering third-degree burns and minor injuries. Unfortunately, a London firefighter, called to fight the blaze, was hit by a stray bullet and has suffered life-threatening injuries. He has undergone surgery in Hillingdon Hospital and is in a critical condition. We are not releasing his name until his next-of-kin have been informed.'

Duckworth turns to Keegan. 'I can't tell you how proud I am to call this man a colleague and a friend. What you did last night, Brendan, your bravery, your professionalism, your courage under fire, is a credit to the Met.'

He pulls Keegan into an embrace and holds him there. Applause breaks out. Embarrassed, Keegan doesn't return the hug.

Duckworth releases him and steps back from the microphones. It is Keegan's turn to keep selling the lie. He braces his hands on either side of the lectern and looks at the battery of microphones with padded covers. He imagines what germs are breeding in the foam. Then he looks up at the expectant faces of the assembled reporters and knows that they *want* to believe the lie.

'Firstly, let me thank my team and Assistant Commissioner Duckworth for the support he's given throughout this investigation. Without his guiding hand, I wouldn't be here now.

'I also want to pay tribute to the young London firefighter, who is fighting for his life in hospital. He went into a burning building alone, under fire, to rescue the young officer who had been abducted.

'For procedural reasons and because there will be an inquest, I cannot give you a full breakdown of the operation, but I will take questions.'

The reporters begin shouting all at once.

'One at a time,' says Duckworth, picking out raised hands.

'What can you tell us about the gang?' asks a reporter from the *Daily Mirror*.

'We believe they are primarily Bulgarian nationals.'

'How many police were involved in the operation?' asks another.

'I can't give you the exact number.'

'Who fired first?'

'They did.'

'How did the warehouse blaze start?'

'It's possible a stray bullet ignited flammable material in the warehouse, but a full investigation is under way involving the London Fire Investigation Unit.'

'How did a London fire crew become involved?'

'The appliance was returning from a call-out on bonfire night.'

'Where is the brigade based?'

'I don't have that information.'

'Can you tell us about the abduction of the police officer?'

'She was working undercover, protecting an important witness.'

'Will you be releasing her name?'

'The officer may wish to continue her undercover work, which will mean keeping her identity secret. I will tell you that this officer has a very bright future in the Metropolitan Police, and Assistant Commissioner Duckworth has already suggested recommending her for the King's Gallantry Medal.'

Duckworth's face is locked in a rictus smile.

The questions continue, becoming more specific, but Keegan's answers grow hazier, blurring the edges of the truth, yet giving the reporters enough to write their headlines and fill their bulletins and feed the news cycle for another day.

# 82

It has been four days since the shooting. I have spent most of that time in the ICU, sitting in the semi-darkness, listening to the machines hum and beep, and watching liquid circulate through tubes that snake across the sheets and twist above Henry's body. He is breathing on his own now and, sometimes, I rest my hand on his chest and feel his heart beating.

Only two visitors are allowed in the ICU, between the hours of two and eight o'clock, but I can stay for as long as I like, which is why I'm still here when everyone else has gone.

There are twelve beds arranged in bays with an emergency care nurse looking after every two patients. I am getting to know some of the other visitors. We nod to each other and smile bravely and listen to whispered conversations and prayers.

I tell Henry stories. I read him the sports pages from the paper and the 'get well soon' cards that could fill a Santa sack. I've also planned a trip to Paris and promised that we'll go on the erotic walking tour and get tickets to the Moulin Rouge and have lots of hotel sex, which is the best kind.

The patient lounge is still full of my family. The hospital director asked them to go home or at least take it in turns, but my uncles and aunts are not the sort to be put off by bureau-cracy and rules. They bring boardgames and knitting, and keep the lounge tidy and swell the profits of the café downstairs.

My mother came yesterday afternoon and stayed for an hour.

Daragh and Clifton took her for a cup of tea, flirting outrageously and making her laugh, which they always could. There was a time, when my parents were together, when my mother loved these men and embraced the McCarthy family, warts and all.

The doctors have given Henry drugs to wake him up, but he has decided to keep sleeping. Maybe he's having a lovely dream. Maybe he doesn't want to come back to me.

He has lost a kidney and half his stomach. Some people pay good money to get their stomach stapled but he got his surgery for free. That's what I'd say to Henry if he woke up. I'd tell him he's not allowed to get skinny because I've been putting on weight eating hospital food and the home-baked cakes and cookies my aunts insist on bringing.

This has become a vigil – Henry-watch – and our collective wills and prayers and wishes are going to bring him back to me. There is only one person missing. My father hasn't visited the hospital or called me, but I know he's getting updates from Constance and the others. He hates hospitals, but that's not the reason. He feels guilty or he doesn't know how to console me.

I sense a presence behind me. DCI Keegan is wearing a surgical mask.

'I hope you don't mind,' he says. 'I was going to wait, but your family said that you never leave his side.'

I point to a chair.

'How is he?'

'The same.'

'I'm sorry.'

'It's not your fault.'

'Yes, it is. The police should have been there. You're one of ours. It shouldn't have been down to Henry and your uncles.'

'Am I one of yours?'

'You're a soon to be decorated officer, albeit anonymously.'

I laugh and look at Henry. 'Hear that? I'm going to be decorated.'

Henry deserves it more than I do, but I don't know if the London Fire Brigade will appreciate his efforts in quite the same way. He stole an appliance and crashed it into a building.

'What about my uncles?' I ask.

'Their names have been suppressed, along with yours. Dimitar Popov has been charged with extortion, robbery and murdering Hugo Desai.'

'He didn't kill Caitlin Kemp-Lowe.'

'That's what he keeps saying. Do you know who did?'

'I have an idea.'

After a long pause, he raises an eyebrow. 'Are you going to tell me?'

'I need to be sure. Can you wait?'

'Until when?'

I look at Henry. 'He wakes up.'

# 83

'Talk to her,' says Constance, unable to stand the silence any longer.

McCarthy is sitting on the terrace with a blanket over his legs, staring across the garden like he's gazing out to sea. He seems to be growing old before her eyes.

'She doesn't want to talk to me.'

'How do you know? Have you asked her? Have you been to the hospital? Have you called?'

'She knows where I am.'

'This isn't some staring contest. You're both as bad as each other. Stubborn. And if you don't talk and forgive you'll go through life living like this.'

'Like what?'

'Regretting.'

McCarthy doesn't respond. Instead, he asks about Henry.

'The same,' says Constance.

'What do the doctors say?'

'He'll wake up when he's ready.'

McCarthy goes back to gazing across the garden.

Constance pulls a chair closer. 'Phil hasn't left his side. I don't know when she sleeps or eats. It's like she's trying to breathe for him.'

'That's what frightens me,' says McCarthy. 'If Henry dies, she'll die with him.'

'No. She'll survive. She's *your* daughter.'

His phone vibrates. It's Clifton. He's been looking after Hope Island, making sure that workers are being paid and the construction is running smoothly. He's also renegotiating their business loans, taking them to a new bank. Carmichael has left him a dozen messages, holding out olive branches and offering better terms, but McCarthy has told the obsequious little toad to shove his money up his arse.

'The police have identified the body they pulled out of the warehouse. They used dental records and the tattoo on his right wrist. It's Damyan Georgiev.'

'What about Popov?'

'He's been put in HMP Belmarsh, high security.'

'You got someone watching him?'

'Yeah.'

Clifton seems to wait for more orders. 'Why didn't you take him out?'

'Because we're better than that.'

'And?'

'Prison is the sort of place where Popov expects he will flourish. A place where the strong overcome the weak and you sleep with one eye open. He likes the jungle – he told me so. Well, we have friends inside who can make him feel very welcome. Men who owe us money, or favours, or want to see their families looked after, or hope to get a job when they're released.

'Popov will not know a single day or a single night or a single hour when he can relax, free from wondering whether it's going to be crushed glass in his food, or a shiv in his guts, or a broom handle up his arse.'

'That would drive a man mad.'

'I hope so.'

# 84

The shifts have changed and a familiar nurse is sitting on the stool behind Henry's bed.

I'm alone again, but the family will be back tomorrow, bringing breakfast and knitting and boardgames and Switches and their indefatigable spirit.

'Do you want me to make up your cot?' asks the nurse, Clayborne. His skin is so dark it looks almost blue black in the diffused light.

'No, I can do it.'

'I'll keep watch, if you want to have a shower.'

'Maybe later.'

'I hear you talking to him. You have a lovely voice.'

'Do you think he can hear me?'

'Absolutely.'

'How do you know?'

'Well, I've been doing this job for twelve years and I've seen more miracles than I can count.'

'I bet you say that to everyone.'

'Yes, but it always makes me wonder how much control we have over our lives, or if we're simply part of a chain reaction – one event crashing into the next.'

'You cannot calm the storm, but the storm will pass.'

'Yeah, something like that.' He slides off his stool. 'I'm going to get a coffee – you want something?'

'No thanks.'

When he's gone, I crawl up on the bed next to Henry and lie down with my head on his chest, careful not to disturb the wires and tubes. I close my eyes and listen to his heart and it reminds me of our little house and Sunday mornings, when we read the papers like this, with my head on his chest, commenting on the stories.

I doze, dreaming, and then hear a voice.

'What happened to your lovely hair?'

'It got burned,' I say, thinking Clayborne has returned.

A hand touches my head.

I try to sit up, but the hand holds me against him. 'Will it grow back?'

'Yes.'

'Why are you crying?'

'No reason.'

'Did I do something wrong?'

'No. You did something right.'

'What's that?'

'You came back to me.'

# 85

'Are you going to tell me now?' asks Keegan when he picks me up from the hospital in an unmarked police car.

'When I'm sure,' I say, doing up my seatbelt.

I glance back at the entrance. This is the first time I've left Henry since he arrived in the back of an ambulance. That was ten days ago, but it feels like years have passed and the world has moved on without me. London hasn't changed. She is still chewing up time. Aging and ageless.

I give Keegan directions as we navigate to Sutherland Avenue in Maida Vale. There is a bag on the back seat — a cotton tote from Hamleys, the toy store, printed with cartoon pictures of London bobbies linked like paper dolls.

'It's for my little boy,' he says. 'I'm seeing him today.'

'How old is he?'

'Three.'

I remember visiting Keegan's house. The unwashed dishes in the sink and the near-empty fridge.

'Are you divorced?'

'Heading that way.'

'I'm sorry.'

'It's not your fault,' he says. 'It's mine.'

For a moment I think he's going to confess some infidelity or unburden himself in some other way, but his demeanour doesn't change.

'I wasn't a very good husband, but I'm trying to be a good father. That's the important thing, right?'

He takes his eyes from the road and looks at me. Is he asking me a question or commenting on my own family situation? Maybe both. I change the subject.

'I know I'm not part of the task force, but can I ask you a few questions?'

'You seem to be running the investigation at the moment,' he replies, in a teasing way.

'The blood on Daisy's pyjamas – who did it belong to?'

'Her mother. Caitlin was struck across the face.'

'Did you compare it with Daisy's DNA?'

'Yes. Why?'

'We'll know soon enough.'

The car has pulled up outside a mansion block, parking beneath the bare branches of a grey-trunked tree.

Amber Culver answers the intercom, sounding surprised. Keegan flashes his warrant card at the camera and the door unlocks. We cross the foyer and enter the garden flat and then the kitchen. There are crayon drawings stuck to the fridge and a bowl of soggy breakfast cereal on the table and clothes are tumbling in the washer dryer.

'Where's Daisy?' I ask.

'I just dropped her at preschool,' says Amber, looking at her phone. 'I have an appointment with a lawyer. I'm applying for custody.'

'How is your health?' I ask.

'I'm going to have surgery. The prognosis looks brighter.'

'I'm glad to hear that. Can I borrow your bathroom?'

Amber nods, less certain than before. As I step into the hallway, I hear her ask Keegan if Russell Kemp-Lowe has been arrested.

'He denies any involvement in his wife's death.'

'He knew about the robbery,' says Amber.

'Maybe so, but we can't prove it.'

'He must have known. And even if he didn't, he shares the blame. It was his gambling that forced Caitlin to take such a risk. He doesn't deserve Daisy.'

Now out of earshot, I walk past the bathroom and enter the second bedroom, which now belongs to Daisy. Her stuffed animals cover the single bed and a dreamcatcher is suspended from the curtain rail. Two enormous chests of drawers, too big for the space, are covered with framed photographs of Daisy as a baby and a toddler. I'm looking for one in particular, which shows her as a newborn, still covered in vernix, eyes closed, swaddled in a sheet and cradled in Caitlin's arms.

Amber is also in the photograph. She is beside Caitlin but has been partially cut off by the framing. Only her face and shoulder are visible, along with the pillow beneath her head. Both women are wearing hospital gowns. Caitlin is seated. Smiling. Amber looks exhausted. Uncertain.

I carry the photograph back to the kitchen but keep it hidden.

'You were at Daisy's birth,' I say to Amber.

'I told you that.'

'Yes, but you didn't say that you *gave* birth.'

Amber's eyes flick to Keegan and back to me. I can almost see her mind working, the cogs and wheels turning, the pins falling into place.

'We can find out easily enough,' I say. 'There will be a record of the birth. The name of the mother and the midwife and hospital registrar.'

Amber, defiantly, 'You're right. Daisy is my child.'

'I'm confused,' says Keegan. 'Who is the mother?'

'I am,' says Amber. 'I gave birth to her.'

'That's true,' I say, 'but you're not her mother. You have the stretch marks and the memories of giving birth, but Daisy doesn't belong to you any more than she belongs to me.'

Keegan looks completely lost.

I explain. 'Caitlin Kemp-Lowe couldn't have children. She tried everything – IVF, hormones, diet, exercise, herbal remedies – but nothing worked.'

'She suffered from chronic endometriosis,' says Keegan. 'The post-mortem showed a hysterectomy, but I thought that happened after Daisy was born.'

I stay focused on Amber, speaking softly. 'You gave your best friend the ultimate gift. You carried her baby. But you're not Daisy's biological mother. It was Caitlin's egg and Russell's sperm implanted in your womb.'

'If she came out of me, she's mine,' says Amber, her voice shaking with emotion.

'I think you transferred legal parenthood to Caitlin and Russell when Daisy was born. And you have no biological link to her. You share no DNA, no blood, no genetic history at all.'

I take the photograph from behind my back and show it to Keegan. It takes him a moment to recognise Amber lying next to Caitlin and to put the pieces together.

Keegan interrupts. 'Caitlin bought you this flat. Commercial surrogacy is illegal in Britain.'

'It was a gift, not a payment,' says Amber. 'I don't know why you're being so mean to me. I *deserve* to be Daisy's mother. She wouldn't be here without me.'

'I understand,' I say. 'That's why you have a special bond with Daisy and why you've stayed so close to her and watched her grow up. You're more than a godparent. More than an aunt.

'The real tragedy is that you haven't had your own children. Your marriage failed and now that you've been diagnosed with cancer, Daisy might be the only baby you ever bring into the world. I know that seems cruel. You did all the hard work, but she doesn't belong to you.'

'What are the alternatives?' asks Amber. 'A gambling-addicted father, an ex-junkie uncle, aging grandparents with dementia? Daisy loves me. I can make her happy.'

'I believe you, but that's not going to happen.'

Amber blinks at me, unsure of what's coming.

'Caitlin told only two people about the home invasion and robbery. Noah, because he contacted the gang, and you – her best friend, her confidante, who had introduced her to Russell and given her the greatest gift – a child.

'You said it was an "intellectual exercise", but you knew she was serious. You also knew when, where and how it was going to happen. And all you had to do was wait until the gang had gone and sneak into the house. You had a spare key. The alarms and security cameras had been disabled.'

Amber gets up. 'This is crazy talk. I really have to go.'

'Sit down,' says Keegan. 'My colleague hasn't finished.'

I feel a little surge of pride and continue. 'You found Caitlin in the kitchen. Bound and gagged. Helpless. Vulnerable. She had what you wanted, what you deserved. A husband, a child, a home. But she had put everything at risk by letting criminals in her house. She didn't deserve to have Daisy. You said it yourself. It wasn't fair. That's why you put the plastic bag over her head and held it around her neck. She struggled. Sucking at the plastic. Dying as you held her.'

Amber shakes her head but doesn't answer.

Keegan picks up the slack. 'There was a partial palmprint on the bag. We haven't been able to connect it to anyone, not yet.'

Amber looks around the kitchen at the crayon drawings on the fridge and the soggy cereal bowl and children's clothes tumbling in the dryer. 'I'm all she has,' she whispers. 'Daisy needs me.'

Amber's head drops forward and her body seems to deflate like a leftover party balloon.

'How did you get into the house that night?' I ask.

'I waited until the gang had gone. They put Russell in a van and drove away. Caitlin had given me a key.'

'Did you talk to Caitlin?'

'I told her I was sorry and I promised to look after Daisy because she was my baby, too.'

'You killed your best friend.'

'I did it for Daisy.'

'You did it for yourself.'

'No. You don't understand. I was protecting her.'

Amber looks from face to face, pleading with her wet eyes.

'Did you see her that night?" I ask.

'I heard the dumb waiter coming and hid in the pantry.'

'Did Daisy see you?'

'No, but I heard her trying to wake Caitlin. It was heart-breaking.'

'You let Daisy leave the house,' I say.

'I wanted to stop her, but that would have meant showing my face and losing my chance. But I was following her. I made sure that she didn't get run over, or freeze to death, or get picked up by some monster.' Amber nods to me. 'I was there when you found her. I saw the police car pull up and you searching for Daisy. Putting the blanket around her shoulders. I knew she was safe then.'

Keegan gets to his feet and takes handcuffs from the belt of his trousers.

'Amber Culver, I am arresting you for the murder of Caitlin Kemp-Lowe. You do not have to say anything but it may harm your defence if you do not mention when questioned something which you later rely on in court. Anything you do say may be given in evidence—'

Amber looks confused. 'But I have to pick up Daisy from preschool. I promised her fish and chips for supper.'

'Her family will look after her,' says Keegan, snapping handcuffs around her wrists.

'But I'm her mother,' says Amber, who continues talking as she is led down the hallway and outside to the waiting police car. 'Daisy needs new pyjamas. She's getting so tall. She's up to my hip now. And I need to cut her fringe . . .'

430

Only later, when I'm back at Henry's bedside, do I remember Keegan's words about family looking after Daisy. When I was most in need, it was my father and my uncles who came to rescue me. And right now, the hospital lounge is full of my aunts and cousins, nieces and nephews, keeping a vigil for Henry.

Family is not the important thing. It's everything.

# 86

Two weeks before Christmas, I wheel Henry from his room at the hospital, into the lift and down to the ground floor. We cross the foyer and the automatic doors open. My family have formed a guard of honour and many of the staff have come to say goodbye – nurses, doctors, cleaners, physiotherapists and counsellors – who have all grown fond of my father and my extended family.

Clayborne is sporting a newly knitted sweater with an elephant motif, and one of the ward sisters has a cable cardigan.

Henry is embarrassed by the attention. It's strange how when we're children it's people's cruelty that makes us cry, but when we're adults it's their kindness.

Henry wanted to walk out of the hospital, but I insisted he take things slowly. He has lost almost a third of his body weight and has to watch what he eats and how much he exercises and what he drinks.

A car has been arranged to take us home. I open the rear door and Henry walks the final few steps, slipping onto the back seat, while I store his suitcase. It's not until I turn around that I realise who is driving. My father looks hollowed out and tormented by things he can't control.

'Hello, Daddy.'

'Philomena.'

'Are you driving us home?'

'I can ask Finbar if you'd prefer.'

'No.'

There are more goodbyes on the footpath. Hugs and kisses and promises to call. Eventually, I climb into the passenger seat. Daddy slips behind the wheel. Henry leans through the seats and shakes his hand, calling him 'Mr McCarthy'.

'For God's sake, call me Eddie, please?'

'Can I call you Edward?' asks Henry. 'You don't seem like an Eddie.'

'You can call me anything you like, Son. You saved my daughter. I owe you a debt I can never repay.'

'I'll repay it,' I say, squeezing Henry's hand, holding it up to my lips.

'How are you going to do that?' asks Henry.

'I'm not talking about *that* in front of my father,' I reply.

Daddy smiles and then grows quiet. His face is a map of accumulated problems and suppressed guilt. He steers us onto the M4, heading east towards Central London. He clears his throat.

'I wanted to say how sorry I am, for what you've been through. I hope you can forgive me.'

'It wasn't your fault,' says Henry.

'Yes, it was,' I say. 'And he doesn't get off that easily.'

Henry goes quiet and the silence is a chasm.

'You can't expect forgiveness,' I say. 'It's not like you've broken a window and had it fixed. Henry almost died. I almost died.'

More silence. I begin again, choosing my words. 'It's your fault, but I don't blame you because that would be like blaming a lion for being a lion. Certain things are in your nature and you're not going to change.'

'I have changed,' he whispers.

'No. You don't stop being a predator by acting like prey.'

He doesn't turn away from the road to look at me, because he's frightened of what he might see.

I love this man, but I can never forgive him. He has taken

433

more than one life in my name and God didn't strike him down. The sun rose. Roosters crowed. Hens laid eggs. Water came out of taps. He did things that were supposed to change him, but he didn't change. He will never change.

# Acknowledgements

When I can't sleep at night, I try to remember the titles of my novels, in order of publication. You think it would be easy because they're supposed to be like my children, but I get my kids' names wrong all the time. Often, I have to run through all three before I get the right one.

When I created the character of Philomena McCarthy in *When You Are Mine*, I thought I was writing a standalone, but I fell in love with Phil and in particular with her father and uncles, who were old-school East End gangsters. Geezers, if you will, who made me laugh.

Some novels come more easily than others and this one was a joy to write because I love these characters and how they interact with a world which is changing so quickly.

I wish to thank Nick Lucas for his advice and expertise on police matters. Any procedural mistakes in this text are mine and made wilfully because sometimes exact protocols slow down the story. That's one great advantage of writing fiction – I get to make stuff up.

I am also indebted to my wonderful agents Mark Lucas, Richard Pine and Nicki Kennedy, and to my editors Tilda Key, Rebecca Saunders and Colin Harrison. Working in the background are my crack publishing teams at Little, Brown Book Group UK, Hachette Australia, the Scribner in the US, as well as my many foreign publishers far and wide, most notably Goldmann in Germany.

Last but not least – never least – I thank my beautiful, perfect, ageless wife, Vivien, who has had to share me with another woman for the past year. We have been out to dinner and she has kicked me under the table saying, 'You're with Philomena, aren't you?'

Guilty as charged.